A Thousand Bones

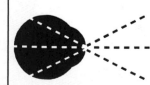

This Large Print Book carries the
Seal of Approval of N.A.V.H.

A THOUSAND BONES

P. J. PARRISH

WHEELER PUBLISHING
An imprint of Thomson Gale, a part of The Thomson Corporation

THOMSON
™
GALE

Detroit • New York • San Francisco • New Haven, Conn. • Waterville, Maine • London

LIBRARY OF CONGRESS CATALOGING-IN-PUBLICATION DATA

Parrish, P. J.
    A thousand bones / by P.J. Parrish.
      p. cm.
    ISBN-13: 978-1-59722-644-8 (lg. print : alk. paper)
    ISBN-10: 1-59722-644-0 (lg. print : alk. paper)
    1. Women detectives — Michigan — Fiction. 2. Serial murder investigation — Fiction. 3. Michigan — Fiction. 4. Large type books.
    I. Title.
    PS3566.A7567T48 2007
    813'.54—dc22   2007032177

Published in 2007 by arrangement with Pocket Books,
a division of Simon & Schuster, Inc.

Printed in the United States of America on permanent paper
10 9 8 7 6 5 4 3 2 1

To Daddy,
who took us up north
and left too soon.
But oh, the memories.

PROLOGUE

Captiva Island, Florida
December 1988

He was waiting for her. She could see him there in the shadows, but he hadn't spotted her yet, hadn't seen her car pull in. She had a few seconds to prepare herself.

God, her heart was hammering.

Her hands, resting lightly on the wheel, had gone cold. She had a sudden flashback to the guy she had busted last week, a PCP-crazed kid who came at her with a cardboard-box cutter, slashing at her face as she and the other detective drove him face-first into the concrete of Biscayne Boulevard while the bankers toting briefcases gaped. The kid could have killed her. It hadn't even fazed her.

But this . . .

Joe Frye looked back at the man waiting in the shadows. This was going to be the hardest thing she had ever faced.

She picked up her Glock from the passenger seat.

The slam of her Bronco's door made him look up. He watched her as she came across the sandy yard, but he didn't move. Except his face. There, in the brightening of Louis Kincaid's eyes and in the slight tilting up of his lips, she saw all his love for her.

"You're late," he said as she came up onto the screened-in porch.

"Paperwork," she said.

He reached down to pick up a glass of red wine from the floor and held it out. "It got a little warm waiting for you."

She clicked the Glock onto her belt and smiled as she came forward to take the glass. One sip told her he had taken the trouble to go to the wine store in Fort Myers to get her favorite, the new Ironstone zinfandel.

Louis was sitting in a wicker lounge, his black cat, Issy, lying on his stomach. She didn't want to make him move the cat, so she bent down to accept his kiss. It was a long, lingering kiss.

"Cherries and pepper," he said, coming away with a smile.

"You've been reading *Wine Spectator*?"

"Just trying to keep up with you."

She kissed him again. He had been gone

only three weeks, but it had been too long.

She dropped down into the chair next to him, kicked off her shoes, and put her legs up across his calves. He was wearing jeans and a heavy sweatshirt, despite the fact it was still eighty degrees at four o'clock. He had told her on the phone that since his return from Michigan, he still felt as if he hadn't been able to warm up. He had told her, too, that he needed to talk to her about something important.

But she had something she needed to tell him first. Maybe it was because he had been in Michigan. Or maybe it was because she had been holding this inside her for so long now that she finally had to tell someone. And maybe it was because she finally trusted him enough that he was the one who had to hear it.

Whatever the reason, there could be no kind of future for them unless she could unlock her heart.

He put his Heineken on the table and reached down to touch her bare ankle, just below the cuff of her slacks. His hand was cold and wet from holding the beer bottle.

"Louis —" she began.

"God, I missed you, Joe."

She closed her eyes.

"When I was up there," he said, "all I

could think about was getting back here, getting home, and seeing you."

She opened her eyes. Not trusting herself to look at Louis, she focused on the gulf, a silver-blue sliver visible through the swaying sea oats in front of the cottage. She loved this place, loved coming over here to be with Louis. Her apartment in Miami was just a three-hour drive across Alligator Alley, but it was like a different world over here on the west coast. The moment she hit the tollbooth at Sanibel Island, she could feel her muscles begin to unclench, feel the adrenaline sting in her blood easing. It was as if her first glimpse of the gulf washed away all the grit and hard glamour of Miami, leaving her feeling cleansed and able to breathe again.

The thought that had been hiding in the corners of her brain for weeks now was pushing forward. Had it come to this? She was the only woman detective in Miami-Dade's homicide division. She had worked hard for this. When had she started hating her job?

"Joe?"

She looked at Louis.

"Something wrong?"

She let out a long breath. "Let's go down to the beach."

Louis got a fresh beer and topped off her wine. Barefoot, they walked through the sea oats and down to the water. Off in the distance, Joe could see a shrimp boat, its net poles extended, making its way back south to its home in Snug Harbor. Silhouetted against the cloud-striated sky, it looked like a water bug skimming across a pond.

"Louis, we have to talk," Joe said.

"I know," he said.

She turned toward him. God, she loved his face. Forceful, high-cheekboned, black brows sitting like emphatic accents over his gray eyes, the left one arching into an exclamation mark when he was amused or surprised. And his skin, smooth and buff-colored, a gift from his beautiful black mother, whose picture he had once shown her, and his white father, whom he had never mentioned.

She brought up a hand to cup his cheek. She squinted against the tears she felt threatening. "I need to talk first," she said. "Please. There is something I have to tell you."

"Should I sit down for this?" he asked.

She let her hand drop and nodded.

They sat down on a low dune. Louis stuck his beer bottle in the sand. Joe cradled the

11

wineglass between her palms as she stared out at the water.

"Before I came to Miami, I worked in Michigan," she said.

"Michigan? I thought you were always with Miami PD?" Louis asked.

She shook her head. "No, my first job was with a sheriff's department in northern Michigan. A small town called Echo Bay. I was only there a short time. Then I got the job down here."

Louis was quiet, waiting.

Joe took a sip of the wine. "Something happened up there," she said. "Something happened to me. And I did something that I have never . . ."

She closed her eyes.

"Joe, what is it?"

"I did something that makes me think I shouldn't be a cop anymore," she said.

"But this was what, ten years ago?" Louis asked.

"Thirteen," she said softly.

"But why now?"

She faced him. "Because I have never told anyone. And if I don't tell you now, I can't do this anymore."

Louis was quiet for a moment. "Do what? The job? Us?"

"Both," she said.

She carefully wedged the wineglass down in the sand and closed her eyes. She heard Louis let out a long breath.

"All right," he said. "I'm listening."

She opened her eyes. The gulf was smooth, the waves coming in with the softest hiss. She concentrated on the sound for a moment, trying to time her heart to it, trying to slow the beating down. She closed her eyes again, this time concentrating on trying to bring it all back — the sounds, the sights, the feelings, every horrible moment.

"I was just a rookie . . ." she began.

■ ■ ■ ■

I
SOMEBODY'S
DAUGHTER

■ ■ ■ ■

1

Echo Bay, Michigan
October 1975

The sharp buzzing noise filled her ears, coming from everywhere and nowhere at the same time. It took her a moment to realize it was coming from somewhere outside her brain.

She looked up into the green lace of the leaves. She knew that was where they were, up there in the trees. That's where the cicadas were hiding as they sang their dying summer song.

A bead of sweat fell from her brow and into her eye. She blinked and looked down to the yellow crime-scene tape hanging limp between the trees. Down to where the men worked over the dirt. Down to where the clean white bone had been found.

"Joe?"

She turned toward the deep voice.

"You want to come take a look?"

Cliff Leach was standing at the bottom of the gully inside the yellow tape. The three other officers had all glanced up when he spoke, looked first at him, then up to her. She wished the sheriff had not singled her out, but her curiosity was stronger than any worries she had about how the others felt about her.

Joe slipped under the tape and came down the hill. The three other deputies didn't give way, and she had to stand behind them to see.

Not that there was really much to look at. Set in a shallow hole with a light covering of pine needles, the bone looked more like a shard of a broken white plate. Joe felt a small stab of disappointment.

When the call had come in that two boys walking in the woods had found the bone, a current had crackled through the station. She had been in the women's bathroom changing into uniform, and through the thin walls she could hear the others talking about it, their deep voices rising in pitch as they speculated about how a human bone had found its way into a remote scrap of woods up by Bass Lake. Things like that didn't happen in places like Echo Bay. Echo Bay was just a mosquito bite on the tip of the little finger of the Michigan mitten. That's how folks in Echo Bay pinpointed their place in the world. They'd hold up their right hand, palm forward and point to the tip of the little finger. "That's where I come from," they'd say, "Echo Bay."

The cicadas had stopped. No sound, not even the rustle of a leaf in the still October air.

"That don't look like no human bone," one of the men said.

"Deer maybe," another said.

"We came all the way out here for a fucking deer carcass?"

Joe glanced at the last man who had spoken. Unlike the rest of them, Julian Mack didn't wear the dark brown uniforms of the Leelanau County sheriff's department. He wore gray Sansabelts, and a thin black tie hung like a dead snake down his sweat-soaked white shirt. Joe knew he was just a deputy like the rest of them, but he was the closest thing the seven-man department had to an investigator, and he affected the casual dress of one.

Mack's brown eyes met hers. For an instant, she could see resentment in them. She had seen it before, whenever Cliff Leach made it a point to include her in conversation or ask her opinion on how something should be handled. Part of that came from her status as a rookie. Most of it was because she was a woman.

She looked back down at the bone, inching closer so she could see better.

Leach squatted down and inserted a stick into one of the bone's cavities, pulling the bone clear of the needles. They all fell silent.

Joe took a deep breath. "Sir?"

He looked up at her.

"I think it's a pelvic bone," she said.

She could feel the damp press of the polyester uniform on her back and thighs. She could feel all their eyes on her.

"And I think it's from a female," she said.

A snort and a chuckle, but she wasn't sure which of them it had come from. She kept her eyes on the sheriff.

"Why female?" Leach asked.

When she hesitated, he motioned her forward with a small nod. She squatted next to him and picked up a stick.

"See this?" She pointed to the base of the butterfly-shaped bone. "This is the pubic arch. In a man, it is real narrow. But a woman's arch is wide, like this one. It's part of the birth canal."

"How do you know that?" he asked.

She shrugged, her eyes willing him not to press it.

Leach tossed his stick aside and let out a

sigh. "Great," he said softly, his eyes wandering over the pine needles and dirt before he looked up to Mack. "This looks like it was dug up. Did the kids do it?"

Mack looked at the other rookie officer standing next to him. "Holt," he said, "you were here first. Who dug it up?"

Holt licked his lips. "I don't know, sir. I just know the two kids and the dog were standing here when I showed up."

Leach grunted to a standing position. He was a burly man, with a halo of sparse white hair surrounding a florid face punctuated by a thick white mustache. Joe suspected he probably got whatever Santa Claus gigs there were in Echo Bay. He had that kind of gentle aura — until you got a good look at the keen gray-green eyes behind the wire-rimmed glasses. She had seen him angry only once, and those eyes had turned as dark as a storm-tossed Lake Michigan.

Holt was getting that look from the sheriff now, and the rookie gave an embarrassed shrug. "I'll go talk to the kids," he said.

"No," Leach said. "You and Mack start looking for more bones." He wiped his sweating face, leaving a smear of dirt near his nose. "Frye can deal with the kids."

Joe stood up, her eyes locked on Leach. What was this? One minute, he was bringing her in, and now he was banishing her to babysitting chores? She tried to catch Leach's eye, but he had turned away.

She took off her hat, wiped her wet hair off her forehead, and put the hat back on. The two boys were still waiting at the top of the ravine. She trudged up to them.

"Okay," she said, "which one of you found the bone?"

They just looked up at her. Even the damn black Lab was staring at her. The cicadas were going at it again, their buzz and the awful heat bringing on a headache.

The kids were still staring. She was twenty-two, unmarried. What did she know about kids? "What are you looking at?" she blurted out.

The older boy looked at his friend, then back at Joe. "You really a policeman?"

"Yeah, I'm really a policeman."

"I ain't never seen a lady policeman before."

"Well, now you have."

Joe realized the kid was staring at her breasts. His eyes flicked to the gun at her hip and back to her chest. She couldn't help it. She laughed. The kid's face went crimson beneath his freckles.

"Okay, okay," she said. She pulled a small pad and pencil from her pocket. "Let's get to work here. You two are witnesses, and I need your statements."

The boy's eyes widened. "Witnesses? Wow."

Joe held back her smile. "Names?"

"I'm R. C. Mellon. That's R.C., like the cola," the boy said.

"And Mellon, like muskmelon brain," the other boy chimed in.

"Shut up, Frankie!"

"Make me."

"All right," Joe broke in. "Spell your names for me, and give me your addresses and phone numbers." Joe wrote it all down. "And who found the bone?"

"Farfel did," R.C. said, patting the Lab's big head. "We were playing, and Farfel ran off. I whistled for him, but he didn't come. We finally saw him over that way." He pointed north to a stand of tall pines. "But when we went after him, he ran off."

"Did he have the bone?"

"Yeah. We chased him, and when we caught up with him, he was down there burying it."

The boy pointed to where Holt was stringing up more yellow crime tape. Joe surveyed the trees. She knew a little bit about this part of the woods, knew it covered a couple of miles, running all the way west to the shore of Lake Michigan. If the dog had found the bone somewhere other than where it lay now, the search for the rest of the bones or for a crime scene would be near impossible.

She closed the notepad. "You guys have been a big help. Wait here, okay?"

Sheriff Leach was standing back at his cruiser, talking on the radio, the coiled cord stretched through the open window. It sounded as if he were making arrangements for the coroner. The coroner would come from Traverse City, if he was in town. And any crime-scene guys would probably travel from Cadillac or even Lansing.

She tapped Leach's shoulder. He held up a finger as he gave directions to their location. She tapped him again. Leach finally told them to stand by for a moment and looked at her. "What is it, Joe?"

"Where we found the bone is not a burial site."

"What do you mean?"

"The kids say the dog picked it up somewhere else."

"We know where?" he asked.

Joe shook her head. Leach let out a sigh and rekeyed the microphone. "Yeah, Augie," he said. "We're going to need more than just the usual team. Give Michigan State a call, and see if they have any criminology students who want to participate in a search for some remains."

Leach signed off and leaned an elbow on the cruiser. He pulled a handkerchief from his pocket and wiped his face.

Joe glanced back at the kids. "I'll see if the kids can show me where the dog found the bone."

The boys were sitting on a log, the Lab sprawled at their feet. When she asked them to show her where they were playing, the boys started off down the incline, the dog following. Joe trailed, kicking softly at the pine needles, her eyes scanning the ground. The kids led her into thicker trees and the shadows deepened as the leaves grew denser, blocking the sun.

"This is it. This is the tree we were climbing on," R.C. said suddenly.

Joe glanced up. It was a majestic old beech tree, set down in a clearing of smaller trees. The canopy was so dense it almost felt like nightfall. Joe looked at the boys. "You're sure this is the tree?"

R.C. nodded and pointed. "Yup. I remember 'cause of those two weird branches that look like arms."

The dog was whining and pawing at the leaves. Joe pulled him away by the collar.

"R.C., hold him back," she said, handing the dog off.

She knelt and brushed away the remaining leaves and needles. The ground seemed untouched underneath. She grabbed a stick and tried to work away some of the dirt. But she quickly realized that if there was a shallow grave here, a stick wasn't going to get her to it. She stuck the stick in the dirt to mark the spot and looked back at the kids.

Their faces were lined with dirty sweat. "I'm tired. Can we go now?" Frankie asked.

"I'm sorry, you guys are probably hungry," she said. "How about I buy you a hamburger on the way home?"

Suddenly, the dog started growling, and Joe turned. He had something in his teeth. As she grabbed for his collar, he dropped what he had at her feet. It was another bone. Long, thin, whitish-brown, and perfectly clean. Maybe an arm or leg bone.

Joe cupped her hands around her mouth and hollered, "Sheriff Leach! Over here!"

She heard footsteps and the snapping of brush, and she glanced back to make sure the kids were still with her. R.C. was holding a third, smaller bone between his fingers, looking at her.

"R.C., drop that, please," she said.

"It's not yucky."

"I know, but please put it down."

The boy dropped it just as Leach, Mack, and Holt reached them. Leach immediately saw the large bone and motioned to Holt.

"Holt, take the kids back to the cruiser and drive them home."

"I promised them a burger," Joe called as Holt herded the kids and the dog back toward the road.

When they were gone, Leach knelt by the two bones. Mack remained standing, his little eyes scooting over the leaves, past the bones, and finally back to Joe.

Leach pulled himself up. "I'm guessing this is an arm bone and maybe a rib."

Joe was scanning the ground around the tree. Something odd and clumped caught her eye. She squatted down for it, then remembered she shouldn't touch it. She carefully cleared away the dead leaves.

"Sheriff," she said.

Both Mack and Leach came up behind her, bending to look over her shoulder.

"What is that?" Leach asked.

"I don't know," Joe said. "Maybe a piece of jewelry?"

Mack picked up a stick and poked at the caked dirt, trying to break it loose from the object. A glint of tarnished silver appeared, and what looked like a tiny cross. He let out a grunt and tossed the stick aside.

Then he turned and walked away. Joe watched him until he disappeared into the trees, then she picked up the stick Mack had left.

Leach touched her shoulder. "Don't touch it," he said. "Let the tech get it."

She stuck the stick in the ground near the piece of silver, then dusted her hands on her trousers. Leach was staring out at the forest.

"What are you thinking, sir?" she asked.

"That this is going to be a helluva investigation," he said.

She knew their small department couldn't handle a homicide and that Leach would ask the state for help. But she hoped he would let her be marginally involved.

"Sir, is there anything I can start doing?" she asked.

Leach smiled, hearing the eagerness in her voice. "Let's relax here a little," he said. "First, we have to let the experts take a look. It doesn't look like she was buried, so her bones could be scattered for miles. We can keep searching for that, at least."

Joe's eyes wandered out over the heavy woods, coming back finally to the tree. She hadn't noticed it before, but now its strange beauty registered.

The tree rose from a base of knotted roots covered by green moss. About ten feet from the ground, its wide, straight trunk split into two thick branches that curved straight upward. Like arms, just as R.C. had said.

Like a woman's arms, Joe thought. The tree looked like a kneeling woman, her emerald skirt spread out and her arms reaching upward as if awaiting rescue or salvation.

2

The sun was low in the sky by the time Joe started back to the station. The forensic crew had set up shop at the prayer tree, as Joe had come to call the spot where the dirt-caked jewelry had been unearthed. The coroner had offered his opinion that the three bones were probably from the same victim, and that they were, indeed, a rib, a humerus, and a female pelvis.

Joe had caught the question again in Leach's eyes: *How did you know?*

Hell, she knew a lot about bones. Like, that there were two hundred and six of them in the human body. She could still name most of them, thanks to an instructor back at Northern Michigan University who had made the art majors memorize all the names. Joe had signed up for the instructor's life drawing class after her roommate said it would be an easy way to see cute guys naked.

Joe's lips turned up in a smile as she drove.

The models all turned out to be fat old women. She didn't see a man fully naked until that January night after her nineteenth birthday when Jack Oberfell took her to the old lighthouse, gave her some Boone's Farm Strawberry Hill, spread his Tau Kappa Epsilon jacket on the hard floor, and efficiently claimed her virginity. The only thing she could clearly remember from the night was the sight of Jack's shivering white body and his pecker retreating like a scared turtle in the cold.

The road took a bend and changed from gravel to pavement as she turned out of the woods and onto M-22 South. Joe kept the cruiser going at a slow speed, savoring the time alone to think and drive. Her partner, Mike, didn't like to relinquish the wheel of the cruiser, so she was glad he had stayed behind to man the station when the call about the bone came in.

The bone . . .

She couldn't get the sight of it — so white against the black dirt — out of her head.

And she couldn't let go of the idea that there were other bones, the rest of that unknown girl, still out there somewhere.

The cruiser rounded Cemetery Point. Soon the woods gave way, and the roadside was dotted with the neat bungalows and cottages that shepherded in Echo Bay.

She wondered what the reaction in town would be once word of the bones got out. Echo Bay was just a village, really, wedged between the meandering wasp-waisted Lake Leelanau to the east and the oceanlike stretch of Lake Michigan to the west. "Downtown" was a blinking-light intersection with a small grocery, a post office, a couple of shops, the white clapboard Riverside Inn, The Bluebird restaurant, and its sister breakfast nook, the Early Bird. Most of the buildings had a soft, weather-beaten look that whispered of Echo Bay's origins as an 1800s fishing settlement. A turn at the blinking light led down to Fishtown, a collection of docks and shanties lining the mouth of the Carp River, which tumbled down, turquoise and cool, from an old mill dam into Lake Michigan.

She stopped at the blinker to let the Wonder Bread truck back out of the grocery store lot.

Brad popped into her thoughts, and what

he had said the first time they had driven into Echo Bay, pulling the U-Haul. It was a dreary April day, with a fog curling in from the lake.

"Looks a little like Brigadoon emerging from the mist," he said.

She had laughed and leaned over to kiss him, surprised by his romanticism. Brad wasn't given to such whimsy. He was a serious man, and she liked that about him. She had liked it from the first moment she met him. She had been waiting tables at Shammy's, three months after having to drop out of Northern. The money had run out; she was lonely, far from home, and maybe, she admitted to herself, a little afraid for the first time in her life. The bar that night was filled with drunken jocks, her feet were throbbing, and someone kept playing "Basketball Jones" on the jukebox, giving her a grinding headache.

She delivered the pitcher of beer with a sharp thud, and the three men had all looked up at her. One of them said something smart, and his friend laughed. But the third man, the blond with the soft brown eyes, was quiet. Through the smoky haze and neon glow, she met those eyes, and it was like sliding into a warm bath after being out in the cold too long.

Later, after she moved into his apartment, Brad joked that "Basketball Jones" was their song. In bed, he would sing the song's stupid words against her neck: "Baby, I need someone to stand beside me. I need someone to set a pick for me at the free-throw line of life, someone I can pass to, someone to hit the open man on the give-and-go and not end up in the popcorn machine."

She loved Brad Schaffer. Loved that he could make her laugh. Loved that he was a veterinarian. Loved that his devotion to his large family came so easily and his roots to his boyhood home in Marquette ran so deep. Loved that his compass seemed so true when her own had always been so unreliable.

Things were perfect for a year as Brad worked in the small clinic in town and she kept waiting tables. Perfect until the day Leach called out of nowhere to offer her a job. He had taught the criminology course that she had taken on a whim. But she had aced it and Leach had noticed her interest. "Had she ever considered being a cop?" he asked during the phone call. Truth was, she hadn't until then. But she was intrigued. Leach told her that he had relocated to Echo Bay and was now county sheriff, and if she could make it through the academy, he had a job for her.

The night she told Brad about it, they had their first real argument. He didn't understand why she wanted to be a cop, he said, why *any* woman would.

"I want to try this, Brad, I *have* to try this," she said. "Can't you understand? Your work means something to you. And that's what I'm trying to find, too. I can't wait tables for the rest of my life. I need to do something I love."

It was February, and a driving sleet was beating against the window. For a long time, it was the only sound in their bedroom. They lay there side by side without touching. Finally, Brad turned toward her. "All right," he said. "We'll go to Echo Bay. We'll give this a try for a year."

"I love you," she said. "Thank you for doing this."

He was quiet again, then, slowly, he smiled. "You'll turn me into a troll. Are you happy?"

A troll was what people from Michigan's Upper Peninsula called anyone who lived "below the bridge," the five-mile-long span that connected the Upper and Lower peninsulas.

"Yes, I am very happy," she said.

She suspected he gave in because he

34

thought this whim of hers would pass. Or that she would never make it through the academy. But when she did, he was there, applauding in the front row on graduation day.

The bread truck pulled out, and Joe glanced at the dashboard clock, remembering that Brad was working an extra shift at the vet clinic down in Traverse City tonight. Nothing to look forward to but an empty cottage and dinner with their dog, Chips.

She pulled into the station lot. The Leelanau County sheriff's department was on the marina road that fronted Lake Michigan, and Joe had always thought it funny that one of the best pieces of real estate had been given to the cops. The old stone building had once been the county library but now housed the sheriff's office on the first floor and the county courthouse on the second. The jail was in the basement, a dank cavern cut into three holding cells that were hardly ever used.

Joe paused just inside the entrance to take off her hat. The interior, now carved up into offices, was softened by its original oak paneling, fireplace, and old milk-glass light fixtures. Augie Feldman, the dispatcher who had ruled over the department for twenty years, had left his own mark — from the spider plants that he hung everywhere to the cinnamon coffee he brewed every morning.

"Hey, Augie," Joe said as she came in the door.

"Joette, *mi amore,*" he said. "So give."

"Nothing to give," Joe said, coming up to Augie's desk to sign off shift.

"What did you guys find out there?" Augie asked.

"Bones. Definitely human, probably a girl."

"Last time we found any bones was somewhere around 1961," Augie said. "Turned out to be a hunter who got drunk and wandered off and passed out. No one found him until spring thaw. And not entirely in one piece."

"Why did it take so long to find him?"

"Took that long for his ex-wife to report him missing."

Usually, Augie's humor made her smile, but not today, not after seeing the bones in the woods. She reached up to the sheet on the wall to sign out, but her eyes caught a two-ringed blue binder on the shelf. It was the missing persons file, a compilation of Teletype bulletins that routinely came from law enforcement all across the state.

Damn. Somebody had to be missing the

girl in the woods. At least she could check the bulletins. Grabbing a cup of coffee, she took the binder back to her desk.

There were so many. She hadn't expected that.

Page after page of faces. A few men, but mostly women, some very young. The photographs were mainly school portraits with a few snapshots thrown in. Some of the faces — the men, mostly — seemed to hold a mild look of resignation or defeat, as if they were saying, "Forget me, I'm gone." But others, the young women, seemed to be looking out with beseeching eyes that said, "I don't know what happened. Find me."

She took a slow sip of coffee, trying to decide how to narrow her search. For lack of a better plan, she looked for any females who had disappeared within a hundred-mile radius of Echo Bay in the last ten years.

"Joette, dear, I am going home," Augie called out. "Do you need anything before I leave?"

Joe looked up to see Augie slipping on his jacket. His replacement, Bea, was behind the dispatch desk, already immersed in her crossword. "No, thanks, Augie, see you tomorrow," Joe said.

Joe turned back to the bulletins. She flipped to the next one.

Name: Virginia McCafferty
Age: 17
Date of birth: 12-5-1956
Height: 5'4"
Weight: 114
Hair: Red
Eyes: Green
Distinguishing marks: Freckles on face
  and shoulders
Missing since: 10-16-1975
Last seen: Leaving Big Boy's Drive-in on
  2nd St. Mackinaw City. Please contact
  the Michigan State Police with informa-
  tion.

Virginia McCafferty had gone missing only a few days ago. This could not be the girl in the woods.

As Joe moved on, it occurred to her that there seemed to be no order to the bulletins, and she guessed someone had once pulled them off the rings but had not put them back in the proper ascending order by date gone missing. The papers needed to be in order. Not just out of respect but because it was the right way to file them. She unsnapped the rings, took all the bulletins off, and started arranging them by date.

"Don't you have a dog to walk or something?"

She turned in her chair. Mike Villella stood in the doorway. He was in civvies, snug jeans and a blue T-shirt emblazoned with a hound dog and the words DON'T LET THE BASTARDS WEAR YOU DOWN. Joe seldom saw Mike out of uniform, and she was struck by how different he looked. He was only five-nine, maybe one-fifty, but wiry with muscle. He had the dark, thick hair of his Italian ancestors and an expressive face that reminded her of those Greek twin masks of tragedy and comedy. One minute Mike's face could be sullen, but in the next it could crease upward to a sudden smile.

Mike was holding a green notebook in his hand.

"What's that?" she asked, nodding toward it.

He wrapped it into a tight tube and stuffed it in his back pocket. "Just my son's homework. Amazing what second-graders are being asked to do now."

Mike went to the small refrigerator, grabbed a Coke, and came over to prop a hip on the desk next to Joe's. "What are you doing?" he asked.

"Researching missing girls."

"This about those bones they found this afternoon?"

Joe nodded.

"How many bones did you find?" he asked.

"Three so far," Joe said. "The sheriff has called in the county search team, but I don't think we'll find too many more. She wasn't buried, and the animals probably scattered her."

"Yeah, and that's rough terrain up there," Mike said. "Mack said he was lucky to find what he did."

Joe looked up. "He was lucky to find what *he* did?"

"He said he was rewalking the area with the kids, and that's when he found the other bones." Mike took a swig of the Coke. "At least, that's what he was saying over at the Riverside tonight."

Joe held his eyes for a moment before she looked away. She knew Mike had caught her disgust, but he didn't say anything more. When his sneakered feet started rhythmically tapping the side of the desk, she finally looked up.

"Don't you have a wife to go home to?" she asked.

Mike grinned. "Mindy's having a Tupperware party tonight. I'm making myself scarce. Want to grab some dinner?"

She was surprised at the offer. In the past

six months, she and Mike had managed to forge a decent partnership, even though she knew he hadn't quite gotten past the stereotype of a female cop as a lesbian looking to kick ass.

For a second, Joe considered taking Mike up on his invitation. But she knew that Mindy was still adjusting to the fact that her husband spent eight hours every day in a car with another woman. And that it took very little to trigger Mindy's imagination.

"No, thanks," she said. "Like you said, I got a dog to walk."

She gathered up the fifteen bulletins she had set aside and went to the Xerox machine. The grind of the copier was the only sound in the office, except for Bea's nasally voice sending the lone swing-shift cruiser to an accident. A Chevy had hit a deer.

A phone rang, and Mike grabbed it. Joe listened as she slapped another paper on the glass. Mike was talking to Sheriff Leach, and she heard Mike tell him that he would deliver the message.

"What message?" she asked when Mike hung up.

"Sheriff wants all of us here tomorrow at ten for a powwow on the bones," he said.

"Did he say if he called in the state investigators?"

"Nope, but he will. What the hell are we going to do? None of us has ever handled anything like this before."

"I thought Mack had."

"Mack's idea of himself and his experience is highly inflated," Mike said. "He's nothing but a small-town cop with big-city dreams that have passed him by."

"Nothing wrong with dreams, Mike. You can't live without them."

"Yeah, but how long do you hang on to one you're never going to have? At some point, you just got to decide that isn't what life had in store for you and move on."

Joe watched him as he finished off the Coke and tossed the can into the trash. She didn't know a lot about Mike Villella, but she knew he had lived in the Leelanau Peninsula his whole life, had two children, a boy seven and a girl eleven, and a wife he called twice a day. Joe could do the math and figure he had married at eighteen.

She went back to her desk, sliding the bulletins back onto the ring binder. Mike was watching her as she stuck the copies in a manila folder.

"What you gonna do with those?" he asked.

"Not sure yet," she said.

He grunted and headed to the door.

"Well, I'm out of here. See you at the pow-wow," he said.

Joe pulled open a desk drawer and started to drop the folder in. But then she closed the drawer. She would take the bulletins home, although she wasn't sure why. Maybe to study them, maybe because she just wanted to keep them close. She gathered up her hat and keys and went outside.

Out in the parking lot, she paused, turning toward the lake. It was still warm, and the sky was a shimmering red curtain behind the black shanties of Fishtown. A gull screamed and disappeared.

She was remembering what she had said to Mike about dreams, but she was thinking about her father now. Thinking about the smoky smell that he carried home with him every night on his fireman's uniform. Thinking about his warmth when she nestled into the crook of his arm and his voice when he read from *Charlotte's Web.* Thinking about the little poem he used to tell her at night: *Hold fast to dreams, for if dreams die, life is a broken-winged bird that cannot fly.*

She brushed her hair back from her face and put on her hat, pulling it snugly down over her ponytail. The fingers of her right hand found the top edge of her holster, and she fingered the leather and the metal beneath it.

A shiver snaked up her spine and she knew immediately what it was. She had been here seven months now, and the most pulse-quickening thing she had done was take a slap to the head as she helped Mike push an unruly drunk into the back of the car.

All those weeks in the academy, she had dreamed of putting on a uniform. But never — not once in her wildest dreams — did she think she would be working a possible homicide. She felt charged by all this, the sight of the yellow tape, the chatter of the radios, the faces of those forgotten girls in the bulletins, and that pelvic bone, its stark whiteness standing out against the dark leaves.

A stab of guilt pierced her, and she looked at the manila folder in her hand.

Was this what it felt like to be a cop? To feel so alive because someone was dead?

3

It was dark by the time she pulled into the gravel drive. She gathered up the folder of bulletins and got out of the Jeep. Propping open the screen door with her hip, she fumbled for her house key in the dark. A scratching sound behind the wooden front door, then a low whine.

"Okay, okay, Chips, I'm coming," she said.

Before she could get the door completely open, a snout thrust through and the rest of the big yellow mutt emerged. The dog's front legs came up on her thighs as his long, skinny tail swung like a racing metronome.

"What's the matter, kiddo? You afraid of the dark?" Joe said, scratching the dog's ears.

She hit the light switch at the left of the door. She had started toward the table when her shoe hit something soft, and she skidded. She looked down.

Shit.

She held up her foot and let out a sigh. Then she saw Chips sitting there, staring at her balefully.

"It's all right," she said. "It's my fault for being late."

She opened the screen door, and Chips ran outside. She hopped into the kitchen, tossed the folder on the counter, and grabbed some paper towels. Once she had cleaned her shoe and the floor, she stood up, wiping her sweaty forehead and looking around the cottage.

The cottage had been closed up all day, and it was hot and stuffy. But it was neat and clean, as usual. The plaid throw was folded over the arm of the sofa, the breakfast mugs were left clean in the sink drainer, and that morning's *Echo Bay Banner* was already rolled into a tight bundle for the winter kindling pile.

Joe stared at the newspaper in consternation. The log newspaper roller was Brad's new toy. He had bought the gadget, which looked like a big pasta maker, out of a catalogue, and every morning, he fed the *Banner* into the roller and added the paper log to the pile by the sink. Problem was, he never seemed to remember that she liked to read the paper at night when she got home.

A scratching at the door. She went to let Chips back in. He followed her into the kitchen, waiting patiently while she dumped a glob of Alpo into his bowl and refreshed his water.

Then she went around the cottage, throwing open the windows to let in the sultry night air. After changing into an old T-shirt and running shorts, she got an icy Stroh's from the refrigerator. She leaned against the counter taking a long drink as she watched Chips lick the empty bowl in the hopeful way that only an ex-stray could. Her eyes drifted to the folder of missing persons bulletins. She opened it and looked at the face of the first girl. Dark hair. Lovely eyes. Sixteen years old.

She turned away from it and took her beer out to the screened-in porch, settling into the wicker lounge. The darkness enveloped her, endless and deep, glittering with a million pinpricks of light. The sky was different up here that way. No city lights to mask the beauty of the stars. No smog to sour the night air. Their rented cottage was about a mile outside town in a stand of pines, and while Joe could sometimes — when the wind was just right — smell the lake, she couldn't see it.

She thought about her mother suddenly, and something she had once told her.

You're an Aquarius, Joe, you should live near water.

Ma, the only water in Cleveland is the Cuyahoga River, and that is more solid than liquid.

Don't get smart. I'm just telling you what your chart says.

The phone rang. She didn't want to get up, but it might be Brad. She was eager to tell him about the bones. She went in to grab the receiver.

"I called earlier. Where were you?"

"Ma! I was just thinking about you."

"I know. That's why I called. I know when my daughter needs me. I can feel it. Don't tell me I can't."

Joe's smile lingered. In addition to doing astrology charts, Florence Frye claimed to have ESP. But only with her daughter, she would always add whenever someone gave her the usual look.

"I'm fine," Joe said, as a way of short-circuiting her mother's inquiries into her personal life.

"Did I say anything?"

"Don't start." Joe took a swig of the beer. Her mother wasn't crazy about Brad, said he wasn't "right" for her, because she had done their charts and said their moons were squared. Joe decided to divert the subject.

"Have you heard from Dennis lately?" she asked.

"Well, you know your brother," Florence said. "Seeing the world on a wing and a prayer. Last I heard, he was working the pipeline in the Yukon or somewhere."

Joe smiled. She missed her older brother.

"But I didn't call to talk about him," Florence said.

Joe waited, hearing some small catch in her mother's voice.

"The divorce is final," Florence finally said.

"Oh, Ma . . ."

"It's okay. I'm okay. He was a horse's ass.

I'm better off without him."

Gus Grandle had been Florence Frye's fifth husband. Joe didn't know Gus well, because Florence had married him while Joe was away at Northern. Joe met him at the wedding in Cleveland and once more at Christmas. He was a gregarious, red-faced truck driver whom Joe remembered as having a too-loud laugh and a penchant for Polack jokes. But the guy doted on Florence, took her to Vegas, bought her a pair of rhinestone earrings the size of ice cubes, and seemed to make her happy. For three years at least.

"I thought you and Gus were trying to work things out," Joe said.

Joe could feel her mother's shrug through the phone. "The magic wore off. He gave me snow tires for my birthday."

Joe laughed. She could hear her mother lighting up one of her Salems. In the long pause Joe could read that her mother was taking this harder than she was letting on. And she knew that Gus wasn't the man foremost in her mother's mind tonight.

"I was thinking about Daddy today," Joe said quietly.

Her mother was silent for a moment. "Yeah, me, too." More silence. "God, I miss him."

"Me, too, Ma."

Joe cradled the phone close, waiting. She could hear the *chit-chit-chit* of her mother's parakeet in the background. Finally, Joe heard the sharp intake of smoky breath as her mother came back from her memories.

"So!" Florence said, coughing. "What's new in your life? Tell me something to get my mind off things. Make it up if you have to."

Joe laughed softly. "We've got a good case," she said, putting her legs up on a table. She went on to tell her mother about the bones.

"Well, you've got to find out who she was."

"Yeah, Ma, I know that.

"I'm not talking about just IDing her. I'm talking about finding out who she really was. You got anything other than bones?"

Joe hesitated. She thought about mentioning the piece of silver they had found but a part of her didn't want to go into this, but a different part of her knew that even when her mother was pressing like this, she could be helpful. Florence Frye had been a cop once, after all. Sometimes Joe had trouble remembering that. Her mother . . . a police-woman on the Cleveland force, one of the first, back in the late fifties. Not a commis-sioned officer, of course. Her mother had been assigned to the jail as a matron and later worked the parking-meter circuit, but she prided herself on the fact that she had a badge. Every time Joe got to thinking how hard she herself had it back in the academy, or even how much crap she had to take from guys like Mack, all she had to do was imagine how much tougher it had been for Officer Florence Frye.

"Joe?"

"Yeah, Ma, I'm here."

"There's always something you can use. You just gotta find it. Find it, and you will find this girl."

Joe almost said it, almost said, *You were a jail matron, Ma, not an investigator.* Sometimes it was just too hard to hear the echo of dead dreams in her mother's voice. Sometimes it was just too hard being the depository for those same dreams.

She took a swig of beer. "I'll try," she said softly.

"You can get to know a victim from something as small as a button," Florence went on, her smoke-rasped voice taking on an edge of excitement. "A button can lead to a blouse and a blouse to a store and to a credit-card receipt."

"They've got a search team out there. Maybe they'll find something."

There was a long pause on Florence's end. "They're not letting you in on this, are they?" she said.

Joe waited too long to answer, and Florence's sigh filled the dead space. "Look, sweetheart, now that the papers are signed and all, I don't have much on my plate," she said. "How about if I come up for a visit?"

Joe was surprised to feel a slight tightening in her throat. She hadn't seen her mother in months. She missed her.

"I'd like that, Ma. When could you come?"

"Hell, I'll throw a suitcase in the Pontiac, get Audrey next door to come in and feed the bird. I can be there in two days."

Joe smiled. "Pack light. We're having a warm fall."

They said their goodbyes, and Joe hung up the phone. She took her beer back out to the porch, switching on a small table lamp to break up the darkness. She pushed Chips aside to make room on the lounge and picked up the *Echo Bay Banner.*

The paper was filled with its usual fare: hopeful predictions for a good winter of skiing at Sugarloaf; the Sutton Bay Norsemen had trounced Benzie Central; the Yarn Barn down on Main was celebrating its fiftieth anniversary; the Ruffed Grouse Society was getting ready for its annual banquet. But the big story was about the cormorants nesting on South Manitou Island. Wildlife officials were considering letting hunters shoot the birds because their droppings were killing off all the native orchids and trillium.

Joe knew the bones would make tomorrow's front page, bumping the cormorants inside. She set the paper aside, rubbing her eyes.

She didn't realize she had dozed off until she heard the crunch of tires on gravel and the thud of a car door. She could tell from the slump of his shoulders that Brad was tired.

"Hey there, why so late?" she asked as he came onto the porch.

"Good Samaritan rescue," Brad said. "They brought in a shepherd that had been hit by a car. Dog had no tags. There ought to be a law against some people having animals."

Joe rose and wrapped her arms around his waist, giving him a kiss. She pulled back to see his face. Brad had the clean features of his Finnish ancestors, a wide smile, sandy blond hair, and pale brown eyes. But when he was tired or upset, an opaqueness could settle over his face like a November fog and he would look suddenly ten years older than his twenty-eight years. As he did now.

"Did you eat?" she asked.

He shook his head. "Wasn't time. Didn't stop all day."

"Come on. I'll fix you something."

Brad followed her into the tiny kitchen, and she saw him stop and look down at the bulletins. She was about to reach over and close the folder, but he picked it up and set it over on a chair near the door, where they put things they didn't want to forget to take back to work.

Joe turned back to the stove, gathering up the things needed to make bacon and eggs. Brad slid into the chair, welcoming Chips's snout on his thigh with a stroke of the dog's head. Joe glanced at Brad and then looked away, easily reading his silences. She knew what this one was about.

"Any progress on getting a new vet?" she asked as she poured the beaten eggs into the skillet.

Brad leaned back in the chair, spreading his long blue-jeaned legs out and shaking his head. "Tom says he can't find anyone. I don't think he's even trying."

Tom was Brad's boss, the vet who owned the clinic in Traverse City. It was a big clinic, always busy. Brad was the only other vet, and he put in long hours, sometimes six days a week. They never seemed to have days off together anymore, not like it had been back in Marquette when she was just waitressing. But Joe knew that wasn't the real source of Brad's discontent.

Brad wanted his own clinic. And not here. She knew he missed the U.P. and wanted to go home. But she also knew he wouldn't bring it up. He had been the one to say they would give Echo Bay one year's try. Still, she wondered sometimes lately if he wasn't marking off the months on his mind's calendar.

Joe set the plate of bacon and eggs in front of Brad, and sat down. Neither of them spoke until Brad pushed the plate away.

"Brad," Joe said softly, covering his hand with hers. "Ask Tom for some time off. Maybe we could go back to Marquette for a few days."

His eyes came up to meet hers. For a second, she could see the man who had swept into her heart like a cyclone and left her ravaged with his sexual energy.

"I've been neglecting you lately," he said softly.

"We've both been busy," she said quickly.

He pulled his hand away, and she leaned back in the chair. She didn't look up as Brad took his plate and went to the sink. He began to wash the dish and the skillet. Joe waited until he was almost done to speak again.

"My mother called today."

"How is she?" Brad asked without turning.

"Fine, fine," Joe said, picking at a paper napkin. "Actually, not so fine. She's getting divorced."

"Is this number six?"

"Five." Joe hesitated. "She wants to come for a visit."

Brad didn't say anything as he stashed the skillet in the stove drawer. Then he turned to face her. "Joe, this isn't a good time," he said. "You just said —"

"I know, I know. She needs me right now, Brad."

He was just standing there, looking at her. The guilt was there again, tugging at her insides. He came over and squatted down in front of her, taking her hands and holding them together in his as if he were saying a prayer for both of them.

"Tomorrow I am going to ask Tom for some time off," he said. "And then you and I are going up to Mackinac Island."

Before she could say anything, he leaned in and kissed her, a deep kiss, the kind of kiss that neither of them seemed to have time for lately.

When he pulled back to look at her, he was smiling. "Mackinac Island? Breakfast in bed? At the Grand Hotel? All the fudge you can eat?"

"We can't afford the Grand Hotel," she said.

"We can afford fudge."

He kissed her again, and this time she felt herself responding. "All right," she said.

"Great. Now I am going in and wash all this dog smell off."

Brad left the kitchen. Chips was whimpering by the door, so she rose and let him out. She followed him onto the porch.

The yard was washed with a silver light. She watched Chips rolling in the grass, watched the tops of the trees dancing in the wind. A voice floated to her, Brad singing "Someone Saved My Life Tonight" off-key in the shower.

She smiled with the sudden recognition that in such a short time, she had grown to love this place, love its beauty, love the fact that they never bothered to lock their doors at night. No one in Echo Bay ever did.

She looked up at the half-moon. It hung above her, waning and white, like a shard of bone in the black sky.

4

He was up high, and he could see everything. Above, the pearly glow of the bone-colored half-moon. Below, the endless black expanse of the lake, moving like oil. And all around him, the rolling mounds of sand that glittered in the moon's light.

The soft pounding of the waves blended with the pounding in his head. This was not where he wanted to be. But it was the only place he could think of that was without people. This time of year, the woods — his woods — had too many hunters and hikers, so he would not have the privacy he needed. This place would have to do this time.

He looked around him. The footprints left in the sand by the tourists were gone now, erased by the shifting winds of Lake Michigan. His own prints would be gone by dawn. Erased here, just as they had always been erased in other places, and other months, by snow.

No snow here. That was wrong, too. And no hunger in the air either.

The hunger . . . it had been with him this morning. It had started as a sour-meat taste rising in his throat as soon as he saw that stupid girl. She had been standing there by his car at the gas pump when he walked up to it. Stupid girl, asking him if he was heading up north. Asking him to do this to her. Stupid, stupid girl.

He closed his eyes, willing the hunger to come back. But it was gone, and he knew why. It was because everything was wrong right now, this time, this place. He had made a mistake this time, and now he had to fix it.

He walked down the sandy slope to his car, his ears alert for human sounds. When he heard none, he unlocked the trunk and threw it open. The moonlight offered him an image of bare skin, tangled rope, and two dark eyes swimming with fear.

Her mouth was covered with a strip of duct tape. He would have liked to remove it so he could hear her beg, but he didn't dare. This place might be patrolled after dark, and it was already risky being here. And despite the sudden hardness in his body as he looked down at her, it still didn't feel right.

She was light as he lifted her from the trunk, balancing her bound body upright against the rear fender. He grabbed the bulky canvas bag and closed the trunk.

She began to whimper, but the cries were absorbed into the tear-soaked duct tape. He glanced toward the dunes, then in the other direction, into the darkness of the footpath that led down into the trees. He needed the trees, but he didn't know how far they went or if there were other parking areas here or if there might even be a ranger station nearby.

Indecision. Ignorance. Stupidity. This was so wrong.

He looked to her, realizing that he could not carry her and the heavy bag that deep into the trees. He would have to cut the ropes on her ankles and make her walk. He set the bag down and unzipped it. When he pulled out his hunting knife, she cried out again and twisted away, falling against the car, then smacking to the sandy asphalt.

He flipped her over. Her skin was damp and gritty, the sliver-moon reflected back at him in her wide, dark eyes. She had been a bitch all day, kicking and screaming, and sometimes when she got mad enough, calling him names, reminding him a little of Ronnie. He had already cut her once on the arm to get her in the trunk. And he thought about cutting her calf now so she couldn't run, but if he didn't do it just right, she wouldn't be able to walk.

He slipped the knife between her ankles and, in one upward jerk, severed the ropes.

"You remember how sharp this knife is," he said, pulling her to her feet. "Now walk."

She stumbled, and he stopped, again trying to find the patience not to slice her up right now and just abandon this whole fucking night.

He gave her a shove toward the trees.

She began to move forward, her head swiveling to scan the darkness around them. Then suddenly she stopped again, spinning to the lake behind her. She couldn't see it, he knew. But she could hear it, maybe even smell it.

He turned, too, a strange idea crossing his mind. Maybe it would be better to do the first part of this out there on the sand, where the moonlight would illuminate her face. It might be interesting, different from the others, who had been in the snow, numbed by the frozen ground. Would she feel different to him if her body was warmer? Would it give him more power to take her that way?

He heard the sudden slap of bare feet and turned back to her. She was gone, running blindly across the parking lot, struggling to keep her balance as she worked furiously to free her hands from the rope.

He threw down the canvas bag and ran after her. She was easy to see, bare skin gleaming in the moonlight, and as he ran, he was washed with an excitement he hadn't felt yet today. Something primitive and savage that came from chasing a woman who was just as naked and untamed as the wilderness in which she sought escape.

She struggled up the dunes, her arms free now, her hands ripping at the tape over her mouth. Her screams fractured the night.

He had to stop her. Now.

But she shocked him by stopping herself. Then he realized she was trapped at the edge of the bluff, nothing below her but darkness and the blind rush of waves against the beach. She spun to him, eyes wide in horror. Her body was so white it already looked dead. His erection pressed painfully against his pants, thickening the taste in his mouth.

He teased her with the knife, flashing in the moonlight. "Here, little girl," he said, holding out his hand. "Come on."

A tiny cry. A look over her shoulder. Then she disappeared.

He ran forward. She hadn't thrown herself over. She was trying to crawl down the steep, sandy slope. Her skin was the same color as the sand, making her almost invisible except for her brown hair.

No. He couldn't let her get down there.

He would never get her back up here to the trees.

He stepped off the edge, digging each footstep into the deep sand so he wouldn't slip, quick but careful to keep himself balanced as he started groping for her arms, knowing that at any second, she could lose her balance and tumble to the beach below.

He finally caught her wrist. She screamed and slapped at him, but she was on her stomach and had no leverage or strength.

"Don't!" she cried. "Let me go! Let me go!"

He twisted her palm upward and slashed her forearm.

She screamed. He stabbed at her shoulder, spewing blood onto her back, his hands, and the sand.

"Stop! Oh, God . . . please . . . please . . ."

She was becoming dead weight, and he dropped to his knee to keep his balance on the shifting sand. She was sobbing, her legs flailing, still fighting him. Blood was everywhere, slicking her arms and his hands. He couldn't hold on to her much longer.

He slashed at her, each stab taking more air from her lungs and weakening her screams. Then a hard plunge that went all the way through her, thudding into the sand.

She stopped moving. It was quiet again,

the sound of the surf coming back in to fill the night.

He pulled back, jerking out the knife. Panting, he stared down at her.

"It wasn't time!" he said. "It wasn't the fucking right time!"

He looked at the moon. A huge sob convulsed his body, and he fell to his knees beside her on the blood-wet sand.

5

Joe had expected the powwow on the bones to be held in Leach's office. But Augie pointed her down the hall to a closed door. There was a sign taped to it in Augie's careful printing: CONFERENCE ROOM.

A table and six chairs had been crowded into the windowless room. A bulletin board and a clock had been hung on the wall, a phone installed on the table. It took Joe a minute to realize this was the room Augie had been using to stow old files and his boxes of Christmas decorations.

There had been no need for a true conference room before. She guessed that Leach had ordered the room prepared only because of the bones.

Joe claimed a chair by the door, setting her pad and folder in front of her. Mack came in five minutes later, giving her a grunt of acknowledgment before dropping into a chair as far away from her as possible.

They sat in silence for several minutes before the door banged open and Mike burst in. He held his leather utility belt in one hand and his hat in the other. His uniform shirt hung open. "Sheriff not here yet?" he asked.

When she shook her head, Mike tossed his belt onto the table and hurriedly started tucking in his shirt, mumbling something about the school bus being late. Behind him, Holt squeezed by and quietly took a chair. After a few seconds, he realized he hadn't brought anything to write on, and he left quickly.

Mike was buckling his belt when Leach came in. Leach walked to the head of the table and set down two folders. Before he could say anything, the door banged open again and Holt slid into a chair.

Leach let the silence hang for a moment. "You don't know what great comfort I get from knowing how prepared we are this morning."

No one said a word. Leach gave a small shake of his head and opened the top folder. "Okay," he said. "First off, I want to make it clear that under no circumstances will we refer to this as a homicide until we know for sure that it is one."

"What else could it be?" Mack asked.

Leach threw him a sharp look, but before he could say a word, Mack slapped open his own folder, grabbed an eight-by-ten glossy, and shoved it down the table toward Leach. Joe caught only a glimpse of it, but she could see it was of a teenage girl with long blond hair.

"It's a homicide, and that's our victim," Mack said, pointing at the photograph. "Annabelle Chapel."

Leach picked up the photo. "For those of you who do not know," he said, "Annabelle Chapel was a sixteen-year-old girl who disappeared from the Petoskey area about seven years ago."

"Six years ago," Mack said. "And when she disappeared, she was wearing a necklace. A crucifix. Her mother told me she never took it off."

Everyone was staring at Mack, except for Leach who was studying the photo. "Mack used to be with the Petoskey PD," Leach said, looking up. "He was the investigator assigned to the Chapel case."

Joe couldn't hide her surprise. She had always thought Mack's crustiness came from walking the streets in a city like Detroit or Flint. Petoskey was a small resort town northeast of Echo Bay. It was a popular second-home spot for moneyed downstaters and Chicagoans. She thought back to Mike's comment about how Mack's big-city dreams had passed him by.

"The Chapels are from Chicago but had a second home in Petoskey," Leach said, drawing her attention back. "The family was up here on vacation in February 1969. Annabelle left the family home with friends to go skiing at Boyne Mountain, about thirty miles away. She never made it home. Her disappearance remains unsolved."

Leach set the photograph of Annabelle Chapel on the table. "Mack," he said, "I assume that sometime between yesterday and this morning, you verified that Annabelle Chapel has never been found, dead or alive?"

"I have," Mack said. "She's still missing."

"And how did you determine that?" Leach asked.

"I called her parents," he said.

Leach looked to the ceiling, furious. "Good Lord, man, we haven't even confirmed we are dealing with a homicide here."

"We are," Mack said.

"Not until the medical examiner signs his name to it," Leach said. "And until he does, we have to consider any and all possibilities. Like, the victim may have gotten lost and died of exposure. Or was attacked by a bear. Or was shot in a hunting accident."

"We found a crucifix," Mack said. "Annabelle wore one. It's her."

Leach leaned down on the table. "Even if you are right, we don't know how she died or if she was murdered. We don't know who killed her. And we won't ever know without real evidence. We still have an investigation to do."

Mack sat back in his chair, crossing his arms.

"And in the meantime, we keep all other possibilities open," Leach said, raising his voice. "Is that understood?"

Mack stared at his folder. Holt looked as if a bomb had gone off, and Mike was looking up at the blank bulletin board. Joe reached across the table and pulled the photograph of Annabelle Chapel close. It was a portrait, and from the white formal gown, Joe guessed it might be a school dance or a debutante type of thing. Annabelle Chapel was gorgeous, long blond hair, a hint of a smile, and wide pale eyes. A delicate crucifix encircled her neck.

"So," Leach said, "I don't want *any* statements made to the press or anyone else that even come close to insinuating this is a homicide. Are we clear?"

"Yes, sir," Joe said, setting the photograph back on the table.

Mike nodded.

Holt hesitated. "Yes, sir."

"Mack?" Leach pressed. "Is that clear?"

"Yeah, it's clear," Mack said.

"All right. Next," Leach said, "I have called the state police, but I have asked them to let us do a preliminary investigation to see if we can identify the victim through other items we might pick up over the next week. Maybe we'll get lucky and get a skull or a wallet. And if the lab can narrow down the time of death to even a few years, we'll have a better idea of what we're looking at."

"Do you know how long it will be before any results come in?" Joe asked.

"On the bones, possibly months," Leach said. "On anything else, like the jewelry, we should have something on that soon. That and a few other items we picked up yesterday have already been sent off. There'll be more items coming in every day as the searchers work the area."

Leach went to the door and called for

Augie. He was there in a second, handing over the large blue binder that held the missing persons bulletins. Joe's eyes flicked to the folder she had brought in. Inside were the copies she had made yesterday.

"Mack is going to be point on this," Leach said. "But no investigation is done without a lot of grunt work. We'll start with the missing persons file."

Joe was watching Mack. He was eyeing the blue binder with something close to contempt.

"If this is not Annabelle Chapel," Leach went on, "my guess is that she was local or semilocal, maybe from within a hundred miles. I doubt she was a tourist. I think we would have heard about something like that. Statistics tell us she was probably between fifteen and forty, more likely on the young side of that. In the absence of forensic verification, I'd also guess she's been dead at least a year."

Leach pushed the binder across the table to Mike. "Mike," Leach said, "I want you to go through these and pull the ones that fit those criteria." He paused. "That is, if you can remember it, since I see you're not choosing to write any of this down."

"Joe already did that," he said.

"Did what?"

"Pulled the possibles and made copies," Mike said.

Everyone looked at Joe.

"What criteria did you use, Joe?" Leach asked.

"Just about the same as you have," Joe said. "I went back ten years and used a hundred-mile radius."

Leach nodded. "Good. Where are the copies now?"

Joe could feel Mack's hard stare as she held the folder out to Leach.

"Give them to Mike," Leach said. "He can narrow them down as to who's turned up and who hasn't, and we'll go from there."

"Can't I do that?" Joe asked.

Leach hesitated, then glanced at Mack, as if he were trying to tell her something he could not say out loud. She guessed Mack had already asked Leach that she be moved to the sidelines.

"I'd appreciate it if you would just carry on with your regular patrol duties, Joe," Leach said. "Mike will ride with you in the morning, but in the afternoon, he's on the phones."

"We'll call you if we need you," Mack added.

Joe looked to him, wanting to lunge across the table and punch him.

"This is going to require some extra hours and hard work on everyone's part," Leach said. "So I'm thanking you in advance for your cooperation. Dismissed."

Joe stayed her seat, her eyes flicking up to Mack as he and the others left the room.

Leach remained. "Joe, you okay?" he asked.

She couldn't look at him. "Not really, sir."

"Look, all we're doing at this point is a preliminary investigation. We both know we'll be turning this over to the state in a few days."

She stood up. Mike had forgotten the folder. She picked it up.

"Is there something else?" Leach asked.

She faced him. "Officers like Holt see what Mack does and they learn from it. That's wrong, Sheriff. You know it is."

Leach rubbed his jaw, his eyes going from Joe to the open conference-room door, then back to her. "You knew coming in this was not going to be easy."

"I don't want it easy," she said. "I just want it fair."

Leach nodded. "I'll talk to Mack."

"But you're not going to tell him to let me in on this."

"No. He's lead because he has the experience. Lead investigators have to make their own calls. I have to let him do his job."

Joe brushed her hair from her forehead. She was not going to win this. "Are we finished, sir?" she asked.

Leach nodded.

She made her way to the front office. Augie was hanging up the phone and waved her over.

"We've got a problem out on Lake Shore," he said.

Joe sighed. "Mrs. Elsinore's grandson?"

"The neighbor says he's been peeking in her windows again."

When she reached for the slip of paper, Augie touched her wrist. "I heard what happened in there," he said. "I'm sorry."

She shrugged. She didn't want Augie — or anyone else, for that matter — to see her disappointment. She went to her desk on the pretense of looking for something in the drawer.

"Joette, do you know anything about wine?" Augie asked.

"Just that three glasses are my limit," she said without looking up.

"I always thought people were like wine," Augie went on.

Joe didn't say anything.

"I mean, you've got your Burgundies," Augie said. "Mature, lots of finesse, easy to swallow, but only after a serious aging process. That's the sheriff. Then you got your Beaujolais. Playful but doesn't stay long on the tongue. That's Mike."

Joe tapped the folder on her palm, her eyes going to the conference door, where Mike was talking to Leach.

"And then there is Medoc. A heavy hitter that can overwhelm everything."

"Mack," Joe said.

"Yeah, but Mack is corked Medoc, just on the edge of going bad."

Joe smiled. "All right, I'll bite. What am I?"

"I'm guessing an austere Burgundy. Good stuff that just needs aging."

Joe laughed softly.

"You know, maybe you should go talk to Theo," Augie said. "Maybe he could help you with the case."

Theo was the editor of the *Echo Bay Banner* and Augie's lover. Joe knew that between the two of them, they probably knew the business of every person who had ever set foot in Echo Bay over the last twenty years.

Before she could answer Augie, Mike came up to the desk. Joe handed him the note Augie had given her.

"Shit, not that creepo grandson again?" Mike asked.

"You got it. We might as well go and get this over with."

Joe followed Mike out the front door. They started toward the cruiser.

"I wouldn't get too close to Augie if I was you," Mike said.

"Why not?"

He shrugged. "You know how those people are."

"What people?"

"Uh-huh. Pretend you don't notice."

"What are you talking about?"

Mike stopped at the driver's door. "Homos."

There was no hate in his tone. It was more of a strange acknowledgment of something foreign that he had chosen to let exist as long as it kept its distance.

She didn't reply, putting on her cap as she started toward the passenger side of the car. Mike opened his door and stopped. "Shit," he said. "I left the bulletins in the conference room."

"I've got them," Joe said, holding up the folder.

As she held it out to him over the roof of the cruiser, she felt as if she were handing over one of her kids for him to babysit.

"Thanks," Mike said, taking it. He opened the door and tossed the folder into the backseat. Joe stared at him. He finally noticed that she hadn't made a move to get into the cruiser.

"What's the matter?" he asked.

"You could show them a little more respect," she said.

He looked confused for a second. "They're just papers, Joe," he said.

She jerked open the door and got in. Mike slid into the driver's seat.

"They're people, Mike," she said without looking at him. "People who are still missing. And someone is still missing them."

6

It took them more than an hour to get out of Mrs. Elsinore's house. The old lady plied them with coffee and Entenmann's Caramel Apple Twist and yakked about everything from the trash clogging the narrows of Lake Leelanau to why "that Sergeant Pepper woman" on *Police Story* dressed like a hooker.

Finally, Mrs. Elsinore promised to keep her grandson away from the neighbor's windows, and they left.

Joe, still angry over Mike's cavalier attitude, had barely said a word during the whole hour. As they stepped off the porch,

76

Mike trailed behind.

"Maybe you should start dressing like Angie Dickinson," he said.

"Shut up," Joe said without turning.

Mike tossed his notebook into the back as he slid behind the wheel of the cruiser.

"You're not even going to write this up?" Joe asked.

"Jeff Elsinore is harmless," Mike said. "By seven tonight, she'll be making him a pot pie and forget we were even there."

"We still need to do a report," Joe said.

"Be my guest."

Mike swung the cruiser back onto the main road. Joe reached down to get the black zippered binder at her feet. In it were her ticket book, log sheets and report forms, her address book, maps of the state and county, and a small spiral notebook. The binder had been a gift from her mother the day Joe graduated from the academy. Florence had used the same binder when she was on the force back in Cleveland.

Joe ran her hand over the scuffed leather and pulled out a report form. She filled it out in her neat handwriting, then zipped the binder closed.

She settled back into the seat and glanced at Mike. He didn't have a binder. He had a giant rubber band. The rubber band held his ticket book and department forms, his coffee-stained maps, and a bright blue spiral notebook that he had probably lifted from his kid.

Mike had put on his sunglasses, and the warm breeze from the open window whipped his long dark hair.

Too long, Joe thought, and she found herself wondering why Leach let him get away with it.

He didn't let her get away with anything. From the first day she met Leach, he had told her that this was not just a job but a career. You were expected to take pride in what you did, and you learned quickly to polish everything from your manners to the toes of your shoes.

Joe closed her eyes, thinking of the long hours she had spent trying to get that mirror shine on her shoes. Her shelf had been cluttered with bottles of things that claimed to add a sparkle or stiffness to every surface she had. Leather. Brass. Cotton. Except her nails. No nail polish on that shelf.

Nails . . . she had a sudden memory of cutting off her own the day she went into the academy.

She had been only one of two women there. Nothing — not her mother's warnings, Brad's protests, or her own imagination — had prepared her for how tough it was. The men didn't give a damn about the new Equal Employment Opportunity Act that gave her the right to be a cop. Not just as her mother had been back in the fifties. But a cop with the same uniform, the same duties, the same pay.

She was five-ten but slender, with no upper-body strength. She gritted through the tactics training, the weight lifting, the pull-ups, the nine-mile morning runs. She endured the sexist jokes, the used Kotex napkin left in her locker, the hits from being slammed to the mat by the guy trying to take her out and make his point. At night, alone in her room, she would cry silently, unable to pull in a full sob because of her bruised ribs.

Four weeks into training, the other woman dropped out. That same morning, during a baton drill, the instructor was called away, and that's when it began. One of the guys started using his night stick in a jerking-off motion. The others howled as the guy started simulating oral sex, moaning her name. That night, when Leach called to ask how she was doing, Joe burst into tears on the phone.

"Joe, there is nothing they can do to run you out. Only you can quit."

Two months later, she graduated. One week after that, she was wearing a Leelanau County sheriff's badge.

"So how long is this silent treatment going to last?" Mike asked, interrupting her thoughts.

"What do you mean?" she asked.

Mike let out a sigh. "Look, if you're mad because the sheriff gave the bulletins to me and not you, that's not my fault."

"I'm not mad."

"You're mad. You just won't admit it."

She was silent.

"When you're mad, your face gets kind of, well, mean-looking," he said.

"Mean?"

"Jesus, I can't say anything right today. What I mean is you're a good-looking woman, Joe. God knows, Mindy gives me enough shit about it." He paused. "But your eyes have a way of turning into little slits that make you look like something, like a cat you don't want to meet in a dark alley."

She wasn't sure how to take that, so she kept quiet. They rode on in silence for several miles. They were coming back into town when Mike finally spoke.

"I'm sorry," he said. "We have to ride together, so whatever the hell I did — or didn't do — I'm sorry." He glanced at her.

"Okay?"

She didn't trust herself to look at him and not say something more that would make things worse. So she just gave him a tight nod and leaned back in the seat, gripping her mother's black leather binder.

Mike went back to the station to go to work on the bulletins. Joe slid behind the wheel of the idling cruiser, and for a moment, she just sat there. The radio was quiet; there was nothing to do, nowhere to go. She pulled away, intending to just cruise the town. As she turned onto Main, the sign for the *Echo Bay Banner* caught her eye.

She thought about what Augie had said. What could it hurt to talk to Theo?

The newspaper office was housed in an old dress shop, with a counter separating the front from the desks, file cabinets, and computer terminals beyond. Carrie, the teenage girl who manned the desk and took classified ads, looked up from her *Glamour* when Joe came in.

"Is Theo here?" Joe asked.

Carrie popped her gum. "He's in the back. You want me to go get him?"

"Please."

A few minutes later, a light-skinned black man appeared, rubbing his hands on an apron. Theo Toussaint was a short, chubby man of about fifty, with close-cropped hair surrounding a harvest-moon face set off with black-framed glasses. He had a ready smile as he approached the counter.

"Augie said you might be coming," he said in a lilting accent Joe had never been able to place. Town gossip said Theo's father was a Haitian doctor who had fled Duvalier's regime in Haiti and settled in Montreal, where he married a British woman. No one knew how Theo had gotten down to Echo Bay, but he was as much a fixture in the town as the smokehouse over in Fishtown.

Theo offered his hand, and Joe took it. When she pulled away, there was something sticky on her palm.

"Oh, *merde,*" Theo said. "I'm sorry. It's the wax. I'm pasting up tomorrow's edition. Come on back, and I'll give you something to clean it off."

The back room was crowded with what looked like small lighted architect tables. Each bank of tables held pages of tomorrow's *Banner,* with headlines, stories, and pictures pasted onto paper grids.

Theo gave Joe a rag wet with acetone. As she wiped her hand, Joe stepped up to look at the paste-up of tomorrow's front page: NO LEADS ON BONES FOUND IN WOODS.

"I don't know why I bother," Theo said. "By the time I can print anything, the whole town already knows more than I do." He walked off to a machine in the corner.

Joe knew that Theo did most of the work himself, writing the stories, taking the pictures, and probably sweeping up at night. She knew, too, that Augie probably told Theo everything that went on inside the station.

Theo came over to the light table, holding out the waxed paper strip like a Christmas garland. Joe watched him as he carefully patted the strip into a blank column on the front page.

"So what can I help you with, Joe?"

"Right now, I'm just gathering information about missing girls," Joe said. "I know you've lived here forever, and newspaper people, well, they know things, hear the gossip."

"Gossip?"

"I was wondering if you might remember anything the police may not have."

"Such as?"

She shrugged. "Some wife who was rumored to have left town in the middle of the night, a runaway no one might have reported."

"You're from Cleveland, right?" he asked.

"Yes, why?"

"Well, things are different in small towns," Theo said. "And Echo Bay is a very small town. Some families have been here for generations, others have come here, drawn to the calm. Here on the peninsula we are very isolated, not just physically but emotionally, from the rest of the world. People here like that."

"But people do disappear, don't they?"

"Yes," he said. "The teenagers get restless and run off looking for jobs or excitement. But they always seem to come back. Like Sheriff Leach did."

Joe nodded. "So anyone come to mind who didn't come back?"

"Just that girl from Petoskey."

"That's about a hundred miles from here, right?" she asked.

"More, metaphorically speaking."

"What do you mean?"

He went back to working on the front page. "Beautiful town, lots of money there, but many outsiders. All those Victorian summer homes left over from the old days, with their pretty porches looking down over the harbor. The Chapels had a home like that, way up on the hill."

"Did you cover Annabelle Chapel's disappearance?"

"The pretty blond daughter of a rich Chicago family goes missing from a Michigan ski lodge?" He smiled. "I put her picture on my front page."

"Can I see what you wrote?" Joe asked.

Theo wiped his hands on his apron. "Come with me."

He led her into a closet-sized room and pulled a large binder off the shelf. He flipped through the pages until he stopped at a *Banner* front page from February 1969. It was the same photograph Mack had tossed onto the table at their briefing. Again, Joe was struck by Annabelle Chapel's beauty. She had the eyes of a girl whose only worry was picking out a new winter coat at Marshall Field.

"Theo, could you make me a copy of this?" she asked.

"You want everything we printed?"

"If it's not too much trouble." She knew Mack wasn't going to share whatever he had in his case file.

Theo pushed his glasses up on the bridge of his nose. "You seem to have a big interest in these bones."

"I'm just doing my job," Joe said.

"Augie thinks you have a special . . . attachment."

Joe was silent, miffed that Augie was talk-

85

ing about not just police business but her.

Theo sensed her coolness. "I'm sorry. Augie can be such a yeti sometimes."

"Yeti?"

Theo frowned. "Yeti. Oh, no, wait. Yeti . . . that's like a Big Foot animal." He smiled. "Yenta, that's the word I want."

"Yeah, Augie's a yenta, all right," Joe said.

Theo closed the binder. "Come. I need a cigarette, so I will walk you out."

They paused outside on the sidewalk. It was hot, the sun a smudge high in the hazy white sky. The summer tourists had all gone now, and the leaf peepers had yet to descend. It was so quiet Joe could hear the wheeze of the grocery's automatic door across the street as someone went in.

She spotted Mack coming out of the Riverside Inn, carrying a Styrofoam takeout carton. Mack had lunch every day at the Riverside, always alone. More than a couple of times, Joe had smelled alcohol on his breath even under the Sen-Sen he popped.

Theo saw Mack, too. "Annabelle Chapel was his case, you know," he said, pointing his cigarette at Mack.

"That's what I hear," Joe said.

"He had a very special . . . attachment to her."

Mack disappeared around a corner, heading to the station.

"Some folks say he was obsessed," Theo said. "And that it cost him his job."

Joe wanted to hear more. But she knew it wasn't right to let Theo go on. How much of it was real, and how much of it was just junk that Augie and Theo cooked up?

The sun was beating down on her. She wiped her forehead and put on her cap. "Thanks for your help, Theo," she said.

"*De rien.* I will send the copies in with Augie tomorrow morning." He took another drag on his Camel. "Maybe I will have something else for you, as well."

"What?" Joe asked.

He smiled. "A little surprise."

7

Joe hadn't been ready for Theo's "little surprise" when it landed on her porch that morning.

Theo had written a second story about the bones. No, not a story, exactly. It was a eulogy for the unknown victim, set off in a black box right on the front page so no one could miss it among the sewer stories and high school football scores.

Joe picked up the copy of the *Banner* from the desk to read the story again. The headline was just two words: SOMEBODY'S DAUGHTER.

They think she was female. They think she was small. But there is nothing else to be gleaned from the shards of bone found just five miles beyond the edge of our village.

Just a girl.

We all know the woods where the bones were found. We've walked there, admiring the autumn colors or gathering firewood. We've hunted there, bringing home venison or rabbit for our tables. Our kids have played there, building imaginary houses in the old trees. How could we have known what lay beneath the bed of leaves and needles? How could we have known that our woods had become a cemetery?

We've all wondered who she is. But we may never know whose small bones these are.

Just a girl.

Somebody's girl. Somebody's daughter.

We should all pray those woods are not her final resting place. Let's pray our police are able to give her a name and a face. Let's pray they can take her home to those who are still missing her. And if not, then we must treat her as one of our own.

She is somebody's daughter.
Maybe our own.

The station door banged open, drawing her attention up. Dried leaves swirled in behind a man wearing a brown uniform. He set a small box on the counter.

"There a Detective Julian Mack here?" he asked.

"He's out," Joe said, tossing the newspaper aside. "Can I sign for it?"

The UPS man glanced at her badge and pushed a clipboard at her. "Right there."

He was gone with another cyclone of leaves. Joe started to take the box over to Mack's desk and then noticed that the return address was a private crime lab in Lansing. The box was light, and when she shook it, it rattled. She had shaken enough Christmas presents to guess what it was. The jewelry recovered near the bones. She was surprised it had come back so quickly.

She glanced at the door and took the box to her desk. She carefully peeled back the brown paper and eased the flaps open. Inside was a clear plastic bag sealed with evidence tape and inked up with several sets of initials. She turned on the desk lamp and spread the bag flat on the blotter.

The silver was badly tarnished, but the

lab had cleaned it so every link was visible. It wasn't a necklace with a crucifix, as Mack had thought. It was a charm bracelet. Joe brought the gooseneck lamp closer. There were seven charms: a windmill, a Christmas tree, a horse and carriage, a teddy bear, a locomotive engine, a cross, and what looked like a Roman soldier's head.

Joe started jerking open drawers. She found a magnifying glass and positioned it over each charm, trying to see the details, or a name or a date. There was something engraved on the back of the Roman soldier one, but it was too small and faint to make out.

Footsteps came up behind her, and she smelled Brut cologne.

"Hey, Mike," she said without looking up. "Heading home for a quick lunch, huh?"

He came around the front of the desk. "How did you know?"

"Just a hunch."

His eyes dropped to the evidence bag. "Is that the jewelry from the woods?"

She nodded, looking at the Roman soldier charm again with the magnifying glass. "It's not a crucifix," she said. "It's a charm brace-let."

Mike picked up the UPS box. "You shouldn't have opened Mack's box," he said.

"I'm not doing anything wrong," she said. "I didn't take it out of the bag. Besides, it's not his box. It belongs to the Leelanau County sheriff's department. I'd get to see it eventually anyway."

"He's still going to be pissed."

"He's going to be even more pissed when he realizes this is not Annabelle's necklace."

Mike bent to look at the bracelet.

"There's something on the back of this charm, but I can't read it," Joe said. She held out the magnifying glass. "See if you can make it out."

Mike didn't even have to take the glass before he spoke. "That's Michigan State," he said, pointing.

"What?"

"They have a Spartan as their mascot," he said.

She looked up at him. "Damn, you're right. And that's another strike against Annabelle Chapel. She was sixteen and probably going to high school somewhere in Chicago."

"Well, if our victim went to MSU, maybe we can ID her," Mike said. "And if we find out something about her, maybe that can help us find out who killed her."

"My mother said the same thing," Joe said.

Mike glanced at his watch but didn't make

a move to leave. "You talk about the job with your mother?" he asked.

Joe was studying the charm and didn't look up. "Sure, she was a cop."

"No shit? I didn't know that."

"She was a cop back in the days when the women wore skirts and wrote parking tickets. She likes to talk to me about my job."

"She likes you being a cop?"

"I didn't say that. But she is very proud of me," Joe said.

"My dad likes that I'm a cop," Mike said. "But my mom . . ."

Joe was still studying the MSU Spartan charm and didn't realize that Mike had fallen quiet. When she finally looked up at him, the sun from the window was full on his face, and he looked every bit of his twenty-nine years. But there was someone else there, too, in his eyes. A boy.

He raked his hair and started toward the door. "Mindy's waiting. See you after lunch."

"Right," Joe said. "Don't wear yourself out."

Mike laughed and pushed open the door. Joe picked the lab's report out of the box and gave it a quick read. The bracelet wasn't real silver, and there was no mention of any attempt to decipher the engraving on the back of the Spartan charm. There was nothing useful in the report at all. No wonder it had come back so quickly. They had done nothing but clean it up.

Joe turned her attention back to the bracelet. It was just a cheap thing, and it didn't seem like the kind of jewelry a rich girl like Annabelle Chapel would wear at any age. And the more Joe thought about it, the more it seemed not to be something even a coed would wear. It was the kind of bracelet a younger girl, making the fragile passage to womanhood, would leave home in a jewelry box when she went off to college and a grown-up life.

Joe stared at the Spartan charm. Every instinct was telling her that the girl who had worn the charm bracelet hadn't been old enough to attend college.

Damn. So why was a Michigan State charm on this bracelet?

She glanced up to the clock. Augie would be back from lunch soon. And Mack could walk in any second. She started to put the evidence bag back into the UPS box. Then she paused.

As soon as Mack realized this was not Annabelle Chapel's crucifix, he would dismiss it and it would be locked up in the evidence room and forgotten.

Her eyes went to the filing cabinet where Augie kept the Polaroid camera. But she quickly discarded that idea. There was no way to raise the detail on the engraving without a close-up lens. And it would have to be done without taking the bracelet out of the plastic bag.

She snatched up the evidence bag, shoved it into her pants pocket and flung the empty UPS box under her desk. It was wrong to do what she was about to do, but she knew it wasn't tampering with evidence or stealing it. She was just going to get it properly photographed. It would be back in its box in thirty minutes, if she was lucky.

Augie came in and looked at her strangely as he took his place back behind his console. "Everything okay, Joe?"

"I'll be right back," she said, pushing out the front door.

8

In the dim glow of the infrared light, Joe couldn't make out Theo's face. Which meant he couldn't see her well, either. Still, as she handed him the evidence bag, she was sure he could read the anxiety in her face.

Theo switched on the overhead light and

held up the bag, frowning. "I thought it was a necklace you found with the bones," he said.

When she didn't reply, he smiled. "Augie told me about it. But don't worry, Mack was blabbing about it to everyone over at the Riverside last night."

Joe didn't want to tell Theo any more than she had to. "I can't take it out of the bag. Can you get good pictures through the plastic?" she asked.

"*Bien sûr,*" he said.

She watched as he spread the bag beneath a Leica on a tripod, positioning each charm under a macro lens. The room was quiet except for the click of the camera. He raised an eyebrow when she asked him to take a close-up of the engraving on the back of the Spartan charm but didn't ask why she wanted it.

"Are you going to tell me why you need this?" Theo asked as he rewound the film and took it out of the camera.

"I can't yet, Theo," Joe said.

"Was the dead girl wearing this bracelet?"

"I don't know."

"But you found it in the woods?" Theo pressed.

Joe hesitated. "Yes."

Theo held up the film canister. "This is

going to take a while to develop," he said. "Why don't you go wait in my office, have a coffee. I will bring the prints out to you."

Joe slid off the stool, thankful to escape the smell of the chemicals. Out in Theo's office, she poured herself a cup of coffee. The phone rang and she looked out to see Carrie taking a subscription order, from the sounds of it. Joe knew that the circulation of the *Banner* increased every fall when the departing summer folks wanted to take a little piece of Leelanau home with them. Theo liked to brag that the circulation of the *Banner* spread from Saginaw to Saskatchewan. Joe listened to Carrie ask the caller how to spell "Grosse Pointe."

Joe looked toward the darkroom door. Finally, she began to wander around in Theo's office, her eyes drifting over the framed *Banner* front pages he had hung on the walls.

SEGREGATION BANNED. 1954.
U.S. MOURNS DEATH OF
ROBERT KENNEDY. 1968.
FIRST MAN ON THE MOON. 1969.
NIXON QUITS. 1974.

Some of the stories were just flakes of memories from her childhood. Nixon's resignation was more vivid, mainly because she and Brad had gotten giddy drunk that night and made love to celebrate.

She let out a slow sigh. Damn, they hadn't made love in a week. They had barely seen each other since the bones had been found, and now Leach had canceled all vacations until further notice.

She stopped at the last newspaper.

LEELANAU HIRES
FIRST FEMALE DEPUTY.
APRIL 1, 1975.

She stared at her picture. It was taken at the academy graduation, and she looked scared to death, her uniform gaping around her neck as if it were made for a football player.

She remembered the day she had gone down to Uniforms Unlimited in Traverse City to get fitted. All they had were men's sizes, so the guy had found a 34 jacket, a man's 14 shirt, and slacks. She had to pay a fortune to have the waist taken in and the rear let out. It was the only time in her life she was thankful for having small boobs. The hat had worked, but the tie . . . it was a clip-on made for a six-foot-tall man, and every time she took a pee she had to make sure it wasn't dangling in the damn toilet.

"Joe," Theo called.

She hurried back into the darkroom. In the infrared gloom, she could see wet prints hanging on a line, all good, clear close-ups of each charm.

"This is the engraving one," he said. "Let's see what comes up." He poked at a paper in a tray of chemicals, humming softly.

She leaned back against the wall. "I liked the story you wrote," she said, for something to break her nervousness over his silence. "The one about somebody's daughter."

"I got a very good response from it," Theo said. "Gerry Hathaway over at the post office has started a collection to buy a cemetery plot."

"They're getting a little ahead of themselves," Joe said.

"They feel sorry for her, that's all."

"She has family somewhere. We'll find them."

"I hope so." Theo slipped the paper into a second tray. "Ah. Come look."

Joe came forward and looked down at the paper floating in the tray. First, there was nothing but the shape of the charm. Then, slowly, the details emerged. It looked to be four letters.

Theo pulled the paper from the tray and used two clothespins to hang it on the line. He switched on the light.

Joe blinked and stared up at the paper. The letters were clear: CHHS.

"Chris?" Theo said.

Joe was smiling. "No . . . CHHS. It's a high school somewhere. I knew it. Now I just have to find out where. Can I take this, Theo?"

"Not yet. It has to dry." He saw her impatience and waved toward the door. "Go use my phone. The number for the Traverse City library is right there in the Rolodex. They'll have a directory of high schools on file. Ask for June. She's very helpful."

Joe thanked him and left the darkroom. A few minutes later, she was talking to June. Five minutes after that, she had the names of three high schools in Michigan that began with CH. Calls to the schools revealed that Cadillac Heritage had a Patriot as its mascot; Chippewa Hills in Remus had the Warriors. And Cherry Hill High School in Inkster had a Spartan for a mascot.

She was just hanging up when Theo came out with the photographs. He handed over the prints and the bracelet, still in its bag.

"Thanks, Theo."

"De rien," he said.

She hesitated. "No one can know about this yet, not even Augie," she said. "I need your discretion on this, Theo."

His eyes were steady on hers. "And you will have it."

She looked down at the bracelet. From the first moment she had seen it, something told her it was important. Now all she had to do was persuade Leach to let her pursue it.

By the time she got back to the office, Leach had left for the day to go to a dentist's appointment. Joe went home, eager to share her theories about the bracelet, and over dinner, Brad had listened patiently. Her energy carried over to the bedroom, arcing and burning bright. For once, Brad was the one left depleted on the damp sheets.

They had made love again in the morning. She had lingered in the shower, convinced she could still smell the scent of sex on herself. She stopped to spray herself with Jean Naté, something she never wore when she was in uniform.

Mike had given her an odd grin this morning when she squeezed by him to take her place in the conference room. It was one of those looks a man gives another guy when he knows he has gotten a quickie from an unexpected source. It didn't feel bad being included in that strange man-type exchange.

The door banged open. Holt set a large cardboard box on the table with a thud. Joe rose to peer inside. Dozens of plastic evidence bags. And not in plastic, a strange metal contraption that looked like a rusted hoist of some kind.

Leach came in, followed by two other deputies and a man Joe didn't know. No badge, but he looked like a state guy.

"Okay," Leach said, drawing a deep breath. "Let me first introduce Detective Norm Rafsky, Michigan State Police investigator. He'll be working with us from here on out."

Rafsky gave a bob of his head. He was a tall, slender man, wearing a plain blue suit under his tan trench coat. He had a long face and a head of ragged sandy-brown hair.

"Joe," Leach said, "would you do me a favor and take meeting notes?"

Joe held his eyes for just a second, then flipped to a new page in her notebook.

Leach looked down at the folder in his hand. "I got the ME's report back," he said. "They have no opinion on the cause or manner of death. None of the bones we found give any indication of blunt-force trauma, stabbing, or cut marks. Until they have more, that opinion is not likely to change."

Leach reached into his pocket and withdrew the plastic bag with the bracelet inside. "Turns out the jewelry we found is not a necklace, it's a charm bracelet," he said, setting the bag on the table. "Mack checked with Annabelle Chapel's parents, and Annabelle never owned a charm bracelet, so —"

"The bracelet isn't important. It doesn't mean Annabelle is not our victim," Mack said.

There was a flicker of irritation in Leach's eyes at being interrupted. "You're right, Mack," he said. "But we have nothing but your insistence — and the one fact that Annabelle Chapel disappeared less than a hundred miles from where we found the bones. You can stay with the Chapel girl, but the rest of us will check out other possible victims. And we still need to keep the bracelet in mind as a possible link to those victims."

Mack sat back in his chair, crossing his arms over his chest.

Joe stared at the bracelet lying on the table. Her hand was resting on a manila envelope that held Theo's pictures of the charms. But before she could say anything,

Leach said, "Mike, where are you on the bulletins?"

Mike gave Joe an odd look, as if he were waiting for her to say something, but then he turned back to Leach. "I've contacted all the agencies or families of the missings Joe pulled," he said. "None have turned up, dead or alive. None had any links to Leelanau County or family up here. And no one could remember any of these girls owning a charm bracelet, either."

"Bracelet? You already asked about the bracelet?" Leach asked.

"Sure."

"How did you know about it?"

"I saw it yesterday on Joe's desk," Mike said.

Mack's eyes shot to her, followed by everyone else's. Leach started to say something, but Mack spoke first.

"You opened my package?" he demanded.

She sat a little taller. "It was addressed to you, but it also said Leelanau County Sheriff's Office," she said. "I wanted to see it. And when I —"

"Joe," Leach interrupted, "you should not have done that. That's how things get messed up with an investigation. Evidence gets lost or mishandled, and before you know it, the case is thrown out."

"But I knew when Mack saw it was not Annabelle's, he would dismiss it as nothing," Joe said.

"You don't know anything," Mack said. "You were out of line, Frye."

"Enough, Mack," Leach said quickly. "Joe, I will talk to you later about this. Let's move on."

"Sheriff?" Joe drew in a breath. "May I say something about the bracelet first?" she asked.

Mack let out a disgusted breath. Leach's hard stare told her he was still upset with her, but he gave her a slow nod.

"One of the charms has an engraving on the back," she said. "I couldn't make it out, so I had it photographed and enlarged."

She pulled the shot of the engraving out of the envelope and slid it across the table. Leach looked at it, and then his eyes went back to Joe.

"Who took this picture?" he asked.

"Theo," Joe said.

Mack leaned across the table. "You shot your mouth off to that frog about what we found?"

"No more than what you did at the Riverside," she said. "The whole town knows about this now."

Mack glared at her, but before he could

say anything, Leach held up a hand. Mack sank back in his chair. Leach picked up the enlargement to look more closely at the CHHS. She took his silence as her cue.

"The engraving says CHHS," she said. "There are only three high schools in the state with those initials and only one has a Spartan as its mascot. It's in Inkster, a suburb of Detroit."

"That bracelet could belong to anyone," Mack said.

"Isn't that the point, to figure out who it belongs to?" she asked.

"The point is," Mack said, "that you overstepped your position. You don't touch evidence."

"So now the bracelet is evidence?" Joe asked. "A minute ago, it was nothing."

Mack looked to Leach. "What the hell is this, Sheriff? She's out of line here. This is my case. My case, damn it, and —"

"Shut up, Mack," Leach said. "Both of you just keep quiet."

Joe sat back in her chair, jaw tight. Her heart was racing, and she hated confrontations like this, but damn it, what else was she supposed to do? She felt a stare and glanced up at the state investigator. He was holding back a small smile.

"Mack," Leach said, "you will treat your

fellow officers with some respect here. And you will keep an open mind about this case."

Joe looked away from the state investigator and back to Leach, trying to relax her shoulders.

"And you, Deputy Frye," Leach said, "you will not investigate one more lead in this case without consulting both me and Mack beforehand. Do you understand?"

She bit back her response, remembering that there were others at the table — including Detective Rafsky — and she knew Leach just needed to make a stand here.

She sat back slowly. "Yes, sir."

"And I don't want to hear about *anyone* talking about this case outside this station without my say-so," Leach said. "Are we all crystal-clear on that?"

Everyone was quiet. Mack wouldn't look up at Leach.

"All right, then," Leach said, turning to Mike. "Mike, I want you to go back through all the bulletins and see if there's anyone from Inkster in there. If there is, let me know."

Joe's eyes snuck to Mike. He mouthed an "I'm sorry." It occurred to her she probably had that mean look on her face again, and she tried to soften it.

"Let's go on," Leach said. "Holt, bring

the box over here."

Holt jumped to his feet and dragged the box over. Leach began to lay the bagged items on the table. Joe leaned closer, but she was at the far end and couldn't see anything clearly.

"These are the other items the search team collected over the last week," Leach said. "Everything was found within a hundred yards of the three bones. While we have bagged *everything* as evidence, I am not convinced that all of this actually is. So we're going to go through this stuff and decide what is worth sending to the lab."

They went through a variety of items. A frying pan with a broken handle. Three empty cans of Dinty Moore stew. A used condom. A pair of rusty scissors. A broken arrow. A pair of men's wire-rimmed glasses. Twenty-seven bullet cartridges of varying calibers. A Diner's Club credit card. Three orange ball caps, muddy. A long piece of lace, blue. A man's wedding ring.

They voted to keep the condom, the cartridges, the credit card, and the piece of lace. The rest would be saved to be analyzed later, if needed.

Leach was about to go on to something else when Joe pointed. "What's that big rusty thing?" she asked.

Leach lifted it out of the box and laid it on the table. "It's a deer hoist, Joe," he said.

It looked like a large metal frame with a set of pulleys and tangled rope. "How is it used?" she asked.

Mack rose and grabbed the frame by a short piece of rope. When the frame hung down, it formed a triangle, like a large, heavy clothes hanger suspended by the pulleys.

"You hang the hoist up in a tree. You hook the hind legs of the deer to these two prongs here on each end," Mack said. "Then you pull the carcass up off the ground and gut it down the belly. The blood drains down. Nice and clean."

She heard a snicker behind her and glanced back, but she couldn't tell who had laughed.

"Are we sending that?" she asked.

Leach shook his head. "Well, it's not a cheap piece of gear, but it's something hunters can forget about and leave in the tree when they get to drinking like they do."

Joe stared at the deer hoist for a moment. There was nothing wrong with not knowing something, but she still felt as if she had made a mistake asking about it.

Leach put the hoist back in the box. "All right," he said. "We need all the heads in this we can get. And that includes Joe. Mack, give her an assignment."

Joe's eyes slipped to Mack. *Throw her a bone.*

"Okay, you like to play with evidence?" Mack said. "Your assignment is to log all the crap that isn't going to the lab, then deliver the rest of it personally to Lansing."

She didn't bother to look at Leach, but she let her gaze slip around the table. The state guy, Rafsky, was watching her, seemingly interested in her reaction. Holt was standing by the box of junk, looking as if he had just witnessed a traffic accident. And Mike . . .

No shock there. Just pity and something else, maybe. Something close to respect and a glimmer in his eyes that gave her a tiny sense of victory. If only between them.

Leach made a few other comments, and the meeting broke up. Rafsky and Leach quickly disappeared. Mack stayed at the table, poking at the evidence bags. He picked up the bag with the blue lace in it and held it up to the light.

"What are you going to do? Take that to Chicago, wave it in front of the Chapels, and ask if it's from their daughter's underwear?" Joe said.

"I might," Mack said.

He dropped it to the table and left the room. Mike glanced after him, then straightened his stack of bulletins.

"Look, Joe," he said, "you found this Inkster connection. If you want to check the bulletins again, I don't mind."

Joe picked up the engraving photograph. "Of course you don't."

She heard the crispness in her voice but didn't look up. Out of the corner of her eye, she saw Mike walk out of the room and knew she should apologize. Having Mike as an ally was better than no one. She would talk to him about it later, but for now, she was going to take him up on his offer.

It took her less than ten minutes to go through the bulletins and determine that there was no girl reported missing from Inkster.

Holt approached, carrying the box of bagged evidence. He set it on her desk with an apologetic look and left. Joe sat there, staring at the box.

Well, hell.

She walked down the short hall to Leach's office. His door was closed, and she could hear voices inside. She leaned against the wall and waited. Five minutes later, the door opened and Rafsky came out. The hall was narrow, and she had to step back against the wall to let him pass. As he did, he paused, in front of her. His trench coat smelled of a recent rain. His eyes were a startling, clear blue.

"The bracelet's a good lead," he said quietly. "Stay with it."

She watched him walk away until he turned the corner at the end of the hall. Then she stepped to the doorway and looked in at Leach. He was standing behind his desk, a bulky silhouette backlit by the sun. She couldn't see his expression.

"Come in, Joe," he said.

She moved forward so she could see his face. It was solemn. But not angry anymore.

"I have a request," she said.

Leach waited.

"Since I have to go to Lansing tomorrow anyway," she said, "may I have permission to drive down to Inkster and visit the high school? Maybe ask some questions?"

"Let's wait until Mike checks on any girls missing from there first," Leach said.

"I already did. There are none."

Leach's mouth pulled into a thin line.

"I'll use my own time," she said. "Even pay for my own gas."

"It's not about the cost, Joe."

"Then what is it about?"

Leach took his time in finding his answer.

111

"It's about protocol. Investigations need to follow procedure. They need a structured format and a single direction."

"How can an investigation have a single direction?" she asked. "Isn't that the same as having only a single line of thought or a single suspect?"

"I'm simply trying to keep things focused."

"On Annabelle Chapel."

"No, but I agree with Mack that she needs to be eliminated before we move on."

She stepped forward. "Sir, we could find a wallet with a girl's ID in it, and Mack wouldn't budge. You know that. Even if we don't find anything, we only have three bones. No one can prove they belong to Annabelle Chapel. We've got to look elsewhere and follow other leads."

"The leads need to be viable."

"And jewelry found near remains is not viable evidence?"

"Of course it is, but —"

Leach stopped himself, studying her for a moment. Then he came out from behind the desk. He stood close to her, and Joe resisted the urge to take a step back. The look on his face was more fatherly than anything else, but it bothered her. Still, she didn't want him to know it. The fact that he had been her instructor at college, even the fact that he had taken a chance on her, still didn't give her the right to expect special treatment.

"Sheriff," she said quietly, "I just have a feeling about this."

He almost smiled. "Women's intuition?"

"Maybe. Maybe that is all it is."

"All right," he said. "Take a couple extra hours tomorrow and visit that high school. And stop by the Inkster police department and see if they know anything."

"Yes, sir," she said.

"If it's a dead end, I don't want to hear anything else about it."

"Yes, sir. Thank you, sir."

She started to the door and had it open when Leach called to her. "And Joe, let's just keep this between you and me."

9

Despite its odd name, Inkster looked like most of the suburbs she had known back in Cleveland. It was a grid of small brick houses whose tiny porches, aluminum awnings, and modestly clad windows gave out the mute scream of white, middle-class respectability.

Joe took the road called Cherry Hill

toward the high school of the same name. She passed clusters of party stores, gas stations, and restaurants and a park that was probably there long before the blocks around it started growing bricks.

Earlier that morning, she had stopped at the lab in Lansing to drop off the search items. The paperwork had taken almost an hour, and when she was finished, she had stood in the parking lot, listening to the whistle of the Chicago-bound train, thinking about Annabelle Chapel and about how Leach had gone out on a limb by letting her go to Inkster. She needed to come back with something that justified his faith in her.

Joe glanced down at the directions. She was on a street called Avondale now. More cookie-cutter houses, the lawns littered with children's bikes and dented trash cans. She eased the car to a stop in front of a low-slung school built in the style typical of the fifties. The sign in front read CHERRY HILL HIGH SCHOOL, HOME OF THE SPARTANS, with a Spartan head symbol that looked exactly like the one in the photograph.

Inside, Joe paused in the tiled lobby. There was an area set off with big windows, trophy cases, chairs, and a huge papier-mâché chariot toting a Spartan head. She headed

toward the office marked ADMINISTRA-
TION.

The woman behind the desk stiffened at the sight of a uniform. "Can I help you?" she asked.

Joe gave her a smile and identified herself. "I'm hoping you can," she said, setting a photograph on the counter. "Is it possible this charm is from your school?"

The woman had a pair of reading glasses on a chain around her neck and set them on her nose to peer at the picture. "I don't think so," she said. "Have you tried Michigan State?"

"It's not from a college," Joe said. "And this looks exactly like the one on your sign out front, and I was hoping —"

"May I ask, please, what this is all about?"

The woman's eyes dipped to the Leelanau County S.O. patch on Joe's sleeve. Joe could tell by her expression she had no idea where Leelanau was, and Joe didn't feel like explaining it. Joe caught sight of a white head in the office behind the woman. The sign on the door said MR. GARRETT PRIN-CIPAL. She had the odd thought, not for the first time, that sometimes men respected the authority of her uniform more than women did. At least outside the station.

"Could you please tell the principal I'd like to talk to him?" she asked.

The woman's face went tighter, and she pivoted to the glass office. The man inside was craning to look at Joe. He came out to the desk. "I'm Mr. Garrett," he said, hand outstretched.

"Deputy Frye. Leelanau County sheriff's department," Joe said, shaking it.

A bell shrieked. Doors banged open, and suddenly the hallways filled with noise and laughter. The principal cocked his head toward the back. "Come into my office so we can hear each other."

Joe took the chair he offered after he closed the door on the noise and the stares of the woman outside.

"Did Georgia give you a hard time?" he asked, sitting down behind his desk.

"I'm used to it. People generally don't like talking to police."

"She's protective, of me and the school." He smiled. "Leelanau County. That's up near Traverse City, right?"

"Yes, sir." Maybe it was that great shock of white hair, but something about Mr. Garrett made her feel as if she were a high school kid again.

"I have a hunting cabin up by Kalkaska. Don't get up there as much as I like." His

116

blue eyes drifted but came back to her. "Now, you're asking about a charm?"

Joe slid the photograph across the desk. "Yes, sir. It might be from your school. It could be connected to a missing girl."

He peered at the photo and nodded. "Yes, that's ours. The pep club thought they could raise money selling them. But no one wanted them. It took us years to get rid of them all."

"Can you remember what year you started selling the charms?"

He shook his head. "They were just one of many things the pep club sold over the years." He handed the picture back to Joe. "You said this is about a missing girl?"

"Actually, we are trying to identify some remains," Joe said. "This charm was on a bracelet found with the bones."

Garrett's affable expression clouded. "Good Lord."

"Can you recall any students going missing over the last decade or so?" she asked.

He thought for a moment, then shook his head slowly.

"Are you sure?" Joe asked. "Someone who maybe didn't come back after summer?"

"That happens all the time," Garrett said. "People move. We don't track them down."

Joe stifled a sigh of disappointment.

"Would it be possible for me to talk to some of your teachers?"

"Well, only the ones on break right now. Most of them are in the teachers' lounge. I'll take you there."

Garrett led her to a room that smelled of cigarettes and tuna fish. Six teachers sat at a table drinking coffee. Two others were over in a corner going over lesson plans. Everyone looked up as Garrett led Joe in, introduced her, and explained what she was looking for. Joe was able to rule out three of the teachers immediately because they had been hired that fall.

Of the remaining ones, the men just shrugged and shook their heads when Joe asked about the charm bracelet. But when Joe took out the photograph of the full bracelet, a woman came forward.

"Can I see it?" she asked. Her voice was nasally from a cold. She was holding a roll of toilet paper and stuck it under her arm to take the photo.

She studied the picture and looked back up at Joe. "I had a girl in one of my English classes who wore a bracelet like this," she said. "I remember it because she jangled it constantly. It used to drive me crazy, so I made her take it off whenever she came into my class. She gave me a lot of lip about it."

"Do you remember her name?" Joe asked.

She handed the photo back. "God, that was years ago. I only remember her because of the bracelet. She wore a lot of jewelry and makeup and always dressed kind of wild, you know, tight skirts and leather."

"Can you remember anything else about her? Did she graduate?" Joe pressed.

The teacher shook her head in mild disgust. "Dropped out, more likely. She was the kind who hated school and couldn't wait to get out of here. You know how kids are. They think the suburbs are a dead-end kind of place."

"Her name," Joe pressed.

The teacher tore off a wad of toilet paper and blew her nose. "I only remember that she went by a nickname, and it was a boy's name. You know, like Mickey or Sammy or Freddie."

Joe pulled out her notebook. "Could I have your name? In case I need to get back in touch."

"Sure. Ellen Brody." She sniffled. "Sorry I can't be more help, but the girl didn't make a big impression. Some kids are more blurry than others, you know?"

Joe thanked her and Mr. Garrett and left, heading back out the front door.

The sun had come out, but there was a

bite to the air now, signaling the end of the long summer. As she walked to the cruiser, she was looking at the small tract houses across the street, thinking about some nameless girl who wanted to break free of the monotony of suburbs, small minds, and straight sidewalks that led to nowhere.

I don't get it, Joe. Why the Upper Peninsula in Michigan? It's so far away. Why there?

Because it's not here, Ma.

Joe got into the cruiser and started the engine. But she just sat there, still staring at the little brick houses. There was one house that was different. It was an old stone place that had probably once been surrounded by apple orchards before the land had been cut up into tiny parcels and paved over. It had been a pretty house once, but now it just looked imprisoned by the bland houses around it.

Dead end . . .

She thought about Leach and his admonition that if she found nothing in Inkster, she had to let the bracelet lead go. She had linked the charm to this place, but there was still nothing to link it to the bones. She was chasing leads that went nowhere, being as stubborn about the unknown owner of the bracelet as Mack was about Annabelle Chapel.

She glanced back at the school. Why couldn't she just let this go?

10

Joe closed her eyes and rubbed her stiff neck. For the last hour, she had been closeted in the evidence room, a ten-by-ten cubbyhole that had served as the men's restroom back in the station's days as a library. There was no room for a chair, so she was perched on the lid of an old toilet, clipboard in her lap.

After her return from Inkster yesterday, Leach had told her to put the bracelet aside. There was nothing to do now but go back to the assignment Mack had given her — logging in the leftover junk from the search.

Joe picked a broken Bic pen out of the box. She tagged it, numbered it, dated it, and entered it on the log.

She thought back to the two suits she had dealt with at the Inkster PD. They had never moved their asses off their desks even to look in a drawer. Just spent the five minutes exchanging glances. On her way out, one of them had suggested that the next time she wanted help with an investigation, she should have her sheriff call.

One rubber band. Date. Place. Time.

One pair of men's wire-rimmed glasses.

"Hey."

She looked up. Mike stood at the door. His tie was stuffed in his pants pocket. "Sheriff said he let you go down to Inkster yesterday."

"Yeah," Joe said, going back to her logging.

"You find out anything?" Mike asked.

"Nothing important."

Mike slid down the doorjamb, sitting on his heels, his green notebook in his lap. He didn't offer to help, so Joe picked up the next item.

One half-filled bottle of sloe gin.

"So tell me about it," Mike said.

Joe knew he didn't care, but she wanted to tell someone. "I found a teacher who remembered a girl who had a charm bracelet like the one we found."

"No name?"

"Nothing that helps."

"Did you talk to the Inkster PD?"

"Oh, yeah. They were a big help."

"Well, maybe it's time to let Mack finish this up."

"Our victim is not Annabelle Chapel," Joe said.

Mike gave her a small smile and stretched to his feet. "I'm hungry," he said. "Let's go to lunch."

She glanced at the pile of junk on the floor and started to shake her head but then decided she needed a break, if nothing else to ease her bad mood. Her disappointment over the trip to Inkster had spilled over last night with Brad. They had argued about something so stupid she couldn't even remember now what it was.

"Come on," Mike pressed. "I'll buy."

"Talked me into it," she said. She closed the door and locked it, wondering why she bothered. Except for the box of junk from the woods, the shelves were nearly bare.

They checked out with Augie and stepped outside. It was sunny, the air alive with eddies of leaves. At the Cove bar in Fishtown, they took a table on the weather-worn deck that overlooked the water. It felt good to be outside after the confinement of the evidence room. Joe turned her face to the sun, but her eyes were drawn to a two-story wood shanty on the other side of the canal. It was bleached gray by the harsh winds of countless winters and festooned with faded fishnetting, bruised white lifesavers, and Christmas lights. The deck was cluttered with junk — pots of geraniums, a flamingo lawn ornament, and a huge rusted deep-sea diver's helmet.

There was a man sitting on the deck, soaking up the sunshine. He had a Buddha belly and two tufts of gray hair — one on his head and one on his chest. There was a pink plastic cup in his hand, a metal milk crate under his feet, and a smile on his face.

Mike saw her looking. "That's Pete," he said. "He's rich."

"Rich from what?"

"No one knows. He spends every day out there. Every morning, he climbs down that ladder, swims with his little poodle, and then climbs back out and goes right back to his chair. What a life."

Joe turned away from Pete and settled into her chair, wondering how much the shanties were, or if they were even for sale. Maybe people rented them. But then she tried to picture Brad lounging with a metal crate under his feet. It didn't sit well.

The waitress appeared. She set a Coke in front of Joe and a Pabst in front of Mike. Joe waited until she had taken their sandwich order and left before speaking.

"Mike, you're on duty," she said, nodding to the beer.

He took a drink. "It's one beer, Joe. I don't get drunk on one beer."

"That's not the point. People don't need to see the person they might need to defend them later drinking at lunch."

"Like someone's going to need us to defend them here."

Joe looked away, not wanting to get into an argument. There was a trio of over-the-hill blondes a few tables away, and she could tell by the tilt of their heads that they had already heard part of the conversation.

Mike leaned across the table. "Joe, I have never pulled my gun. I've only been in two or three tussles. This is not Detroit. Shit, it isn't even Traverse City."

"Things can happen, even here," she said softly, "and you need to know you could defend someone if you had to."

His smile vanished.

"Don't you ever think about it?" she asked.

"Think about what?"

"How you would handle yourself in a life-or-death situation," she said. "If you could pull the trigger, especially in defense of someone else."

"No," he said, taking a drink.

She let him see her shock.

"I don't think about it," he said, "because I know I could do it. I got the same training for the same number of weeks you did."

"It's more than training," she said. "It's something inside you. I don't believe everyone could pull a trigger. Not even police officers."

"Then maybe they shouldn't be cops."

He settled back in his chair, stiffly, looking out at the water. She thought about letting this go, but she couldn't. Still, she didn't want to rag on him, either, not about his cop masculinity, as she had come to think of male officers' peculiar brand of machismo.

"You know," she said, "there was this sign I saw up in the academy that I never forgot. It's a quote from Hemingway. It goes, 'There is no hunting like the hunting of man and those who have hunted armed men long enough and liked it, never really care for anything else.' "

"So what, now you're saying that because I've never had to use my gun, I'm a lousy cop?"

"I don't think you're a lousy cop, Mike," she said with a sigh. "I think you're a careless one, and I think that one day that carelessness is going to get you hurt."

He finished his beer in three long swallows, then set the can on the table, silent. Their sandwiches appeared. Mike ordered a 7 Up.

"I don't hunt, Joe, never liked it," he said, taking the lettuce off the ham slices. "I don't see much point in killing something that hasn't done anything to you. But my dad was a hunter, so I understand the mentality."

The three blondes broke up their party and waddled off the deck. When Joe looked back at Mike, he was holding out his green notebook.

"Here," he said.

"What?"

"I want you to see something."

She took the notebook. The papers were filled with handwritten entries, all done in black ink. The page he had folded over for her was titled "Indian Summer."

In the heat of Indian summer, I sit quiet in
    still hot air.
My child's eye watches my father as he
    becomes another man
I do not know.

A man who touches his bullets the way
    other men fondle gold,
A man who holds his rifle the way other
    men hold a son,
A man who draws his strength from the
    sharpness of the pines
And the lingering scent of an animal on
    the run.

In the heat of Indian summer, I am alone
   within the woods.
My child's mind wonders what it is my
   father seeks,
I do not know.

I wonder if he fears the strength of the
   animals he stalks,
I wonder what he feels as he stands and
   watches them die,
I wonder if he takes their breath and keeps
   it as his own,
And I wonder if he is the animal, and if he
   is, what am I?

In the heat of Indian summer, I sit with a
   rifle in my arms.
My man's eye watches a white feather
   scamper through the trees.
I do not shoot.

She closed the book and pushed it back
across the table.

"You didn't laugh," he said.

"Why would I?" she asked.

Mike was silent for a moment. "It's bad,
isn't it?"

"No, it's not." She couldn't think of
anything else to say because she was so
shocked that the man sitting across from

her even knew what poetry was.

"I write essays, too," Mike said. "But mostly just thoughts. I have another note-book with the beginnings of a short story."

She was still staring at him.

"I started them when I was riding alone, back five or six years ago," he said. "I have, like, twenty notebooks hidden in the garage."

"Hidden? Mindy doesn't know you do this?"

He had taken a bite of his sandwich, and he almost choked. "Hell, no," he said.

Joe watched him. He was wiping mayonnaise off his lip, his cheeks pink. She pulled the photographs of the charms from her pants pocket. She kept them with her now all the time, afraid Mack would dump them in the nearest trash can if he got the chance. She pushed her plate aside and spread them in front of Mike.

"I've seen the bracelet, Joe," he said.

"Yes, but now I want you to look again," she said. "Tell me what you think they mean."

"Mean? What do you mean 'mean'?"

"Mike, you see things. Maybe more than you want to admit. So what do you see in these charms?"

He stared at the photos for a moment.

"Well, you know they're like souvenirs, right?"

"Souvenirs?"

He pointed to the first one. "This windmill is probably from Holland."

"Holland?"

"It's a town down by Grand Rapids. We took the kids there once. They have a lot of tulips with all this Dutch stuff."

Mike sifted through the other shots. "These are all Michigan tourist places. The Christmas tree is from Frankenmuth, and the carriage is from Mackinac Island. The train is probably Greenfield Village, that museum down near Detroit. The teddy bear, maybe Sleeping Bear Dunes?"

Joe could only stare blankly. "What about the cross?" she asked.

"That's probably the Cross in the Woods," he said.

"Where is that?"

"Indian River, not far from here," he said. "It's this outdoor Catholic shrine with this giant cross and a seven-ton bronze Jesus."

"How do you know all that?"

"Been there too many times to count," he said. "My dad took me to the woods to hunt, my mom took me to the woods to pray. It's the Italian Catholic thing."

Joe turned the photos over and wrote the

names of the places on the backs.

Mike was wiping his hands on the paper napkin. "I think you're right about Annabelle Chapel," he said.

"What do you mean?"

"This bracelet didn't belong to some girl from Chicago," Mike said. "Coming up north is a Michigan thing. It's a summer ritual. Dad gets a week off from Ford Motor, and the family goes up north to rent a cabin somewhere. They pay to catch fish in the trout ponds, climb the dunes. By the time they're fifteen, they've seen it all."

"So you think she was definitely from downstate?"

"Well, no one from up here would collect charms from places we see all the time."

She started to gather up the pictures, then stopped. "What kind of girl do you think would collect these?"

"You're the female here," he said.

"You're the poet," she said.

He blushed again, but his eyes drifted back to the photos. Then he drew the one of the carriage to him. "Okay, on Mackinac Island, they have a dozen possible symbols — bicycles, cannons from the fort, ferries, the lighthouse, probably even little fudge boxes. But she chose a horse and carriage. Kind of a romantic charm, right?"

131

Joe was quiet, listening.

"And see this locomotive? Something of the past. Same with the windmill."

"Okay."

"And one more thing," Mike said. "All of these charms are from places. There's not one thing on the bracelet to represent her family, like brothers or sisters." He paused. "Come to think of it, there's nothing even personal about herself, like a musical instrument or a doll. Just places."

Joe sat back. "Except for a charm from a school she wanted to escape. She wanted to be somewhere else."

Mike gave a shrug and wadded up his napkin.

Across the canal, Joe heard a woman's laughter, and she glanced over at Pete. One of the blond martini grannies was on his balcony, serving him a tray of cheese and a glass of wine. Pete gave her a pat on the rump, and she disappeared back inside his shanty.

It took Joe a moment to understand what it was about the scene that bothered her. It was the attention the woman was giving Pete, and she tried to remember the last time she had brought Brad anything on a tray.

"Joe," Mike said, "promise me you won't

say anything about the notebooks."

"I promise."

"I mean to the guys."

"God, I promise." She shook her head and smiled. "You know, you should share them with Mindy. Wives love seeing that softer side of their men."

He shook his head. "Trust me, Mindy has all the softness my house needs."

Joe was putting the photographs away when Mike's radio paged them. He grabbed it with a sigh of annoyance.

Sheriff Leach's voice snapped from it. "Where are you two?"

"Over at Fishtown."

"Get back out to the woods now."

Joe stood up, keying her radio. "Sir, can I ask the reason?"

"They've found another bone, Joe."

11

It lay atop a bed of brown oak leaves, a small half-moon thing that looked like a piece of carved ivory jewelry.

Except for the teeth.

It was a jawbone. Joe could see that clearly even from her vantage point behind Mack and Sheriff Leach. And when the sun came out from behind a cloud, she saw a glint of metal.

"Braces?" Leach said.

Mack took a step forward. "Damn right it's braces. And that means we're looking at Annabelle Chapel here. She wore braces. This is my girl."

Leach looked at each of them. His eyes lingered on Joe before he spoke. "Okay, we will proceed now on the assumption that this may be Annabelle Chapel." He looked at Mack. "How do you want to handle this?"

"We need to get the searchers back for a new grid," Mack said. "And we should call down to Davison for some dogs."

"Dogs?" Mike said.

"Canine search units," Mack said, drawing the words out just enough to sound condescending. "If there's more bones out there, the dogs will find them."

"We'd better get this taped off," Leach said. "Hundred-yard-square perimeter."

"Holt," Mack said quickly.

"Yes, sir." Holt was gone, heading to the cruiser.

"And flag some trees leading back to the road so the searchers can find this place," Mack yelled after him.

Leach was looking around at the woods, and Joe could almost read what he was thinking. They were about a half-mile from the prayer tree where the first set of bones had been found by the kids. This new bone confirmed that the body had never been buried, or at least not very deep, because the only way this jawbone could have traveled so far would have been in the teeth of a scavenger.

She spotted a flash of red in the far trees. Then she realized it had to be the flags that marked the boundary of the grid from the original search last week. The team had worked out from the prayer tree and marked the far boundary with the red flags. That's why they had missed the jawbone, even though it was a mere ten yards or so beyond the search perimeter.

"Damn," Leach said, almost to himself. "We're going to need more men out here."

Joe knew what he was thinking. Their department couldn't handle what now needed to be done. Although they had kept the area around the prayer tree taped off, there had been no effective way to keep people out. The woods were open country, not part of a state park with a gate that could be conveniently locked. Since the word of the bones discovery, a steady stream of curiosity seekers had been tramping through the area. That was how the jawbone had been found — by a couple of hikers who had read Theo's story and had come up from Traverse City to poke around.

Joe knew there would be others. The past week of colder weather had accelerated the changing leaves. The annual influx of leaf peepers was just beginning and would make their jobs even harder.

"Mike," Mack said, drawing her attention back. "As soon as you get back to the station, I want you on the phone to Chicago. I want Annabelle Chapel's dental records."

Mike nodded. The four of them just stood for a moment, letting the soft silence of the woods surround them. The temperature had dropped a good ten degrees in the last hour, and the sun was struggling against the gray clouds advancing from the north.

She glanced at Mike. He was hunched down into his jacket, hands thrust in his pockets, his eyes riveted on the jawbone. His face was strangely slack. She was watching him so intently she didn't hear Mack the first time he addressed her.

"Frye."

She looked up.

"I want you to stay here and wait for the search team."

Joe knew the team had to come from Lansing. That meant two to three hours.

Mack was pushing her to the margins again. She caught a blink of sympathy from Mike before he turned away.

Joe followed him up a small hill. He stopped at the base of a tree, staring down at the leaves.

"What's the matter?" she asked.

"Nothing."

"Don't tell me that. What's wrong?"

He didn't look up at her. "Jenny has braces," he said.

It didn't register at first. Then she remembered Jenny was Mike's daughter. Joe let out a quiet sigh. She moved closer and touched his sleeve.

"Mike —"

His shrug wasn't rough, but it was definite. He walked a few yards off and lit a cigarette.

"Mike, you shouldn't —"

He silenced her with a stare and looked away.

Joe zipped her windbreaker higher and stuffed her hands into her pockets. Mack and Leach were already heading back to the road, their brown jackets two specks that blended in with the falling leaves. Damn, it was getting cold. She glanced at her watch. Going on four.

She started to wander, her eyes scanning the ground, her toe gently kicking at the leaves. She knew she wasn't supposed to be searching, and the chances of seeing anything under the leaves was slim, but she couldn't help herself.

A squawking sound drew her eyes up, and she watched a wedge of geese pressing south, their black wings ticking off retreating checkmarks against the gray sky.

When she finally wandered back to Mike forty minutes later, he was looking at his watch.

"Where the hell is Holt?" he said.

On cue, the crunch of leaves announced Holt's return. He was red-faced and out of breath, and his shoes and cuffs were mud-caked.

"What happened to you?" Mike asked.

"There's a big-ass hill over there," he said, pointing. "And a big-ass ravine down there with a big-ass mud hole."

He wiped at his face and took a half-hearted swipe at the muddy seat of his pants. "I'm going home," he muttered, rolling up the yellow crime tape. He started off toward the logging road.

"I'll come with you," Mike said.

"You're not staying with me?" Joe asked.

He shrugged. "You can handle things. And you heard Mack. I have to get going with the dental records. And Mindy is expecting me home early tonight —"

"Go," Joe said quickly. More quickly than she intended.

"You keep the unit. I'll ride back with Holt."

Joe listened to the crunch of Mike's boots through the leaves as he ran to catch up with Holt. She heard the distant cough of the cruiser starting up and then nothing. The sudden quiet of the deep woods was engulfing. No birds or animals, no hum of human activity. Not even a trace of wind stirring the leaves.

She glanced again at her watch and then up to the west. The sun was a pale face imprisoned behind the bars of pine trees.

It bugged her that Mike had cut out. Not that he just left her alone but that he seemed so eager to get away from this place. It wasn't just the thing about his daughter, either. It was the whole case. It was the whole damn thing about being a cop. Then the real source of her irritation hit her: How could he take for granted something she so desperately wanted?

Joe looked up at the tree where the jaw-bone had been found. It was a huge old oak. For a second, she thought about getting down on her knees, clearing away the leaves, and digging for more bones.

She kicked the oak's trunk. "Fuck you, Mack," she muttered.

She had to get outside the search perimeter before her frustration made her do something stupid and contaminate the scene.

Stuffing her cold hands into her pockets, she headed west toward the copse of pines. Ducking under the yellow tape, she paused to retie one end that was coming loose. The tape went left, stretching south into heavier trees. She headed that way to make sure Holt had tied the other ends tightly.

She walked slowly, staying near the tape so she wouldn't get lost in the fading light. Holt had taped off a very rough square that proceeded south up a rocky hill and through a thick stand of trees. She was breathing hard by the time she crested the hill. As the tape turned east, the hill dipped sharply into heavy brush, and the ground grew wet and slippery. She had to grab a sapling to keep from sliding downhill until the ground bottomed out into a morass of mud. Finally, the ground dried out in a carpet of needles and leaves as she headed back toward her starting point.

She came to a stop back at the oak. Still no sign of the searchers, and it was too cold to stop, so she just kept walking. She walked the perimeter once more, her eyes checking her watch and her ears pricked for the sound of a car. Nothing. After the third time, she reversed her course out of sheer boredom.

It was when she rounded the western edge of the tape that she saw it. Something carved in the huge oak tree slightly above eye level. She hadn't seen it the first two times because it was on the back of the tree. She moved toward it.

It looked like a man standing in a boat. It was definitely some kind of design, because whoever had carved it had taken their time, making it even and clear and deep. And it didn't seem like a casual memento, like lovers leaving their initials in a heart. Why was this here? And did it mean anything?

Her mother's voice was suddenly in her head. A button can lead to a blouse and a blouse to a store and to a credit card receipt . . .

Joe glanced up at the thickening clouds.

She knew what she needed to do. She walked quickly, relying on the yellow markers Holt had left to find her way back to the lone cruiser parked on the logging road. Inside, she paused to warm her hands and then radioed in.

Augie told her he would call down to Lansing and find out what had happened to the search crew.

"Is Mike still there?" she asked.

"I just heard him radio in that he was off duty at home," Augie said.

Damn.

Joe clicked off and popped open the glove box, taking out the Instamatic camera they kept for recording accident scenes. Grabbing a flashlight, she got out of the cruiser, forgetting about Augie until she heard his voice.

"Joe, the searchers aren't coming tonight," he said. "They didn't get started soon enough to make any daylight. Sheriff says for you to come back in, and he'll send a swing-shift deputy out tonight to check on things."

"Thanks."

She slipped from the cruiser and followed Holt's markers back to the oak tree.

She snapped two photos of the carving, then checked how many exposures were left

— two. She brought the camera up to take another shot, then paused, peering into the darkness.

The prayer tree. She concentrated, trying to remember every detail from the tree where they had found the other bones. She had not seen a carving there, but there hadn't been any reason to notice one before.

Shining the flashlight toward the far trees, she started off in what she was sure was a southward direction, knowing what she was doing was foolhardy and a long shot. The night was moonlit, moving like a current of cold gray water around her. The flashlight beam picked up the tree trunks and the ghostly exhalations of her quickening breath.

Had she gone a half-mile? She had no idea. And she had the crazy thought that by the time the swing-shift deputy got here, she was going to end up yelling for rescue, looking like a fool.

She stopped suddenly, not sure why, and moved the flashlight beam higher. She let out a breath as the sweeping arms of the prayer tree emerged from the darkness.

Moving forward, she trained the flashlight at the rough bark. No carvings. No marks at all.

She stepped around to the back of the

tree. It was faint, so faint that if she hadn't been looking for it, she never would have noticed it. But it was there.

It was not carved as deeply as the other one, and it looked worn by weather and time. It was different from the first one, except maybe for the U shape on the bottom.

She set the flashlight on the ground, stepped back and took a picture. The flash was blinding, and she had to blink the trunk back into focus. She took one more shot before the clicking confirmed the film was used up.

The darkness seemed thicker in the aftermath of the flash. For a second, she couldn't see the tree, couldn't see anything.

She knelt, grabbing the flashlight from the leaves. She swung it up to the prayer tree. The odd carving stared back at her like a taunting smile.

12

It was late by the time she got back to the station. She had been so cold and muddy that she took a quick shower in the deserted men's locker room and then waited until Augie got off shift so he could drive her home.

There was a light burning in the window of the cottage when they pulled up.

"Isn't that sweet," Augie said.

"Don't be such a cynic, Augie."

"A cynic is someone who knows the cost of everything but the value of nothing. I, my dear Joette, am a romantic. I just wish Theo was. He never leaves candles burning when I'm late."

She had called Brad from the station, but there had been no answer. As she gazed at the candle in the window, it occurred to her that its meaning was as mysterious to her as those carvings in the woods. Was it a conciliatory signal after their argument last night?

She started to get out of the car, then paused, looking down at the Instamatic in her hand. Her initial thought had been to drop it off at the Rexall tomorrow for old man Dirksen to develop, just as they always did. But she couldn't risk anyone seeing the carvings before she talked to Leach.

Joe popped the film out. "Augie, I need a favor. Would you ask Theo to develop this for me?"

She could see Augie cock an eyebrow in the dim dome light given out by his ancient VW. "Don't ask?" he asked.

"Don't ask. Thanks for the ride, Augie."

They exchanged good nights, and the VW sputtered off down the road.

Inside the cottage, she heard the shower running. Something was simmering on the stove, and the smell made her stomach churn with hunger. A fire was burning in the stone hearth, trying to hold back the cold creeping under the poorly caulked windows. She shrugged out of her windbreaker and took off her mud-caked shoes. She got a Stroh's from the fridge and took it to the bedroom, where she hung her gun belt on its hook behind the door. She stripped and put on her robe. She picked up a brush to comb the tangles out of her hair, still wet from the hasty shower back at the station.

The bathroom door was open, and the shower had fogged up the mirror over the bureau in their bedroom. She wiped it with her bathrobe sleeve.

Her face stared back at her, pale and indistinct, the way the sun had looked earlier as it sank in the cold, clouded sky. She moved away as she slowly brushed her hair.

She had never liked her face very much, never seeing any beauty in its clean architecture. She had always wanted the pug noses and Barbie-doll eyes of the cheerleader girls. Or maybe a girl like Annabelle Chapel. She had a sudden flash of memory, of sitting next to her dad in a gymnasium, watching her older brother, Dennis, in a basketball game.

I'm ugly, Daddy.

You're beautiful.

Not like them, I'm not.

No. They're easy to add up. They're plain old arithmetic.

So what am I?

Geometry, Joey. Not everyone gets it.

Arms came around her waist. "Hey, baby."

She closed her eyes. Brad's breath was warm and toothpaste-tangy at her neck. His body was hard against her back. She leaned into him.

"Does this mean I am forgiven?" she asked.

"For what?"

She faced him. "For being a bitch last night?"

"You're working too hard," Brad said.

She hesitated, then nodded.

"Why didn't you call?" he said.

"I did. You weren't here."

"Had to work late again."

"So did I. We found another bone in the woods, and —"

She could feel him growing hard against her.

"You hungry?" he asked.

"No," she lied. "Brad, out in the woods, there were these carvings —"

He silenced her with a kiss. At first, she didn't respond. It was the fatigue and everything about the day in the way. But then . . . he kissed her again, and slowly, things began to fade away, and she was left with nothing but his mouth covering hers and the hard press of his hips warming her cold bones.

He moved her to the bed and took off her robe. He exposed her, opened her, filled her, and emptied her mind. He was licking, tasting, teasing her, making her forget about everything but his mouth and hands and how his hardness made her feel soft again.

He told her he loved her, and she believed him.

He told her she was beautiful, and she believed him.

When he moved her onto her back and

slipped below her waist, she grabbed his hair, moving her hips in a rhythm with his tongue. When she came, she cried out.

"Joe?"

She opened her eyes.

He was sweating above her. His face was contorted, like the carving in the tree.

"Joe?"

His lips came down, and she could taste the mossy-sea taste of herself on them. He came in a thrusting torrent, and she wrapped her legs around his back, holding him until the convulsions stopped and he was quiet again.

She lay silent and still beneath him. Slowly, one sense at a time, the world came back to her. First the smell of the chili out in the kitchen. Then the weird call of the great horned owl in the tree just outside the window, a call that had always sounded so human to her.

How long was it that she lay there not moving? She felt a weight on her feet. When she moved her legs, Chips groaned and moved away.

Finally, Brad shifted to the side and rolled onto his back, eyes closed. She molded herself into his side, resting her head in the crook of his shoulder, and pulled the blanket up over their shoulders. She could see the candle burning low in the window out in the living room.

"All right, who is he?" Brad whispered.

"What?"

"Your hair smells like Brut."

"I showered at the station. I had to use Mike's shampoo."

He laughed softly. A weary exhalation followed.

She waited a beat, then slowly extricated herself from Brad's embrace.

"Where you going?" he asked.

"I'm hungry," she said.

"I made some chili." Sleep was heavy in his voice.

"I know. Thanks." She found her robe and put it on. She pulled the blanket up over Brad's shoulder and kissed his cheek. "I'll be in soon."

"I can't fall asleep without you."

"I know."

She stopped to plug in the space heater. Brad's breath had deepened into the beginnings of sleep by the time she made her way out of the bedroom. Chips followed her to the kitchen and sat at her feet while she ladled out a bowl of chili. Joe dropped a saltine cracker to the floor, and Chips sniffed in the dark trying to find it. He was still looking as she took the chili out to the living room.

The fire had burned down to a soft glow, and the cabin was cold, but she didn't want to bother starting a new fire. Pulling a blanket around her, she curled her legs under her on the sofa. Chips jumped up and laid his snout on her ankles, staring up at her as she slowly ate the chili.

The owl called again. No, a different one this time, with the distinct sound of the barred owl. She had lived here in the woods only six months, and already she could tell the owls apart. Ma would get a kick out of that.

Her eyes drifted to the phone. She set the bowl aside, reached over and brought the phone to her lap, and dialed.

"Hello?"

"Ma?"

"Joe?" Her mother's voice sounded raspy, but more from Salems than sleep. Joe knew her mother would be awake. She never went to bed before two.

"Something the matter?"

"No, why do you say that, Ma?"

"I dunno. You're usually in bed by ten."

"I just wanted to talk."

Joe heard the crumple of cellophane and a sharp inhalation as her mother lit a cigarette. There was a TV on in the background.

"What you watching?" Joe asked.

"*Now, Voyager.* Hold on a minute . . ."

Joe stroked Chips's head in the dark.

"Okay. It's over. Damn, I love that movie."

"I know, Ma. You made me watch it every time it came on."

And they both recited the line at the same time: "Oh, Jerry, don't let's ask for the moon. We have the stars."

Joe laughed softly.

A pause. "So where's Brad?"

"In bed."

"And you're not?"

"I was, Ma. For the last hour."

A deep chuckle. "He's that good, huh?"

Joe hesitated, surprised at her mother's boldness. They had never talked about sex before, at least not since that one awkward time after Joe had started her period. Joe smiled slightly.

"I didn't call you to talk about Brad."

There was a silence on the other end.

"What? No smart comeback, Ma?"

"I wasn't going to say anything about him, Joe."

"But you were thinking it."

Another silence. Joe pulled the blanket tighter around her.

"Joe, what's the matter?"

She let out a sigh. "I don't know. I just

feel . . . restless."

"You sound tired."

"I'm tired *and* restless."

"Don't bite my head off. I just want to know if things are okay between you two."

"Yeah, Ma. Things are fine. It's . . . this case, that's all."

"The bones thing?"

"Yeah." She brought her mother up to date on the case, telling her about the carvings and even about Mack. "They're still not letting me in on it, Ma," she finished.

Her mother was quiet for a moment. "They get like that. You have to be smarter than them."

"I'm trying, Ma. I've been trying to do things, but . . ."

"But what?"

"I think Mack is going in the wrong direction. I've . . . taken some shortcuts, and I've pissed him off. Maybe Sheriff Leach, too."

"You can't do it that way, honey," her mother said.

"I know," Joe said softly.

"If you don't follow the rules, you won't survive."

Joe stared hard at the dying fire.

"Joe?"

"Yeah, yeah . . . you're right."

"You have to trust your sheriff."

"I know."

"Can you?"

"I think so. He's a good man. It's just . . ." She shook her head slowly.

"Hard," her mother said.

Joe gave a small laugh.

"Good. At least you're laughing," Florence said.

They were quiet. Joe could hear the owl call again.

"So, when can I come up and see you?" her mother asked.

Joe hesitated. "Ma, I think Brad and I need some time together right now. Work has been, you know . . ."

"I know," Florence said. "I may not have done the job exactly as you do it, but I know the problems. I understand."

Joe heard a twinge of loneliness in her mother's voice. "I'll make time soon, Ma. I promise."

The fire was gone now, and the cabin was dark and growing colder. "I better go, I have to get up early," Joe said softly.

"Okay." A pause. "I love you, honey."

"I love you, too, Ma."

Joe hung up and set the phone back on the end table. She looked toward the bedroom. She could see the pulsing glow of the space heater. Chips got up slowly and gave a soft whine, looking to the door.

Joe rose with a sigh and went to the door, opening it. Chips trotted out into the yard, and she followed him.

The clouds had moved in, and the darkness was so solid it seemed to press against her. It was very cold. She shivered, pulling the blanket tighter around her shoulders.

Chips had disappeared. She whistled softly. It took a few moments, but finally she saw him emerge from the shadows.

"Chips, get in here," she said.

The dog followed her inside. Joe paused to look back out at the blackness. She closed the door and hesitated, looking at the lock. They never bothered with it usually. No one did in Echo Bay.

She turned the lock. The click of it seemed too loud in her ears.

13

He stood at the edge of the trees, watching the floating rectangles of yellow light. Everything else — the cabin, the shed, the car — was absorbed into the blackness of the night.

The people were still inside. They were always inside. There had not been one minute in the last few days when they had left the cabin. Not one chance for him to do what he needed to do.

He reached into his back pocket and withdrew the folded newspaper. He had read the story a hundred times, but he felt the sudden need to look at it again now. He turned his back to the cabin, stepped behind a tree, and flicked a match to life.

SOMEBODY'S DAUGHTER.

The flame wavered and died in the cold air. He lit another match, but it, too, quickly died.

Fuck this.

A sound drew his eyes back to the cabin. There was a new rectangle of yellow, an open door. Someone had come outside.

A girl . . .

He had not seen her before. He had thought only the man and the woman lived inside. Where had she come from?

A man's silhouette appeared at the door.

"Terry? You out there?"

"I just wanna look at the stars!" the girl said.

From his position behind the tree, he looked up. There were no stars tonight. She was lying. He respected her for that, lying to her father. That took guts.

She said something about coming back in a minute, and her father closed the door.

The girl scampered to the shed, slipping behind it. She was close to him now, so close her sweet smell drifted to him in the cold air. She couldn't see him. She was too busy searching for something in her pockets.

He moved to the other side of the tree, trying to get a better look. Wondered if maybe, just maybe, this opportunity was being offered to him as a replacement for the girl in the dunes.

This was as perfect as it could get.

This place. In these woods.

Suddenly, the girl's face lit up in the glow of a match. Heart-shaped with mischievous eyes. A cigarette in her mouth. She drew nervous puffs, blowing the smoke out over her head and quickly waving at the air to dispel it.

He felt a small churning in his gut.

This was somebody's daughter, too.

Somebody's very lucky daughter.

He would not kill her. He'd been stupid once already in the dunes. He couldn't let it happen here again. Christ, what was wrong with him? What was happening to him?

The bang of the screen door drew his head up. The girl was gone. It was time for him to be gone, too.

He started back through the woods to where he had left his car. It was almost a mile, and as he wove through the dark trees, he began to wonder what else could go wrong. What if the cops had found his car? What if they searched it?

He came back out onto the road and let out a breath as he saw the car. No cops waiting in ambush.

He could smell it even before he reached the car, smell the body in the truck. It was worse than it had been this morning.

He had wrapped her in a plastic sheet and bundled her up tight. All the bags of ice had kept her cool, but he wondered now if decomposing body fluids could eat through the plastic. It would be just his luck to be barreling down I-75 spraying this shit under the tires of some eager state trooper.

He kicked the bumper of the car.

Damn her. Damn those people in the cabin.

He needed to go home, but he couldn't leave her here. The cops were already looking at the old bones, and if they found a fresh body, they'd make the connection easily. They'd start asking questions at the motels, and he couldn't let that happen.

This girl could not be found here. Not ever.

He got into the car and started down the deserted dirt road. Soon he was back on the main road, passing only one car before he got to the M-22 turnoff. He waited at the stop sign for a motor home to pass, then he pulled out and headed south.

Two hours downstate, the car was thick with the smell of rotted flesh. He drove at a steady pace, his eyes on the speedometer, his heart kicking into a higher gear every time he saw headlights approaching in his rearview mirror.

When the green reflective sign for the Houghton Lake exit came into view, he swung off the freeway. He had to find a place to finish this.

He pulled into the gravel lot of a boarded-up Dairy Queen and thrust the car into park. He rolled down the window and took a gulp of clean air. He studied the motel across the highway. Some kids were playing shuffleboard under the mosquito-clouded floodlights. And further on, he could see the lights of a miniature golf place, and he could hear the putter of go-karts.

This place was for families. He didn't like it here.

He drove away, turning back the way he had come. But before he got back to the freeway, he spotted a side road heading south, away from town, and took it. Soon the road turned from asphalt to dirt and

the comforting darkness of the woods surrounded him.

Miles of black. Then suddenly, something
drew his foot from the accelerator. The eerie
glint of eyes floating in the trees.

He stopped the car.

A deer. Standing in the trees by the side
of the road. It was staring straight at him.

*Shoot it! Shoot it! What's the matter with
you? Shoot it, you little pansy!*

He shut his eyes tight against the voice in
his head, against the images coming. His
nostrils burned with the smell of rotting
flesh. He turned off the engine, yanked open
the door, and stumbled from the car.

The deer was still there, watching him.

He wiped his face and sucked the pine-
scented air deep into his lungs. Finally, he
walked slowly back to the trunk and popped
it open.

The smell made him work quickly. He
pulled the plastic lump out, careful not to
let it touch any part of him. He looked
around at the darkness and then dragged
the body toward the trees.

He pulled out his knife and he sliced the
ropes. Then, grabbing the plastic, he gave it
a hard jerk. The body rolled onto the grass.
He couldn't see it clearly, didn't even want
to anymore. But he had to check one last

thing, because he wasn't sure anymore if he had even done this part right back in the dunes.

He came closer, holding a hand to his nose, and looked down. Yes, yes . . . the hand was gone. He had not fucked that up, at least. He grabbed the plastic and started for the car.

He sensed something, someone watching him, and looked up in panic. He let out a long, shaking breath.

Eyes in the dark. Just the deer? Or maybe some other animal?

He allowed himself a small smile, the first one in a long time, because at least this part was right. He nodded at the animal in silent acknowledgment. Then he backed slowly away, inching out of the woods.

He stowed the plastic in the trunk, got back into the car, and started the engine. The headlights split the darkness, lighting the road south. He put the car in gear and started home.

14

Joe crossed the street, dipping her head against the sharp wind coming off the lake. There had been hopeful talk in the station that morning of an Indian summer that might let them prolong the search for more bones before the snows came and put an end to everything. But the cold that had moved in yesterday had deepened during the night. And suddenly, small talk in the Early Bird had turned from fishing and Octoberfests to storm windows and the stocking of woodpiles.

Earlier, Theo had called to tell her he had developed the film from her Instamatic. She left Mike waiting for a call back from a dentist in Chicago. Annabelle Chapel's dentist had died four years ago, and the man who had bought his practice was having trouble locating the old records. Mack had already contacted Annabelle's parents to prepare them.

When she stepped inside the *Banner* office, there was no one manning the counter. "Theo?" she called out.

"Be right there." His voice came from behind a door.

She leaned on the counter, pulling over that morning's *Banner* to read as she waited. Theo had run a story about the finding of the jawbone, even mentioning the braces. She wondered who had told him that. Augie, probably. The sheriff was going to be pissed when he saw it.

Theo appeared, carrying some prints and

her camera.

"Did they come out okay?" she asked.

"Very good, considering the cheap camera," Theo said, handing over a small stack of prints. The four shots of the two carvings were on top.

"So where did you take these?" Theo asked.

"Can't tell you yet, Theo."

"But you will."

She looked up and realized he was asking her to strike a bargain. "As soon as I can talk about it, Theo, you'll be the first to know. To be honest, I'm not sure they mean a thing."

"They look like they might be Indian to me," Theo said.

"Indian? Why do you say that?"

Theo shrugged. "Just a guess. But about the exact symbolism, I would have no idea. The library in Traverse City has a good collection on local tribes."

A phone rang, and Theo left. Joe labeled the backs of the photos with the names of the trees on which she had found them, the first two "Prayer Tree" and the other two "Oak Tree."

She sifted quickly through the other photos of routine accidents, separating them so she could take them back to the station.

But when she got to the final one, she drew back. It was a photo of a teenager sitting on the trunk of a department cruiser. Skimpy white top, cutoff denim shorts, long bare legs, head thrown back with a sexy smile. It was not Mindy and was too old to be Mike's daughter Jenny.

"Was this one on the roll, too?" Joe asked, holding it up.

Theo was coming back to her, carrying a manila envelope and the Instamatic. "Yes," he said. "I don't know her? Do you?"

Joe shook her head, looking again at the photo. The background was green and leafy, so the snapshot probably had been taken sometime last summer. The fact that Theo didn't recognize her meant she wasn't a local.

"Is this your personal camera?" Theo asked, handing it to her.

"No," Joe said. "It's been in the cruiser for months."

"Well, seems your partner has a little friend."

Joe slipped the print of the girl behind the others. How was she going to handle this? She knew it wasn't any of her business, but she also knew that eventually she wouldn't be able to resist saying something to Mike.

"So how is Mack treating you?" Theo asked.

"Like an old dog he hopes will croak soon," she said with a shrug.

"I did some research on him. Would you like to hear what I found out?"

When she hesitated, Theo pushed the manila envelope across the counter. "Here, you can read for yourself."

She opened the envelope, pulling out the Xeroxed papers. They were copies of articles from the *Petoskey News-Review.* Her eyes went right to the headline on the first article: DEDICATED DETECTIVE REFUSES TO GIVE UP SEARCH.

The story gave the usual details about Annabelle Chapel's disappearance but it focused more on Mack and his dogged pursuit of her case — despite the fact the local district attorney and the police chief had publicly criticized him for it. The story was written thirteen months after Annabelle had vanished.

"Interesting, *n'est-ce pas?*" Theo asked.

She didn't answer as she moved on to the second article, dated a few months later and headlined: DETECTIVE FIRED. The story quoted a chief named Linden, who said he had no choice but to let Mack go because he had "crossed the line too many times" and that his record with the Petoskey PD was "riddled with problems, both personal and professional."

The last paragraph stated that Mack had also been fired from the East Lansing PD Traffic Division when he was twenty-five and had once been on a long medical leave of absence for unknown reasons.

"I called a friend down there," Theo said. "The leave of absence was alcohol. Mack used to drink on the job."

Joe set the articles on the counter. "Why did you show me these, Theo?"

"Augie told me Mack is not being good to you. I don't know, I thought maybe this could help you somehow."

Joe suppressed a sigh. "I appreciate the thought, Theo. But throw them away, okay?" she said.

Theo wadded up the copies and tossed them into a trash can. "Done," he said.

Back at the station, the office was empty, except for Augie, who was watering his plants. Joe was tempted to talk to him about Theo but decided not to bring it up.

"Where's Mike?" she asked.

Augie shrugged. "Lunch, I think."

Joe tapped the manila envelope on her

palm. At least she didn't have to confront Mike with the photograph right now.

"Oh, by the way, our friend Mack left you a present," Augie called out.

She spotted a large box on her desk and knew immediately what it was: more junk from the woods, gathered up last night and this morning. And it had been left for her to log.

She peered into the box. It held an array of muddy clothing, cigarette packs, shoes, cans, and gloves. It looked as if Mack had already culled out anything that could be remotely connected to a female or a possible homicide.

"Augie, is the sheriff in?" she asked.

"Back in his office."

She pulled out the snapshot of the girl from the envelope and slipped it into her desk drawer. At Leach's door, she tapped lightly and pushed it open.

Leach set down his coffee as his eyes came up. "What is it, Joe?"

"I have something I think you need to see, sir," she said, coming forward and holding out the photos of the carvings.

Leach took the photos. "What am I looking at here?" he asked.

"I found these last night on the trees closest to where we found the bones."

"What kind of carvings are these?" he asked.

"I'm not sure, maybe Indian," she said.

He looked up at her. "Do you know anything about our Indians here?"

"No."

He sighed, setting the photos on the desk. "Joe . . ."

"All right, maybe they aren't Indian symbols," she said. "But they might be important, maybe even something left by the killer. Maybe it's how he marked the spots."

"Why? And why on more than one tree?" Leach asked. "And why carve kid's stuff like this? If our killer left anything, it would most likely be the girl's name or a date or some message."

Joe was quiet, staring at the top picture, trying to see something in it besides a man standing in a rowboat. But she couldn't, and with every second of silence that passed, she felt more like a fool.

"Listen, Joe," Leach said. "Hopefully, we'll match the jawbone to Annabelle Chapel's dental records soon, and we can close this damn case. Or at least our end of it. We'll let the state police figure out what happened to the poor girl."

"Yes, sir," Joe said softly. She picked up

the photographs.

Leach pushed himself up from his chair and came around to her.

"Joe, I brought you in here because I saw a special hunger in you, the kind of thing that makes a great investigator," he said. "And I know one day you'll be one. Hell, you'll probably be a detective in a place bigger and better than this place before you're thirty."

"Sir, please —"

"But right now, you just don't have the experience, and you need to play by the rules," he said. "One of the rules is you don't let emotion blind you to the case at hand. As a woman, you're going to feel passionate about your victims, but you can't get emotional when you're working a case."

"Mack's not emotional?" she asked.

"Yes, but he's also probably right."

"So that excuses it?"

"When you're in charge and you're on the right track, lots of things are excused."

Joe tried to hold his eyes, but she didn't want him to see the disappointment in her own, so she looked out his window at the lake.

Leach gestured toward the photos. "Go ahead and file those along with all the other things you've logged. And I don't want to see them in the newspaper," he said.

Joe forced her eyes back to Leach. "Thank you for your time, sir."

She left his office and went to her desk, shoving the photos into a drawer. She stared at the box for a moment, then snatched up the evidence log clipboard and threw it on top of the junk. Grabbing the box, she started to the evidence room. As she pushed through the door with her knee, the box caught the edge of a shelf. The box's bottom split open, and the shelf gave way, sending everything clattering to the floor. The jagged edge of the rusted deer hoist smacked her wrist as it hit.

"Damn it!" she hissed.

A trickle of blood was already oozing from the cut on her wrist. She glanced down at the box, then kicked it. Gloves, hats, and empty cigarette packs skittered across the floor.

"Joe?" Augie hollered.

"What?"

"There's someone out here you should speak to."

She went back to the front office, her chest still heaving. The small round woman was standing in a slant of sunlight. Her blondish-gray hair and the matronly style of her blue coat placed her about forty-five. She looked tired, yet there was something oddly hope-ful about her powdered face.

Joe came forward slowly. "May I help you?"

The woman laid a copy of the *Echo Bay Banner* on the counter. It was folded to the story Theo had written about the bones early last week.

"My name is Dorothy Newton," she said. "I think the bones you found may belong to my daughter, Natalie. She disappeared seven years ago."

15

The last thing Joe wanted to do was overstep her bounds again, so she took Mrs. Newton back to see Sheriff Leach. Joe could tell by Leach's expression that he wasn't pleased with the prospect of having to deal with the grieving mother of a missing girl. But he welcomed Mrs. Newton into his office and motioned for her to sit down. Joe took a position near the bookshelf before Leach could dismiss her.

Dorothy Newton's eyes flicked nervously around the room. Leach brought her back to him with a gentle clearing of his throat.

"What can I do for you, Mrs. Newton?" Leach asked.

Dorothy Newton glanced at Joe and repeated that her daughter had disappeared seven years ago, in 1968. Leach's eyes went up to Joe and back to Dorothy Newton.

"Where did she disappear from?" Leach asked.

"We're from Indianapolis, but Natalie was a student at Western Michigan," Dorothy Newton said. "She had a trip planned to Florida for spring break, and I hadn't talked to her for weeks before and didn't really get concerned for a few weeks after."

"Did you report it?"

"Yes," Dorothy Newton said. "But not right away, because I didn't know she was even missing. I called, and her roommates told me she never made the trip to Florida. And they just assumed she went home to visit me instead."

"How old was she?"

"Twenty-one."

Joe wondered how much of the case he would share with this woman, or if he should share anything at all. Then she tried to remember if she had seen Natalie Newton among the missing persons bulletins. She didn't think she had.

"The newspaper said you found bones," Dorothy Newton said. "I have a picture of Natalie here. Perhaps . . ."

Dorothy Newton pulled a folded piece of paper from her purse and laid it gently on Leach's desk. Joe stepped forward to see it better. It looked like a homemade missing persons flyer, the top printed with HAVE YOU SEEN HER?

Joe looked at the face on the paper. Natalie Newton was a brunette, with long, straight hair and a round face with cupid-bow lips. She wore a puffy peasant blouse, wire-rimmed glasses, and hoop earrings that looked large enough to fit around Joe's wrist. She wasn't smiling in the picture, and Joe realized they could eliminate Natalie Newton with one simple question.

"Mrs. Newton," Joe asked, "did Natalie wear braces?"

"No, Natalie had perfect teeth."

When Joe said nothing, Dorothy Newton's soft brown eyes glistened with tears, and she lowered her head, fingering the edge of the newspaper. "The girl you found," she said. "She has braces, doesn't she?"

"Yes."

"Then it's not Natalie."

"No," Joe said softly. "I'm sorry."

Dorothy Newton gathered the newspaper to her chest. She shut her eyes and lost a tear down her cheek.

"Mrs. Newton," Leach said, "may we get

you a glass of water?"

She shook her head, and rose slowly. Joe picked up the flyer. "May we keep this?" she asked.

Dorothy Newton frowned. "Why?"

"So we can keep looking for her," Joe said. "It would be very helpful."

"I have plenty more," she said. "There's a phone number on there you can call. I'm almost always there, except when I travel, and I always leave the answering machine on and —"

"Those are all good things to do," Joe said. "We'll call you if we come across anything you should know."

Dorothy Newton glanced around the office, as if she weren't sure where the door was. Joe went to open it for her. She touched Dorothy Newton's arm as she passed, but she didn't think the woman felt it.

Joe closed the door and turned back to Leach.

"You handled that well," he said. He let out a long breath. "You'd better prepare yourself. We're likely to have more of them."

"Mothers?" Joe asked.

"Yes," Leach said. "That's what publicity gets you."

Joe didn't reply as she folded the old flyer carefully and slipped it into her shirt pocket so she could put it with the bulletins. Then she looked around, postponing her return to the evidence room. There was still a sadness in the air, hanging like the drifting sunlight. Joe wished she could have given Dorothy Newton something, and she thought about how macabre that was — to wish you could tell someone you've found their daughter's bones.

She looked back at Leach, something else churning in her brain. They had four bones, but only one, the jawbone, could ever be definitively linked to a victim. And everything they had done so far was based on the jawbone and the braces, including the assumption that they had only one victim.

But what if the other three bones were not from the same skeleton as the jawbone? What if there was a second victim?

Joe came forward slowly. "Sir, may I offer something?"

"Certainly."

"Do you think there's a chance we may have two victims?"

Leach looked at her. "Why would you suggest that?"

"We have braces and the charm bracelet, and we haven't been able to link those two items to any single victim. It's like each one belonged to someone else."

"It's possible we have not yet identified the girl who had both."

"But there were two different carvings on two different trees."

"Carvings that may mean nothing."

"Why do you discount them?" she asked.

"I'm not discounting them," Leach said. "I'm simply being cautious. When a cop is not objective, it becomes easy to fall into the trap of seeing only the evidence that supports his theory of the crime."

"Can't more than one theory be followed at the same time?"

He finally gave her a smile. "Yes," he said, "but theories have to be logical. The odds are astronomical we'd have two victims killed by the same man. It would mean a multiple killer was working in our midst, and that just doesn't happen in places like this."

"A multiple killer?" she asked.

"Yes," Leach said. "You know, someone like John Norman Collins, the coed killer."

She remembered the name vaguely, someone at the academy mentioning a series of murders down in the Ann Arbor area. But if she remembered right, Collins was now serving a life sentence in prison.

"When did Collins do his crimes?" she asked.

Leach took a long pause, and his answer came slowly, as if something had just occurred to him. "Sixty-seven to sixty-nine," he said.

Joe was quiet, suddenly realizing what Leach was thinking. Natalie Newton disappeared in sixty-eight, from a college only a few hours' drive from Ann Arbor.

Leach pushed from the chair and walked to the bookshelf, pulling down a black binder. He held it out to Joe. "Take a look at this."

She set it on the desk and opened it. Taped to the first page was a photograph of a good-looking, dark-haired young man wearing a jacket, shirt, and tie. The next page was a newspaper clipping from the August 8, 1967, edition of the *Ann Arbor News.*

"A body found yesterday afternoon on a Superior Township farm was tentatively identified as that of a 19-year-old Eastern Michigan University coed who disappeared without a trace July 10."

Joe flipped through the pages. They were mostly newspaper articles, a few police reports Leach had managed to get his hands on, some handwritten notes and magazine articles on Collins's life.

"Were you part of that case?" she asked.

"No," Leach said. "I was a sergeant in Marquette County and teaching at Northern at the time. We all heard about the student murders down in Ann Arbor and Ypsi. But when I saw how the fear stretched to a campus hundreds of miles away, I started paying more attention to the case."

Joe continued to look through the scrapbook, scanning the headlines. A year between the first and second bodies. Then a third and a fourth and a fifth. Seven victims total, with speculation of more. All raped, slashed, mutilated. Two years into the spree, a psychic was called in, a man named Peter Hurkos. Then, finally, the arrest. Collins had been turned in by his uncle, a state trooper. Collins had murdered one of the coeds in the uncle's basement while the uncle was on vacation.

She closed the book. "Was there ever any indication Collins spent time up here?"

Leach gave her a slow nod. "There's a town north of Petoskey. They found an entire family murdered in their home there in 1968. Collins was a friend of one of the teenage sons, but no one was ever able to link Collins to that crime. It remains unsolved."

Leach picked up the phone and asked Augie to get him an investigator with the

Ann Arbor police. As he waited, he looked at Joe.

"I still believe our case is a solitary homicide," he said. "But it's protocol to alert the investigators of even a possible connection."

"I understand, sir."

Joe looked back at Leach's scrapbook, still seeing the graphic crime scenes in her head. She felt a soft flip of her stomach.

Something else was hitting her. The fact that their girl — or girls — were so young left one other obvious conclusion. Like Collins's victims, they had probably been raped.

"You can keep that awhile," Leach said, covering the receiver with his hand and nodding toward the scrapbook. "Study up on the way they conducted their investigation. Get a little insight into a man like Collins. It'll help you later, if this is what you are suggesting it is."

It took a moment for what Leach had said to register. He was keeping his mind open that she might be right about the bones.

Leach finally started talking to someone. As Joe left the office, she heard him begin the conversation with the words "This is probably nothing, but . . ."

She grabbed the missing persons binder off the shelf. She pulled Natalie Newton's flyer from her pocket and carefully smoothed it with her palm. She paused to take one last look at Natalie's face.

She was dressed in the style popular in the late sixties, right down to the wire-rimmed glasses hippies wore and the center-parted straight hair of the English fashion models.

Joe focused on the glasses. She was thinking about the glasses they had found in the woods during the first search. They had dismissed them then, thinking they belonged to an old man.

Joe hurried back to the evidence room. She was scanning the shelves for the glasses she had tagged days ago when she remembered she had put them in a shoe box with some other small articles. She found the box on the floor, the contents toppled. The glasses were right on top.

She spread Natalie's flyer out on the shelf and held the glasses next to the pair in the picture. They looked exactly the same.

16

Everything had changed. Since the discovery of the jawbone two days ago and the matching of the glasses with Natalie Newton's flyer, the leap had been made that they might now have more than one victim. And once Joe found out from Dorothy Newton that Natalie had never owned a charm bracelet, there was also the possibility that they could have three victims.

As Leach had told Joe this morning, one victim probably meant they were dealing with something isolated and personal, like a relative or an angry boyfriend. But two or more — that meant they could be looking at a psychopath who killed for no reason other than his sick needs.

The volunteer searchers from the university were now gone, replaced with an army of blue uniforms from the state police. The sagging tape printed with POLICE LINE that Holt had strung had been ripped down, and a squared-off grid had been marked with taut barriers of wide yellow tape that shouted CRIME SCENE DO NOT CROSS.

Even the trees were different. The cold front that had crept down from Canada had triggered the trees to begin their change. The leaves, which had gorged all spring and summer on green chlorophyll, now were starting their slow starvation.

Joe looked up. The colors had seemed to appear from nowhere. The red-purple of the sumacs, the brilliant orange of the sugar maples, the russet brown of the oaks, the gold of the birches. She squinted, and it blurred into one Impressionist swirl.

How many bones were still out there? How many more would they find? How many girls had he killed?

The sharp bark of a dog drew her eyes to the distance. The technicians were out by the oak tree, and she wanted desperately to go there and watch them work. But Leach had told her to stay here, at the northern boundary of the tape, to make sure no gawkers intruded. The state police had set up a roadblock out on the logging road to keep the curious out, but a few hikers had managed to sneak in already this morning before she and Holt threw them out.

A search dog broke through the trees. The grim-faced state cop at the other end of the leash gave Joe a nod as he went by.

"They really expect the dogs to find anyone?" Holt asked.

Joe looked at Holt. "What do you mean?"

"It's not like we have bodies or something here."

Joe turned back to watch the German shepherd. "A dog's sense of smell is forty times better than ours, and humans are smelly creatures. So to a dog we smell as powerful as a just-baked apple pie."

"Your boyfriend tell you that?" Holt asked.

"As a matter of fact, yeah," Joe said, remembering how excited she had been telling Brad about the case last night.

"Well, there's nothing here for a dog to smell," Holt said.

"A dog can pick up a scent from a bone or even skin cells. We shed cells all the time, Holt. You're shedding all over the place right now, in fact."

He gave a grunt of disbelief as he watched the dog.

Joe was quiet, the same doubt Holt felt swirling in her head. Hell, Chips was so dumb he couldn't find a saltine cracker in the kitchen. And increasingly it appeared that there was nothing else out here to find.

She had been watching all morning as the state police set up a command post and marked off an elaborate search grid. She had watched the teams of men carefully clearing away the blankets of leaves, depositing them in heaping mounds that looked like so many benign yard piles raked to the curb for burning. They were searching for patches of ground that looked disturbed or different, anything that might be evidence of a shallow grave. Crews with hand trowels and screened sifting boxes were at work where the two sets of bones had been found. But so far, nothing had been unearthed.

Not a shred of clothing. Not a bone. Not a tooth.

Mack had put in an appearance that morning. He stood watching, unable to hide his anger at the state police taking over. He was still waiting for the dentist in Chicago to report back. He wasn't convinced that the glasses were important. As he told Leach, they looked exactly like the ones old man Dirksen at the Rexall wore.

"Jesus, how are these people getting in here?" Holt said.

Joe watched as Holt moved to the tape to chase four teenagers away. Leach was just coming up the hill as the kids left. There was a tall man in a tan trench coat with him. The sheriff ducked under the tape. The sandy-haired man had to stop and collapse his gangly frame to get under the same tape Leach had so easily broached.

The man's long, pale face slowly registered in Joe's memory. It was the state investigator who had shown up at the station two weeks ago. Joe couldn't remember the guy's name. All she could remember was the odd color of his eyes, blue shot through with white stress lines, like a frozen lake.

"Joe, you remember Detective Norm Rafsky," Leach said. "He's here to advise and assist."

Joe gave a curt nod with a finger to the brim of her hat. As the state investigator's eyes focused on her, she found herself wondering how eyes the color of ice could look so warm.

"Norm was asking me about the carvings," Leach said.

"Sheriff Leach said you found them," Rafsky said. His speech had the flat, nasally vowels of a native Michigander.

"Yes, sir," Joe said. "One on that tree over there." She pointed into the woods. "The other one is maybe a half-mile off that way."

"Why don't you show me?"

"Yes, sir."

They went to the prayer tree, stepping carefully around the area where the dirt was being sifted. At the back of the trunk, she pointed.

Rafsky stepped up next to her. His long, bony fingers came up to trace the faded carving lightly before he looked back at Joe.

"Any ideas?"

"Sir?"

"What this might mean?"

Joe felt Leach's eyes on her. "No, sir. Could be anything or nothing. Maybe just kid's stuff."

"I think they are too high for kids to have made them," Rafsky said.

She hesitated. "That was my thought as well, sir."

"And your other thoughts?"

Again, she hesitated, thinking now of what her mother had said about toeing the line. "I have a feeling they are Indian markings of some kind," she said.

Rafsky smiled slightly. "I think you're right. I saw something similar once when I was working in Alpena."

Joe glanced at Leach. He didn't seem upset with her. In fact, there was something close to pride in his eyes.

"Deputy Frye, does the second carving look like this one?" Rafsky asked.

"It has the same U shape," she said, pointing to the bottom of the carving. "But the other one looks like a man standing in a boat."

"A boat? You're sure?"

"That's what it looks like to me, sir."

"Any rivers, streams around here?" Rafsky asked Leach.

"Just Houdek Creek. But it's a good ways from here."

A gust of cold wind poured in from the west, sending a fresh shower of leaves swirling down on them.

"We need to find out what this means," Rafsky said, tapping the bark. "You have any locals who will talk to us?"

"Lots of Ojibwa around here," Leach said. "But they don't trust us, and we don't really trust them."

"Well, let's try." Rafsky turned up his collar against another gust of wind. "I'll need to hang around here a couple days. Maybe you could recommend a place, Sheriff?"

"Sure, come back to the cruiser," Leach said. "I'll radio back to Augie to call the Riverside."

Joe followed them back to the yellow tape perimeter where Holt waited. She watched Rafsky and Leach duck under and head down to the logging road.

"What do you think?"

She turned to Holt. "About what?"

"That Rafsky guy."

Joe gave a shrug, still hanging on to what she had felt when Rafsky said she was right about the carvings, still seeing the gleam of respect in the investigator's eyes. She was hoping now, more than ever, that Leach would keep his word about letting her work on the case, if Rafsky allowed it.

"He seems okay," she said.

"Did he know what the carvings were?" Holt asked.

"He thinks they might be Indian," Joe said. "And he wants Leach to find an Indian who might talk to us."

"I know somebody," Holt said.

Joe faced him.

"Well, I don't know any Indians," he said. "But I know somebody who knows somebody."

There was an eagerness in Holt's voice. Joe could tell he felt left out, and she felt a twinge of sympathy. Holt wasn't the sharpest crayon in the box, as her dad used to say, and now that the state police had taken over, Holt would be pushed even further to the margins.

"Go tell the sheriff," Joe said.

Holt grinned, ducked under the tape, and hurried off down the hill toward the logging road.

She turned back to watch the searchers. The German shepherd was sitting obediently at its handler's feet, ears pricked. The steady scrap of the trowels went on. The leaf mounds were growing larger.

Another gust of wind blew in from the west, sending the birches sighing. The German shepherd raised its snout. Joe looked up as a shower of leaves fell. The ground that the men had cleared just a half-hour before was already covered again. Winter was moving in. It was now a race against time and weather.

She heard a sound, the shuffle of feet through leaves, and looked to her left. Far down the yellow line of crime tape, she saw a woman. She started to go to her to tell her she had to leave. But then she stopped.

It was Dorothy Newton. She was standing there huddled down into her blue wool coat, a bright scarf covering her head. She was watching the men digging in the dirt.

17

They entered a tunnel of blood red. For a moment, the sun was gone, and then it was back, sifting down through the red leaves of the sugar maples arching over the road.

Joe blinked against the sun as she stared out the window. She was in the passenger seat, and Rafsky was driving, his long body relaxed in the soft leather seat of the Chrysler sedan. He wore a long-sleeved white shirt and navy tie. His dark blue suit jacket and trench coat were draped over the seat between them.

They were heading away from Echo Bay, down the thin finger of land that separated Lake Leelanau from Lake Michigan. Rafsky had his window cracked, and the crisp pine-scented air swirled around them.

"This is beautiful country," Rafsky said.

Joe glanced over at him. "You haven't been here before?"

He shook his head. "Never had reason to. I was born in Bay City, and when I joined the state police, I got assigned to Saginaw. I was sent to Gaylord two years ago. Never been over in this neck of the woods before."

They were quiet for a few miles.

"Leelanau," Rafsky said. "That's Indian. Means 'delight of life.' "

"I didn't know that," Joe said.

"Me, either, until the waitress at the Early Bird told me this morning."

Rafsky turned left onto a county road that jagged east across the peninsula. The hardwood and pines soon fell away, and they entered a new landscape of cherry orchards and vacant land, cut through with dirt roads that seem to lead nowhere. Every so often, Joe could spot a cabin or a small house. She knew that many of the people here were poor, that for every dazzling sand-duned vista or pristine pine forest, there was a ramshackle trailer or shingled shanty stuck back in the woods. For every family hauling the camper up from Detroit or for every leaf peeper who rented a cabin on the shore, there was a local who had to live through long winters on the crumbs left over from the too-short summers.

She knew this. But she didn't know it the way the locals did. She didn't know it with the cold certainty of living through a winter here. Not yet.

Joe pulled up the collar of her jacket. Rafsky glanced over and rolled up the window.

"Thank you for bringing me," Joe said.

Rafsky smiled. "No problem," he said. "I enjoy the company. And it never hurts to have a different viewpoint on things."

They were almost to the eastern shore of the peninsula, and the trees were thickening again, the narrow blacktop road providing a stage for a frenzied ballet of leaves. She picked up the folder from the seat and opened it to the photographs of the carvings.

Holt's friend had hooked them up with an Ojibwa man named Thomas Ahanu, who said he would be willing to talk to the police. Joe didn't know too much about Indians. Most of her perceptions had come from TV or movies. Or what she had heard up at Northern. It had seemed to her that most of the students — who, like her, were almost all white Michiganders — had no interest in the Indians. And it seemed the Indians had little interest in them.

The car slowed, and she looked up. A small green sign told them they were entering Peshawbestown. At first, she saw nothing, then finally a store, a gas station, and a smattering of houses. Two men standing at the gas pumps watched the Chrysler as it cruised by.

Rafsky stopped the car in front of a white frame church to check his directions. Joe rolled down her window. The church looked oddly out of place here where there was so little else. Or maybe it wasn't. She had no idea if the Indians were Christian or anything else.

Rafsky took a side road through a woods so thick she couldn't see a glimmer of a sunray. He made another turn onto a dirt road, then another, and as he pushed the heavy car up a hill, branches clawed at the car doors.

She smelled the burning firewood first, then saw the curl of gray smoke above the trees. As they rounded a corner, she saw the house. Part wood, part metal siding, a stovepipe chimney on the tar-paper roof.

Rafsky stopped the car and killed the engine.

The silence dropped over them, heavy at first, then lightening with the chirp of birds and the far-off bark of a dog.

"You ready?" Rafsky asked, grabbing his jacket.

She nodded and followed Rafsky across the grass to the house. There were two aluminum lawn chairs on the porch, draped with Indian blankets. Between them was a ceramic pot, filled with dirt and stabbed with cigarette butts.

The front door opened, and a man stepped out. A broad, burnt-brown face, a wide nose, and a suspicious set to his jaw. His onyx hair was pulled back in a ponytail. A nickel-plated handgun sat in a woven leather holster on his hip.

"You Mr. Rafsky?" the man asked.

"Yes, sir," Rafsky said. "And you are Thomas Ahanu?"

Ahanu's black eyes cut to Joe, and he said nothing.

Rafsky extended a hand to him. "How do you do?"

Ahanu turned away from Rafsky and walked back inside his house, leaving the door open. Rafsky gave Joe a look, then motioned that they should follow.

The inside of the house was dim, lit only by oil lamps that gave a sheen to the bare floor and the trunk-like legs of the wood chair and table in the middle of the room. A fire was burning in a fieldstone hearth that was coated with years of thick black ash. The mantel held colorful Indian dolls and stone sculptures of animals.

Joe's eyes were riveted on Thomas Ahanu. He moved to the kitchen and was stirring a pot at the stove, sending the scent of something gamey into the air.

"So talk," he said.

Rafsky stepped closer to him, but he didn't say anything. Joe knew he was waiting for Ahanu to look at him, demanding his attention as politely as he could. Ahanu stayed at the stove for almost a full minute before he finally turned. He was a big man, but he made no sound as he came toward them across the planked floor.

"Talk."

Rafsky held out a hand to Joe and she gave him the photographs of the two carvings. Rafsky offered them to Ahanu, but he refused to take them. But he did look at the one on top. His eyes came up to Joe before moving to Rafsky.

"You want to know what that is," Ahanu said.

"Yes," Rafsky said.

"Where did you find it?" Ahanu asked.

"Near a crime scene over by Echo Bay," Rafsky said.

Ahanu wiped his fleshy hands on his blue jeans and took the photos, moving closer to the oil lamp on the table. He held them down to the flicker of light.

"What kind of crime scene?" he asked.

Rafsky hesitated and Ahanu tilted his head with suspicion. "Someone is dead?" he asked.

"Yes, possibly murdered," Rafsky said. "We found human remains not far from these carvings."

Ahanu came back to them, slapping the photos against Rafsky's chest, forcing him to take them. "You see a carving on a tree, and you come here to accuse an Indian of murder?"

"No," Rafsky said quickly.

Ahanu walked back to the stove, stirring the pot. Rafsky gave him a moment, then went to him, smoothing the wrinkled photos.

"My apologies, Mr. Ahanu," he said. "The fact is, we believe a white man did this."

"Then why do you ask about the carvings?" Ahanu asked without turning.

"Because they were found on trees nearby," Rafsky said. "That's the only reason. They probably have nothing to do with the remains, but we need to know if they are Indian and what they symbolize." Rafsky held out the carving from the oak tree. "Please take another look."

Ahanu set the wooden spoon on the stove

and faced them. "It is a symbol of the moon, the Hunger Moon."

"And this one?" Rafsky said, holding up the second photograph.

"I do not know," Ahanu said. "It could be one of the others."

"How many are there?" Joe asked.

Ahanu looked to her as if he were surprised she could speak. "Twelve months, twelve moons," he said.

"Do the symbols have any other meaning besides the months?" Joe asked.

Ahanu's black eyes studied her before he answered and she had the sense he thought her stupid. "There is much meaning in them," he said. "There are many things to be seen in the moon symbols."

She was glad she hadn't told him she thought it was a man standing in a boat. "Tell me," she said.

Maybe it was just the shifting of the lamp lights, but the hardness of his brow seemed to soften. So did his voice. "As in many cultures, there is a belief that every woman holds in her body the ancient mysteries of the moon." His black eyes held hers. "It is the same with your astrology."

He seemed to be waiting, watching her for a reaction.

"Please go on," she said.

"The blood cycle of a woman flows like the changes in the moon, waxing and waning as the moon does," Ahanu said. "And the blood cycle is what the woman herself is. And the woman who sees the moon and seeks herself in it will never be lost. The woman who sees the moon will hear the wisdom of her ancestors and learn to honor what she is."

The cabin fell silent. A log dropped in the fireplace, filling Ahanu's black eyes with a glitter of cinders. He seemed to be searching her face for something, and she suddenly felt exposed, like she did sometimes when her mother got into her head.

Rafsky cleared his throat. "Mr. Ahanu," he said, "is there any sinister meaning behind the symbols?" he asked.

"Sinister?" Ahanu asked, turning to him.

"Yes," Rafsky said. "Can they represent a hunting kill or a sacrifice?"

Ahanu went back to the stove and took a large wooden bowl from the shelf. As he ladled his meaty stew into it, he spoke. "There is nothing sinister in the symbols," he said. "They are folklore, long forgotten now by our children."

"So there would be no reason for a killer to leave them near a body?"

Ahanu's hand paused in midair. Then,

slowly, he finished filling his bowl. "I am finished talking," he said.

Rafsky gave a sigh and handed Joe the photos. She slipped them into the folder, watching Ahanu. He took a spoon from a drawer and sat down at the table.

"The victim was a young woman," Joe said. "Does that change how her killer would see or use a symbol?"

Ahanu shut his eyes. "How much of her did you find?" he asked.

Joe exchanged a quick look with Rafsky, then slipped into a chair across from Ahanu. "Just a few bones," she said.

Ahanu's eyes were still shut. The smell of the animal stew was everywhere, thick and almost sickening.

"Where exactly did you find the bones?" he asked.

"In the deep woods," Joe said.

He was silent. And even though he was sitting right across from her, Joe had the sense that a part of him had suddenly left the cabin.

"There is nothing else I can tell you," Ahanu said softly.

Joe leaned across the table. "Then why did you ask how much of her body was left?"

"Leave."

Joe didn't move. Ahanu started to eat, his

movements slow, his jaw grinding against the meat.

"Mr. Ahanu," Joe said, "we may have several victims. Please, if you know —"

Ahanu pushed away from the table and walked to the screen door off the kitchen, pushing through it so hard it back-slapped against the house. Through the window, Joe watched him step off the back porch. A few seconds later, he disappeared into the dark folds of the forest.

"I pushed him too hard," Joe said, rising.

"No," Rafsky said. "You did fine. You saw something there that got a reaction. And sometimes, getting a reaction is all we need."

She glanced back at the window. Ahanu was gone.

"Come on," Rafsky said.

Joe followed him back to the car, her head still stuck on the odd expression on Ahanu's face when she spoke of the bones.

"Something scared him," she said.

"The symbols could be just a time marker, like the killer was leaving a mark of what month he killed."

"There could be more carvings," Joe said.

Rafsky nodded. "I already told the search team to look for others. Nothing yet."

Joe was quiet.

"What it is?" Rafsky asked.

"I don't know. Just a feeling. I just know he was scared of something."

Rafsky opened the car door, laid his jacket inside, and leaned his elbows on the roof. "We need to find the other symbols and what they mean. You want that assignment?"

"Sure," she said.

"You got it, then."

18

"Ojibwa or Ottawa?"

Joe stared at the librarian. "I'm not sure."

The woman behind the counter looked at Joe over her glasses. "We have several tribes that are indigenous to the peninsula. Maybe if you could be more specific?"

Joe sighed. "I'm sorry. How about if you just give me everything you have?"

The librarian gave a small shrug. "All right, but it might take me a while. Why don't you take one of those study carrels over there?"

Joe looked to a series of doors with pebbled glass windows. The inside was just big enough for a wooden table and chair. Joe took off her hat and set it on the table. She could hear the hiss of the steam heat rising from the old radiator, and after a moment, she unsnapped her windbreaker and took it off.

She sat there, waiting, sweating, wondering how long this old stone fortress of a library had been here. The library was on Sixth Street in Traverse City, set down among the dowager mansions built in the nineteenth century by the city's logging barons. She was thinking, too, about Brad. His clinic was only a couple of blocks away. They had made a date to meet for lunch after she was done.

The fluorescent light flickered and hummed. Joe was about to go find the librarian when the woman came in and dropped a big stack of books on the table.

"This is everything we have on Indian lore. There's Ojibwa, Ottawa, Peshaba, and Anishinabeg."

Fifteen books. Joe thanked the woman, the door closed, and she was alone.

The small room grew close and hot as she labored through the books. Most were arid scholarly accounts of Leelanau's history. Others were picaresque personal records of the Indian culture written by settlers, interesting but nothing that illuminated what Thomas Ahanu had offered. Joe was about to give up when she found a slim, tattered volume written by an Ojibwa chief reprinted by the local historical society. It talked about how the Ojibwas were descendants of the Anishinabegs, an ancient tribe whose name meant "the real people" of the Great Lakes basin and whose unifying native language was Algonquian.

The close heat of the room was lulling, and she was about to close the book when a paragraph caught her eye:

Anishinabeg life revolved around an annual cycle of activities determined by the seasons and food supplies. With the coming of the heavy snows and the bitter cold of winter, came the Hunger Moon, with its limited supply of fish and the ice cover that stopped all lake and river canoe travel.

Joe sat upright. She quickly scanned the account, but there was nothing more about moons. She flipped through the rest of the slender book and then stopped. Drawings. Twelve of them, one for each month.

She let out a breath as she stared at the February Hunger Moon symbol. That was the one carved on the oak tree, that much she was sure of. The other one? It didn't seem to match any of the symbols in the book. She tore off a piece of scrap paper to mark the page.

She was gathering up the books when a

JANUARY
Snow Moon

FEBRUARY
Hunger Moon

MARCH
Crow Moon

APRIL
Wild Goose
Moon

MAY
Planting Moon

JUNE
Rose Moon

JULY
Thunder Moon

AUGUST
Green Corn
Moon

SEPTEMBER
Hunting Moon

OCTOBER
Falling Leaf Moon

NOVEMBER
Mad Moon

DECEMBER
Long Night
Moon

pamphlet caught her eye. The title was "Lore and Customs of the Algonquian Speaking Tribes." She flipped through it, looking for more moon references. She stopped at a heading called "Mad with Hunger."

In the depths of the forest, deep down into no man's land, are tales of terror that would make the boldest of men shiver. Tales of inhuman things, supernatural things, savage things. Strange creatures dwell in the deepest, darkest forests in the world, but stranger still are the ones that live inside of man, inner beasts more fearsome than anything else. One such creature is the Windigo. Or as the Algonquian root word calls it, "Witiku."

The legend of the Windigo is well known among the Algonquian speaking tribes. No monster or "evil spirit" evokes so much fear in these people. Windigo is usually associated with winter, what the Algonquian tribes call the Hunger Moon. Most "cases" of Windigos are heard of during these cold months, probably because the lack of food is felt the most during these times, bringing cannibalism along with them. Most tales say that the Windigo rides with the winter wind, howling inhuman screams, others that the Windigo is made of ice and cold, a creature with a heart of ice, incapable of feeling human emotions.

Joe sat back in her chair, staring at the title: "Mad with Hunger." No way could she bring this back to Rafsky. He'd laugh her right off the case.

She flipped the page and went back to skim-reading the other entries about Ojibwa lore. She paused again, a familiar word in the chapter about language catching her eyes: "Leelanau."

There are many theories about the origin of the name Leelanau, and many attribute it to a corruption of an ancient Indian word meaning "Delight of Life."

Joe thought of Rafsky getting his local history lesson with his morning coffee from the waitress at the Early Bird. She read on:

But many people believe the true origin of the name Leelanau came from an old Ojibwa legend about a beautiful Indian maiden who ran away from home to spend time in a sacred grove deep in the woods by Lake Michigan. On one trip, she said a prayer:

Spirit of the dancing leaves,
Hear a throbbing heart that grieves
Not for joys this world can give
But for the life that spirits live.

Her prayer was answered, and she disappeared from her home forever and went to live in her enchanted haunted grove. The name of the legend was Leelinau or "The Lost Daughter."

Joe stared at the book in stunned silence.

Maybe it was just the closed room, but she suddenly felt as if she couldn't breathe. She gathered up all the books and quickly left.

19

Joe pulled open the door to the Early Bird, her eyes tearing in the sudden burst of warm air. She blinked and scanned the row of booths for Rafsky. He was seated near the back, staring out the window.

She shivered as she walked to him. She had thought Cleveland was cold when the winds came off Lake Erie, but it was nothing like the gusts off Lake Michigan. Bigger and bluer and deeper, Lake Michigan could bestow soul-warming sunsets but it was equally capable of unleashing wrathful winter screams that could drive men mad.

Joe dropped into the booth, shoving her pile of library books to the side as she unwrapped the scarf from her neck.

"Sorry I'm late," she said, trying to tuck her hair back into the ponytail. She gave up, looking around for a cup of coffee.

Rafsky signaled the waitress, and she appeared instantly with a cup. Joe grabbed it with both hands, taking small sips. Over the rim, she saw Rafsky watching her, a small smile tipping his lips.

"You look half frozen," he said.

"So much for an Indian summer," she said, taking two gulps of the coffee and looking around for the waitress for a refill.

"Speaking of Indians," Rafsky said, "what did you find out?"

Joe pulled out the book written by the Ojibwa chief. She opened it to the page with the twelve moon symbols and pushed it across the table.

"Twelve months, twelve symbols, just like Thomas Ahanu said," Joe said.

"So this is Hunger Moon," Rafsky said, pointing. "That's definitely the carving on the big oak tree. You got a photo of the other carving, the one that looks like a jack-o'-lantern?"

Joe dug through the papers she had stuck in one of the books and found the photograph of the second carving. Rafsky studied it before looking up at her. "What's your thought?" he asked.

She tapped the book page. "It could be this one, for September, Hunting Moon."

"Or it might just be a crude version of the Hunger Moon," he said.

"That would give us two carvings for February," Joe said.

"When did the Newton girl disappear?"

"We don't know exactly. But Dorothy

Newton told us she last talked to Natalie sometime in early February. But then Natalie was supposed to be going away for spring break. We haven't tracked down the roommates yet to verify anything."

"I'll get one of the men to handle that." Rafsky took a drink of his coffee.

"The charm bracelet doesn't belong to either Natalie or Annabelle," Joe said.

Rafsky just nodded.

Joe sat back in the booth, feeling another shiver ripple her shoulders despite the fact she hadn't taken off her jacket. She let her gaze drift to the window and for a few minutes she watched the people. Most of the leaf peepers were gone now, leaving only those hearty souls who lived here year-round to brave the coming winter.

Joe spotted Mindy Villella crossing the street, holding the collar of her parka closed against the wind. The photograph that Theo had developed of the teenage girl on the hood of the cruiser flashed back to Joe and she wondered again about Mike and his off-duty life. She still hadn't had the chance to tell him she had the picture.

"I need to eat," Rafsky said, pulling her attention back. "You want something? My treat."

Joe thought about Brad. After finding the

books in the library, she had immediately called Rafsky. He had asked to meet her for lunch so they could go over them. Brad had tried to sound understanding when she called to cancel their lunch date. Then he told her he had to work late again tonight. She promised him she'd wait so they could have a late dinner together.

"I'll have a ham and Swiss on rye," she said.

Rafsky flagged the waitress again and gave her their orders. When he turned back to Joe, he seemed to be studying her, and it made her uncomfortable. She used the excuse of taking off her jacket so as to not look at him.

Rafsky opened the book again, and Joe sipped her coffee as he thumbed through. "You find anything else in here we can use?"

"Well, like Ahanu said, the Hunger Moon is a symbol of survival in a season of starvation," she said.

Rafsky's eyes came up when she didn't go on. "I hear an 'and' in your voice."

When the waitress brought their food, Joe was glad for the interruption. A part of her wanted to tell him about the Windigo myth, but what was she supposed to say? *Well, sir, I think we have a cannibalistic monster that lives in the forest and is driven beyond all hu-*

man comprehension to eat his victims.

Rafsky was carefully taking apart his BLT and arranging the bacon and tomatoes in different layers. "Tell me what's on your mind, Frye," he said without looking up. "I won't bite."

She cleared her throat. "Well, sir, there's this Algonquian legend. It's about this creature that lives in the woods, and —" She pulled in a breath. "The creature stalks people during winter, eating them to survive."

Rafsky looked up.

"The Algonquins call it the Witiku, or the Windigo."

He slowly put the toasted bread atop the sandwich. His pale blue eyes, interested but cautious, gave her hope that he wasn't going to laugh at her.

"The Windigo is considered just a folklore story by white people, like Big Foot," she said. "But for many centuries, the Indians believed Windigos really existed."

"If you were reading Thomas Ahanu right, some still do," Rafsky said.

She pointed to the photograph of the carving. "The Windigo hunts during the Hunger Moon, when survival is hardest for animals or humans. It's too big a coincidence to have the symbol for February on the tree closest to the bones."

Rafsky took a bite of his sandwich and then a long drink of coffee. "So this creature is supposed to be what, like a werewolf?" he asked.

She shook her head. "Similar but different. Creatures like the Windigo show up in many cultures. Did you have to read *Beowulf* in college?"

Rafsky smiled slightly. "Didn't go to college."

She smiled back before she continued. "Well, you were saved from Grendel."

"Grendel was a Windigo?"

"Distant relative."

Rafsky took another bite of his BLT. "Go on."

"The Windigo legend is unique to this area and Canada. The details vary from tribe to tribe, but the basic idea is always the same. The Windigo starts out as a normal human being. Maybe a hunter who gets lost in the woods, or someone who gets stranded, runs out of food during the long winter, and has to turn to cannibalism to survive."

Joe noticed he had put down his sandwich.

"Once they have eaten human flesh, they become inhabited by the victim's spirit and then are forever drawn to cannibalism," she said. "They become violent, and even if they try to be normal, the need to eat human flesh always comes back. Some people who believe they are Windigo-possessed try to stop by isolating themselves in the deep woods, away from people. Some commit suicide to stop."

Rafsky leaned back in the booth. "You just made an important leap there."

"What's that, sir?"

"From mythological beast to human behavior."

"I was getting to that. There is a medical condition called Windigo psychosis."

"You're kidding."

Joe shook her head. "It's a mental illness where patients show signs of extreme violence, antisocial behavior, and cannibalistic urges. I couldn't find much on it in the library, but I'll keep looking."

Rafsky pushed his plate aside and pulled the book over, looking again at the moon symbols. "So how do we kill this bastard when we find him — a silver bullet?" he said.

Joe sat back. He was dismissing the Windigo theory — and her. She should have never brought it up.

He looked up. "I'm kidding, Frye." He smiled. It was a kind smile.

The waitress appeared to refill their coffees. Joe took the moment to wolf down a couple of bites of her sandwich, watching Rafsky joke with the waitress. When he held out his coffee mug, Joe found herself looking at his left hand. He was wearing a gold wedding band.

"All right, so let's stay with this Windigo psychosis idea," Rafsky said, lowering his voice when they were alone again. "You're saying we could have someone killing and eating his victims. That could explain why we haven't found any graves."

Joe nodded. "Any theories, sir? I mean, on what kind of person we're looking for?"

"As I told Ahanu, a white male is my guess."

Joe stayed silent.

"A white male who abducts a girl, brings her up here and kills her, and leaves her in the woods in winter, knowing her bones will be scattered by scavengers," Rafsky went on. "He's a typical sexual predator with no special thoughts or powers. And the carvings are meaningless, probably just stuff done by some Indian trying out a new knife."

Joe fought to hide her disappointment.

"Theory two," Rafsky went on. "A white man who abducts, kills, and leaves his victims in the woods. An Indian comes along and finds the remains after they have been partially devoured. The Indian believes a Windigo is at work and leaves the carvings as some kind of warning to other woodsmen."

Rafsky was looking at her, waiting for her reaction.

"Theory three," he said. "White killer leaves his victims in woods, then does the carvings himself to make us think it's related to some weird Indian myth, knowing that the police up this way will quickly arrest an Indian on almost any evidence."

Joe nodded.

"Theory four. We are dealing with someone who really does believe he's a Windigo and commits his crimes up here because he feels the land is sacred to his mission. And he carves the moon symbols as a way to feel he is somehow part of the Indian culture."

"That would make him a true monster," Joe said.

"A true monster?" Rafsky said. "Do you believe there are such things?"

"I don't know."

He offered another of his easy smiles. "Neither do I. Although I've had a few cases where I had doubts I was dealing with a human being."

Rafsky finished off his coffee and started looking for the waitress to get the check. She wanted to ask him more about his cases, but he seemed in a sudden hurry to get going. When he turned back to Joe, his expression had settled back into business mode.

"Okay, I need you to do something for me," he said.

"Anything, sir."

"Make some copies of the twelve moon symbols and drive them out to the search team. Tell them to look for anything resembling any of the symbols."

She closed the library book and started to stack up the photographs. Rafsky tossed a twenty onto the table. They went out into the cold wind, pausing just outside the restaurant door.

"I have a question," Joe said.

"Ask."

"You sound convinced this is a white man. You don't think he could be Indian?"

"Do you?"

"I read an account of an actual Windigo trial among the Ottawas in the 1800s," Joe said. "A young hunter confessed he wanted to eat his sister's flesh, so the tribal council condemned him to death. He willingly submitted to a hanging."

Rafsky pursed his lips. "Case history tells us multiple killers are almost always white men. But if you want to look further into this Windigo thing, go ahead."

Joe nodded. She put on her hat, tugging it down over her ponytail. "Thanks for the lunch, sir."

Rafsky was looking at her, head cocked. "One more thing I need you to do."

"Anything, sir."

"Drop the 'sir' thing."

Joe blinked. "I . . . what do I call you, then?"

He looked equally confused for a moment, his eyes wandering out over the street before coming back to her. "Rafsky. I'll call you Frye. How about that?"

Joe looked down.

"What?"

She looked back up. "It wouldn't look right. Around the other men."

He sighed. "Okay. 'Sir' in public. 'Rafsky' when we're alone. Can you do that?"

"Yes, sir."

He smiled and nodded to her books. "Get those copies out to the searchers."

He turned, slumped down into his collar against the wind, and started away. Joe headed in the opposite direction.

"Frye!"

She turned.

"In that stuff you read," Rafsky said, "you read anything about how they killed Windigos?"

"No, sir," Joe said.

Rafsky nodded and turned, disappearing around a corner.

She parked the cruiser on the side of the road behind a blue van marked with the Michigan state flag and headed down a hill, the copies of the moon symbols in her hand. Some men were sifting leaves with a large screened frame. She started with them. They listened intently, dutifully studying the moon symbols before folding the copies and putting them in their pockets.

Joe moved on to two men in Michigan state police vests. They were working with rakes and three large metal cans. One looked up as she approached, then elbowed the other.

Their gaze dipped to the patches on her jacket before their faces pained with annoyance. She could guess where it came from. Mack had probably spent a good part of the last few days here, and these men were just tired of dealing with the local idiots.

"Afternoon, officers," she said.

One of them went back to raking. The

other propped his hand on the rake handle and looked at her. His name badge read T. ELKINS.

"You got something else you want us to do, you need to ask my supervisor first," he said. "He says we don't answer to you guys."

"I know that, Officer Elkins," she said. "And we appreciate all your efforts. I don't know what small towns like ours would do without the experts to step in and offer a hand sometimes."

Elkins stared at her, the half-sneer on his lips fading. "Well, that's our job," he said.

"And you do it well."

He shifted the rake and tipped back his blue ball cap. "You a fully commissioned officer here?"

"You mean, am I a real cop?" she asked.

He gave her a weak grin. "Yeah."

"Yes," she said. "Went to the real academy and everything. Just like you."

He took that with a flex of his jaw, then cocked his head toward the envelope. "What do you have there?"

"You know about the tree carvings, right?"

Elkins nodded. "We've been told to watch for marks in trees, yeah."

She held out one of the copies. "This is exactly what they should look like."

He took the paper, studied it, and smacked

the officer working next to him on the arm. "Nick," he said, "look at these."

Nick came up from his pile of leaves, and they looked at the symbols for a moment. "That's Indian stuff," he said.

"Yes," Joe said. "But it's best if we don't broadcast that to everyone. They could make the wrong assumptions too early."

"Right," Elkins said. He stepped to the nearest tree and took a slow walk around it. He came back, a hint of disappointment on his face. "If there's more of these out here, we'll find them for you, Deputy," he said.

Joe smiled. "Thanks."

She moved on to the next group of searchers, and then the next, passing out the copies, advising them not to speculate, especially in public. It became increasingly easy to win them over. Even the veteran officers seemed intrigued by the symbols, and she knew that they would not be able to keep them a secret very long. Theo and other reporters would be intrigued, too, and before long, the word *Windigo* would somehow make it into some headline. And Echo Bay — and Detective Rafsky — could be the laughingstock of the state.

Joe found herself back by the prayer tree, and she paused, wishing she had a warmer jacket. The sun was slipping away, and the eastern sky was deepening in color. The searchers were starting to pack up for the night, and she watched as a trio of officers began arranging sleeping bags inside the back of the blue van.

That surprised her. She didn't know Rafsky had posted anyone here all night, but it made sense. It was important that they keep wanderers out. But maybe Rafsky was also thinking that with the colder weather, their killer might return.

She turned a half-circle, struck with the feeling that he may have already come back. Maybe lived up here. Or was here even now.

Something cried above her, and she looked up, trying to see what kind of bird it was. The branches were black against the pink sky, the remaining leaves flittering in the breeze like shreds of tissue paper. She heard the cry again but saw no bird, and she had started to look away when something else caught her eye.

She stepped away from the tree, trying to find a different slant of light so she could see it better. It appeared to be just a broken branch caught in the other limbs, but it was awfully thin. And perfectly straight.

She moved again and stopped.

It was no branch. It was a piece of rope. And it was hanging straight down from a thick limb about thirty feet over her head.

She changed position again, and the rope caught a lingering ray of sun and brightened for just a moment. How had they missed it before?

But then she realized the tree had shed most of its leaves in the last couple of weeks. The branches were now exposed.

She stared at the rope, a part of her knowing it could easily be something a hunter used or maybe even the remains of a swing strung up by a kid. But it was so high, and as she looked closer, she could tell the end was frayed.

The hoist. There was a piece of rope attached to the hoist that had also been frayed.

And it came to her in that instant.

Oh, my God . . .

He hung them.

He tied them to the deer hoist and pulled them up into the trees. She closed her eyes. She could see it. She could see them, tied by the ankles, legs spread, suspended upside down.

She grabbed her radio.

"Augie," she said, "find Detective Rafsky and have him meet me out here immediately."

20

The leaves were still green downstate. And she hadn't noticed it on her last trip, but the air smelled different here, too. It was heavier, thick with the smells of humanity, exhaust, and the dreariness of the coming winter.

Yesterday, after the piece of rope was retrieved from the tree, Rafsky had pronounced it a good enough match to the rope on the hoist to be sent off to Lansing. The hoist itself, underneath its layers of rust, still had a serial number. It had taken Holt three hours of phone work to find the manufacturer. The hoist had been made in Wisconsin but shipped to a sporting goods store called Hunter's Haven in August 1962. The address was on Middlebelt Road, in Inkster, Michigan.

Now they were in Rafsky's Chrysler, on the way back to Inkster. Joe had been surprised when Rafsky asked her to come along. So had the others, especially Mack. But when Rafsky explained to Leach that Joe had been the one to make the hoist connection and that he wanted her on the case, Leach had been quick to give his assent.

"That hoist bothered you from the start,

didn't it?" Rafsky said.

She nodded. "It just didn't seem like something someone would leave behind, but I never hunted, so I didn't take it any further. Then when I saw that piece of rope in the tree so high up . . ." She let her voice trail off. "Just a hunch, I guess."

"No, it wasn't," Rafsky said.

He eased the car toward the freeway exit. She listened to the *plink* of the blinker and looked back out the window.

"So, tell me more about this charm bracelet no one thought was important, either," Rafsky said.

Joe began with the discovery of the bracelet and why she thought it didn't belong to Annabelle Chapel. She told Rafsky about her first trip to Inkster, the high school Spartan head, and the bracelet's possible owner — an unknown girl with a boyish nickname.

"I tried to talk to the Inkster police," she said. "They were less than helpful."

"I think they'll talk to us now," Rafsky said.

Joe watched the landscape change again, as the cornfields gave way to the brick enclaves of suburbia. The Inkster PD would talk now only because Rafsky was with her, and that bothered her.

"Thank you for coming along," Rafsky said.

Joe glanced at him. But suddenly she was seeing Brad, standing in the bathroom doorway this morning, dripping with soapy water, a towel held around his waist. *You're going all the way to Inkster with this state investigator?*

"I appreciate you asking Sheriff Leach if I could," she said. "I'm learning a lot."

Rafsky turned the Chrysler onto Middlebelt Road. Joe knew they were somewhere near Cherry Hill High School.

"Sheriff Leach speaks highly of you," Rafsky said. "And I haven't worked with a partner for a long time."

Partner? She wasn't sure what to say, and she decided on something bland. "Thank you."

The Hunter's Haven sign came into view, nestled between a party store and a Marathon gas station. Inside was a sea of broad shoulders, blue jeans, and ball caps. The place was packed with merchandise: racks bulging with quilted jackets and vests, targets, glass cases of rifles, end caps of boots.

Joe rounded a corner and stopped abruptly. A giant stuffed brown bear loomed in front of her, teeth bared. "Jesus," she

whispered.

Rafsky laughed softly and placed a hand on her back, leading her to the counter. The man behind it was ringing up boxes of shotgun shells. Rafsky eased his way through the bodies to the front. The man's face crinkled in annoyance when he saw Rafsky's offered badge, and he whispered, "Shit." He motioned Rafsky to the corner next to a rack of fishing poles. Joe could feel all the eyes on her as she followed. Rafsky introduced her to the owner, Randall Geren.

"Look, if you guys are here to see my gun registrations again —" Geren began.

"No," Rafsky interrupted, pulling out a copy of an invoice. "We just want to find out who bought this hoist from you."

Geren took the paper and rubbed his forehead. "This is from 1962. How am I supposed to remember who I sold something to that long ago?"

"You keep records, don't you?" Rafsky said.

"Man," Geren said. "Even if I knew where to find it, it might not have a name on it."

"We'd like you to look anyway."

Geren glanced toward the cash register, where the pimply clerk was struggling to find a price on a pair of long johns. He sighed and shook his head. "I'll look next

week when —"

"You'll look today," Rafsky said. "Please."

"What's the big hurry?" Geren asked. "It's not like poaching is a real big deal, you know."

"It's not a poaching case, it's a homicide."

Geren's shoulders slumped, and his eyes drifted back to the register. "Can you guys cut me some slack and look yourselves? I'm losing money here, and this is my best week."

"Your records on-site?"

"Yeah, twenty years' worth. I got audited once, so I keep every friggin' scrap of paper."

"You game?" Rafsky asked Joe.

"You bet."

Geren led them to the back room and unlocked the door, shoving it open with one hand. The walls of the room were yellowed by years of cigarette smoke and dust. A desk, heaped with gun and hunting magazines, took up half the room. A line of file cabinets owned the other half. A deer head looked down at Joe with baleful eyes, a black bra draped on its antlers. Geren saw her looking at it, yanked the bra down, and made a quick exit.

Joe stacked up the magazines and catalogues and dropped them into a box, clear-

ing the desk. Rafsky opened a drawer labeled 1960–1970 and pulled out a manila folder labeled 1962.

"Damn, he's got the whole year's worth just crammed in one file," Rafsky said. "We'll have to go through all of them." He separated the invoices into two piles and pushed one over to Joe.

They were standard preprinted invoices, all handwritten. The one she held listed thirteen items. Two shotguns, three boxes of ammo, gloves, hat, primers, and several items that she couldn't read because the handwriting was illegible. The tiny scrawled serial numbers — when they were even listed — were even harder to decipher.

"This is going to take a while," she said.

Rafsky pulled up a metal crate and sat down. "This part always does."

Joe looked around for a crate, and seeing none, she slid her hip onto the desk and started through the invoices.

It took three hours to find it. Joe spotted it because it was the only item listed on the invoice, and it was a special order. "One Hansen's Heavy Duty Poly Rope Hoist."

The name on the invoice was Kenneth Snider. It meant nothing. But the address did. Joe stared at the street's name.

Avondale. She had been there once before.

21

It was the same house she had noticed before, the old stone one that had caught her eye because it had looked so out of place among the cookie-cutter tract houses. But now it didn't seem quaint so much as creepily convenient.

Joe turned and looked across the street to the high school.

"That the school you traced the charm to?" Rafsky asked.

She nodded. "Yes, but I didn't get anything really solid."

"Maybe we can try later. But first let's go pay a visit to Mr. Snider."

They got out of the Chrysler, and Joe followed Rafsky up to the porch, waiting while he rang the bell. The porch's dark green boards were peeling and slightly warped. The windows were dirty, and the glazier's putty around the panes was cracked and falling out. A pair of muddy work boots sat next to a frayed welcome mat.

Rafsky was on his third ring when the door finally jerked open. The man standing behind the screen door was tall, wearing jeans and a Lions sweatshirt and holding a can of Pabst.

"Yeah?"

"Kenneth Snider?"

"Yeah, that's me." The man's eyes had found Joe, and he was staring at her uniform.

Rafsky showed his state ID badge and made sure Snider got a look at the shield before he put it away. "I'm State Investigator Rafsky. This is Deputy Frye, Leelanau sheriff's office. May we ask you a few questions?"

Snider was staring at Joe. "Leelanau?"

"Yes."

It took effort for him to pull his eyes back to Rafsky. "What about?"

"About some hunting equipment."

"Hunting equipment?"

Rafsky held up the invoice from Hunter's Haven. "This piece of equipment."

Snider pushed open the screen door, and Rafsky gave him the invoice. Snider squinted at it and blew out a strange sigh that sounded to Joe like relief.

"I remember this hoist," Snider said.

"Yes, we need to talk to you about when you bought it."

"I didn't buy it. That's my father's name on that invoice. I'm Ken Junior."

"Can we speak to your father?"

"He's dead," Snider said.

Joe took a step forward. "Could we come

in, Mr. Snider?"

Snider gave a small shrug and opened the door wider. "Sure, sure. No point in heating the outdoors."

They entered the gloomy living room. *The Price Is Right* was blaring on the TV, and Snider went to the old Zenith and switched it off. With the TV off, the room felt as dark as a cave. Joe quickly took in the details: a plaid sofa covered with a blue sheet, end tables coated with dust and water glass stains, the dull glint of bowling trophies on the mantel of a red-brick fireplace. There was a closed-up, fusty smell to the house, like mildewed laundry or a wet dog.

She took a moment to assess Kenneth Snider. He looked to be in his late twenties, a big guy, dark-haired, well over six feet, and broad-chested as if he had once played football. His long face was off just enough to be short of handsome, with brown sloping eyes beneath heavy black brows. She was close enough to get a look at his hand grasping the Pabst can. His fingers were chapped, chewed-up-looking, as if he worked with his hands.

Rafsky was asking Snider about his father. "He died eleven years ago?"

"That's what I said," Snider said.

"Did you ever use the hoist?"

Snider shook his head and then took a drink of beer.

"You don't hunt?" Rafsky asked.

"Used to. Gave it up a long time ago." Snider's eyes were going from Rafsky to Joe and back to Rafsky. "Look, maybe if you told me why you're here, I could be more help."

"The hoist was found recently up in Leelanau County near a crime scene," Rafsky said.

Joe was watching Snider carefully, but the only thing that registered in the man's face was confusion.

"You must got something wrong, then," Snider said, "because my dad's hoist is down in the basement."

"Could you show it to us, please?" Rafsky asked.

Snider shrugged again and waved a hand. "This way."

He tossed the beer can into a huge trash can as they passed through the small kitchen. A row of cereal boxes lined the old Formica counter, and the avocado-colored appliances were rust-pocked and missing knobs. But at least someone had tried to clean; there were no crusted dishes in the sink or stains on the stove. Still, Joe had the impression that Snider lived here alone.

Whatever the hell that smell was, no woman would stand for it.

The wood stairs creaked as they headed down into the basement. The air grew cold, the musty smell stronger. Snider hit a switch as they neared the bottom.

Concrete water-stained walls. A furnace crouching like a hulking beast off in the shadows. Lines of thin rope strung across the room. Joe was wondering what they were for when she saw an old wringer-style washing machine. Snider apparently hung his laundry down here to dry. She was breathing in the moldy wet-dog smell, imagining it clinging to Snider's shirts.

"Over here," Snider said, heading under the stairs.

There was a large workbench fronting heavy shelves holding an assortment of power tools. A pegboard behind the bench was filled with carefully arranged jars of bolts and nails and gleaming hand tools. A carpenter's belt was folded on the bench, its leather soft and well maintained. As old and dingy as everything in the rest of the house was, everything on this workbench was clean, and precisely arranged.

"What do you do for a living, Mr. Snider?" she asked.

He was pulling cardboard boxes out from

the space under the stairs and glanced back at her. "Construction," he said flatly.

"Is that a scraping plane?" Joe asked, pointing to an elegant-looking tool.

"Yeah." He hesitated. "I use to do cabinetry work." He pulled out a large, battered footlocker. Kneeling, he opened it and began rummaging through it. Joe saw two shotguns resting in the corner. The barrels were spotted with rust.

Joe and Rafsky waited as Snider brought out what looked like two bedrolls and a rusted deer-gutting knife. Some tin camping pans clanked on the floor as Snider tossed them aside.

Snider stopped and looked up at them. "It's not here," he said.

"You're sure?" Rafsky said, stepping forward to peer in the empty locker.

"Yeah, I'm fucking sure."

Snider's eyes darted into the shadows beneath the stairs, and he rose slowly, wiping his hands on his jeans.

"Did you loan it out?" Rafsky asked.

Snider shook his head. "I haven't touched this stuff in ten years."

Rafsky stepped closer to the locker. "Did all this belong to your father?"

Snider nodded, his eyes moving slowly across the heap of camping gear.

"Maybe we could look around for the hoist," Rafsky said. "Maybe it's upstairs or in a garage."

Joe saw something flit across Snider's face. Confusion for sure, but there was a hardening, as if the man were slowly figuring something out. Or trying to.

"You got a warrant?" Snider said.

Rafsky paused just a beat. "No."

"Then I don't have to let you look at anything, do I?" Snider asked.

Rafsky glanced at Joe. Then he looked back at Kenneth Snider and gave a curt nod. "Thank you for your time, Mr. Snider. We'll find our way out."

They were sitting in the Chrysler still parked in front of the stone house. Snider had not reappeared after they left him in the basement, hadn't even come to the window to watch them.

"I don't think he knew the hoist was missing," Rafsky said.

"But it bothered him."

Rafsky nodded, his eyes drifting to the school across the street. It was only four, but the low-hanging gray sky made it feel like dusk. Rafsky saw Joe turn up the collar of her jacket. He turned on the ignition and hit the heater.

"How come you asked him about that carpentry tool?" he asked.

"He said he worked construction. But those weren't your basic tools on his workbench. He had a lot of stuff furniture makers use. My dad did cabinetry as a hobby, and he had a plane just like the one Snider has."

Rafsky waited while she gathered her thoughts.

"Snider says he works construction, but his house is falling apart." She looked at Rafsky. "You notice the window panes? They all need recaulking."

"My mom cleaned hotel rooms for a living. But our house was always a mess," Rafsky said. "Maybe it's the same thing."

Joe was looking at the stone house. "I just get the feeling something's off about the guy."

Rafsky didn't answer her. He was staring at the school. The front doors burst open, and a trio of girls emerged. They looked like the girls on *The Brady Bunch* — straight blond hair, too-pink cheeks, and pastel parkas above low-riding jeans. The girls crossed the street, too absorbed in their chatting even to look for traffic, and disappeared around the corner.

Joe glanced back at the house, expecting

to see Snider at his window. He wasn't.

"What was the name of the girl who might have had the charm bracelet?" Rafsky asked.

"No name," Joe said. "The teacher could only remember that it was a boy's nickname. Could be Sam for Samantha, or Georgie for Georgia, or —"

"Let's see if the school will let us look at some yearbooks," Rafsky said. "Maybe we'll get a hit."

The principal, Mr. Garrett, led them to an empty room behind the office. He brought the yearbooks himself, 1962 through 1974. Then he hung for a while near the door, hands clasped behind his back, trying not to look interested. Rafsky glanced back at him.

"Thank you, Mr. Garrett," he said. "I'm sure we'll be fine."

Garrett left, closing the door behind him. Rafsky handed Joe three books and settled uncomfortably into one of the small plastic chairs.

Joe opened the first book, from 1962, thinking the year the hoist was bought was the logical place to start. Rafsky took the book for 1963. It was tedious going, because they couldn't assume the girl they were looking for was a senior and therefore merited an individual portrait. They had to scrutinize the group photographs for each class, running their fingers along the lines of small type under each. They also checked the pictures of each student activity or event.

Joe turned the pages slowly, staring at all the girls' faces, even the ones without captions. The faces that stared back looked like a collection of sixties dolls, the girls wearing everything from stiff flips to the long straight hair of the British models. Most of the names were traditional.

Linda. Debra. Carol. Gail. Christine. Marsha.

She heard a sharp thud and looked up. Rafsky had tossed the 1963 yearbook down and had picked up 1964. "You know our chances of finding her aren't good," he murmured, not looking up. "Even if she's in one of these somewhere, it is probably under her real name, not some nickname."

"I remember the teacher I talked to told me she was a wild type, one of the fringe students," Joe said. "Something tells me we aren't going to find her in the usual club activities or National Honor Society pictures."

Rafsky nodded, and Joe went back to work. From the corner of her eye, she spotted Mr. Garrett watching them, and she realized the outer office was dark. Everyone had gone home. It was nearly five p.m.

Finally, she closed the 1962 yearbook and picked up the 1965 volume. She flipped to the back, starting with the senior pictures. Betty. Anne. Joan. Ruth. Her eyes stopped on a picture in the upper righthand corner. Dark bouffant hair. Bright doe eyes heavily outlined in black. A big Hollywood smile.

"I found something," Joe said softly.

Rafsky looked up.

"I have a girl named Ronnie," Joe said. "Her name is Veronica Langford, but it says here she went by Ronnie."

Joe slid the book to Rafsky. The caption under the picture said: "Veronica 'Ronnie' Langford. She's Ready for Her Close-up!"

"How old do you think Ken Snider is?" Joe asked.

Rafsky shrugged. "Twenty-nine or thirty."

"So he could have been in school with her."

He quickly flipped to the S section of the senior pictures. She was right. Kenneth Snider's picture showed a good-looking boy with a tentative smile. The caption read: "Kenneth Snider. Kissed the Girls and Made Them Cry!" The activities listed for him were Varsity Football, Ski Club, and Drama Club.

"Would you go ask Mr. Garrett if he can pull up the family's address?" Rafsky asked.

"We're going to see the Langfords now?" Joe asked. "We have nine other books to go through."

"We'll take them with us," Rafsky said. "But I'd like to move on this one. I don't like the fact that a girl with a boy's name and maybe a charm bracelet attended this school with Ken Snider, who just happened to have access to a deer hoist found in Echo Bay."

Rafsky handed the yearbook back to Joe. She stared at the picture of the young Ken Snider. But in her head, she was seeing him as he was now. Seeing him in that stone house across the street, hiding behind those ugly drapes, peering out at the young girls walking by his front door every day.

22

The Langford home was a small yellow brick ranch house. In the front yard, a plaster Virgin Mary statue with a broken right hand stood in a bed of unraked leaves. The house was only three streets away from Ken Snider's home.

Joe and Rafsky were halfway up the walk when a woman in a sweater came out to the porch, holding open the screen door.

"Can I help you?" she asked.

Rafsky showed her his ID, introduced Joe, and waited at the bottom step of the porch while Marie Langford studied them. There was no hint in her face that she suspected cops were here to talk about a missing daughter.

"Do you have a daughter named Ronnie?"

Marie Langford came down the steps slowly, holding her sweater closed across her thin housedress. "I do," she said. "But I haven't seen or talked to Ronnie in years."

"When was the last time you spoke to her?" Rafsky asked.

Marie Langford thought for a moment. "It was just before Valentine's Day, 1965," she said.

"How do you remember the date so well, Mrs. Langford?" Joe asked.

"I remember because Ronnie told me she had quit her job and she was going to quit school. Four months away from graduation, you know? We had this big argument right out here on the lawn."

"Why did she want to quit school?" Joe asked.

"Why do they all want to quit?" Marie Langford said. "She found herself some man who promised to take her away."

"Do you recall his name?"

She didn't have to think too long this time. "Mitch Haskell. A trucker who did long hauls. Older than her, too. Probably had a wife and kids stashed somewhere, if you ask me."

"Do you know if Ronnie knew a man named Ken Snider?" Joe asked.

Marie Langford shook her head. "Not that I ever heard. She had a lot of boyfriends. But Mitch Haskell . . . she told me he was the one and that she was hitting the road with him."

"And you didn't hear from her again?" Rafsky asked.

"Nope. I figured someday Ronnie would grow up and at least give me a call or come home pregnant or something. But she never did. I guess maybe her and that Haskell guy made it after all."

Marie Langford fell quiet, and Joe looked up at her, expecting to see some sort of sadness in her eyes. But there was just a tired resignation, as if what Ronnie had done was how Marie Langford expected all daughters to act.

"Did Ronnie have a charm bracelet?" Joe asked.

Marie cocked her head. "Huh. Haven't thought about that in years. She sure did, never took it off."

Joe caught Rafsky's eye. "What kind of charms were on it?" she asked Marie Langford.

"Souvenir stuff. Like from places we took her as a kid, before her father died. He was a big one for going up north, but I couldn't afford to take the girls anywhere after he passed." She paused. "Ronnie, she sure loved going to those places. It was hard on her after her dad passed. She was only thirteen. Started acting up after he . . ."

Marie Langford shook her head, her eyes drifting.

Joe reached into her jacket for the photographs of the charms and held them out. "Do you recognize any of these?" she asked.

Marie sifted through the photos slowly. "The dunes, Frankenmuth, the Cross in the Woods. Yeah, we went to all these places." Her eyes came up slowly. "Where did you find her bracelet?"

Rafsky gave Joe a second to answer, and when she didn't, he spoke. "Up near Echo Bay, in Leelanau County."

Marie Langford held his eye, her face hardening as she realized why two cops were standing on her sidewalk. "Is Ronnie dead?"

"We don't know," Rafsky said gently. "We have bones and some other pieces of evidence. This bracelet was close by."

"So she was murdered?" Marie Langford asked.

Joe thought it strange that Marie Langford had made that assumption so quickly. Before she could say anything, Rafsky went on. "We just don't know enough yet, Mrs. Langford."

He pulled out a business card and handed it to her. "Feel free to call anytime," he said. "And we'll let you know when we find out more."

He arched a brow at Joe. It was a look she was getting to know, his way of asking her if she had anything else to ask. It seemed cruel to prolong the interview now that Rafsky had told the woman her daughter might be dead. But all of this was just too big a coincidence — the school, the bracelet, Snider's house, and Ronnie's disappearance in February of 1965.

"Mrs. Langford," Joe said, "I'm sorry, but I have a few more questions. Are you sure Ronnie never mentioned a Ken or a Kenneth or a boy who lived across from the high school?"

"I'm sure."

"You mentioned earlier you never took the girls on vacation after their father passed? So Ronnie has a sister?"

"Yes, Valerie, two years older," Marie said. "She's out in California. Do you want her phone number?"

Joe nodded, and Marie Langford reeled it off. Joe wrote it down, hoping maybe Ronnie had shared something with her sister that she had not shared with her mother.

"Can you remember any of the names of her other boyfriends before Mitch Haskell?" Joe asked.

Marie thought for a moment, then offered a few names — just first names. Joe had started to close her notebook when she thought of one last thing. "You mentioned Ronnie quit her job. Where did she work?"

Marie Langford gestured over her shoulder. "Up there on the corner at the bowling alley, Cherry Hill Lanes. She worked the snack bar on weekends."

Joe scribbled the name, but she was seeing the dusty bowling trophies on Ken Snider's mantel.

Marie Langford was staring at the card Rafsky had given her. Her eyes came up, and Joe followed them to the two girls coming down the street, books clutched to their chests. When Marie Langford's pale brown eyes came back to Joe, she saw a shadow of sadness in them, but she didn't think Marie Langford would cry.

"If you see Ronnie, I mean, find her . . ." Her voice trailed off. "Tell her to call her mother, will you?"

The smell was the same as she remembered it. A mix of beer, frying grease, cigarette smoke, and sweaty shoes. And the sound, always in the background, of clattering wooden pins.

Joe paused on the dirty red carpet just inside the door of Cherry Hill Lanes, waiting for Rafsky to catch up. The snack bar was to the left, with the pro shop tucked into a dark corner near the restrooms. It looked exactly like the place her dad had taken her and Dennis to back in Cleveland.

The kid at the counter paused long enough from his chore of giving out shoes and score sheets to tell Rafsky the manager was off today. The kid didn't know if the manager worked here ten years ago and didn't seem to care. He also didn't know a Ken Snider.

Rafsky came back to Joe, gesturing to the old woman behind the snack bar. "Maybe she's been here long enough."

"Those jobs change weekly. I have a better idea."

Joe led Rafsky to the pro shop, which was thick with dust and the smell of burned rubber. The man in the back gave them a quick look over his shoulder.

"Be right there," he called over the whine of a drill.

Joe glanced around. Behind the glass counter was a wall of framed photos. "Rafsky," she said. "Look at the third picture."

He reached over the counter and took it off the wall. The photo showed five men in yellow and black shirts, holding a trophy. The middle man was Ken Snider.

"Whatcha need?"

The pro shop guy wore an old lime green bowling shirt, the name GREG HUNT embroidered on the chest.

Rafsky again made the introductions, then asked Hunt how long he had worked at the bowling alley. Hunt glanced at the framed photo in Rafsky's hand.

"Twenty-two years come April," Hunt said.

"Do you know this man?" Rafsky asked, pointing to Snider.

"That's Kenny," Hunt said. "Been bowling here since he was about fifteen or sixteen. I taught him most everything he knows."

"Do you recall a high school girl named Ronnie Langford?" Rafsky asked. "She worked in the snack bar here in sixty-five."

Hunt scratched his chin, his eyes still on the photo Rafsky held. "We get a lot of girls working here."

Joe reached into her pocket. Back at the high school, she had made a copy of Ronnie's yearbook picture, and she held it out to Hunt. "This is Ronnie Langford," she said.

Hunt's eyes widened. "Oh, yeah, I remember her now."

Hunt offered nothing else, but there was something in his face that told Joe he now remembered Ronnie vividly, and Joe wanted to know why. "What was she like?" she asked.

"She was, well . . ." Hunt sighed, looking at Rafsky as he talked. "She was a bitch and kind of a tease. Played around and was always getting the guys worked up, you know? Had a few fights in here because of her."

"Was Ken Snider one of the men she got worked up?" Joe asked.

"Kenny was only eighteen then, and he hung on her like a horny dog," Hunt said, still keeping his eyes on Rafsky. "They dated most of that season, if I remember right, even though he caught her a couple of times doing other guys in the parking lot."

"Was he ever violent toward her?" Rafsky asked.

Hunt shook his head. "It was the other way around. One night, they had a helluva fight in the bar. But it was her doing all the throwing. Glasses and bottles. I recall it was something about her leaving to go on the road with Mitch."

"Mitch Haskell."

"Yeah, Haskell, that's him. He bowled on Tuesdays." Hunt was nodding, as if things were coming back to him suddenly. "Oh, man, I remember now. Kenny came in that night with this ring and said he was going to ask Ronnie to marry him. But then Ronnie told him she was leaving town with Mitch. Man, it was ugly."

"Mr. Hunt," Joe said, "can you be more exact about the date of the fight?"

Hunt thought for a moment. "Maybe late January, early February? I know the Christmas decorations were down, but there was still snow outside."

Rafsky tapped the bowling photograph. "May we have this?"

Hunt nodded. "Is Kenny in trouble?" he asked.

"We really can't give you any more information," Rafsky said. "But I would ask that if you see him, please don't tell him we were here, and don't mention Ronnie Langford."

They left Greg Hunt with an expression of confusion on his face. Out in the parking lot, Rafsky paused as he opened the driver's-side door.

"I need to tell you," he said, "you did a damn fine job at Mrs. Langford's. I didn't think to ask her where Ronnie worked."

"Thank you."

"I don't usually miss things like that."

Rafsky looked up at the neon bowling alley sign. Joe wondered for a moment if he felt she had shown him up somehow, as Mack did when she pointed something out. But she didn't think that's what prompted his distant look now.

"Where to now?" she asked.

"Inkster police for a search warrant."

"Do we have enough?" she asked.

Rafsky shrugged. "I think so. We have the hoist and the bracelet found in the same area. A girl missing for ten years. A stormy relationship between our suspect and the victim."

"Can't we just get the warrant through your office?" Joe asked.

"It'll be quicker this way, and my guys won't have to drive down here to help with the search. Besides, it's the Inkster PD's jurisdiction, and I want to show them the proper respect." He gave her a smile. "I like protocol, Frye."

Rafsky strolled the length of the small room, took a peek out the only window, and wandered to the water cooler, where he poured himself a third cup of water. Joe had never seen him this agitated. She felt it, too. To calm down, she went to the window and looked out at the row of police cars parked in the lot. The Inkster police department, with ten times the number of officers as Echo Bay, was housed in a brick building that reminded her a lot of a high school.

The heating unit under the window kicked on again, puffing more hot air into the already sweltering room. Joe took off her jacket and laid it over the chair. Rafsky did the same, using a handkerchief to wipe a sheen of sweat off his brow. The gesture spiked a few strands of his damp hair straight up.

"I'd be treated with more respect in a whorehouse," Rafsky said, checking his watch again.

Joe slipped her hip onto the table and put her feet on a chair. "You think Snider is thinking about running?" she asked.

"They all think about it," Rafsky said. "Until today, he probably had no reason to think he would ever have to. If he killed Ronnie Langford, he got away with it for ten years. A man can get awful comfortable with that."

"And he kept killing."

Rafsky stopped pacing and faced her.

"The yearbook picture we have of Ronnie," Joe said. "She isn't wearing braces. Or glasses."

Rafsky nodded. "So now we have three victims. The odds are astronomical that more than one killer would leave remains so close together in a remote area like Echo Bay."

"Do you think Ronnie was his first?"

"I believe most killers start with someone they know. Ronnie sounded like the kind of girl who could make a man snap. My guess is that's what Snider did. Probably right inside that house."

The door opened, and a detective came in. He was the same man they had talked to earlier, Lieutenant Mumsley. Barrel-chested, with a hard jaw and dark ice-pick eyes. He held a few sheets of paper and an affidavit Rafsky had filled out earlier.

"Your man's got no criminal record," Mumsley said, holding out Snider's sheet. "Just a couple of traffic tickets, all in Inkster. Nothing up north."

"Any sign Ronnie turned up somewhere?"

Mumsley shook his head. "Can't locate an employer, social security number, driver's license, or any warrants or tickets," he said. "And no reports of her death anywhere. It looks like she's still missing."

"And the warrant?" Rafsky asked.

"Judge is seeing us tomorrow at nine across the street at the courthouse. I got six officers lined up to go with you."

"We're not going to go tonight?" Rafsky asked.

"Judge says unless you can tell him there's a girl in that house right now, he'll sign it in the morning."

Rafsky let out a long breath of annoyance.

"You might as well get a room and cool your jets, Detective," Mumsley said. "Even calling Lansing isn't going to get you a team tonight."

Rafsky snatched his affidavit from Mumsley and grabbed his coat from the chair. "This is unbelievable."

"Look," Mumsley said, "if it makes you feel better, we'll stick a car down the block. Make sure Snider doesn't bail during the night. That suit you okay?"

Rafsky finally drew a breath and managed a nod. "Thanks."

Mumsley left the room without a word to

Joe. Rafsky raked his hair, spiking it even more.

"I'm sorry," he said. "I don't lose my temper often. I just hate unnecessary delays. And cops who have no sense of urgency."

Joe pulled her jacket on, her eyes moving to the darkness of the window. She thought about tomorrow morning and what it was going to be like to stand in front of a judge to secure a search warrant and how it was going to feel to walk inside Ken Snider's house. And she was thinking about what they might find down in that basement.

"I suppose we should go get a motel and check in with our respective departments," Rafsky said.

"A motel?"

He gave her a teasing smile. "Unless you want to sleep in the car a block down from Snider's house."

"Sorry," Joe said. "My mind was drifting. Of course we need a place."

As they headed out, she was already working on what she was going to tell Sheriff Leach and wondering what his reaction would be when she told them they had a suspect. And she was trying to imagine what Brad was going to say when she told him she wasn't coming home tonight. As they hit the cold air of the parking lot, Rafsky touched her arm.

"I'm starved. How about Italian?" he asked, pointing down the road.

She turned. A red neon sign flickered in the darkness about a half-block down. RECCHI'S. Behind it, another sign read MICHIGAN AVENUE INN. Ice Cold Rooms. Free TV.

There was a small knot in her stomach. She wasn't sure what it was from. She wasn't even sure if she was hungry.

"Italian sounds good," she said.

23

They were halfway through the antipasto plate before Rafsky brought up the case.

"I know this isn't very exciting," he said. He saw her puzzled expression and went on. "But this is the way real investigations are done. Lots of sorting through receipts, lots of waiting around, lots of talking to people, lots more waiting around, lots of bad food."

Joe picked up a grilled pepper. "These aren't bad."

Rafsky smiled. They were one of only three couples in the restaurant, sharing a booth in the back. The place was a cave of cheesy clichés, from the plastic red-checkered tablecloth to the Chianti-bottle candles to the faded poster of the Trevi Fountain over the bar. The bearded owner was washing glasses behind the bar, humming along as Sinatra wended his way through "In the Wee Small Hours of the Morning."

"What's your take on Marie Langford?" Joe asked.

"What do you mean?"

Joe shrugged. "I don't know. I was thinking how different she is from Natalie Newton's mother. Hasn't seen her daughter in ten years, and now we show up saying she could be dead. It was almost like she didn't care."

"People give up," Rafsky said.

Joe shook her head slowly. "Dorothy Newton hasn't given up. She still wants her daughter home. Even if she's dead."

Rafsky picked up the carafe and poured out two glasses of Chianti. He pushed the glass across the table to her. Sinatra had moved on to "I'll Be Around." The piano was mingling with the tinkle of glass as the owner stacked goblets behind the bar. For a long time, they sat there just sipping their wine.

"So how you dealing with this?" Rafsky asked finally.

Joe wasn't sure what he was referring to, so she didn't answer.

"Snider, the missing girls," he said. "It can start to get to you after a while. Especially if you've never worked something like this before."

He was being protective. But she heard no condescension in his voice.

"Sheriff Leach gave me his files on John Norman Collins," she said. "Photos, everything. I was okay with that. I'll be okay with this."

Rafsky raised a brow in interest. "How did Collins come up?"

Joe shrugged. "We thought for a while he may have killed our victims, but the Ann Arbor PD didn't think so. And now we have Snider."

"Collins was one of the first people I checked," Rafsky said. "I didn't think he did these murders up there, either. Guys like Collins tend to stay within a comfort zone, and he never dumped far from where he abducted."

Rafsky pointed to the last peppers and salami on the antipasto plate, and Joe gave a wave that he should finish it. As he ate, she was tempted to fill in the silence by responding further to his concern that the case might be bothering her. It was bothering her on some level.

She was seeing the photograph of Mary Fleszar, the nineteen-year-old coed who had been John Norman Collins's first victim. A blackish-brown object lying in a field. She was thinking about the statement of the farmer who had found Fleszar, his description of smelling something foul and thinking he had happened upon a decomposing deer. The August heat, the carcass in a cloud of flies, the head so shapeless only the ear told of its humanity. She was thinking of Collins's victims — seven official but maybe fifteen — thinking of the other gruesome photographs.

And she was thinking about the bones lying somewhere in the Lansing crime lab. So clean and white. So unconnected to anything real — yet.

"What's the matter?" Rafsky asked.

She toyed with the stem of her wineglass. "Nothing."

Rafsky was studying her, but with a gentleness in his eyes that made her feel uncomfortable.

"Can I say something?" he said. "It's personal, and we don't know each other very well, but I think I need to say it."

She nodded.

He took a drink of wine before speaking.

"When I asked you how you were taking things? I only asked that because I've been doing this a long time, and I have worked with a lot of cops, big departments and small departments. And I have seen some cops invest too much of themselves emotionally in their work."

Joe could feel the heat of a blush working its way up her face and was glad it was dark.

"You have to be careful," Rafsky said. "You have to have another life. You can't let this be your life. A lot of cops do that, let their work become their life. And my God, that will kill you."

She just stared at him. "Are you telling me this because I'm a rookie or because I'm a woman?"

He held her eyes. "Neither. I'm telling you this because I think you are very good at what you do. And I can tell you love doing it."

She took a drink of wine, looking away.

The waitress brought two big plates of spaghetti. Joe stared at hers for a moment and picked up a fork. She twirled it into the steaming red mass but didn't raise the fork to her mouth. Finally, she set the fork down and took another drink of the Chianti.

"You reach Sheriff Leach?" Rafsky asked. He was digging into his spaghetti with gusto, and the unease of the personal moment was gone.

"Yeah," Joe said, picking up her fork again. "He was surprised about Snider. I don't think he expected anything out of this trip."

"He wasn't the only one," Rafsky said with a small smile.

It could have been the wine or the long day spent together, the compliment he had given her, or the advice he had shared. But suddenly, for the first time, Joe felt on equal enough ground to ask something personal. "Your boss was surprised, too?"

"A suspect in four days? Surprised is putting it mildly."

The waitress came by with a basket of garlic bread. They ate in silence for a while. Rafsky was on to his second meatball and his third glass of wine.

"So how'd you get into this?" he asked suddenly.

"This?"

He nodded at her badge. "The job."

Joe smiled. "God, I'm not even sure anymore."

"What, don't all little girls want to be cops when they grow up?"

He was teasing her. She didn't mind. "My mom was a cop back in Cleveland," she said. She saw the shock on his face and went on. "She never wanted me to be one. And to be honest, I didn't want it, either, growing up. I guess I really wanted to be a fireman like my dad."

"How'd he feel about that?"

"He died when I was ten."

Rafsky hesitated. "On duty?"

She nodded. She finished off the last of her wine. Rafsky picked up the bottle with an arch of the eyebrow. When she nodded, he poured her a fresh glass.

"Leach was the one who really made me think about being a cop," Joe said.

Rafsky nodded. "He told me you were a student in his criminology class," he said. "He said you were an art student at the time."

"Yeah, that's what I went up to Northern for. But then my stepdad died, and the money ran out, and I had to drop out."

"So you were an artist?"

"A bad one."

"The art world's loss. Law enforcement's gain."

She took a bite of spaghetti, not trusting herself to look directly into the face of another compliment.

"Leach said you did well in the academy," he said.

"I worked hard."

"Couldn't have been easy."

"I survived."

She was smiling. He saw it, and his fork stopped its twisting in the pasta. "What's so funny?"

"I was thinking about the two-hundred-fifty-pound man in the alley," she said.

"Ah, yes," he said, smiling. "He's put on weight. He used to be two hundred."

She laughed. The guy in the alley was part of cop lore, the symbol of what female officers faced in terms of prejudice from the public and their male counterparts. The alley was the testing ground, and the man was the faceless beast, the ultimate symbol of your vulnerability. The question was always there: What are you going to do when you find yourself alone, squared off against the big crazy fucker in that dark alley?

"It used to bug me, the alley thing," Joe said. "But then I realized something. Women have always walked around with the threat of physical harm, from rapists, molesters, abusive husbands. That alley has always been there for us. But when I became a cop, that changed. I felt . . ."

Rafsky was listening, waiting.

"I don't know, I felt empowered," she went on. "Now I have a radio, a gun, skills, backup, the power to arrest someone. Now

261

if I meet some guy in the alley, he has to watch out for me." She couldn't read his expression in the flickering light of the candle. "You said before you started out working in Saginaw?" Joe asked, partly to deflect the intensity of his eyes.

"I was a patrolman there before I got with the state," he said, nodding. "Never met the two-hundred-pound guy in the alley and didn't want to. I always wanted to be an investigator, so I applied to the state, did my time as a trooper, and worked my way up to investigator. Been in homicide a few years."

"Have you dealt with many?" Joe asked.

"Mostly I help small towns deal with theirs," he said. "I seem to have a way with the chiefs and sheriffs."

Joe thought back to the way Rafsky had handled himself in Leach's station and in the Inkster PD. He had honored the local authority but had still managed to convey who was really in control. She was thinking, too, about how different Rafsky was from Leach — smoother and more commanding. And she was thinking about how differently Rafsky treated her. There was none of Leach's paternalism in Rafsky's attitude, no attempt to rein her in. Mike popped into her head, and the comparisons went on.

Mike so lackadaisical about his job, so disinterested in the bones case. And Rafsky . . .

"So you're close to your mom?" Rafsky asked.

The change of subject caught her off-guard.

"I heard something in your voice when you mentioned her," he added.

"She drives me crazy sometimes. What mother doesn't?" Joe smiled. "But yeah, we're close."

"Anyone else?"

"I have an older brother, Dennis. He's up in Alaska somewhere laying oil pipe. Next year, he'll be somewhere else. That's Dennis. Always on the move."

"And your mother is —"

"Back in Cleveland."

Joe took a final bite of the spaghetti and pushed the plate away. She needed to call her mother when she got home.

And Brad . . .

She had called home as soon as they checked into the motel, but there had been no answer.

Rafsky was looking at his watch. "I should call home," he said.

Joe heard a softening in his voice. Her eyes dropped to the gold band on his left hand.

"There's a pay phone out front," she said.

He shook his head. "I'll wait until I get back to the room."

She wanted to ask, but before she did, he went on. "Gina and I live in Gaylord, but my son, Ryan, is in private school down near Lansing."

"How old is he?" she asked.

"Twelve. I know what you're thinking, what's a little guy doing away from his home?" Rafsky's blue eyes warmed. "I get transferred a lot. Gina doesn't mind it, she's great about it, in fact, but kids . . . they need to stay put. So we enrolled him in a private school near his grandparents."

"You get to see him often?"

"Not often enough." His smile was rueful, tinged with guilt. "You want to see his picture?"

He had gone for his wallet before Joe could even nod. He flipped open the plastic holders and held it out, tipping it to the candle.

Ryan was a small replica of his father, right down to the spiky, sandy hair. Rafsky flipped the plastic sleeves back but not before Joe caught a glimpse of a dark-haired woman. The waitress came by and slipped the check under Rafsky's plate. Joe watched him as he pulled out two twenties to pay.

The two other couples had left. The owner had finished washing up and was hunched over the bar, slowing turning the pages of the *Free Press* sports section. In the silence, Joe could hear every word Sinatra sang: "Look at yourself. Do you still believe the rumor that romance is simply grand?"

She watched Rafsky's hands as he carefully folded the receipt and put it in his wallet. Long fingers, no motion wasted, and a glint of gold in the candlelight.

It hit her hard, coming out of nowhere. She was attracted to this man.

She stood up. "We have an early day tomorrow," she said. "We'd better get going."

They walked across the parking lot. The small motel was dark, except for the two rooms on the end. Numbers seven and eight.

He stayed with her all the way to her door, waiting while she dug the key from her pocket. She flashed to a memory from high school. Her mother, helping her get ready for her first date.

Make sure they come to the door to pick you up and wait for you to get safely inside when they drop you off. That's what gentlemen do.

Joe looked up at Rafsky, feeling as if she

should thank him again for including her on the trip. Or at least for dinner. But when she met his eyes, she had no words. And neither did he.

She looked away, slipping the key in the door. "Good night, Rafsky."

"Good night, Frye."

24

The first thing Rafsky did was open the drapes. The morning sunshine lit up Ken Snider's living room in all its dusty glory.

Joe stayed just inside the door, and two Inkster officers disappeared down the hall. Mumsley and another detective wandered to the kitchen. A fifth uniformed officer stood outside on the porch.

Ken Snider was frozen on the green shag carpet, sleep impressions on his face and confusion in his eyes. He was barefoot, wearing only a pair of old blue jeans. The search warrant hung limply in his hand.

"What *are* you looking for here?" he asked.

"Evidence of a homicide," Rafsky said.

"Who's dead?" Snider asked.

Rafsky looked to Joe, making a motion toward his shirt pocket, and she knew he wanted her to take notes. She snatched her notebook from her jacket and pulled the cap off her pen with her teeth.

Rafsky was holding a file folder, and he opened it, slipping a copy of Ronnie Langford's yearbook photo from inside. He held it up to Snider. "Know this girl?"

Snider's eyes widened. "That's Ronnie. She's dead?"

Rafsky produced a photo of the charm bracelet. "This look familiar?"

Snider stared at it, barely managing a nod. "That was hers. Is Ronnie dead or not?"

"We think you already know the answer to that, Mr. Snider," Rafsky said.

"I haven't seen Ronnie in ten years," Snider said, glancing down the hall as the sounds of drawers opening and closing drifted to him. "She left me. She went off with Mitch . . . in a truck. I never heard from her again. What's going on here? Why are the cops in my bedroom?"

Joe watched Snider, trying to hear something in his denials that would tell her if he really was the monster they thought he was. And she flashed on the killer John Norman Collins, and how his clean-cut good looks and good manners had allowed him to move through college campuses without suspicion.

Ken Snider didn't look like a killer, either. He was a blue-collar guy with no criminal record, living alone in the house he probably grew up in. By all accounts, a decent human being. Not a man anyone thought could kill young women, string them up, and maybe cannibalize them.

Rafsky moved across the room as he talked. "Echo Bay mean anything to you, Mr. Snider?" he asked.

"What?"

"Leelanau County," Rafsky said.

"I've been there," Snider said. "My dad used to . . ." He shut his mouth suddenly.

"Your dad used to what?" Joe asked.

Snider didn't even look at her. He glanced down the hall to his bedroom. When he came back to them, he had a flush of red up his neck. The warrant was crushed in his hand.

"I'm done talking to you," he said.

"You could help yourself by answering some questions," Rafsky said, still walking circles around Snider, forcing Snider to turn with him.

"Does the name Annabelle Chapel mean anything to you?" Rafsky asked.

"Who?"

"Annabelle Chapel," Rafsky repeated. "What about Natalie Newton?"

Snider stared at Rafsky. Joe could tell by the expression on Snider's face that he knew the names being thrown at him must be other victims, but he couldn't find an answer. Or even a strong denial.

"When was the last time you were in Leelanau County?" Rafsky asked.

"I don't remember," he said. "I was . . . I was . . ."

"You were what?"

Snider shook his head, opening the warrant to reread it. Joe knew it specified any evidence possibly connected to a homicide and/or the whereabouts of Veronica Langford. It also allowed them to take any weapons and any evidence that Snider had traveled up north in the last ten years.

"When were you last up north?" Rafsky asked. "Anywhere up north. Echo Bay, Petoskey, anywhere."

Snider finally faced him, feet planted. "Stop asking me questions," he said. "I want a lawyer."

"We don't have to give you a lawyer until you're under arrest," Rafsky said. "You want one, call one."

Snider threw Rafsky a glare, then dropped into a chair, eyes on the floor. Then he shut them and put his face in his hands.

"Detective Rafsky," a voice called from the bedroom.

Rafsky walked to the hallway and met a

uniformed officer as he came into the living room. The officer was holding something in the palm of his gloved hand. Joe stepped over to him quickly. He had found a heart-shaped charm, the engraving on it clear. RONNIE.

Rafsky looked back at Snider. He had risen from the chair but had not ventured over to them. He knew what they were looking at.

"Why do you have this?" Rafsky asked.

"She . . . she . . . I don't know."

"Of course you know," Rafsky said. "Why is it here in your bedroom instead of on her bracelet?"

"She gave it back to me," he said.

"Why?"

"She . . . she was . . . leaving with Mitch. She —"

"And I bet that really pissed you off," Rafsky said.

"No," Snider said. "No . . ."

Snider started to pace, edging to the door, and the officer on the porch stepped in to block the way. Snider stared at him for a moment, then spun back, his movements jerky. He opened his mouth to say something to Rafsky, then clamped it shut. He walked stiffly to the kitchen and snatched the phone receiver off the wall. A few minutes later, he hung up and came back to the living room.

"I'm not saying anything else."

Rafsky gave him a shrug and looked to Joe, motioning to the basement stairs.

Joe went down first, hitting the switch. A single bare bulb offered thin shadowy light. She stopped at the bottom of the steps, looking around for another switch, but saw none. A flashlight clicked on behind her. Detective Mumsley. She stepped aside to let him pass.

Rafsky tapped her shoulder and held out a pair of latex gloves. She tugged them on, feeling slightly embarrassed she had not thought to keep a pair with her. But she couldn't remember a time in Echo Bay when she even needed them.

Mumsley went to the footlocker under the stairs. Joe stayed near the steps, her eyes moving over the basement, the damp stench filling her nose.

"Go on," Rafsky said.

She wasn't sure what he meant at first, but then she felt his hand press gently against her back. She was going to be allowed to search, and she took a step, wondering where to go first. Her eyes moved over the wall of shelves that held paint and lawn tools. Over the old wringer washer, the crumbled boxes in the corner, the monstrous furnace, and the dark cubbyholes behind it. Finally, she focused on the workbench.

She walked to the workbench and took a long look at the hammers and screwdrivers hanging on the pegboard. She grabbed a breath to focus and plucked a routerlike tool from its hook.

"He could have used something like this to carve the symbols in the trees," she said.

Rafsky was behind her, and he leaned closer. "We don't have that link yet," he said.

Joe nodded, letting her gaze drift over the workbench, looking for old bloodstains on the wood. But the wood was clean. She picked up the leather carpenter belt and removed the tools one by one, examining their edges. They were clean and well cared for, some brand new.

She dropped to one knee to look beneath the bench and saw two large plastic paint buckets. She pulled one out. It was stuffed with rusted tools. She wiggled the first tool loose from the tangle of claws and prongs. It was a hacksaw. When she went to set it down, Rafsky held out a few sheets of newspaper.

"Start two separate piles," he said. "One for the things you want to keep for the lab and one for the others."

She spread out two sheets of newspaper and set the hacksaw down. As she reached in for the next tool, she could hear Rafsky trying to work open a basement window behind her. A few seconds later, the basement was washed with new light. And a fresh, cold breeze.

A tack hammer. Clean.

A wrench. Oily. She set that one on the other newspaper.

A Phillips head screwdriver. Muddy. She set it next to the wrench.

A metal ruler. Clean. She laid it next to the tack hammer.

The process went on, and by the time she got to the second bucket, she had four sheets of newspaper spread out on the floor. Under the stairs, Mumsley was gathering the old shotguns, and she could hear him saying something about blood. She looked over her shoulder. Mumsley was holding up a knife — the deer-gutting knife she and Rafsky had seen on their first trip.

"Looks like blood to me," Mumsley said.

"Bag it," Rafsky said.

Mumsley called the other detective over, and they dropped the knife into an evidence bag. Joe noticed Mumsley had tagged the shotguns, too. Mumsley started to unroll the sleeping bags.

She turned back to the bucket, reaching for another tool. She got a strong whiff of soap, and she looked up to see Rafsky standing over her. He was holding three small books, turning them so she could read the spines.

The Birchbark Canoe.
Running Deer's Adventures.
The Winter of the Windigo.

She took the last book from him and looked at the cover illustration. It showed a full moon against a navy-blue sky with silhouettes of pine trees. And in the center, a teeth-baring creature with ragged blue fur.

"Open it," Rafsky said.

She opened the book to the first page. The inscription read: "To Kenny from Mommie."

He bagged the books, and she went back to her bucket, but her head was still inside the Windigo book. She wondered what kind of story it told and how someone could write a children's story about flesh-eating monsters. She shook away the thoughts and focused on her tools.

One left. Long, with a wooden handle. She drew it out. In the thin light, it looked like a clawhammer, but as she turned it, she could see it wasn't. It had a hammerhead on one side, but the other side was shaped more like a small hatchet, as if the tool were used to chop at something. The rusty edge of the hatchet part was black and crusty, but there was something else on it, too. She stood up, taking the tool to the window. Backlit by the sun, five or six tiny hairs were clearly visible.

"Rafsky," she called.

He crossed the basement quickly and peered up at the hammer. For several seconds, they were both quiet, then Rafsky looked down at her.

"We got him," he said softly.

He called to someone upstairs, and an officer appeared with a camera. They took photos of the tool lying flat against a ruler and others with Joe holding it up against the light. Then more pictures of the bucket and the workbench. When they were finished, Rafsky held out an evidence bag to her. She set the tool inside the bag and took a step back, glad finally to get it out of her hands.

Rafsky laid the bag on the workbench, sealed it with orange evidence tape, and reached into his shirt pocket for a pen to fill in the required information on the strip of tape. Then he turned, holding his pen out to Joe. He motioned to the bag.

"Tag your evidence, Deputy Frye," he said.

25

Joe stood at the pay phone in the hallway near the men's room. Behind her, three Inkster PD uniformed officers were talking about the arrest of Ken Snider. Rafsky had disappeared, along with Mumsley and a local prosecutor, but not before telling her to join them in the conference room when she was finished with her phone call.

She leaned against the wall, listening to the silence on the other end of the phone. She tucked a few stray hairs back into her sagging ponytail and started to wonder just how bad her uniform must smell. She had bought some toiletries at the drugstore near the motel last night, but there wasn't much she could do about her clothes. Last night, she had washed out her underwear in her room and put them on the heating unit to dry, but they had fallen off during the night and were still wet.

Finally, she heard the click on the extension as someone at the vet clinic picked up. Brad's voice was suddenly in her ear.

"Joe?"

"Hi," she said. "Listen, we're still in Inkster, and —"

"It's almost three," he said. "You coming home tonight?"

"I don't think so."

"Why not?"

"We made an arrest," she said. "There are questions and paperwork and —"

"And I suppose this Rafsky guy needs you there to help him do all that?"

"No, not really, but —"

"Then come home."

She shut her eyes, and in the silence she could hear dogs barking and another phone ringing. "I can't just come home," she said. "I'm on a case. And even if I wanted to, I have no way to get there. He's in charge, Brad."

"So you don't want to come home."

"It's got nothing to do with want. It's my job."

The phone went quiet for a long time, but when he did speak, there was no anger. Just a surprising softness. "Maybe you should rethink your job, Joe," he said. "It's coming between us, and I miss you."

"I'll be home tomorrow. We'll talk about it then."

More barking and voices in the background.

"Brad?"

"Yeah, okay. I have to go. We have an emergency here. I'll see you when you get here." He hung up.

Joe set the receiver down slowly. She spotted Rafsky coming toward her. There was a glaze to his eyes that didn't come from fatigue.

"We have a problem," he said.

"What?"

Rafsky took her elbow and led her away. They stopped near a door labeled NO EXIT. He started to say something, then paused.

"What's wrong?" he asked.

"Wrong?"

"You look upset," he said. "Did you get bad news on your phone call? Do you need to go home?"

"No," she said.

"I could have you flown home," he said. "You'd be there in a couple of hours."

"No, I'm fine. Tell me what the problem is here."

He glanced behind him, then his eyes came back to her. "A few minutes ago, an analyst working at the Snider house found what he thinks is old blood on the floor of the basement."

"But why is that a problem?" she asked. "That's great evidence, right?"

"Yes, but not for us. That and the bloody

hammer put the scene of the crime here. In Inkster."

It took a second to hit, and when it did, she blew out a breath that emptied her. They were not going to be able to take Snider back to Echo Bay. Where a murder took place — not where the remains were found — determined jurisdiction.

She instantly tried to ease her disappointment by telling herself Wayne County and a larger city like Inkster could do a thorough investigation, and a seasoned prosecutor could take Snider to trial with a sure conviction in sight. But then she thought about the other bones up in Echo Bay and the carvings on the trees. If Ronnie Langford had been only one of Snider's victims, where had the others been killed?

"Well," she said, "at least he's in jail now."

Rafsky shook his head. "Maybe not for long. The DA doesn't want to file murder charges without a body."

"What?"

Rafsky raked back his hair. "He has fourteen days until the preliminary hearing, at which time he has to show probable cause to bind Snider over for trial. No body, no case. He says he won't take it to the judge."

Joe leaned against the wall.

"We don't have any proof Ronnie Langford is even dead," Rafsky said. "All we have is the bracelet."

"And no way to prove any of the bones are hers," Joe said.

"Right."

"This stinks."

Rafsky sighed. "Yeah."

She stared at the floor, her mind still trying to find something in all the information they had collected that would show Ronnie Langford was dead. But she was seeing only the scattering of bones left in the woods. All they had were disconnected pieces.

"Did they search his car for blood?" she asked.

"Yeah, but he's only had the car a few years. His old car was repossessed, and we have no idea where it is."

"Nothing else in the basement?" she asked.

"Not yet."

Joe rubbed her face, her gaze drifting to the hallway. Detective Mumsley was talking to another man she guessed was the prosecutor. Mumsley seemed agitated, pointing to a door farther down the hall. The prosecutor finally nodded and left.

"What's going on?" Rafsky asked as Mumsley came toward them.

"Snider's back there hollering his head off

about being innocent," Mumsley said. "And now get this. He wants to take a lie detector test."

"That's a gift," Rafsky said. "What are we waiting for?"

"The guy we use is in Detroit today on another case," Mumsley said. "And I don't want to give Snider one extra minute to reconsider what he just asked for. You know anyone?"

Rafsky nodded, reaching into his inside pocket for a small black notebook. Five minutes later, they were standing in Mumsley's cluttered work cubicle, and Rafsky was talking to someone in Dearborn, a nearby suburb. When Rafsky hung up, he had a tired smile on his lips.

"He'll be here in forty minutes."

Joe was in the dark, watching the action in the harshly lit room beyond the one-way glass. Snider was sitting in a chair, his left arm resting on a table connected to the polygraph. He was sweating so heavily his hair was matted and damp.

Rafsky came up beside her, holding out a Styrofoam cup. She took the coffee gratefully. "Ever seen one of these tests before?" he asked.

She shook her head, watching as the

281

examiner made notations on the paper spewing from his machine.

"You know how they work?" he asked.

"Body responses," she said.

Rafsky nodded. Inside the other room, the examiner glanced toward the window. Snider's gaze followed, but Joe knew he was only looking into a mirror. He looked drugged with fear.

The first questions were easy — name, place of birth, father's name — all asked so the examiner could determine Snider's response to known truths. Joe knew polygraphs were not admissible in court, and she used to wonder why they were administered. But standing here now and seeing the jumpy panic in Snider's eyes, she understood. It was one of the few times police got this kind of face-to-face interrogation with a suspect. And it was the only chance to convince a suspect you knew he was lying.

A noise made Joe look back. Two men had come in, backlit by the hall light. The first silhouette was easy to make out — garrison cap, bulky gun belt — a cop. The second man wore a suit and held a briefcase.

"Stop this immediately," the man said. "I'm his lawyer."

"Shit," Mumsley said. He hit an intercom button on the wall and ordered the examiner to stop asking questions. Someone hit a switch, and a light flickered on overhead.

The man in the suit stepped forward. He was a few inches shorter than Rafsky, brown hair cut close. There was a boyish, smooth roundness to his face and a glimmer of arrogance in the way he tipped it to the light.

The lawyer moved past Joe, sized up Rafsky, and decided on Mumsley. "I want to talk to my client," he said. "Now."

The room was too small, too warm, and too filled with smells. Stale cigarettes, rain-wet wool, cop sweat, and the tang of anxiety. Ken Snider hadn't been brought in yet. The lawyer, Roland Trader, stood stiffly against the wall near the door, coat over his arm, briefcase at his side, one foot crossed over the other. He was studying them, and not discreetly. Joe watched the lawyer's opaque brown eyes as they settled on the Wayne County prosecutor and seemingly dismissed him as a man of no importance, maybe one with too many cases and too little energy. The lawyer's gaze moved on to Mumsley and the gold badge on his coat, seeing in him maybe what Joe had seen: hardened determination.

Rafsky seemed to be of more interest to the lawyer than anyone. Rafsky must have sensed the stare, because he looked up, and the two stood in a silent eye-lock. They held it so long Joe started counting off the seconds in her head. She was still counting when the door opened and a cop brought Ken Snider in.

Snider gave Roland Trader a quick glance, then slid into a chair and clasped his cuffed hands in his lap, head down. Mumsley stepped forward and turned on a tape recorder.

He recited the preliminary information of time, date, and those present. Then he took a breath. "Kenneth Snider has requested he be allowed to make a statement."

Snider looked at the tape recorder, then leaned forward to speak into it. "This is Kenneth Snider," he said in a hoarse voice. "Any crimes I may have committed were committed in the jurisdiction of Echo Bay or Leelanau County, Michigan. No crimes were committed in Inkster, Michigan, or anywhere else."

He sat back in his chair. For several seconds, the room was quiet, except for the soft clink of handcuffs.

"That's it?" Rafsky asked.

Ken Snider looked up at him, then away. His lawyer stepped forward. "If he is allowed to return to Echo Bay, he will be available to you for additional interviews and will provide, under certain conditions and considerations, more information."

Joe watched their faces. The prosecutor seemed relieved, and after another few seconds, he grabbed Mumsley and motioned for Joe and Rafsky to follow him from the room.

Outside in the hall, Mumsley spoke first. "Fucking lawyers," he said. "He killed that girl in that basement as sure as shit. What's he gain by taking his licks up north?"

Rafsky was looking at the closed door to the interview room. "I think Trader wants his client facing a small-town police department and a small-town prosecutor," he said. "He knows we don't have much time to put the evidence together, and he's betting we won't be able to do it."

Mumsley shook his head. "Shit, we were about to let Snider walk until we could get something solid. If Trader hadn't opened his mouth, his client would have been out of here by tonight."

"But now he's given us another gift," Rafsky said. "The only question is, are we going to take it?"

He looked to Joe for an answer. She realized she was the one who would have to take custody of Ken Snider if they were going to return him to Leelanau County. It would be her name on the arrest warrant.

"I don't want him to walk," she said. "He's coming back to Echo Bay with us."

■ ■ ■ ■ ■

II
A WALK IN THE WOODS

■ ■ ■ ■ ■

26

Things were not normal in Echo Bay. The first indication was the NO VACANCY sign at the Carp River Motel. The place was always shuttered right after Labor Day, old man Stocker closing up to go visit his kids in Georgia for the winter. But now the muddy lot was filled with cars and vans. All nine rooms had been booked by reporters or state police.

Dorothy Newton was still staying at the Riverside Inn. Two other mothers had checked in as well, drawn to Echo Bay by the ever-widening scope of the press coverage. One woman had come from Detroit looking for her fifteen-year-old daughter who had disappeared in July 1973. The other woman's teenage girl had left her Toledo home in February 1972 to go to the store and had never returned. The mothers took to meeting each morning at the Riverside Inn's restaurant. Joe saw them once, sitting at a table in the corner. They sat silent, motionless, their faces cast in the gray light coming from the window. They formed a trinity of grief, like statues in a cemetery.

Joe and Rafsky had stayed a third night in Inkster, waiting for the Inkster PD to process the transfer paperwork. Saturday morning, Rafsky called for a marked state police cruiser, and Snider had made the five-hour trip to Echo Bay in the backseat behind a steel grate. Rafsky had ridden with the trooper, hoping Snider would talk. Joe followed in Rafsky's Chrysler.

By the time Rafsky dropped Joe off at her cottage, she felt both empty and elated, and desperately in need of something to replace the images of bloody hammers and hanging bodies. But inside, there was an empty bed and a note on the table from Brad. He said he was going home to Marquette for a couple of days for his mother's birthday. Joe fed Chips, ate a TV dinner and slept alone. The phone woke her at eight. Leach told her the prosecutor wanted everyone at the station by ten for a meeting.

She got there fifteen minutes early, nursing her coffee and watching the others file in and take their places around the table in the suddenly crowded conference room.

Holt sat with his hands clasped before him

on the table. His young face seemed to have lost some of the uncertainty it usually held. He had been assigned the task of caring for Snider's needs, things like meals, showers, and phone calls. Mack sat next to him, his hand resting on Annabelle Chapel's tattered folder. Leach sat at the head of the table, his gaze distant, fingers tapping on copies of Joe's and Rafsky's statements from their Inkster trip. Rafsky was next to Leach, sitting back in his chair, ankle crossed over his knee, eyes on a pad of paper in front of him.

The door banged open. Mike came in, and threw everyone an apologetic look as he slid into a chair across from Joe. Leach shut his eyes in annoyance but said nothing.

Everyone fell silent, waiting for the prosecutor. Joe looked at the items spread out on the table. Photographs of Ronnie Langford, Annabelle Chapel, and Natalie Newton. The glasses they thought belonged to Natalie. The charm bracelet. The rope from the tree limb. And the rusty hoist.

It all belonged to Echo Bay now. It was their case again, given to them only because Ken Snider had promised them more information. What exactly, no one knew. Snider had said nothing on the drive back to Echo Bay.

Joe's eyes went to Leach. Even though

Snider's lawyer wanted Snider tried in Leelanau County, Joe wondered if Leach would just turn everything over to the state, given the pressure they would be under when the trial neared.

She glanced at Mack. The smug smile on his face led her to believe that would never happen. Mack would die before he let this case go.

The door opened again, and a chubby bald man came in. Leach introduced him as the county prosecutor, Gordon Adderly. Adderly went to the head of the table and threw down four newspapers. "Look, I know we can't keep this out of the press," he said, "but I really hate this kind of sentimental shit."

Joe eased forward to look at the top newspaper. It was the Sunday edition of the *Echo Bay Banner.* She had read the story Adderly was talking about, a moving piece by Theo about Echo Bay adopting the unknown girl, buying a cemetery plot, and planning a memorial. He peppered the feature with quotes from the grieving mothers, who had all pledged to stay in Echo Bay until their daughters' killer was brought to justice.

She knew Theo hadn't broken the story about Snider's arrest. That had come from a beat reporter working the cop shop in Inkster. The story was picked up by the wires and printed in papers across the state, leaving Theo playing catchup.

"Sheriff," Adderly said, jabbing at the paper. "See if you can rein in this Toussaint guy and get him on our side. The last thing we need is more mothers holding vigil outside the jail."

Leach nodded, making a note.

"Who have you assigned the task of keeping the reporters at bay, Sheriff?" Adderly asked.

"Myself," Leach said. "I talked to them this morning and told them there's nothing new."

"Keep it that way," Adderly said. "And if they hit you with any news you don't already have, refer them to my office."

Adderly sat down, shoving the newspapers aside and jerking a file folder out of his briefcase. "Okay, let's get started," he said. "I need someone to bring me up to speed here on what we've got."

When no one answered, Adderly lowered his glasses, his eyes looking for a target. They stopped on Joe. "Talk to me, Deputy Frye."

Joe began a summary of their trip to Inkster, wondering what Adderly thought she could offer that wasn't in their reports. Then it occurred to her that he probably hadn't read them. She ended with Ken Snider's statement that any crimes he had committed had been done in Echo Bay, and his lawyer Roland Trader's promise that Snider would provide additional information "under certain conditions."

"But his lawyer didn't say what those conditions were?" Adderly asked.

"No," Joe said.

"I tried to reach this lawyer last night and couldn't locate him." Adderly said. "Anyone know if he's even in town?"

"He hasn't contacted us," Joe answered. "We don't think he's here yet."

"Well," Adderly said, "Snider's being arraigned Wednesday. I'll assume his lawyer will show up for that."

Adderly looked down at his file, a pencil seesawing between his fingers. "So absent his lawyer, I assume you've had no opportunity to speak with Snider. Am I correct?"

"Right," Mack said. "The fucker's not talking."

"Other than this semiconfession, what else do we have?"

Again, no one spoke, and Joe felt she needed to take the lead. "We have a bloody hammer with what we think are human

294

hairs —"

"Found in Snider's house in Inkster," Adderly said.

"Yes, and spots on the basement floor that may be blood and a history of arguments with Ronnie Langford and —"

Adderly tapped his pencil on the table. "But what do we have up here?"

"Up here?" Joe asked.

"Yes, Deputy. What do you have to link Snider to Leelanau County?"

She felt a knot growing in her stomach, and she snuck at a glance at Mack, suddenly realizing why he hadn't said anything. Adderly was about to rip their case apart, and Mack wasn't going to step anywhere near the fray. She looked back at Adderly.

"Snider said he committed his crimes up here," she said.

"He didn't say he actually committed a crime," Adderly said.

"He as much as said it," Joe said.

"But he didn't say it," Adderly said, pointing his pencil at her. "And I'm surprised as hell his lawyer even let you put cuffs on his client. What did you think you could possibly charge him with up here?"

"Ronnie Langford's murder," Joe said.

Adderly's voice was suddenly sharper. "A ten-year-old crime on the basis of a bloody hammer found three hundred miles away? It'll take weeks to get the typing back on the blood, and we haven't yet proven the hair is the same color as Ronnie Langford's, let alone even human."

"But she disappeared the same week she broke up with him," Joe said.

Adderly leaned forward. "But where is the body?"

Joe lowered her eyes, a wash of warmth in her cheeks. It was the same thing the prosecutor in Inkster had said: no body, no case.

The conference room door opened, and Augie stuck his head in. "Sheriff," he said. "Sorry to interrupt, but I have a phone call for you from Chicago."

"Annabelle Chapel's parents?" Leach asked.

"No," Augie said. "It's about the dental records."

"I'll take it in here."

Leach punched the blinking button. He was quiet for a moment, said thank you, and replaced the receiver. "The jawbone is definitely Annabelle Chapel's," Leach said.

Everyone at the table looked to Mack. His eyes glinted with satisfaction. "I knew it," he said. "I fucking knew it. I told you all this weeks ago. She was always the key to this."

"But she's not the only victim," Joe said.

Mack stood up, snatching up his file and holding it up to Adderly. "But she's the only victim we can put a name to. Hers is the murder we charge Snider with."

"There's no more evidence for her —" Joe started.

Adderly slapped the table. "Would everyone shut up for a minute?"

The room fell silent.

"This news may be the saving grace for your case," Adderly said. "Refresh my memory. When did this Chapel girl disappear?"

Mack didn't have to look it up. "February 2, 1969."

"Where did she disappear from?" Adderly asked.

"A ski lodge at Boyne Mountain," Mack said.

"Wait, I just remembered something," Joe said. "In Snider's high school yearbook, it said he was a member of the ski club."

Adderly was twirling the pencil in his fingers. "Can someone place them together at the ski lodge in February 1969?"

No one answered.

"Then can anyone place Annabelle Chapel in Inkster — ever?"

"No," Mack said. "I know everywhere that

girl went. She was never in Inkster."

Adderly pulled at his jaw, then ran a hand over his head. "Does anyone have anything that even places Ken Snider anywhere up north during his adult life?"

"Now that I have his picture and a time line," Mack said, "I can make a damn connection."

Adderly tossed him a weary look. "You are all missing the point," he said. "You should have found these connections before you arrested him."

Joe leaned forward. "But the Inkster PD was going to let him go," she said. "We had to keep him in custody."

"You didn't have to do anything," Adderly snapped. "You could have watched him, investigated his background, continued to build the evidence. Hell, sometimes it takes years to get enough evidence to go to trial."

The flush in Joe's face that had started as embarrassment was growing to a burn of anger, her head popping with snippets about John Norman Collins and the two years it took to build a case against him. That case had all been circumstantial, but Collins had been convicted and was now serving his life sentence in Marquette. So why wasn't the evidence against Snider enough for Adderly?

"You made a mistake," Adderly said.

"Your arrest was premature, and because of that, I'm going to have to tell three grieving mothers and a pack of reporters that I'm letting Ken Snider go."

Joe looked up quickly. She had to blink Adderly back into focus. His face suddenly softened with something close to pity.

"Like all inexperienced cops, Deputy Frye, you let your emotions rule your head," he said. "And I understand that."

Adderly turned to Rafsky. "But you, Detective Rafsky. You're a seasoned investigator. Why didn't you stop her? You had to see this was a bad arrest."

Rafsky set down his pen on the blank pad, his gaze going first to Joe, then to Adderly. "You are right," he said. "But Deputy Frye and I took a chance. To leave Snider in Inkster would have probably resulted in him being released and then running. We hoped that if he spent five hours in the car with us and if he saw the area where he says he committed his crimes, he would break. He didn't."

"And he won't," Adderly said.

Rafsky gave a small shrug. "I admit it may have been a lapse in judgment on my part."

Mack snorted. "Maybe that judgment was a little clouded."

Rafsky swiveled in his chair toward Mack.

"Clouded?"

"Yeah," Mack said. "Three nights on the road and a hot little rookie maybe you wanted to impress?"

Rafsky's lips drew into a thin line, an angry spark to his eyes. Joe wanted to say something — no, throw something at Mack — but she knew if she did, it would embarrass both her and Rafsky. She could see a creep of color on Rafsky's neck, but he said nothing, just turned his chair back toward Adderly.

"Mack, enough," Leach said. "Let's stay on topic here."

"The topic seems to be their incompetence," Mack said. "Nothing wrong with calling a spade a spade."

"Then let's call this what it is as well," Adderly said, shoving his chair back and standing. "A mess."

"Gordon, wait," Mack said. "I'll find you a connection between Annabelle and Snider. I'll go to Petoskey today. I'll place that fucker in that town, damn it."

Adderly closed all the files he had in front of him. "We don't have time, Mack. Snider's entitled to a probable cause hearing within fourteen days, and I'd bet my ass when his lawyer gets here, he'll scream for one as soon as possible. And I might as well walk in there naked holding my dick with what you guys have given me."

"So you're going to just let him go?" Joe asked.

Adderly hesitated. "Yes."

Mack started to say something, but Joe cut him off. "Mr. Adderly, please don't do this."

Adderly snapped his briefcase shut. "If I file cause now and then drop the charges the day before the preliminary hearing, I'll look like a monster to every mother and a fool to every reporter out there. My office loses all credibility."

He jerked the briefcase off the table and took a step toward the door before looking back at Leach. "I'm sorry, Cliff," he said. "I really am."

Joe stood quickly. "Mr. Adderly."

Adderly stopped again, drew a breath that lifted his round shoulders, and turned to her. She pushed back her chair and came around the table, toward the pile of evidence stacked on the table.

"He takes them," she said tightly. "He rapes them. And he hangs them."

She picked up the deer hoist by the frayed rope and held it up above the table. "With this."

Adderly didn't move. Joe felt the eyes of

the others, and she turned, looking around the table. The five men were looking back at her with the expression of people at a funeral who did not really know the deceased. Solemn. Sad, maybe, but with a determined detachment that kept the pain from getting too close.

"Mr. Adderly," Joe said, "please give us our fourteen days."

Adderly blew out a tired breath. "You have forty-eight hours," he said. "Find me something."

27

A cold wind was moving across Lake Michigan and up the mouth of the river. It was blowing so hard the water was being forced backward against the dam, creating tiny whitecaps. Joe watched a lone gull struggle against the wind until it finally gave up and took shelter on the leeward side of a Fishtown shanty, where it sat, forlorn and rumple-feathered.

"I got you a beer."

Rafsky sat down across from her, setting two plastic glasses on the table. Joe didn't look at him as she reached out to take the cup. She took a drink and looked back out at the water.

"Can we go inside?" Rafsky asked.

"No, I need to be out here."

They were the only ones out on the deck. Rafsky turned up the collar of his trench coat. "Okay, you need to cool off," he said. "But do I have to freeze my ass off in the meantime?"

She didn't answer.

"Frye."

"What?"

"We'll find something. We won't let Snider walk."

She was silent, staring at the shanty house across the canal, the one where Pete the Buddha-bellied Romeo held sway over his ramshackle little realm. She was staring at the smoke curling up from his chimney, envisioning him inside with a drink, his dog, and his woman.

"I want to live over there," she said, pointing. "I want to dive off the dock in summer, sit by the fire in winter, with my only worry being who's going out to buy beer and the next cord of wood."

Rafsky laughed. "No, you don't."

She finally looked at him. It took a moment, but she smiled, then burrowed down into her coat. "No, I don't."

Her eyes went back to the water as she thought about how hard it was going to be to find something to appease Adderly. Mack was already on his way to the Boyne Mountain ski resort. Armed with a photo of Snider, he was looking for anything that could connect him to Annabelle Chapel — a hotel receipt, lift ticket records, a witness with a good memory.

Mike had been given the task of sorting through the personal items taken from Snider's Inkster home and was pushing the lab for a quick analysis of the hammer, the deer knife, and the shotguns from the basement. Holt had been assigned to deal with the mothers, a task that put his gentleness to good use. Leach had been the one to call Annabelle Chapel's parents in Chicago to tell them about the jawbone being a match. Then he had given Joe and Rafsky their assignment with one simple sentence: Find some way to connect Snider to Echo Bay.

The first thing they had done was run a check of property records in Leelanau and three nearby counties. There was no record of Snider owning anything.

Joe took a sip of her beer. "Rafsky, what are we going to do?" she asked quietly.

"Snider had to have a place to go here," Rafsky said. "He didn't just dump them and then check into the Carp River Motel."

Joe was quiet for a long time, thinking.

"You have an idea?" Rafsky asked.

"Not sure, just a fragment of one. Something Snider said the first time we were at his house. When we were questioning him, he started to say something about his father. Something like, 'Dad had —' "

"Had what?" Rafsky asked.

"My partner, Mike, he says even the most humble slob on the Ford line has a place up north. Maybe Ken Snider Senior did. He was a hunter."

"No Sniders showed up on the real estate rolls."

"Maybe he had a place but Ken sold it after the father died."

"We could go back to the county, but without a year, we aren't going to find it in forty-eight hours."

Joe was watching the shanty across the canal. Pete appeared, scampering out in his bathrobe to grab his newspaper off the dock. She rose quickly.

"Come on," she said. "I've got an idea."

Theo took his time coming out to the front counter to talk to them. Joe could see in his face that he was miffed at her.

"Give me one good reason why I should help you, Joette," he said.

"Look, Theo, I had no control over that

305

story being printed," she said.

"How do you think I feel getting scooped by some lousy beat reporter on some stinking downstate rag?" Theo said. "I mean, maybe the *Detroit Free Press,* but the *Inkster Gazette*?"

Theo was pouting. Joe couldn't really blame him. The bones had been his story since the start, something beyond the church bake sales and routine break-ins. He got the same adrenaline rush from being involved in this as she did as a cop.

"Your story today was good," she said.

He sniffed. "It was just a follow-up. But tomorrow, the big boys are going to be eating my dust."

Rafsky had been quiet, but now he stepped forward. "What are you printing?"

Theo hesitated, then smiled. "Why not? Come back and see."

He led them to the back, where the pasted-up pages of tomorrow's front page lay on light tables. SNIDER LINKED TO 2ND MISSING GIRL; TEEN DISAPPEARED FROM BOYNE SKI RESORT.

"Shit," Rafsky muttered, turning away. "Mack."

Joe turned to Theo. "Theo, you can't release this yet."

"You see all those reporters in town?"

Theo said. "No more playing catchup for me."

Rafsky came forward. "Okay, then let's make a deal here. You hold this story about the positive ID on Annabelle Chapel, and we'll give you the next break we get."

Theo eyed them both. "Sorry, no deal."

Rafsky looked to Joe, and she took the lead. "Okay, but can we look at your back issues, Theo."

"For what?"

"I can't tell you yet. If we find something, you'll be the first to get it."

Theo pursed his lips. "All right. Follow me."

He led them to the room with the bound copies and left them alone. Joe pulled out the binder for 1969.

"What are we looking for?" Rafsky asked.

"Real estate transactions," Joe said. "You can't do anything in this town without Theo printing it. You have a baby, get married, break your collarbone playing football, buy a cake or a cottage, it will be in the *Banner*."

They sat side by side at the table and opened the 1969 book to January. Joe was aware of Rafsky's closeness, the mix of smells — soap, the starch of his shirt, and the peppermint he had popped after drinking his beer. She felt the slight press of his thigh against her own under the table.

The real estate transfers were wedged in between the obituaries and the church announcements under the heading LEELANAU LOG. They were listed only in the Thursday edition, so it didn't take long for them to work their way into February. She was watching Rafsky's long finger work its way down the column of type when it suddenly stopped.

Feb. 1, 1969. Kenneth H. Snider Jr. to Donald and Jean Collier, Section 42, Echo Bay Township.

Rafsky's eyes came up to hers. There was hope there, but it was restrained. Back out in Theo's office, Rafsky called the county appraiser. Joe watched as he wrote something on a pad. He thanked the clerk and hung up the phone.

"We've got the address," he said. "Let's go."

The cabin was on Bass Lake about eight miles northwest of Echo Bay. It was several miles from the original site of the bones but just outside the eastern border of the expanded search grid. The cabin was isolated, set back in a stand of beeches and poplars, with no other houses visible.

Joe took note of the place as they drove up the gravel road. An old-style dark log cabin, small but well maintained. Too well, Joe thought, her spirits falling slightly. She had been hoping to find the cabin in the same state it had been six years ago — and empty. But it was neither. There were some tenacious pink fall asters in the window boxes. And there was a shiny green Scout 4x4 in the drive.

Don and Jean Collier were in their forties, the wife plump and bubbly, the husband lean and red-faced from working thirty years delivering mail. They listened, with solemn attentive faces, to Rafsky's explanation of why he and Joe were there. Rafsky kept his words general, but Joe could see the morbid curiosity and horror in their eyes. They had read the papers. They had heard the stories about what had been going on almost in their backyard.

"We couldn't believe it when we saw his name in the paper," Don Collier said.

"Kenny Snider seemed like such a nice boy," Jean added.

They were sitting straight-backed on the sofa together. Joe was perched on a bench in front of a spinet piano, notebook and pen out. Rafsky had positioned himself closer to the Colliers, sitting on the edge of a blue La-Z-Boy.

"So you bought the cabin from Snider?" Rafsky asked.

"Nope, from an agent," Don said. "I saw a listing in the Charlevoix paper. I was working up there but we always wanted to live down in this neck of the woods. We bought it in sixty-nine but didn't move in until last spring when I finally retired. I used to come down here every weekend to work on the place. Shoot, took a couple years to make this place livable."

His wife jumped in. "The cabin was a mess."

Don nodded. "But it was on the lake, and there's only so much lake frontage, you know."

"But you met Snider, right?" Rafsky asked.

"Yeah, at the closing in the title office in Petoskey. February 1," Don said.

Joe caught Rafsky's eye. They had placed Snider in Petoskey the day before Annabelle Chapel disappeared. And from Petoskey, it was a quick fifteen-mile trip down US-331 to the ski resort where Annabelle was last seen.

"Did Ken Snider tell you why he was selling?" Rafsky asked.

"Oh, yes," Jean said. "He didn't want to sell because the cabin had been in his family for three generations. But now that his father had died, he said he needed the money." She shook her head slowly. "I still can't believe what I am reading about him."

"So you changed the place a lot after you bought it?" Rafsky asked.

"Had to," Don said. "It was nothing but a shell, partitioned off into a couple rooms. Just a hunting cabin, no plumbing to speak of, just a well out back. Like I said, I did everything myself, all the insulation and drywall, re-sanded the floors, everything."

"I painted and did the decorating," Jean added.

Joe was looking around. "You did a beautiful job, Mrs. Collier," she said.

She smiled. "Would you like to see the rest of the house?"

Rafsky gave Joe a discreet nod, and Joe rose, following Jean Collier into the kitchen. Everything was clean and new. Joe tried to hide her disappointment as she trailed Jean back to the bathroom and into the main bedroom. The door to the second bedroom was closed, and Joe could hear music inside. She recognized Elton John singing "Bennie and the Jets."

Jean knocked once and then opened the

door. A girl was sprawled on a bed with some books and a looseleaf binder. Somewhere around sixteen, a slender version of Jean Collier.

"Terry, please," Jean begged.

The girl rolled her eyes, reached over to the tape deck, and turned down the music.

"This room was just awful," Jean said, lowering her voice. "I think it was the boys' room. They left it such a mess, old furniture, dirty clothes piled up. I wanted to refinish the wood floor in here like we did with the rest of the house, you know, a nice natural look with some nice braid rugs. But the floor in here was so stained I couldn't save it."

Joe's eyes traveled over the pink shag carpeting and up the soft pink walls. If Ken Snider had brought any of his victims here, there was no way to tell now. Any secrets this cabin harbored had been erased by the Colliers' remodeling zeal.

"Close the door when you leave, please!"

Jean Collier heaved a sigh of exasperation at her daughter and closed the door. They went back to the living room. Rafsky was standing near the door, wrapping things up with Don Collier.

"If there's anything we can do, just let us know," Don said.

"You've been a help already, Mr. Collier."

Outside, Rafsky waited for Joe as she zipped her jacket against the cold.

"You get anything?" she asked.

"Collier remembered that when they were at the title office, Snider asked if he could hang on to the key," Rafsky said. "Snider said he wanted to go back and pick up some stuff. Said he'd leave the key on the mantel. When the Colliers got to the cabin two days later, the key was there." Rafsky turned up his collar. "You get anything else?"

"Jean Collier said Snider left the place a mess."

"So why did he need the key for two extra days?" Rafsky asked, turning to scan the trees. "Let's look around some."

"What are we looking for?"

"Damned if I know."

They walked around the side of the house, past the Scout. There was a large object under a heavy tarp. Rafsky lifted the tarp to reveal a Ski-Doo.

"Mrs. Collier isn't going to be very happy about us digging up her yard," Rafsky said.

"You think there might be bodies here?" Joe asked.

"I don't think we'll find anything more of Annabelle. We're too far from the oak tree for that. But if Ronnie was his first, isn't it logical he came here, someplace he knew, to get rid of the body?"

"But the bracelet?" Joe said.

Rafsky just shook his head.

They continued around the back of the cabin. Joe noted that the trees had been cleared back at least fifty feet around the cabin, leaving a stand of tall white birches on the fringe of the yard. There was a small shed, old but freshly painted white, and pile of chopped wood along the back of the cabin, stacked roof-high in anticipation of the coming winter. Rafsky had gone on toward the shed, but Joe's eyes were drawn to a spot near the wood stack, something on one of the cabin's logs.

She went closer, kneeling to get a better look. It was faint but definite, about two feet off the ground.

"Rafsky!" she yelled.

He was at her side in a second. She heard him let out a long, slow breath.

"Jesus," he said softly.

28

The morning fog had not yet burned off, and it hovered just above the ground, obscuring the bases of the trees and leaving them levitating like dark ghosts.

Other small clouds hung in the still, cold air — the labored exhalations of the searchers as they worked the grounds of the Collier cabin on the edge of Bass Lake.

Joe watched them from her position near the tarp-covered Ski-Doo. The officers wore heavy boots, insulated pants, and bulky parkas stenciled with MICHIGAN STATE POLICE. They carried shovels, pickaxes, and sifting boxes. One officer was already staking out the first of what would be many grids, stringing tape and stabbing flags into the ground. Another had a county map spread out across the trunk of a cruiser.

"Coffee, ma'am?"

She looked back at a young trooper who was holding out a cardboard tray of Styrofoam cups.

"Thanks," she said, taking a cup. She peeled off the top and closed her eyes as she took a sip of the strong coffee.

It didn't help. It was so damn cold. She shivered and tucked her scarf tighter into the neck of her parka. The scarf was an old fuzzy red thing that left bits of yarn in her hair, but it was warm.

She heard Mike's voice and turned to see him standing near a cruiser, hands stuffed in the pockets of his pants, boots covered in mud. Leach had given Mike the assignment of supervising the search, working with the state lieutenant to cover the first square mile, the approximate boundaries of the Collier property. Mike didn't look happy to be here, and Joe realized there had been no time lately to talk to him about the case or anything else. She wondered how he was handling things. Wondered, too, how Mindy was taking his long hours. Probably not much better than Brad was dealing with hers.

She took another drink of coffee. Brad had called late last night to tell her he wasn't coming home until tomorrow. It was snowing hard up in Marquette, he said, those big, fat flakes that stuck to everything. The same kind of snow that had been falling the first time he kissed her on a walk through Presque Isle Park, he had added.

She shut her eyes, telling herself there would be time later to make things better with Brad.

When Joe opened her eyes, she saw Jean Collier standing at the kitchen window again, her expression strained. Joe guessed it was horrifying for her, seeing cops digging in her yard for the bones of young girls. Earlier, Joe had caught the face of Jean's daughter, Terry, peeking out from between her pink curtains. Her expression was one of bland curiosity.

Joe heard the slam of a car door and turned to see Leach and Rafsky making their way up the drive. As Rafsky drew closer, Joe saw his face was wan. He had a wad of Kleenex at his nose.

"You okay?" she asked.

"Caught a bug," he said. "I'll be all right."

"Okay, where is it?" Leach asked.

"In the back, Sheriff," Joe said.

The three of them went behind the cabin. Joe moved aside the garbage can she and Rafsky had placed there yesterday to prevent anyone from seeing the carving. None of the searchers or other cops had been told about it yet. Rafsky didn't want it prematurely released to anyone.

Leach squatted to get a better look. He traced it lightly with his gloved finger, then looked up at Joe. "You're sure this is the same as the other one?"

"See for yourself, sir," she said. She pulled a paper from her jacket and handed it to Leach.

He looked at the photo. "Okay, so this one on the cabin here looks like the carving on the tree where we found the Chapel girl's jawbone." Leach pulled himself to his feet with a soft groan. "Do we have any idea how long this one has been here?"

"Don Collier told me it was there when they bought the place six years ago," Joe said. "I think it looks like it's been here longer than that, but I'm no expert."

"Sheriff," Rafsky said, "Frye and I have some other things we need to fill you in on. Let's take a walk."

She put the garbage can back in front of the carving and led them away from the cabin, under the yellow perimeter tape and deeper into the birch trees. As Joe walked, her eyes flicked from the tree trunks looking for carvings and up into the bare branches for ropes, but there was nothing. She walked until she could no longer hear the voices of the searchers. When she turned to face them, she looked to Rafsky to see if he wanted to start. He gave her a nod, the Kleenex again at his nose.

Joe pulled another paper from her jacket and unfolded it. It was a copy of the twelve moon symbols from the book she had found in the library.

"Remember when I brought you the

photographs of the first two carvings?" When Leach nodded, she went on. "Well, there are twelve symbols, sir, one for each month."

She handed him the paper. Leach looked at it and compared it to the photograph of the carving he was still holding. "Okay, so the Chapel carving and now the one on the cabin — they look like the February symbol to me."

"Yes, sir, we agree."

"What about the other carving, the one you found on the prayer tree?"

Joe handed him a third photograph. "This is it, sir."

Again, Leach compared them to the twelve symbols. "This one looks different to me."

"Detective Rafsky and I thought it might be the symbol for September. Now we think it is just a badly done version of February."

Leach looked slowly from each photograph to the paper with the twelve symbols, then up at Joe. "So you're suggesting February has some significance?"

Joe nodded. "Annabelle disappeared February second. Ronnie Langford around Valentine's Day. And Dorothy Newton last spoke to her daughter in February before spring break."

Rafsky blew out a sneeze.

"Bless you," Joe said.

He managed a nod as he turned up the collar of his trench coat. She hadn't noticed before, but now as the wind rippled his coat, it seemed far too thin for the weather. She realized he hadn't had time to go home to Gaylord to pick up a heavier one.

"Okay, any ideas on why February?" Leach asked.

Joe hesitated.

"You'd better show him the book," Rafsky said.

Joe reached into her jacket, pulled out a plastic evidence bag containing a small blue book, and handed it to Leach.

"Have you ever heard the term *Windigo,* sir?" she asked.

Leach was staring at the title. "Yes."

"We found this in Ken Snider's basement. It's a children's book called *Winter of the Windigo.* It's a story based on an Indian legend."

Leach turned the book over and read the back. Joe knew it said something about a young brave called Blackfeather who saves his tribe by defeating the fearsome Windigo.

"The legend says the Windigo comes out during the harshest time of winter when food is scarce and animals are starving," Joe went on. "The February symbol is called the Hunger Moon."

Leach's eyes came up to her, watering from the cold. "And you two think this all means something to Snider?"

"This is Snider's book. It is inscribed to him from his mother." She hesitated, looking for Rafsky, who urged her on with his eyes. "I think Snider might have studied Indian lore, might have come across the moon symbols. Killers of multiple victims often leave signs. Maybe this is part of his weird psychology. Maybe the carving is his way of marking his territory, asserting his strength."

"He thinks he actually is one?" Leach asked.

"I found out there is a medical condition called Windigo psychosis, where mentally ill people actually think they are possessed with an evil spirit," Joe said. "Has Snider crossed that line? We can't say, sir. Maybe a doctor could."

"Shit," Leach said, the word escaping in a slow hiss of vapor.

Rafsky sneezed, and Joe glanced at him. He looked miserable.

"If I recall my local history," Leach said, "Windigos cannibalize their victims."

Joe nodded.

"And it begins with someone in their own tribe."

Joe nodded again. "Ronnie Langford was almost a relative. Snider was planning to ask her to marry him and she refused because she was leaving town with another man."

"So he killed Ronnie Langford in a jealous rage," Leach said. "But why would he bring her body all the way up here?"

"Jean Collier told me the cabin had been in the Snider family for three generations," Joe said.

"So he probably spent a lot of time up here as a boy," Leach said, staring off toward the Collier cabin. "Hard to break those kinds of attachments."

Joe started to say something, but Leach seemed preoccupied, lost in a memory she wasn't sure he would share.

Leach let out a sigh. "I grew up here, you know, not very far from this place, in fact. I used to go off alone into the woods. I was always looking for someplace or something — I don't know — magical. I still do it, go for walks deep into the woods alone. I figured out finally there is no magic place. Except the one in your head when you see a ray of sun breaking through the trees or watch a leaf dance in the air."

He looked to both of them. "It can be almost a mystical experience, if you're open to it."

"Or if you're very young and lonely," Rafsky added.

"Or just plain twisted," Joe said.

Rafsky laughed softly, then lost it in a cough.

Leach held out the book and the copies of the photographs.

"So what do you think?" Joe asked, taking them back.

"I never close my mind to anything," Leach said. "But I want *you* to keep one thing in yours. No matter what we uncover, no matter what we find out he did to these girls, remember, he is just a man. He is not some fanged creature with super powers."

Leach looked toward the cabin. "Let's head back," he said.

"Sheriff," Joe said, "can I suggest something to you?"

Leach nodded.

"I don't think we should tell Mack about the Windigo part of this," she said. "Mack's obsession with Annabelle Chapel is beyond normal. You know if he leaked this, it would make national news. And the mothers can't hear something like this. Not even the suggestion of it until we know for sure."

Leach nodded again. "All right."

They started back to the cabin. She stayed with Leach, and Rafsky fell into step behind them. After a few feet, she heard Rafsky sneeze again. She stopped to let him catch up.

His hands were tucked into his pockets, his shoulders hunched against the wind. She untied the red scarf from around her neck and stepped back to him. He stopped abruptly, and she looped the scarf over his neck and crossed it under his chin.

"Thanks, Frye," he said.

"You're welcome, Rafsky."

29

It started to snow as they made their way back to the Collier cabin. Leach had asked Joe to find Holt. She found him standing guard at the yellow tape in the driveway, and asked him to follow her to the backyard. When she moved the garbage can aside to reveal the carving, Holt's eyes widened.

"Sheriff wants to know if you can figure out how to cut this out of the cabin wall without leaving a huge hole," she said.

"You want to take the actual carving as evidence?" Holt asked.

"Yes. And keep it a secret."

Holt leaned in and touched the carving.

"Holt, you hear me?" Joe said. "No one can find out about this carving being here until the sheriff tells you it's okay. No one. That includes everyone at the station, including Mack."

He looked at her solemnly and nodded. "I gotta go home to get the tool I need."

"Make it quick," she said, moving the can back in front of the carving.

Holt hustled off, and Joe turned back to the scene. The searchers had already finished with the area directly around the cabin. There were mounds of leaves, piles of displaced dirt and rocks. But the evidence boxes and bags still sat empty.

If they didn't find something, their theory that Ken Snider started his murderous career closer to home might not hold up. Just finding the cabin and the carving and putting Snider in Petoskey was more than Adderly expected. But Adderly had told them he wanted more — bones on the cabin grounds.

A familiar laugh rose up to her left, and she turned to see Mike. He stood near the corner of the cabin, his cap tipped back on his head, his cheeks red, smile wide. There was a young girl standing next to him, and Joe's first thought was that she shouldn't be inside the tape, but then Joe realized it was Terry Collier.

The girl said something about David Bowie. Mike said something about Mick Jagger.

Joe thought of the photograph of the girl stretched on the hood of Mike's cruiser. She couldn't remember now what she had done with the picture, but she made a mental note to look for it.

"Mike," she called.

He gave Joe a *Don't bother me* look, and she called again. He pushed off the cabin and walked over to her.

"How's the search coming?" she asked.

"They haven't found anything but a dead raccoon."

"How far are they into the trees?"

He shrugged. "Twenty feet or so."

Joe didn't hide her annoyance. "Maybe you should go keep on an eye on things, help the lieutenant out."

He was going to say something, but he didn't, turning on his heel and walking off toward the trees. He gave Terry a small wave as he passed and disappeared into the pack of blue jackets. He had just made it past the shed when Joe caught the chatter on a nearby radio. Something about a rope.

She broke into a run, sprinting past Mike

and breaking into the trees. Ahead, she saw a trio of officers huddled near a tall tree, faces turned to the sky. She stopped and looked up.

It was about thirty feet up, maybe five feet long, tied to a heavy limb — a piece of old rope with a frayed end.

Her eyes swung to the ground. It was covered with wet leaves. "Be careful in here," she said. "No more people than absolutely needed."

The others who had followed her to the tree started backing away. Mike grabbed a roll of yellow tape and strung it between two pine trees, blocking off the path back to the cabin. Rafsky emerged from the cluster of cops. He had traded his trench coat for a bulky blue state jacket. Joe's red scarf was still around his neck.

He stepped carefully to her and looked up. After a moment, he sighed. "You hope for breaks like this," he said, "but then you get one and you realize what it really means."

Another victim, Joe thought.

Already the officers were starting a ground search, carefully raking away leaves and putting them into containers to be searched by others.

Joe stepped around the tree slowly, scanning the rough bark for any sign of a carving. It was easy to spot. About chest high to an adult man.

She turned to call out to Rafsky, but he was right behind her. "I see it," he said.

He called for a camera, a chain saw, and a ladder, then pulled off his gloves and traced the carving with the tip of his finger. "This is an old one," he said. "Weather-worn and smooth."

"An early one?" Joe asked.

"Maybe. Definitely another February Hunger Moon."

They both turned to watch the searchers. In minutes, they had reorganized. Flags marked the edge of a new perimeter. Wood posts and string set the individual search areas, laid out like lanes in a swimming pool. The photographer appeared. His flash popped in the gray like headlights on high beam. Then someone brought a ladder, and ten minutes later, there was a man with a chain saw going up into the tree.

"I got something," one of the searchers called. "Come in behind me, not in front."

Rafsky took Joe's elbow, and they walked up behind the officer. He was on his knees in a circle cleared of leaves. At first, Joe didn't see anything but clumped mud. Then a small spot of red came into focus. She stepped closer. It was the fingertip of a glove.

A second officer appeared. His black jacket had ANALYST stamped on the back. He carried a leather case, and he carefully began extricating the glove from the dirt. As he dug around it, Joe could see the rest of the glove was blackened and moldy, worn so thin that some tiny threads were floating into the air as the tech worked around it.

The analyst cursed and took another approach, gently scooping the whole dirt clot. The dirt started to crumble, and the glove came apart. A cluster of tiny white bones spilled onto the ground.

"Oh, God," Joe whispered.

The analyst started picking the bones out of the dirt. He took the longer ones first, then the smaller ones. Joe counted them as he dropped them into a box. Twenty-seven.

"What's that?" Rafsky asked over her shoulder.

The analyst turned over the glove, exposing a bracelet. It was gold once, now black with tarnish, but Joe recognized it immediately. It was an ID bracelet, a fad from the sixties, usually engraved with the owner's name — or her boyfriend's.

"Is there an engraving?" Joe asked.

"You want me to clean this bracelet here?"

"It might have a name on it, on the flat part," Joe said.

The analyst swept off the mud with a small brush, then held the bracelet out to her. The engraved letters were still visible: SUSIE-Q.

"Number four," Joe whispered, turning away.

Rafsky came up behind her. "We need to find out everything we can about who had access to this cabin."

"It was in the Snider family for three generations before the Colliers," Joe said, reminding him.

He nodded. "Okay, then we need to find out everything we can about the Sniders, starting with the father."

"I'll let Leach know." She went back to the tree with the carving. Above her, she could hear the chain saw rumble to life. Somewhere behind her, a man was shouting out more search directives, but she suddenly didn't want to hear any of it. She kept walking, dipping under the tape, heading toward the cabin.

She spotted Holt, standing by the cabin, a power tool in his hand, waiting for direction.

"I heard on the radio they found another carving out there," he said. He pointed to the carving on the cabin. "So why are we keeping this one secret?"

"Because it's on Snider's childhood home," Joe said. "It's the best connection we've got to him. I don't know much about the law, but I don't want his lawyer to know we have this until he has to."

Holt nodded and went to work. Joe watched him, but she was thinking about Susie-Q. Wondering who she was, how long she had been missing, and who was missing her. Trying not to think what had happened to her out there and how cold she must have been before she finally died.

They had never talked about *how* he killed them. Did he strangle them? Shoot them? Or simply hang them up and gut them, as the deer hoist suggested? And she wondered something else, too. If they were right about Snider killing for eleven years and Leelanau being his dumping grounds, why had they found so few bones?

Holt's saw cut off, leaving the air vibrating with a sudden silence.

"I'm done," he said.

She gave him a brown bag, and he slipped the slab of wood inside, dutifully filling out all the required blanks on the evidence tape.

"You want me to take it in myself?" he asked.

She nodded, her gaze drawn back toward where they had unearthed Susie-Q's ID bracelet. She wondered how deep into the woods this search would go. They weren't that far from the first search area. The entire peninsula was only about five miles wide. If they went far enough, the first search area would meet this one.

"You okay, Joe?" Holt asked.

She nodded again, thinking she needed to go inside and tell Mrs. Collier they had cut a gouge in her cabin. She followed Holt around the side of the cabin. Holt was rambling about how Ken Snider just sat in his cell, sometimes laid out on his bunk so still and silent that Holt was afraid he might be dead. But Snider always came forward to get his food, Holt said, like a beaten but hungry dog.

As they neared the front porch, Joe stopped suddenly. Parked about a quarter-mile down the road, she saw a black sedan with tinted windows. It wasn't a police car, and both of the Collier vehicles were here in the drive.

"Holt," she said, "do you know who that is?"

He looked toward the car and shook his head. "It wasn't there when I drove back in here. I'll run them off when I leave."

"No," Joe said. "Just drive by and run the plate. Radio the owner back to me."

Holt hurried off, and she watched as he climbed into one of the cruisers. She heard Rafsky's voice behind her and turned.

He had a thin film on his forehead. He was running a fever. "Listen," he said, "I just got done telling the crews how important it is to keep these carvings quiet."

"We've told them that all along," she said.

"Yeah, but this is going to get out of control pretty quick. Leach and I made a decision. We're going to release copies of the carvings to all neighboring law enforcement agencies with orders to look for any similar carvings. They will be told that under no circumstances are they to discuss their findings with anyone outside their departments."

Holt's voice bubbled from the radio on her belt. "Frye?"

She grabbed her radio. "Go ahead."

"Subject vehicle belongs to a Roland Trader."

"Thanks, Holt."

Rafsky frowned, and Joe motioned discreetly toward the black sedan still parked down the road.

"What the hell is he doing out here?" Rafsky asked.

"Watching us," she said.

30

It looked different. It was still a log cabin. But not *their* log cabin. He hadn't noticed the difference in his first three times here just last week. He had been too worried about the dead girl in the trunk to notice anything. But now he realized the cabin no longer looked like the one he had known as a boy.

There were lots of cops, and as he watched them, he bit the ragged cuticles of his right hand. What would they find? And how would it affect what he needed to do now? He knew he should probably leave before they saw him, but he couldn't stop looking at the cabin.

That couple who owned it had put flower boxes out front. They were empty now, but he wondered briefly what kind of flowers grew there in the summertime. He couldn't remember much about the summers up here. Except for that one summer before that one winter. He was young then and the pictures in his head weren't clear anymore, except for that one image of her up in the tree. That had never left him.

Roland Trader reached down into the bag on the passenger seat and took out a baby Tootsie Roll.

He unwrapped it, careful to get all the paper off the chocolate. Sometimes it stuck, and if he didn't see it, he would taste it later in his mouth, and he hated picking things off his tongue. He popped the Tootsie Roll into his mouth, rolled the paper into a tiny ball, and put it in the ashtray.

His eyes moved back to the cabin.

They had electricity. It would be warm now inside his old bedroom in winter. Whoever slept in there now wouldn't have to scrounge for more blankets or sleep in the same bed with someone else just to keep from freezing.

Roland shut his eyes for a moment, feeling the small ripple of cold air on his neck.

He and Kenny used to do that, sit in the darkness waiting for the gin to take hold of Dad so they could sneak into the same bed. Dad was funny about things like that. Hugging. Whispering. Sleeping together just to stay warm. Dad said it would make queers out of them.

It hadn't.

But it had brought him and Kenny closer together. Long nights, shivering together in the darkness, wrapped in old wool blankets, sharing fears and dreams and stories, Kenny trying to help him keep alive memories of a woman whose face he couldn't see anymore. Sometimes, if it had been a bad day or if Roland was hurting too much, Kenny would go get the old ladder from the shed and they would climb up on the roof, where Dad never looked for them. It was their special place. They would lie up there looking at the stars, and Kenny would tell him that everything would be all right, that he would take care of him. And each time, before the season was over, Kenny would always promise that this would be the last year he would let Dad bring them up here.

But it wasn't. The seasons kept coming. Nineteen fifty-eight. Fifty-nine. Sixty.

And then 1961, when Dad said Roland was damn well big enough to sleep alone in the bedroom. Big enough to shoot a shotgun and not have it knock him over. Big enough to gut a deer. Big enough to take his whippings like a man.

More seasons. More gray mornings with the smell of burning firewood and gunpowder and death in the air. Then, finally, in 1964, Kenny kept his promise.

The Tootsie Roll was losing its flavor, drying up the way they sometimes did when you chewed on them too long. Roland swallowed it, turning his gaze back to the cabin.

Kenny was in big trouble now. He had hoped, maybe foolishly, that bringing Kenny back here and handing him over to the mom-and-pop Echo Bay department would be the right move. Now he wasn't sure.

He watched the cops moving around the front of the cabin. That tall cop was here, the one with the tan trench coat and ice-blue eyes. He was a strange man, but the kind of man it was a pleasure to study. There was a stillness about him, even when his body was in motion. But when Roland looked into the man's eyes, as he had back in Inkster, he could almost see the constant movement of his mind. The man was always thinking. He would have to watch him carefully.

He would have to watch Kenny carefully, too.

Roland picked out another Tootsie Roll. He could still see Kenny as he had looked in Inkster, slumped over the tape recorder, head bowed. At that moment, he seemed very small and weak. It was odd for Roland to see him that way, and he had the sensation, for the first time in his life, that they had somehow traded places. Maybe even traded souls, as if what Kenny once was Roland had become.

Strong.

It was his turn to help Kenny. His turn to protect his brother. Kenny had kept his promise all those years ago. Now it was his turn to keep his.

31

Joe scanned the copy of Ken Snider's driver's license that she had just peeled off the Telecopier. Full name: Kenneth David Snider. Date of birth: April 3, 1946. That meant Snider was now twenty-nine, which made his first killing — if his first was Ronnie Langford — at age eighteen.

Her gaze cut to Rafsky, sitting at Mike's desk. Since their arrival back at the station, he had been working the phones trying to find out more about Ken Snider, Sr., or anyone else who might have had access to the cabin.

Rafsky's radio sputtered to life, and she cocked an ear. A report in from the searchers. Nothing but an old boot.

Her eyes moved to the closed-circuit

monitor on Mack's desk. Until three days ago, it had sat in Leach's office, unused because they never had a prisoner worth watching. But Leach had brought the monitor out and ordered Snider watched around the clock, afraid Snider would attempt suicide. Leach had also extended the shifts of all the deputies to make sure the office and the jail were never left unattended. All days off and vacations had been canceled.

Joe adjusted her chair so she could see the monitor better. Snider was hunched on his bunk, a blanket over his shoulders, his food tray nearby. The basement cell wasn't bad by modern standards, and there was an alarm button just outside the cell that Snider could activate in an emergency. Anyone could hear if he yelled, since the back offices were right at the top of the stairs.

But it was still a basement, a place that held the cold even in the summertime. The screen's image was blurry, but Joe could see that Snider was shivering. She wondered now if this was even the best place for him, wondered if their small department would be able to handle the media pressure and keep Snider secure. Maybe it would be better to move Snider to the larger county jail down in Traverse City.

She heard Rafsky hang up the phone and looked over. He had discarded the bulky blue state police parka, but Joe's red scarf still hung over his wrinkled white dress shirt.

"Telecopier still on?" he asked.

She went to the machine. Augie scooted his chair over to allow her room, and Joe connected the phone receiver on the modem.

"What's coming?" she asked.

"Ken Snider Senior's death certificate," he said.

Joe glanced at Augie. He was talking to Mrs. Elsinore, something about her grandson Jeff stealing her binoculars. Joe had the passing thought that since the first bone had been found, she had spent no time patrolling the town.

The Telecopier came to life with a soft, steady clacking. The transmission would take at least five minutes, so she went to the coffee station, poured out two mugs, and set one in front of Rafsky. He gave her a tired smile of thanks.

The Telecopier finally stopped. Joe took out the cylinder, peeled the document off the imaging paper, and turned slowly, her eyes already moving down the page.

"Kenneth Snider Senior died November 20, 1964," she said.

"Three months before Ronnie Langford disappeared," Rafsky said. "Where did he die?"

"Up here in Leelanau County," Joe said. "At the family cabin, it looks like." She skimmed the death certificate and looked up. "Gunshot wound. Local doctor wrote in 'hunting accident.' "

"Who shot him?" Rafsky asked.

Joe shrugged. "It doesn't say, but the reporting party was Kenneth Snider Junior."

"I want to know more about this accident," Rafsky said.

"Responding department was the Leelanau SO," Joe read off.

Augie jumped to his feet. "I'll go get it." He disappeared down the hall to the records room.

Joe began making copies of the death certificate for the file. She knew hunting accidents were common given that for two or three weeks a year, the woods were full of drunks with guns. So the Snider accident probably had no bearing on the current cases. But the fact that Ken Snider's father died just months before Ronnie Langford disappeared was too big a coincidence to ignore.

She moved back to her desk, slipping the copies of the death certificate into the thickening accordion file Leach had started weeks ago. She considered looking back through the file but then changed her mind and sank into her chair.

Holt was preparing reports for Lansing. Rafsky had his head down on his arms. It was an oddly quiet moment given the activities going on a few miles away at the Collier cabin and the quickening pace of the investigation.

The quiet ended with the ringing of Augie's phone. She picked it up. Their order of sandwiches was ready at The Bluebird. She told the waitress she'd be right there.

"I'll go," Holt offered.

She shook her head. "No, I'll go. I need the fresh air."

Outside the station, she saw a group of women standing in front of the Riverside Inn. The mothers. There were a couple more of them now, Holt had told her earlier. He had gently questioned them all about Susie-Q. None of the mothers claimed her. Joe had done a check through the missing persons files, but there was no one with the nickname or any variation of it.

She hurried to The Bluebird. The place was packed with reporters and cops, and it took a while to get the order. At the last minute, she remembered Rafsky hadn't ordered anything, and she added a BLT.

Rafsky was snoring softly at Mike's desk when she got back. She left his food on his desk and went to eat her own sandwich but stopped when she saw that Augie had left Ken Snider, Sr.'s accident report on her desk.

It was a two-page deputy's report, done by a man named Miller, whom she had never heard of.

November 20, 1964. Four-fifteen p.m.

When I entered the yard, I saw a white male juvenile standing approximately thirty feet south of the rear door to the cabin. He identified himself as Kenneth Snider, age 18, son of the man who owned the cabin, one Ken Snider Sr. He stated he had accidentally shot his father and led me to the scene, located approximately fifteen more feet south into the woods. I observed one white male, approximate age forty-five, lying on his back with an obvious shotgun wound to the face. He was deceased. A second shotgun was near his right hand. At that time I noted blood on the grass and the bark of a nearby tree. (See photographs 1–9).

Kenneth Snider stated he and his

father were setting off on a hunt when a buck unexpectedly entered their location. Kenneth Snider Jr. stated he aimed and fired just as his father stepped into his sights. Kenneth Snider Jr. appeared distressed and emotional. He was extremely cooperative and willingly accompanied me to the sheriff's office. See attached statement from second witness.

A second witness? Joe sifted quickly to the second page.

Witness name: Roland J. Snider. Age: 16.
  Relationship to deceased: Son.

Roland? Ken Snider's brother? Joe moved quickly to the accordion file to get Kenneth Snider, Sr.'s death certificate. It took her a moment to find it: NAME OF DECEDENT'S HUSBAND/WIFE: Mary Trader Snider. Roland had taken his mother's maiden name. Why?

She went back to the accident report and found the witness statement Roland had given to Deputy Miller:

Witness name: Roland J. Snider. Age: 16.

Relationship to deceased: Son.

Roland Snider stated to me he and his father and brother were heading to the woods when suddenly he heard a shotgun blast. He heard his brother scream and saw his father lying on the ground, bleeding from the face. Roland Snider stated his brother notified the sheriff's department by CB radio. Roland Snider was distraught and tearful and for most of the interview, incoherent. When I asked them if either had knelt next to or held their father's body, they stated they had not. I confiscated two Remington 870 pump shotguns, one identified as the weapon Ken Jr. was carrying, the other identified as the father's gun. End report.

She went to Mike's desk. "Rafsky," she said. "Wake up."

He lifted his head and blinked.

"Roland Trader is Roland Snider," she said. "They're brothers."

He wiped his nose and picked up the report she had set in front of him. Her eyes cut back to the jail-cell monitor. Snider was huddled under his blanket.

"I'll be right back," she said.

"Where are you going?"

"Downstairs."

"You can't question him."

"I know."

The cold air hit her as soon as she descended the stairs. Holt had asked if he could bring a space heater down for himself and the other officers who sat watch, but so far no one had bothered.

The two cells were on the left side. Everything was gray — bars, walls, blankets, and bunks. The only windows were narrow panes of glass high on the walls. Holt had told her that when it snowed, the windows got blocked, making the basement feel like a cave sunk deep into the earth.

She paused at the small desk and pretended to be looking for something. Behind her, she heard the shuffle of feet, then a sniffle.

"Hey," Snider said.

She glanced at him over her shoulder. "What?"

"Can I have another blanket?"

She pulled a blanket off a storage shelf and handed it to him through the bars. He wrapped the blanket around his shoulders and stepped back, his face pasty, his eyes empty.

"Have you seen my lawyer?" he asked.

Roland Trader still hadn't put in an appearance at the station, and Joe wondered if he was still sitting outside the Collier cabin. She couldn't tell Snider she knew Roland was his brother. One wrong comment, and Roland Trader would claim they were interrogating him without counsel.

A sound drew her eye to the stairs. Holt was coming down. Roland Trader was two steps behind. Snider saw Roland, shrugged off the blanket, and came to the bars.

"Where have you been?" he demanded.

"Quiet," Roland said. His eyes lasered to Joe. "You're not supposed to be talking to my client."

"You mean your brother?" Joe said.

A flicker of surprise passed over Roland's eyes and was gone. "My client," he said evenly.

Holt was staring at Roland dumbfounded.

"I need to speak with my client alone," Roland said. He focused on the TV monitor. "With that off."

Joe reached up and switched the camera off. When she turned to Roland, he was looking around at the cells. It struck her how wrong her first impression of the man had been. Back in Inkster, she had guessed Roland Trader to be in his thirties. But a quick mental calculation told her he was in his mid-twenties.

Damn. Probably not old enough even to be a lawyer.

"You want to talk inside the cell or out?" Joe asked.

Roland glanced back at the cell. "Inside."

Holt unlocked the door. Roland moved inside, and Holt locked the door behind him, the clunk of the heavy lock echoing in the basement.

"Just press that button when you're done," Joe said, motioning to the alarm on the wall.

Roland looked at her through the bars. The thin fluorescent light gave his brown eyes a dull, liquidy sheen, as if things were moving beneath but unable to get out.

"Please leave us alone," he said.

32

He could smell the drifting scent of sewer water from the drain on the floor. And the stink of sweat and mildew from the thin mattresses on the bunks. There was something familiar about it all. He did not like being here.

Roland turned slowly, taking in the rest of the cell.

The walls were cinder block, newly painted gray. The light was fluorescent but softer than he was used to seeing, as if they hoped the gentleness of it would work to calm their prisoners. His eyes stopped on Ken, perched on the edge of the bunk, hands clasped between his knees.

"Where the hell have you been?" Ken demanded. "You leave me sitting here for four days all alone?"

Roland looked back at the stairs. He wondered if the cops were up there, listening. He should have asked for a conference room, but he wasn't sure the rooms upstairs weren't bugged. He didn't trust cops.

"Roland," Ken said, "talk to me."

Roland came back to his brother.

"You said these cops up here were stupid," Ken said. "You said they wouldn't find out anything, you said —"

"The only thing they've found out is that we're brothers," Roland said. "That was inevitable."

"But why are we even doing all this?" Ken asked. "Why couldn't I just tell them back in Inkster I didn't kill anyone? Why didn't you let me take the lie detector test?"

Roland glanced at the bunk opposite Ken, then decided instead to sit next to Ken so they could keep their voices lower.

"Because anything can come up on those things," Roland said. "Lies can be truths, and truths can be lies, and the cops only see what they want to see. And a polygraph isn't admissible anyway. What's the point of a good test result if a jury never sees it?"

Ken nodded slowly, but Roland could see the fear in his eyes. Roland knew fear was a funny thing sometimes. It ate away at the mind's ability to reason and react, and maybe right now, for Ken, that was the best thing that could happen.

"Besides," Roland said, "the evidence against you in Ronnie's murder is very circumstantial."

"What evidence?" Ken asked. "You haven't even told me what they arrested me on! All I know is that they found her —"

Roland placed a hand on Ken's shoulder. He could feel the rush of Ken's panicked breaths, almost feel the race of blood through his veins.

"Calm down, Kenny," Roland said.

Ken hung his head, quiet.

"This is what they have," Roland said. "Ronnie's charm bracelet was found up here in the woods. The charm you gave her, that heart-shaped one, was found in your drawer."

"But she gave that charm back to me," Ken said.

"Yes, I know that," Roland said.

Ken put his head in his hands. "I would

never have hurt Ronnie over that damn charm. Or anything else."

"They also found a bloody hammer with hairs on it," Roland said.

Ken's face shot up.

"They found it in the basement with some other old tools," Roland said.

"You knew this in Inkster and you didn't tell me?" Ken stood up quickly, took two steps, and spun back. "I don't understand this. First the hoist is missing, and now —"

Ken stopped himself, shaking his head.

Roland thought Ken had that look on his face that he used to get when he didn't understand his geometry homework and he'd just sit and stare at it, trying like hell to figure something out for himself before he'd ask Roland for help. Sometimes he did figure it out. Most times he didn't.

"Roland," Ken whispered, "how did blood get on that hammer?"

"Maybe I used it to kill a rat."

"Even I know the cops can tell the difference between animal blood and human blood," Ken said. "If it came from an animal, we wouldn't have anything to worry about."

"You're right," Roland said. "It is human."

"Whose is it?"

"Ronnie's."

Ken stared at him, his eyes glazed with shock. "You killed Ronnie?"

Roland held up a hand. "Keep your voice down."

Ken came closer, leaning over him. "You killed Ronnie?"

Roland grabbed the blanket and pulled him back down onto the bunk. Ken sat rigid, looking at him, waiting.

"It was an accident," Roland whispered.

"Jesus," Ken said, "but what — ?" He shook his head. "Jesus, Jesus. How? What happened?"

Roland wiped his face, listening for the sounds of footsteps or voices on the stairs. He heard nothing but a soft, steady drip of water.

"She came back to the house to get her clothes," Roland said. "You were at work, and I didn't want to let her in, but you know what a bitch she was. She practically shoved her way inside."

Ken was shaking his head, his eyes glistening.

"She . . ." Roland paused, hearing a hollowness in his voice. He cleared his throat and went on. "You know how she used to hang her underwear on the clothesline in the basement, right?"

"Yeah."

"She went down there, and I was helping her, you know, taking things off the line and tossing them into this cardboard box she had brought."

"Go on," Ken said, his voice strained.

"I look up, and I see her staring at me," Roland said. "It was the same look she used to have when you brought her home from the bowling alley drunk. But that day she wasn't drunk. She took the panties down off the line, and she came over to me and started touching me."

"What?"

"Ken —"

"Fuck, Roland."

"Ken, please, listen to me."

"I don't fucking believe this. I don't fucking believe this . . ."

"She was touching me, rubbing herself up against me." Roland pulled in a deep breath. He dropped his eyes to the floor. "I didn't know what to do, Kenny. I was only sixteen, for God's sake."

Ken was quiet. Roland's eyes found the drain on the floor, and he stared at it. It was the same kind of drain they had in their basement back in Inkster. The hole in the floor where he used to sweep the water from the washer overflow. The same hole he had to piss in sometimes when he was locked down there too long. The same hole Ronnie's blood had run into.

"I got scared," Roland said. "I never even kissed a girl before and here she was, clawing at me like some kind of animal who needed . . ." He looked up. "I pushed her away."

"She got mad?" Ken asked.

Roland nodded. "And she started screaming. She was calling me a loser, saying I was just like you. Saying that's why she was dumping you."

Roland heard Ken draw a deep breath, and he looked over at him. His eyes were closed.

"She was throwing things and screaming that she hated the way her clothes always smelled like the basement and that you . . ."

Roland stopped.

"Go on, Roland. Finish."

"She told me she never loved you, that she was just with you until someone better came along."

Ken got up slowly and walked to the other side of the cell. He pulled the blanket tight around his shoulders and leaned his head against the bars.

Roland looked back at the drain. The basement stench was stronger now, and he pulled in a breath, keeping the smell in his nose to mix in his memories. Something else was there, too, something familiar, a feeling. He was getting aroused, and for a moment, he shut his eyes and let himself enjoy it.

"How did you do it?" Ken asked without turning around.

Roland opened his eyes, using the drain to tighten his focus and will the erection away.

Ken faced him. "Roland?"

"I grabbed the hammer and hit her with it," Roland said. "I only meant to hit her once, but I couldn't stop myself. Then suddenly, I was standing there, looking down at her. She was dead."

"Oh, God, Roland."

"I put her in the trunk of Dad's car, that old Chevy we had back then. And I cleaned up the basement. I burned her clothes in a can out back. And you never knew."

"How did her bracelet get all the way up north?" Ken asked.

"The next day, it was the day after Valentine's Day, remember?" Roland said. "I told you I was staying overnight at Danny's house? I lied. I brought her up here and dumped her in the woods."

"Why up here, why Echo Bay?"

Roland looked up. "You know why, Ken."

Roland didn't blink as Ken stared at him.

And when Ken finally came back and sat down on the bunk next to him, Roland was careful not to move. They sat, elbows on their knees, heads down. Roland glanced at Ken, another memory easing its way back.

Cold. A sleety snow. The house on Avondale quiet, their father's empty bedroom, holding only boxes of his clothes, bowling trophies, and three pairs of old leather shoes. From Ken's bedroom, the grunts and groans of rushed sex. His brother's voice. *I love you, Ronnie. I want to marry you, Ronnie.*

Roland wondered what Ken was thinking now. Wondered if after everything Ken had done for him, could he do this one last thing?

"Roland," Ken said quietly, "the cops, when they were searching the house, they mentioned other names. Did you kill other girls?"

Roland shook his head. "I don't know anything about other girls."

"Tell me the truth, Roland."

"You know how hard those years were for me, Ken. And you always thought it was because of Dad dying, but it wasn't. It was her and what I did. I've always hated myself for what I did."

Ken hid his face in his hands.

"It was only Ronnie, Ken. I swear it. I'd

never lie to you. You know that."

Ken finally looked at him, his face drawn with pain and confusion. "I don't know what to do here, Ro," he said. "You know I'd do anything for you. But they're talking life here."

"Listen to me," Roland said. "You won't have to go to prison. I understand the law, and you have one thing going for you. It's really hard to get a conviction without a body."

"They don't have Ronnie's body?"

"No," Roland said. "And they never will."

"Why not?" Ken asked. "Did you bury her?"

Roland shook his head slowly. Ken was staring at him, and Roland knew he was seeing things he didn't want to see, because Ken understood the woods and animals and what they did when they were hungry.

Ken's head dropped lower, and his hands came up to his face. He gave out a soft sob, and Roland stayed quiet, letting his brother have his tears and his memories of Ronnie, a part of him bothered by the fact Ken did not see the beauty of Ronnie dying the way she did.

"I need you to trust me on this, Kenny," Roland said. "I know if we can just hang tough a little longer, we can get out of this.

There's not a judge in the state who will take this to trial without a body, especially on the other evidence they have."

Ken was staring at the floor. "You need to turn yourself in, Roland," he said softly.

"Kenny."

Ken looked up, his eyes catching the light streaming in from the small window outside the bars. The fear was gone, replaced by disbelief and disgust. Disgust for him and what he had done. Roland needed to get the fear back.

"I can't turn myself in," Roland said. "I will never survive in prison."

Ken held his gaze, silent.

"When we were little, you always protected me, Kenny, because you were the strong one," Roland said. "Now you've got to let me protect you because I'm the smart one."

Ken was still quiet. The fear was back in his face. And it was there in his body now, in the broken way he slumped back to the bunk. Roland could almost feel it against his own skin.

"So what do we do?" Ken asked.

"We wait," Roland said. "When they can't produce the evidence at the hearing, we'll walk. Or even if they get enough to take it to trial, we ask for bail. Then we run."

■ ■ ■ ■

The cop named Holt came downstairs to let him out. Roland went upstairs and down the hall to the main office. He paused in the doorway, coat over his arm, briefcase in hand. They hadn't noticed him, and he took those few seconds to study them.

There was an Italian-looking deputy leafing through a magazine. A nobody.

Roland looked to the tall man seated at the desk, head bent over some paperwork. Roland had seen him in Inkster and again at the cabin this morning. Roland couldn't see a badge, but he knew the man was a state investigator. He wondered if the rumpled hair and wrinkled clothes were from self-neglect or simply the result of long hours. Roland guessed it was the latter, and that gave him a small measure of respect for the cop. He liked tenacity.

The last cop in the room was the same woman who had been downstairs earlier. She had been there in Inkster with the state investigator, too. And like the investigator, she looked tired. She was thin, with high, sharp cheekbones and shadowed gray eyes she tried hard to color with toughness. But there was a warmth beneath them, a depth to be plumbed, a weakness to be exploited. He didn't know what it was. But he would find it.

She looked up unexpectedly.

Those weird eyes stayed on him, then went to the state investigator. The investigator felt the stare, and his gaze came up, first to her, then to Roland.

The two cops shared something that needed no words. Roland could tell she liked the investigator. But her affection was colored with respect and uncertainty. And, Roland realized, awe. She was a rookie. He knew how he would use that.

Roland looked back at the investigator. His eyes were like a lake frozen over in winter. On the surface, opaque and safe. But if you went too far, things cracked, and you fell through. This was his opponent.

The investigator stood slowly. "Can we ask you some questions, Mr. Trader?"

Roland held his gaze. It was difficult.

"What do you think you're doing representing your own brother on a murder charge?" the investigator asked.

"It's perfectly legal."

"Legal but stupid," the investigator said. "And it's a conflict of interest since you were living in the Inkster house at the time of Ronnie Langford's disappearance. You're a potential witness. Or maybe an accomplice."

Roland forced a small smile.

"The prosecutor is probably going to make a motion to remove you as counsel," the investigator said.

Roland held his smile, but he let his eyes move away from the investigator, trying to find an answer the man would believe, because in the long run, it didn't really matter what they did in court. It was never going to get that far.

He saw a newspaper lying on the desk, the headline striped across the top: SNIDER LINKED TO 2ND MISSING GIRL; TEEN DISAPPEARED FROM BOYNE SKI RESORT.

He stared at it, jarred by a sudden image that flashed like a streak of lightning in his head. Long blond hair. A screaming mouth and, in the frozen moonlight, the glint of silver off her teeth.

"Mr. Trader?" the investigator asked.

"Do what you have to do," Roland said. He picked up the newspaper. There was another one beneath it with a different headline: A MOTHER'S SEARCH FOR A LOST DAUGHTER.

Roland held up the newspapers. "May I have these?" he asked the woman cop.

Her eyes shifted to the investigator, again, Roland noted, looking for confirmation. She finally nodded.

Roland tucked the newspapers under his arm and walked toward the door. He heard the investigator say something about a prosecutor named Adderly and an arraignment on Wednesday, but Roland ignored him, pushing open the front door and stepping out into the cold gray afternoon.

He scanned the newspapers as he walked. He should have had this information sooner, but there was no way to get it unless he had been willing to sit down with the prosecutor. But this was good enough. Maybe even more than the prosecutor would give him anyway.

Roland's eyes slipped to the byline on the stories: Theo Toussaint, Editor-in-Chief.

He would go talk to this Toussaint. He'd bet there was a lot more he could learn. About this town, the mothers, the cops, and the man with the blue eyes.

33

It was near seven when Joe pulled up to the Riverside Inn. She was tired, dirty, and hungry. She glanced over at Rafsky sitting in the passenger seat. He was hunched down into the blue parka, his eyes closed, his nose red. However bad she felt, she knew he felt a hundred times worse.

"We're here," she said.

His eyes popped open. "Oh . . . yeah. Thanks." He didn't make a move to get out. Joe could tell he was bothered by something.

"You still angry about the brother?" Joe said.

Rafsky nodded. "Trader, Snider, whatever the hell he wants to call himself. He's playing us."

"He's within the law," Joe said.

Rafsky was shaking his head. "I don't care. Something's not right." He sniffled and went for the door handle. "See you tomorrow," he said.

"Rafsky, wait," she said.

He looked back at her with watery eyes.

"What are you doing for food tonight?" she asked.

"I don't know," he said with a sigh. "I have some leftover pizza in my room."

She looked out the windshield of the cruiser. The snow that had started at the cabin earlier had turned to a sleety rain. "I have a better idea." She put the cruiser in gear and pulled away from the inn.

Ten minutes later, she pulled into the drive of her cottage. Brad's truck wasn't there, but she knew he wasn't due home from Marquette until tomorrow. Rafsky didn't say a word as he got out and followed her up onto the porch, waiting as she unlocked the door.

He followed her into the dark living room. Joe went to turn on a lamp.

"Jesus!" he said.

"What's the matter?"

"I stepped in something."

The lamp came on. Joe looked back at the door where Rafsky stood, holding up his foot. Chips sat nearby, looking up at them.

"Take off your shoes and leave them there," Joe said. She let Chips outside. When she came back, Rafsky was standing there in the parka and stocking feet, coughing.

"Oh, for God's sake, get in here," Joe said.

Rafsky came in, slipping out of the parka. Joe took it and her red scarf and draped them on the hook on the back of the door.

"Where's your bathroom?" Rafsky asked softly.

"That way," she said, pointing. "There's some cough syrup in the medicine chest."

He disappeared. From behind the closed door, she could hear honks, sniffles, and running water. She cleaned up Chips's mess and Rafsky's shoe and then went to the kitchen, pulling out the egg tray, a package of bacon, and some bread. Rafsky still hadn't emerged by the time she had the bacon frying, the coffee brewing, toast going, and the eggs whipped in a bowl. She had time to toss some kibble into the dog bowl and start a fire before Chips scratched at the front door and she let him in. The wet dog went straight to his bowl, scarfed his food, and then trotted to the hearth and plopped down in front of the fire.

Joe was working on the scrambled eggs when Rafsky came into the kitchen.

"Smells good," he said.

"Go sit down," she said. "I'll bring it in."

She wasn't a good cook — Brad had always been the one to make any real meals they ate — but she had a way with eggs. A little chopped onion, some cheddar, and a dash of Tabasco. She made two plates, taking care to arrange the buttered toast, bacon, and a wedge of orange on each. When she brought the plates into the big main room where the table was, she drew up short.

Rafsky was sitting at the table, head down on his folded arms. There was a bottle of Robitussin on the table, and the paper napkins she had set out were wadded at his elbow. The poor guy looked like a drunk after a bender.

"Hey," she said softly.

He sat up slowly and focused red eyes on her face. "An angel of mercy," he said.

She set the plates on the mats and sat down across from him. Joe watched as he carefully stacked some eggs on a slice of toast, layered some bacon on the eggs, and topped it off with a second toast slice. He picked it up and took a bite. He closed his eyes in pleasure. He took another bite and another.

"Good," he murmured.

She smiled. "Your speech is steadily deteriorating. Next you're going to be grunting."

"Men devolve to a primitive state when they are sick."

"More like a pathetic state."

"It's all an act to get sympathy. At least, that's what my wife says."

Joe ate some eggs and drank some coffee. The sleet pinged off the window near the table. But the room was slowly warming from the fire now blazing in the hearth. Joe watched Rafsky as he lifted a mug of coffee to drink. His color seemed a little less gray. She found herself focusing on his wedding ring.

"Does your wife get upset with you being away so much?" she asked.

Rafsky set the mug down. "She was an Army brat, so she moved around a lot." He took another bite of his makeshift sandwich. "What about you? What about . . ."

"Brad," she finished for him. "How'd you know — ?"

"Saw his stuff in the bathroom. Very neat fellow, isn't he?"

Joe laughed. "He arranges his vitamins alphabetically."

"And always puts the seat down, right?"

Joe laughed again and nodded.

Rafsky shook his head. "He's giving the rest of us a bad name. I might have to run him in."

"On what charge?" She was smiling.

"Decent exposure."

"But that's just a misdemeanor."

"I could get him on male fraud."

She laughed. "But he'd get a trial by his male peers."

"Ah, yes, a hung jury."

"Nah, he'd probably just pee-bargain."

Rafsky stared at her for a second, then burst out laughing. He was coughing and laughing, his face reddening. He picked up his napkin and tossed it at her, hitting her in the face.

She sat up straight with a look of mock horror, holding her fork of scrambled eggs.

She didn't think; it just happened. She flicked the egg at Rafsky.

It stuck on his wrinkled white shirt. He looked down at it slowly, then up at her. He calmly picked up his toast, ripped off a piece, and flung it back at her.

The giggles started — her laughing, him coughing — in a furious cross fire of eggs, bits of bacon, and shredded toast. Chips was jumping and barking, scarfing up every crumb of food that hit the floor.

They were both laughing so hard they didn't hear the door open. Then Rafsky's eyes went past Joe's head. She turned.

Brad was standing at the front door, staring at them.

"Brad," Joe said, getting up and going to him.

He dropped his duffle on the floor, his eyes going from her to Rafsky and back to her. He pulled her to him and gave her a quick kiss. But his eyes went right back to Rafsky, who was just sitting there, wiping his face with a napkin.

"You're home early," Joe said.

"Yeah, the roads were bad at home, and I didn't want to get stuck." Brad was still looking at Rafsky.

"Brad, this is Detective Rafsky," Joe said, gesturing.

Rafsky rose, a bit unsteadily, and held out his hand. Brad shook it and stepped back. An uncomfortable silence filled the small room. Chips whined and nuzzled his snout into Brad's hand. Brad petted him, but his eyes stayed on Rafsky.

"Well," Rafsky said softly. "I think I should get going. But I need to use your bathroom one more time."

When Rafsky had left the room, Brad took off his anorak. He started to hang it on the hook on the door, but Rafsky's state police parka was there, so he draped it carefully across a chair.

"So that's the famous Rafsky," he said, smiling.

"I don't think I ever called him famous, Brad," Joe said.

He came to her, still smiling. He gently wiped a bit of egg off her face and kissed her again.

"I missed you," he said.

"I missed you, too," Joe said.

"You look tired."

She knew he meant bedraggled. "It was a long day," she said. She was about to tell him about the search at the Collier cabin when Rafsky emerged from the bathroom, a fresh wad of blue Kleenex clutched in his hand.

Joe got her coat off the door hook and reached for her keys. Brad's eyes swung to her questioningly.

"I have to drive him back to his hotel," Joe said.

Rafsky came forward to Brad. "I just realized I shouldn't have shaken your hand. I have a bad cold."

"That's okay," Brad said with an easy smile. "I'll take an extra vitamin C tonight."

Rafsky's eyes slid to Joe, and she had to look away to keep from smiling. He put on his parka, paused, then wrapped Joe's red scarf around his neck. He turned back to Brad. "Good to meet you."

"Likewise," Brad said with a nod.

"I'll be right back," Joe said to Brad.

They rode the ten minutes back to the Riverside in silence. When Joe pulled up to the curb, Rafsky turned in the seat to face her. In the reflected light of the dash, she couid see something in his eyes that told her he had something to say.

"What is it?" she asked.

He hesitated, then shook his head. He unwrapped her scarf from his neck, folded it, and set it on the seat. He opened the door and got out, then stooped down to look in at her. That same odd look was there in his expression, but he smiled and it was gone.

"See you tomorrow," he said.

"Feel better," she said.

She watched him hurry through the sleet and disappear into the inn.

When she got home, the fire was burning low, and Chips was snoring in his dog bed. Brad had cleaned up the food mess and was finishing up the dishes. He came into the living room as she was pulling off her boots.

"I was going to have a beer," he said. "You want one?"

She shook her head. "I'm too tired. I'm going to shower and fall into bed."

She could feel Brad's eyes on her as she went into the bedroom. Undressing quickly in the cold room, she went to the bathroom and ran the shower until the water heated. She stepped in and closed her eyes, turning her face up into the spray. She washed, scrubbing her skin hard, shampooing her hair twice. Slowly, very slowly, she could feel the knots in her neck loosening. The image of those tiny bones spilling from the red glove kept pushing its way to the front of her mind, and she had to fight to push it back.

The door to the bathroom opened. Through the plastic of the shower curtain she could see Brad's blurred naked body.

He drew back the curtain and got into the shower.

She turned to him, surprised. He never liked to share a shower or bath.

He turned her around so her back was to him, and his arms encircled her waist. His mouth was at her neck, and she could feel him growing hard, pressing against her with an urgency she had never felt from him before. It felt suddenly strange. They had never made love in the shower before. Everything felt strange — the streaming water, his hands almost rough on her breasts, not being able to see his face — so strange, as if it weren't Brad at all.

She closed her eyes, giving in to it.

The water started to turn cold.

"Come on." Brad's voice was husky in her ear. "Let's finish this right."

He got out first, grabbing a towel. His face was flushed, his eyes intense as he looked back at her, waiting.

"I have to take my pill," she said. "I forgot to this morning."

"Make it quick, babe," he said. He left the door open, letting out the steam.

Joe reached for a towel and wrapped it around herself. She could hear Brad in the bedroom. She opened the medicine chest and pulled out the pink container that held her birth-control pills. She took one and was about to put the container back when something caught her eye.

The row of vitamins on Brad's shelf above hers. The bottle of zinc was in the first position, the bottle of vitamin A in the last.

Joe stared at them for a long time, frowning. Then a slow smile tipped her lips. Rafsky. She closed the medicine chest and went into the bedroom.

34

The dunes stretched four hundred feet high, hundreds of miles long, and back in time more than two thousand years. To some, they looked like a woman lying seductively on her side at the water's edge. But most liked the image that had given them their name: Sleeping Bear. A mother bear and her two cubs were driven into the lake to escape a forest fire, the Ojibwa legend said, and the cubs grew tired and drowned. The mother bear reached the shore, climbed to the top, and lay down to wait forever for her doomed offspring.

Joe stood on a bluff, looking out at Lake Michigan. The sun was high in a cornflower sky, and the air was so cold and clear that in the distance, she could see the green

mounds of North and South Manitou Is-
lands.

"What are you looking at?" Rafsky said,
coming up beside her.

"The two dead cubs," she said.

"What?"

She turned and gave him a small smile.
"Nothing. God, you look terrible."

"I think it's the flu. I was up all night."

"You should see a doctor. Doc Lyle in
town —"

"No time for that now," Rafsky interrupted. "And don't tell anyone, please."

Joe was going to press it, but she knew he
wouldn't go. Not today, at least. Not with
the news they had just gotten.

The call had come in just after dawn. A
park ranger on routine patrol had found a
carving on a tree that he thought matched
the flyer he had been carrying in his truck.

The Sleeping Bear Dunes were about
thirty miles south of the original search
areas, but nothing could be discounted at
this point. Joe knew that if the carving could
be linked to their case, everything would
change once again. The dunes had been
designated a national lakeshore park five
years ago. That might mean FBI involve-
ment.

"Is the sheriff here yet?" Joe asked.

"Just pulled in. He asked me to come up and get you."

Joe followed Rafsky down to the road. He led her to where Leach and a park ranger waited. There was another man in an overcoat she didn't recognize, but she suspected he was another state investigator.

"You see it yet?" Leach asked, falling in step with Joe and Rafsky. They were following the ranger down the slope of beach grass and sand cherry plants.

"No, we just got here," Joe said.

They entered the shade of beech trees, moving steadily downward. The trees grew thicker, the light thinner. Joe had been to the dunes before, a sweet afternoon of sightseeing and sweaty kisses last August with Brad. She knew the park was more than dunes, that it encompassed everything from apple orchards to serpentine streams. But she was unprepared for the sight that greeted them as the ranger walked on.

They were entering a thick stand of trees, a mix of beeches, maples, and birches. It looked very similar to the woods of the original search area, but the air was very different here — swirling and gritty with wind-borne sand.

The ranger had stopped at a thick birch tree. Joe and Rafsky broke through the brush and stepped forward.

"Is that what you were looking for?" the ranger asked.

Rafsky nodded and glanced at Joe. She knew what he was thinking, that this carving looked very different from the others, which meant they might now be dealing with copycats.

She scanned the surrounding trees. But what if this was the real thing? There were more than seventy thousand acres in the park, most of it sandy bluffs, but there were other pockets of woodlands. There were even trees in the dunes themselves, half-buried black, spindly trunks. The constant winds and the shifting sands made for an ever-changing landscape. Finding any bones here would be near impossible.

"Ranger, can you give me any estimate how old this carving might be?" Rafsky asked.

Joe felt Leach, Mack, and the other state investigator crowding in to listen. The young ranger looked nervously at them. "Well, sir, this is an old tree as far as birches go, and they have a life span of about a hundred years."

"We're thinking of something more recent," Rafsky said.

"I'd say within a couple of weeks."

"How can you be sure?" Joe asked.

"Birch has a very soft bark, ma'am," the ranger said. "Heck, you can make a mark in it with your thumbnail." He pointed to the carving. "And it scars up easy, just like human skin. You cut something in it, and then the scar forms and gets thick and ropy. The tree keeps growing around the cut marks, which makes the lines expand and distort. This has no scar, and it's still fresh. Hasn't been here but a month or so."

"You seem to know a lot about this," Rafsky said.

The ranger gave a quick nod. "I study arborglyphs, sir. In my spare time, I mean."

"Arbor what?" Leach asked.

"Tree carvings, sir. They've been used for centuries by all kinds of cultures. Art, messages, or just a way to keep from going crazy in the wilderness." His smooth face colored slightly. "Tree carvings aren't just kid's stuff."

"No, they're not," Rafsky said quietly. He

walked a few paces away. The other state guy followed him.

"Can I ask what this is about?" the ranger asked. "All the flyer said was it was in connection with a crime."

"It's a homicide, son," Leach said. "Is your boss on his way?"

"Yes, sir. He's coming from Empire. Should be here any time."

Leach nodded and motioned for Joe and Mack to follow him over to where Rafsky stood with the other investigator. As Joe got closer, she heard Rafsky call the other man Captain.

Rafsky did a quick round of introductions, first offering the name of the older man, Captain Kellerman. When Rafsky got to Joe, he added that she was the one to grab onto the carvings' significance. Rafsky went on to give his captain a short update. Joe could tell by Kellerman's slightly disapproving expression that he knew about the search at the Collier cabin but did not know Rafsky and Leach had sent flyers to other agencies.

"You think that was wise?" Kellerman asked.

Rafsky nodded. "I do. And it got us some results."

The brisk wind was blowing Kellerman's comb-over into his eyes, and he held it down with his gloved hand. "It's also going to get a lot of press," he said.

"It already has," Mack said. "The *Chicago Tribune* guy got here this morning. Annabelle Chapel's father is on his way."

"We might need to rethink our investigative structure on this," Kellerman said.

Joe's eyes went to Rafsky. Was he being replaced by someone more media-savvy? Or was Kellerman looking to take over?

"Now wait a minute," Mack said.

Kellerman glanced at Mack as if he were an intruder, then looked back at Rafsky. "It's the right move, as I'm sure you all can appreciate," he said. "Do you agree, Norm?"

Before Rafsky could answer, Mack stepped forward. "This has been our case —"

Kellerman's eyes cut to Mack. "Who are you again?"

"Detective Julian Mack," he said. "I've been working this case for six years, and I —"

Sheriff Leach quieted him with a raised hand. "Captain Kellerman," he said, "we're a small department, but we've made good progress in only a few weeks on a case no one thought would ever get this big. I would like —"

"No one cares what you would like, Sheriff," Kellerman said. "The bottom line here is you just can't handle this. You don't have the manpower, the resources, the —"

Rafsky started to speak, but Mack was first. "Maybe not," he said. "But we have one thing you don't. The *only* positively identified victim in this whole mess. All you got is that carving back there."

"Look," Kellerman hissed, "that carving is going to blow this wide open. This is a fucking national park. What are you going to do when they start finding carvings in other counties and other cities?"

"Captain —" Rafsky started.

"I don't care about other agencies," Mack said. "They can solve their own homicides with their own carvings. I have two goddamn carvings and one jawbone that belongs to Annabelle Chapel. And that makes the Chapel case our damn case!"

"Listen to me," Kellerman said through clenched teeth. "You can't make your case without the cooperation of other agencies."

"I don't need other agencies," Mack said. "I got Ken Snider in my jail. And you got no authority to take him anywhere."

"Mack, back off," Leach interrupted, taking a step between the two men.

But Kellerman already had a finger pointed in Mack's face. "You're going to screw this up," he said. "And it's going to blow apart any chance for any of us to put this asshole away."

"We caught him," Mack said. "He's ours."

Kellerman drew in a slow breath and held up his hands. "Okay, go ahead," he said. "Keep Chapel. Keep Snider. Get your goddamn headlines. But don't expect any more help from the state. No more searchers, no more forensics, no more investigators. No more nothing."

"Who needs you?" Mack shot back.

"Stop," Rafsky said suddenly. He drew a ragged breath that brought a small cough. "Captain, may we speak privately?"

Kellerman had a hard time pulling his glare from Mack, but he nodded and followed Rafsky to the top of a small hill a few yards away. Joe watched them as they stopped under a beech tree, talking quietly, heads down. Every few seconds, Kellerman would look over at Mack and Leach. Then his eyes found her. She knew Rafsky was talking about her. Knew it was good.

Kellerman tightened his shoulders, his eyes drifting to the sky. Rafsky said something else, gesturing back to Joe and the others. After a moment, they came back down the hill.

"Sheriff," Kellerman said with a stiff nod, and he walked off toward his car.

They all looked at Rafsky.

"I made a deal," he said.

"What kind?" Mack asked.

Rafsky coughed again, a deep, hacking rumble that made his eyes water. "I get to stay in Leelanau, in the same capacity I am now."

"Advisor," Mack said.

"Whatever." Rafsky sighed. "In any event, things can remain as they have been. In exchange, Kellerman asks one thing. That you transfer Ken Snider to Grand Traverse County jail in Traverse City."

"Why?" Mack asked.

"Security, mostly," Rafsky said. "It's bigger and better controlled. Pretty quick, the details of what Snider has done will come out, and people will get crazy. And I don't think you have the capability to fully protect him if someone wanted to take matters into their own hands."

"Well," Leach said, "he's being arraigned here tomorrow. We'll take him right from court down there. I'll give the sheriff there a call this afternoon."

"Good," Rafsky said.

Mack shook his head and wandered off toward the cruisers. Leach thanked Rafsky and followed Mack. Rafsky turned and walked back to the ranger, still waiting by the carved birch tree for further instructions. Rafsky spoke to him for about five minutes, then came back to Joe.

"I came down here with Kellerman," Rafsky said. "Would you mind dropping me back at the Riverside so I can get some rest? I want to be at the arraignment in the morning."

Joe nodded, and they started back to her cruiser. "Can I ask you something?" she asked.

Rafsky had a Kleenex to his nose and nodded.

"Were you going to get pulled off this?" she asked.

Rafsky took a moment to blow his nose. "You're very perceptive," he said.

"Why did he want to remove you?"

"Not photogenic enough for the TV cameras, I suppose."

"What did you say to get him to let you stay with us?" she asked.

"I told him you'd transfer Snider."

"It was more than that," she said.

He hesitated and sighed. "I promised him I would not let Mack blow it."

Joe was quiet. She knew it wasn't just Mack that Rafsky was talking about. It was all of them.

"That carving doesn't look anything like the Hunger Moon ones," she said. "You think it's a copycat?"

Rafsky shook his head slowly. "I don't know."

"If it's not, it shoots our theory to hell that Snider only killed in February," she said.

Rafsky pulled in a deep breath before he looked at her. "Sometimes these bastards change their MO," he said. "Their urges get stronger, or something happens that sets them off. Maybe that's what we're looking at here."

Joe was quiet, looking out at the trees and beyond to the dunes.

"What's the matter?" Rafsky asked.

"I don't know," she said softly. "This one isn't like the others. It's so fresh, so new. I keep seeing Snider up here just a few weeks ago and some girl —" She looked up at him. "This one happened while I was here in Echo Bay, and I just can't stop thinking about what she must have felt."

Rafsky hesitated. "Frye, we've got Snider. If he killed someone here, she was probably the last one. It's over."

35

Joe stepped from her cruiser and paused. The mothers were huddled outside the station entrance, facing a man with a micro-phone. Behind him was another man hold-ing a large camera. On the side of it, Joe could see the letters WLS — Chicago.

She ducked in through the back door. She was heading down the hall toward Leach's office when the scream came from the base-ment.

"Where's my fucking lawyer?"

Snider.

"Where is he, damn it!"

Joe bolted down the stairs. Holt was standing in front of Snider's cell, his expres-sion helpless. Snider spun to Joe. "I want my brother, and I want him fucking now!"

Snider's cell was strewn with newspapers. He snatched up one and waved it at her.

"What is this shit?" he demanded. "What the hell are you people trying to do to me?"

Joe motioned Holt to go get Leach, then moved closer, trying to figure out a way to question Snider without breaking any rules. "We'll get your lawyer," she said calmly.

"Fuck him!" Snider shouted. "Fuck him and all of you!"

Snider threw the paper at the bars, then sank to his bunk, shoulders heaving with angry pants. The paper landed front-page up. It was that morning's *Banner,* and on the front was a photo of one of the Febru-

ary carvings and Theo's headline: MYSTERI-
OUS CARVINGS LINKED TO GIRLS' MUR-
DERS.

Joe drew in an angry breath. *Damn it.*

"Joe?" Leach called. "Get up here, now."

When she got upstairs, everyone — Augie,
Holt, Mike, and Mack — was standing in a
semicircle in the hallway. Leach held up the
newspaper.

"Who leaked this?" he demanded. When
no one spoke, Leach's eyes went to Mack.

"You think I did it?" Mack asked.

"You've done it before," Leach said.

"I never leaked a goddamn thing," Mack
said.

"I swear, Mack, if I find out —"

"I ain't the one sleeping with the goddamn editor of the stinkin' rag," Mack said.

Leach's eyes swung to Augie.

Augie went pale, and drew in his lower
lip. Joe knew Augie had seen them making
copies of the flyers yesterday, and maybe
Holt told Augie about the carving he had
sawed off the Colliers' cabin. But Leach had
seemingly forgotten that Theo had developed her pictures of the carvings weeks ago.
Even without Augie's help, Theo would have
made the connection eventually. This was
partly her fault.

"Sir," Joe said.

Leach ignored her. "Augie, have you shared any information on this case with Theo?"

Augie hung his head and crossed his arms. "Yes," he said softly. "I didn't know the flyers were confidential."

"It clearly stated on them that they were for law enforcement eyes only," Leach said. "I know you know what that means."

Augie nodded.

"Sir," Joe said again.

"What?"

"Theo had pictures of the carvings weeks ago," she said. "He's the one who developed my film, remember?"

Leach stared at her.

"I had no idea of the meaning of them then," she said. "None of us did. I'm not surprised Theo put things together."

Leach gestured to the newspaper. "The carvings were our link to both Snider and the bones," he said.

"We still have that link," Joe said.

"Yes," Leach said. "But what do we do when copycat carvings start popping up all over the state? Send a team after every one?" Leach sighed in angry frustration. "It was the only thing we had to hold back from the public."

They were quiet. A phone was ringing

somewhere. From the basement, Joe could hear Snider hollering again.

"His damn lawyer even gave Theo a quote," Leach said, holding up the paper. "Listen to this: 'These carvings are just old Indian lore,' attorney Roland Trader said. 'The police are using them to scare people into believing my client is some kind of monster. This is all nonsense. The next thing you know, they'll be bringing in a psychic.' "

"He knows the carvings aren't nonsense," Joe said.

"That's not the point," Leach said. "The point is that Roland Trader has made us look like fools to the whole state."

"Maybe we are," Mike said.

Leach's eyes shot to Mike.

"Maybe we should've let this go a long time ago," Mike said. "Maybe we're in over our heads."

Leach started to fire something back but stopped himself, and Joe sensed that he agreed with Mike. Leach had seen the mothers and the Chicago reporter outside. She never thought she'd admit it, but now she was glad that Ken Snider was being transferred. Maybe some of these people would go home.

"Augie," Leach said, "you're on suspension."

Augie nodded and slipped away down the hall to his radio console. Leach looked at Joe. "We will talk later."

Snider let out another holler.

"Mike," Leach said, "shut that damn door to the basement, and then hook up with the search teams at the Collier cabin. Get me an update."

"It's supposed to snow tonight. I think the search is winding down," Mike said.

"Don't think, find out," Leach said through gritted teeth. He turned to Holt and Joe. "Holt, find Adderly and tell him I need to talk to him immediately. Joe, call Roland Trader at his hotel and tell him his brother is screaming for him."

"You want me to tell him we're transferring Snider tomorrow?" she asked.

Leach nodded. "Maybe that will get the weasel over here."

Joe went to her desk, shrugged out of her jacket, and called the Dunes Motel. Roland wasn't in his room, and she left a message with the clerk, telling her it was urgent. As she hung up, she heard Augie frantically telling someone he was not allowed in the rear of the station. She stepped into the hall.

A man. Tall and heavyset, in a camel cashmere coat. Variegated brown and gray hair. He was pulling off black leather gloves, searching for someone to talk to.

"Can I help you?" she asked.

"I'm Arthur Chapel. I want to see Detective Mack, please."

Before Joe could reply, Leach appeared. Chapel looked at Leach's badge, then to his face. "Are you in charge here?" Chapel asked.

Leach nodded, introduced himself, and motioned to his office. "We can talk in —"

Leach was interrupted by Snider, screaming again from the basement. It was muted now behind a door but clearly audible.

"Where the fuck is my lawyer?"

"Who is that?" Chapel asked.

"Let's just go to my —"

"Is that the man who killed my daughter?"

"Mr. Chapel —"

"I want to see him," Chapel said.

"You can't do that," Leach said. "It's —"

Chapel pushed past Leach and started toward the stairs. Joe stepped forward, blocking his way. "Please, Mr. Chapel," she said.

Chapel stared down at her. His eyes were swimming with everything from confusion to anger — and a dull pain. He shut them as he tried to gather his composure. Snider's voice drifted again through the hall, then fell silent.

"This is unbearable," Chapel said. He turned back to Leach. "I don't understand. My daughter's been missing for six years. Then I get a phone call from someone telling me a bone has been found and it's hers. Now I have reporters asking me what I know about other bones and other girls and carvings on trees, and I have to tell them that I know nothing."

"Mr. Chapel," Leach said, "we couldn't share those details with you. Not then."

"Share them now," Chapel said.

Leach motioned to his open door. Then he tipped his head, indicating that Joe should follow. Chapel sank into a chair, and Joe stayed back near the bookcase, hands clasped behind her back.

"The papers said you have bones," Chapel said. "How many?"

"Only a few," Leach said. "We have a jawbone, an arm bone, a rib, a pelvic bone, and —"

"Where were they found?"

"All but the last set — hand bones — were found in the general proximity of where we found your daughter's jawbone."

"But you haven't identified any of these other bones as belonging to Annabelle?" Chapel asked.

"There's no way to do that," Leach said.

"The best we could do is have an expert assemble what we have and try to determine which bones may be similar enough to suggest they could belong to one victim. But since we think we are dealing with girls of the same age and race, it's going to be near impossible."

Chapel was quiet for a moment. There was a fractured sense about him that made him hard to look at, and Joe shifted her gaze to the window behind Leach. The line between the gray lake and the sky was broken only by the lace of whitecaps curling toward the shore.

"You're telling me all I have to take home to my wife is one bone?" Chapel asked.

Leach hesitated. "Well, yes. All we can identify for sure is the jawbone, but I'm afraid you won't be able to . . ." Leach paused. "You won't be able to take possession of your daughter's remains for a long time."

"Why not?"

Leach cleared his throat. "We suspect there are as many as eleven victims, and we could be finding bones for months, even years. It would help us, sir, if we could keep Annabelle's jawbone for future comparison. Maybe at some point, our technology . . ."

Chapel lowered his head, and Leach fell

quiet. Joe looked out again at the lake, her ears picking up the soft rush of wind at the glass. She realized Snider was finally quiet.

"Do you know yet how she was killed?" Chapel asked softly.

Leach glanced at Joe, holding her eyes for a moment before he spoke to Chapel. "No, the suspect's not talking."

Chapel opened the newspaper he had in his hand and stared at the photograph of the carving for a moment before looking back up at Leach.

"I've never seen such incompetence," Chapel said. "A man kills for more than a decade unnoticed. Bodies are left in the woods, unfound. Bones are left piled in a lab somewhere because no one can put a name to them."

Leach rose slowly. "We are sorry, Mr. Chapel," he said.

Chapel shook his head. "You said there may be eleven victims. If that's true, which number was my daughter?"

"We believe number five," Leach said.

Chapel stared at Leach for a moment. He set the folded newspaper on the desk, turned, and left, leaving the door open.

Down in the basement, Snider started to yell again. Joe stayed where she was, listening to him and watching Leach. She remembered something Rafsky had said to her in Inkster. *It can start to get to you after a while. Especially if you've never worked something like this before.*

"Can I get you anything, sir?" she asked.

Leach looked up and tried a smile. He didn't quite make it.

"Did you eat today, sir?" she asked gently. He shook his head numbly.

"How about a ham on rye from The Blue-bird?"

He hesitated, then nodded. She left his office, closing the door behind her. She was walking through the front office when she stopped.

Roland Trader was standing at the counter. No suit today. Corduroy pants, a shirt and sweater under a dark green parka, the kind of coat city guys ordered from L. L. Bean catalogues hoping it made them look rustic. He set his briefcase on the counter with a thud.

"I want to see my client," he said. "And this time, not in that damn basement."

36

Roland circled the table, scanning the conference room for surveillance equipment.

"Roland," Ken said.

"Be quiet."

"If you're afraid of being bugged, why'd you ask for this room? Why not just talk in my cell?"

"I have my reasons."

"Damn it, Roland, talk to me!"

Roland grabbed a chair, pulled it close to Ken, and sat down. Ken stared at him, still angry about the newspaper stories, still waiting for answers.

Roland leaned on the table, head down, finding a small scar in the tabletop to focus on. He knew he couldn't let Ken look into his eyes when he told his story.

"I killed that Chapel girl," Roland whispered.

"Jesus," Ken said.

"It happened the weekend we came up to sell Dad's cabin."

"But you . . . you told me you went skiing."

Roland heard his brother let out a long breath, as if he were trying to remember.

"Wait," Ken said. "You . . . did you just *take* her from there?"

Roland shut his eyes as a cold burn started to rise in his face. The same kind of burn that hit his face when he raced down the slopes in a blinding rush of wind and snow.

The burn that stayed with him as he followed her, watched her laughing with her friends, waited until the one moment when she was alone outside. The same burn that built to an icy heat as he grabbed her, dragged her to his car, and threw her into the trunk.

"I didn't take her," Roland said, his head still down. "She went with me. She wanted to have sex, and the only place I could think of was the cabin."

Ken was quiet, but Roland was conscious of Ken's leg next to his, could even feel the nervous tremble in his muscles.

"When we got there," Roland said, "I couldn't do it at first. She got mad and started making fun of me."

"No," Ken said, standing. "I'm not hearing this again about how some girl called you names and —"

Roland grabbed Ken's sleeve and pulled him down. "Sit down and shut up," he hissed.

Ken sat down so hard the chair scraped across the floor.

"She told me she changed her mind and she wanted to go home," Roland said, head down again. He could hear Ken's breathing. It sounded just like Annabelle's had inside the cabin. Fast and thin at first. Then later, when she started screaming, her breaths changed to something terrified and primitive. Almost like a hungry animal in the night.

"I don't believe this," Ken said. "I don't understand it. What's wrong with you? How could you murder two girls?"

"I lost it," Roland said. "I was never good enough, never big enough, never . . . you know what Dad used to say, Kenny, you know what —"

Ken pushed away from the table again. Roland let him go this time, watching him out of the corner of his eye. The jerky panic in Ken's pacing seemed familiar. Almost like hers that day in the cabin. And Ken had that same caged look in the eyes now, like hers when he locked the door.

Suddenly, Ken was at his side. "You killed them all, didn't you? All the girls they're talking about in the newspapers."

Roland nodded slowly.

"Jesus Christ!" Ken said, spinning away from him.

"Kenny," Roland said.

Ken turned back to him, finger pointed. "I'm not going to prison for you," he said. "You're just going to have to —"

"Have to what, Ken?" Roland asked.

"You have to tell them what you did, tell

them I didn't —"

"Sit down."

"I am not —"

Roland stood up, grabbed the front of Ken's jumpsuit, and pushed him roughly onto the chair, almost tipping it. Ken batted at his hand, then doubled his own hand into a fist. Roland held up an open palm, taking a step back.

"Relax," he said. "And listen to me."

Ken clenched his jaw.

"If you say a word to the cops about what I've told you," Roland said, "I will tell them what happened to Dad."

"What?"

"I'll tell them exactly what you did."

Ken's eyes teared up. "You son of a bitch."

"I'm sorry, Kenny."

"We made a promise never to tell anyone," Ken whispered. "And you know I did it for you. You know that. He was going to leave you out there all night tied to that —"

"Don't talk about the hoist, Kenny."

Ken leaned on his knees, head down. For a long time, he didn't move. Then his face came up into the harsh fluorescent light, wet with tears. "I don't know what you want from me, Roland," Ken said. "I don't know anything anymore."

"I have a plan that will get both of us out

of everything," Roland said. "But I need your help to make it happen."

"Nothing will get you out of what you've done, Roland."

"This will. And if you can pull off your end, three hours later, you and I will both be safe in Canada."

"And then what? You go on killing up there?"

"It won't be your concern what I do after," Roland said. "You'll be free."

Ken stared at the floor, hands clasped between his knees.

"I need a decision now, Kenny," Roland said. "What we have to do needs to happen tonight."

"Why?"

"Tomorrow morning, you're being moved to Traverse City," Roland said. "And when that happens, there will be nothing I can do for you."

"You'd leave me here?" Ken asked. "Just go to Canada and leave me here?"

"I'd have to," Roland said.

Ken rubbed his face and looked up with a sigh. "What do I have to do?"

"Remember back in high school, Kenny?" Roland said. "Remember when you were in that play and how much you liked it? You were good at it, Kenny. Remember how good you were at it?"

Ken was quiet.

Roland leaned forward and cupped his brother's face firmly in his hands. He wiped one of Ken's tears with his thumb.

"It will be just like that, Kenny," Roland said gently. "Only this time, you're going to play the part of your lifetime."

Joe was filing folders when she heard the first thump from the conference room down the hall. She stepped out into the hall and listened. Another bump, then voices. Loud.

"You bastard!"

It was Ken Snider yelling. And Roland shouting, "Shut up!"

Joe moved closer, tipping an ear to the closed door. She heard the scrape of a chair, then Ken again.

"You let me sit in here for four days and you don't come to see me and you don't talk to me and you don't —"

"Shut up, Ken. They'll hear you."

A crash, as if a chair had been thrown. Leach appeared in his office doorway farther down the hall. "What the hell is going on?" he asked.

"They're fighting," Joe said.

Leach joined her outside the door, and they both listened for a moment longer.

"I'm telling you to shut up, Ken!"

"No! I want to tell them what really happened."

"They won't believe you, and they'll use it against you, and they'll hit you with every murder this side of Lansing once you tell what you know."

"Fuck you!" Ken yelled.

Then the sound of fist against flesh and thumps against the wall.

Leach pushed open the door. Ken was standing near the table, fists clenched. Roland was slumped on the floor, holding the back of his hand to a split lip.

"What's going on in here?" Leach demanded.

Ken just stared at him.

Leach reached down to help Roland to his feet. Roland shoved him away, drew a handkerchief from his pocket, and wiped his mouth.

"You're going to blow everything, Ken," he said.

Ken hesitated, then looked at Leach. "Get him out of here," he said. "He's not even a real lawyer. He flunked out."

"Don't do this," Roland said.

"Shut up," Ken said.

Joe looked from one to the other. There

were tears in Ken's eyes. Sheer fury in Roland's.

Ken looked around the cell in confusion, and finally his eyes found Leach. "I want to talk to you guys," he said. "Without him."

"You'll need new counsel first," Leach said.

"I'll sign a waiver," Ken said. "I'll sign anything you want me to. No more goddamn lawyers."

Leach looked to Roland. "I guess you're fired," he said.

Roland grabbed his briefcase and started to leave. Then he leaned back toward Ken one last time. "You're one stupid motherfucker."

Roland pushed past Joe, almost knocking her over as he stormed down the hall. When Leach was sure he was gone, he looked at Ken.

"What are we going to talk about, Mr. Snider?"

Ken was staring after Roland, his face sweaty. "Annabelle Chapel," he said.

37

Leach told Joe to call Adderly and tell him Ken Snider had fired Roland and wanted to make a statement. The first thing Adderly said was to make damn sure they had Snider's waiver signed before asking him one question.

Joe hung up and started back to the conference room, then stopped. She picked up the phone and dialed the Riverside, asking for Rafsky's room. When the clerk told Joe he had asked not to be disturbed, Joe told him to deliver the message that Rafsky was needed at the sheriff's office.

"Joe?" Leach called out.

She hurried back to the conference room. Mack was setting up a tape recorder. Mike was leaning over Snider, telling him where to sign the waiver. Snider signed it and pushed it away.

"Can I have a pop?" he asked.

Joe looked at Leach sitting across from Snider. He nodded, and she left, returning with a Pepsi from the office fridge. Snider held the can in his hands a long time before taking a drink.

A couple of minutes later, she heard Adderly's voice in the front office. He appeared in the room, face red from the quick trip down from the second floor. He set his briefcase on the table, picked up the waiver, and read it.

Snider took a long swig of his Pepsi, looking at the wall clock over the can.

Adderly handed the waiver to Mike with the direction to make copies. Then he motioned to Mack to turn on the tape recorder. The snap of the record key sounded like a hammer drawing back on a revolver. Mack stated the date, location, and purpose of the interview. Then he listed the names of those present. He asked Ken Snider to reaffirm that his statement was without counsel and of his own volition. Snider said it was.

"First question," Leach said. "Why'd you fire your brother?"

Snider brought up a hand to wipe his mouth. "Because the fucker wouldn't believe me when I told him the truth."

"So you've decided to tell us the truth, I take it?" Leach said.

"He told me I should just shut up, go to court, and let the evidence talk for me." Snider set the Pepsi can down with a thud. "Fuck that, man. I didn't kill anyone. If anyone's going to talk, it's going to be me. I'll talk to you. And I don't want anyone in between."

Leach glanced up at Adderly. "Okay, then, start talking."

Snider leaned forward and stared at the microphone. Everyone waited, and it was almost a full minute before Joe realized she had been holding her breath. She let it out to relax herself, but it didn't help much.

"Mr. Snider," Leach said, "would it be easier if we asked you some questions first?"

Snider shook his head quickly, drawing his hands into his lap. He was not handcuffed, and Joe could see him twisting his fingers under the table.

"We don't have all day, Mr. Snider," Leach said.

Snider's eyes flicked to the clock and down again. Finally, he took a breath and cleared his throat.

"There's someone else," Snider said.

Leach stiffened his shoulders. "You had an accomplice?"

Snider's head came up. "No, I didn't kill anybody. *He* killed Annabelle Chapel."

Mack stepped forward. "Who?"

"A buddy of mine," Snider said.

"What's his name?"

"I can't give you that 'til I get some guarantees."

"What kind of guarantees?" Mack asked.

"I want that immunity or whatever you call it."

"No way," Mack said.

Snider clenched his teeth. Under the table, Joe could see him digging the nails of one hand into the flesh of the other.

"This other guy did it all," Snider said. "I can testify against him."

Mack leaned over the table, in Snider's face. "Liar. You killed her yourself."

"I didn't!" Snider said. "I swear, I'll tell you how it happened. I'll tell you all of it. But I want something in return."

"All right, Mr. Snider," Adderly said. "Tell us how the Chapel girl was killed, and if we like what we hear, we'll talk about things like immunity."

Joe watched as Snider shut his eyes for a moment, as if he had to dig down inside himself and find the memory. Leach tapped the table.

"Mr. Snider."

"I had to come up here to sign some papers." Snider started slowly. "It was February 1969."

"The papers were for the sale of your father's property here?" Leach prompted.

Snider nodded. "Yeah. My buddy and me drove up in my truck. We didn't have much money, so we stayed at the cabin the night before. We were planning to stay the next night, too. That's why I asked Mrs. Collier if I could keep the key."

Joe caught Leach's eye before he looked back at Snider.

"Go on," Leach said.

"The next day, we drove up to Petoskey, and my buddy dropped me off at the title company, and he took off in the truck. He didn't come back until late afternoon, and I was pissed because I had to hang around in town all day."

"What did you do?" Mack asked.

Snider sighed. "It was cold. I sat in a bar, watched TV, and drank beer. By the time he picked me up, I was wasted."

"Go on," Leach said.

"So I get in the truck, and I see his clothes are bloody and he's kinda freaked out, you know? I ask him what happened, and he tells me he did something horrible and starts driving back to the cabin, talking to me but not making no sense."

Snider raised his hand to his face. Joe saw that it was scratched from where he had dug his nail into his palm. As Snider wiped spittle from his mouth, he left a faint smear of blood on his chin.

"Go on," Leach said.

"We get back to the cabin about five-thirty, and it's already dark, so I light up some kerosene lamps so I can see what the hell he's talking about, and that's when I see her."

"Annabelle Chapel?"

Snider nodded, eyes closed again. "She

was on the floor . . . naked . . . bloody." Snider finished in a hoarse whisper. "She didn't have a head."

For a few seconds, no one spoke. Finally, Leach cleared his throat. "Go on."

Snider wrapped his arms around himself. "I was scared," he said. "I asked him what he did with her head, and he told me he took it out in the woods and left it."

"He tell you why?"

"No," Snider said. "And I didn't ask any more questions. I was drunk, freaking out, you know? But I'm scared, and he's waving around this shotgun like he might shoot me with it."

"What do you know about the other girls?" Leach asked.

"Nothing," Snider said. "But afterwards, I got to thinking that maybe he killed Ronnie, too, because we both knew her from the bowling alley, and I never believed she just left. But no way was I going to ask him nothing."

"And you never told anyone this?" Leach asked.

"Hell no," Snider said. "It happened in my cabin. It was my truck, and it had blood in it. I was up here that day. No one was going believe I didn't help kill that girl."

The room was silent except for the tick of

the clock on the wall.

"Well, do we have a deal?" Snider asked, his eyes darting among them. "If I give you his name, do we have a deal?"

Mack walked away from Snider, then turned back. "You're full of shit. You could give us any name. You could give us some dead guy who can't tell his side of the story."

For the first time during the interview, Snider met Mack's hard stare. "He's alive," Snider said. "And you won't have any trouble finding him."

"Then give us something to convince us you're telling the truth," Leach said. "Give us something we don't already know."

Snider looked across the table at Leach. "He's Indian."

Leach tried to keep his face expressionless, but his eyes drifted up to Joe.

"Gordon, do you have today's paper?" Leach asked Adderly.

Adderly reached into his briefcase and pulled out the *Echo Bay Banner.* Leach set it on the table in front of Ken. "Have you seen this before?" Leach asked, pointing to the photograph of the carving.

Ken stared at it and nodded. "Yeah, it's an Indian symbol."

"He saw the paper this morning, Sheriff," Joe said.

"Yeah, but there's a carving just like this on the back of the cabin," Snider said quickly. "That part wasn't in the paper. He carved it after he killed her."

Joe found Leach's eyes. The carving on the Collier cabin was the one thing they had been able to keep out of the press.

"What about the place where he left the head?" Joe asked. "Did he carve something there, too?"

Snider shook his head. "I don't know about that."

The room was quiet, then Adderly stood up suddenly. "I don't like this," he muttered. He tossed his pad and pen into his briefcase. "It's not enough."

Snider's eyes swung up to him. "I know where she is," he said.

Leach leaned in. "What do you mean?"

"Annabelle Chapel. I know where the rest of her is," Snider said. "I'll show you and you'll see I'm telling the truth."

"How do you know?" Leach asked.

"He wanted to get rid of the rest of her body," Snider said, "so we took her and drove into the woods. We buried her."

Leach leaned in. "You're lying. We don't believe any of the girls were buried."

Snider clenched his teeth. "I don't know what he did with the others," he hissed.

"But I'm telling you we buried Annabelle Chapel, and I can show you where."

"Where?" Mack asked.

Snider was shaking his head. "You give me a deal, and I'll take you to that girl's bones. And I'll give you the name of the guy who killed her."

Mack started to say something, but Leach silenced him with a hand. "Just tell us where she is," Leach said to Snider. "And if we find her remains —"

Snider slumped back in his chair. "You'd never find the place. It was six years ago, man. I have to try and find it."

Mack turned away in disgust, muttering something Joe couldn't hear. She watched Adderly, who was staring at Snider with contempt.

Leach stood up. "Let's take this outside," he said.

They left Snider sitting at the table, Holt guarding him. Joe closed the door, and they huddled together down the hall.

"Talk to me, Cliff," Adderly said.

Leach sighed. "Part of me believes him. He looked sick when he talked about seeing no head, and that can't be faked. I just don't know how much to believe."

Adderly pursed his lips. "What do you make of this Indian friend angle?"

"Snider had books about Indians when he was a kid," Joe said, "so he could have known about the carvings from that."

"Or he could be telling the truth," Mack said. "The bottom line is, we have nothing to lose here. If he's telling the truth, we get the killer's name and the evidence to convict him before we ever arrest the sucker. If we don't have the bones when that happens, he'll try to use them as a bargaining tool."

They were all quiet for a moment.

"So, what do we do?" Adderly said.

"I say we take him out there now," Mack said.

"No," Leach said. "There's something wrong with all of this, and I can't put my finger on it, but —"

"He's being transferred to Traverse City tomorrow," Mack said quickly. "If we try to take him anywhere after that, the state will stick its nose in, and we'll lose every opportunity we have to nail this bastard."

Leach was quiet, glancing back at the conference room door. Then his eyes came back to Joe.

"What do you think?" he asked.

Joe was surprised that he asked, but she had an opinion. For the first time since she'd been here, she agreed with Mack.

"I don't see what we have to lose, either,"

she said. "He'll be shackled and escorted. He hasn't made any calls since he's been here, so there's little chance this accomplice knows that Snider is going to show us anything."

"What about Roland?" Leach asked.

"Roland was just a kid when Snider killed Ronnie," Mack said. "I don't think he knew about that then, and I don't think he wants anything to do with his brother now."

Still, Leach was quiet.

"Look," Mack said. "We've already had a slew of leaks on this case. If it gets out that we had a chance to get Annabelle Chapel's remains and we didn't take it, Arthur Chapel will use every connection and all his money to make us look incompetent. This man has the power to destroy us."

Joe was looking at Leach. Mack was right. A man like Chapel would make someone pay, starting with a recall of Leach.

"Sheriff," she said, "there's the other mothers to think about, too. If we find this accomplice, maybe he can give us names, or at least tell us how many for sure. This could be the first step in bringing all the girls home."

Mack pushed forward. "This sort of thing is done all the time," he said. "You know that, Sheriff. It's routine procedure."

"Not in our department," Leach said quietly.

"Sheriff," Mack said, "it's a simple walk in the woods."

Leach looked at Joe again and let out a long breath. "Okay. But we do this quietly and quickly. And I want someone to keep an eye on Roland Trader. If he so much as makes a move to leave town tonight, I want to know about it. He's still Snider's brother and I just don't trust him."

Adderly gave a nod, and he and Mack headed back to the interview room. Leach motioned to Joe to follow him to the front office. Mike was just coming through the front door, carrying a bag from The Bluebird.

"Mike," Leach said, "I want you to dress up Snider for some time outside and shackle him from head to toe. Then grab your winter gear and pull a cruiser with a cage up to the back door and stick him in it."

"We moving him to Traverse City now?" Mike asked.

Leach quickly outlined the plan for Mike and turned back to Joe. "Joe, I want you and Holt to set yourselves up outside the Dunes Motel to watch Roland Trader."

"I want to go with you," Joe said.

Leach shook his head. "Taking a prisoner

out of the station is never completely safe. Mike is more experienced."

"But I've earned the right to go," Joe said.

Leach drew back quickly, surprised at her tone. Joe thought about apologizing, even begging, but she didn't do either. For a few seconds, no one said anything.

Mike stepped forward. "Sir, I'll go with Holt. Let Joe go with you. She *has* earned it."

Leach looked at her, but then gave a slow nod. "All right. Get your gear."

She hurried to get her winter parka and boots. As she was pulling them on, she heard the clink of chains as they led Snider out. She was zipping the parka as she headed quickly down the hall to the back door. She walked right into Rafsky. He caught her shoulders.

"I got your message. What the hell are you guys doing?" he asked.

"He's taking us to Annabelle's remains," she said.

"In exchange for what?" Rafsky said.

She strained to look over Rafsky's shoulder to make sure they weren't going to leave her. Snider was in the cruiser. Mack was getting in on the driver's side.

"I don't have time to explain it," she said.

"No," he said. "I won't allow this."

"I don't think you have the authority to stop us," she said, moving around him.

He grabbed the sleeve of her parka and forced her to turn back. "I don't want you to go," he said.

"Me or us?" she asked.

Rafsky hesitated only a second. "You."

Joe held his eyes. "It's my job," she said.

Rafsky let go of her, and for a moment, neither of them moved. Then she hurried to catch up with the others. Rafsky grabbed a parka and followed.

38

More snow was coming. Everyone knew it. There was an ozone bite in the air, and the gray clouds that had been on a slow march across the lake since dawn now lay motionless, waiting.

They were twenty miles south of town, on a narrow county road surrounded by trees. The leading cruiser's taillights came on, and they stopped. Joe and Rafsky were following in a second cruiser, Joe driving. She could see Ken Snider's head in the caged backseat of the car ahead.

She keyed the radio. "What's the holdup?" she asked.

Leach's voice came back to her from the

front cruiser. "He's not sure of the direction."

Joe let out a tense sigh.

"Where are we?" Rafsky asked.

"South end of Lake Leelanau," Joe said. "Maybe down by Pere Marquette State Forest. I'm not sure. Not a lot of roads down here, just hiking trails."

Rafsky shook his head. "I don't like this," he said quietly.

It started to snow. Big lacy flakes drifting down in the still air. When Joe switched on the wipers, the taillights ahead had gone off. They were moving again.

The radio crackled to life. It was Mike reporting in to Leach from his post with Holt outside the Dunes Motel. The motel owner had said Roland had put some duffle bags in his trunk earlier but hadn't emerged since, and his black sedan was still parked right outside his door. He was paid up for the week.

"If he even gets in that car, let me know," Leach said, and signed off.

The road was moving steadily uphill. Joe could feel the tires straining for traction.

Suddenly, the cruiser ahead braked hard and swung left into the trees. Joe followed, slowing to a crawl on the narrow road. She could almost hear Rafsky grinding his teeth in agitation.

They were entering a stand of young pines that surrounded them like a pressing crowd. The branches were already wearing epaulettes of fresh snow. Then the lead cruiser stopped.

The radio sputtered. "This is as far as we can go," Leach said. "He says we have to walk from here."

Joe got out of the cruiser, zipping her parka. Rafsky zipped his, too, and turned up the collar.

The soft hiss of the falling snow was broken by the thud of the car door closing in front of them. Leach and Mack had gotten out of the front. Mack yanked open the back door.

Snider slid out. He was wearing a sheriff's parka over his jail jumpsuit. He stood there for a moment, his eyes scanning the pine trees. Mack grabbed a fistful of Snider's jacket, but the guy wasn't going anywhere. The chains strung around him allowed him to walk at no more than a shuffle and gave him just enough freedom to wipe his face if he bent over.

"Which way?" Leach asked him.

Snider was still looking around. As Joe approached, she could see something she read as fear in Snider's eyes. Despite the cold, there was a sheen of sweat on his forehead.

"Up there," Snider said, nodding toward a tree-dense hill.

"Let's go," Mack said, giving him a slight shove.

Leach and Mack led the way, with Snider between them. Joe and Rafsky trailed, Joe pulling on her leather gloves as they walked. The hill was a steady climb upward, and the gathering snow made for tough going, even though she was wearing boots. She looked to Rafsky in his lace-up shoes. His face still wore the red tint of a low fever.

A soft, muffled *crack.*

Joe's eyes shot up, but then she relaxed as she recognized the distant echo of a hunter's rifle. She knew the woods were filled with hunters this time of year, but there was no hunting allowed in the state forest. She glanced at Rafsky and guessed he was thinking the same thing.

She looked up at the tin-colored clouds and then at her watch. Near four. They had only about an hour of good light left.

They walked on, the only sound the *chink* of Snider's shackles. Then, suddenly, she picked up a second sound, a faint rushing. It grew louder as they crested the hill.

A stream, dotted with rocks. It led back to a rocky, snow-dusted bluff and a waterfall.

Maybe six feet high, the water crystal clear.

"This is it," Snider said.

"Where'd you bury her?" Mack asked.

Snider tried to make a motion, but he couldn't lift his hands high enough and finally just tilted his head toward the water. "Behind the waterfall," he said. "There's a cave back there. The ground was too hard, so we covered her up with some rocks."

Leach's face darkened with suspicion. Joe and Rafsky came up behind them. "Mack, you go look," Leach said.

Mack pulled out his flashlight and stepped into the water, spreading his arms to keep his balance as he made his way across. On her radio, Joe heard Mike check in. Roland hadn't moved from his motel, and Mike said he could see the lights and TV on inside. Joe gave Mike a quick ten-four and checked off, her eyes drifting to the snowcapped hill, the dusted trees, and the waterfall. The awful incongruity of it hit her: such a beautiful place for such a gruesome tomb.

Shick-shuck. BOOM!

Joe's eyes lasered to the waterfall, the explosion of the gunshot deafening her ears.

A man on the opposite bank. Holding a long gun. Mack was in the water. Leach was —

Shick-shuck. BOOM!

Leach fell.

Joe ducked and stumbled, grabbing for her weapon, her gloves stiff, her bulky parka covering her holster. She couldn't get to her gun.

Shick-shuck. BOOM!

A blur of brown. Rafsky jerking to his left, yelling something, then falling to the ground.

She dropped to her knees, ripping off her gloves and wrenching her revolver free. She crawled, desperate to find cover. But there was nothing but Rafsky's body.

Quiet.

Rushing water.

Then a rustle of wet leaves.

A knee dropped hard into her back, knocking her flat to the ground, pushing the air from her lungs. He stayed on her, using his weight to keep her still as he ripped her gun from her hand.

She blinked, the snow in her face, trying to slow her heart and bring things into focus. But she saw only the snow and Rafsky's brown shoes. She shut her eyes, fighting tears and the thunder of her heart.

Suddenly, the pressure on her back lifted. With a jerk on her jacket, he flipped her over onto her back.

Roland Trader was kneeling above her, the

barrel of his shotgun pointed at her head. His face was slick with sweat.

Behind him, she could see Ken Snider rising slowly to his feet. Not wounded but wet and scared.

Shick-shuck.

Her eyes shot back to Roland.

"Please don't," she said.

He stood up slowly and lowered the shotgun barrel until it was pressing gently against her lips.

"Kenny," Roland said. "Go get the hoist from the cave."

Ken didn't move.

Roland turned sharply. "Kenny!"

"What?"

"Go get the fucking hoist."

Joe heard the clanking of chains as Ken shuffled away. Snow was falling onto her face, and she blinked against it, keeping her eyes on Roland. He smiled and started to circle her slowly, teasing her face with the gun barrel.

More clanking as Ken came back, hunched over as he dragged the hoist closer. He let it fall next to her head. She looked at it. Steel. A jangle of ropes. And pulleys.

She closed her eyes, sick, breathless.

Roland reached down to grab the hoist.

"Roland," Ken said. "What are you do-ing?"

"Shut up."

Roland dropped to his knees and set the shotgun on the ground next to him. He started to unlace her boot. She looked back to Ken, hunched in the falling snow, his shackled hands balled into fists.

Roland leaned over her to untie her other boot, his hands busy, the shotgun lying near her leg. She knew it was her only chance.

She jerked her foot free and kicked him in the face. He tumbled backward, and she tried to scramble up, but his fist came down hard against her temple, slamming her head to the ground.

"Don't you hit me!" Roland yelled, punch-ing her again in the mouth. "Don't you ever fucking hit me!"

He shoved her back to the ground, a knee on her belly. Her head was spinning, a new wave of nausea rising up inside her.

"Kenny!" he said. "Get a belt from one of those dead cops and tie up her hands."

Joe tasted blood. She could feel Roland's hands on her skin as he tied her ankles to the hoist. She fought to clear her head, and when she did, she saw Ken kneeling above her. Felt him now, as he wound the leather belt around her hands, cinching it awkwardly with shaking fingers.

"Ken," she whispered.

He looked at her.

"Help me," she mouthed.

Roland suddenly stood up and grabbed the center bar of the hoist with one hand and the shotgun with the other. He trudged toward the nearest tree, dragging Joe behind him. The ground was cold and sharp, scraping against her back.

"Roland!" Ken said. "Roland! What the fuck are you doing?"

Roland dropped the hoist and spun toward his brother. "Shut the fuck up!"

Joe couldn't see Ken, but the *chink* of his chains grew louder. Near her head.

"You're sick!" Ken yelled. "You're a fucking animal! What the hell is wrong with you?"

Roland started dragging Joe again, jerking her body toward the tree with angry yanks. Then Ken was there, trying to grab Roland with his shackled hands.

"No more, no more!" Ken hissed.

Roland shoved him away. Ken stumbled, managed to find his footing, and came right back at Roland.

"I won't —"

BOOM!

Ken collapsed to the ground near Joe's

shoulder. Moaning. Gasping. Hands trembling. Then the clinking of his chains stopped, leaving nothing in the air but the bite of cordite and the drifting concussion of the explosion.

A splatter of something warm and wet on her face. She clenched her teeth against a scream as she realized it was Ken's blood. In the drifting flakes of white, Roland came back into focus.

He was standing above her but looking at Ken, a look of disbelief on his sweating face.

His gaze came back to her. Eyes glistening with tears but still empty of anything human.

The moment was frozen. Every image crystal clear, every sound amplified. The hiss of the falling snow. The hot burn of her tears. The hammering of her heart. The black hole of the gun barrel staring back at her.

She closed her eyes.

Then . . .

Nothing.

She opened her eyes.

He had dropped to one knee beside her. He set the shotgun on the ground and roughly unzipped her jacket, throwing it open. With a slow drawing of breath, he slipped a hunting knife from his belt and grabbed the collar of her uniform shirt.

He sliced it open.

39

Cold. Something cold on her face.

Warm. Something warm on her face.

She opened her eyes. Nothing but blackness.

Dizziness. A sickening swirl in her head and her stomach.

Cold . . . warm.

But why couldn't she bring up her hands to feel her face?

Why couldn't she see anything?

Where was she?

Then . . . the pain. It began in her gut, a dull, long ache along her ribs streaming up to her breasts.

Cold. Warm. On her face. Wet.

She tried to move her lips. More pain. But then a trickle of something on her tongue.

Blood.

Cold. Warm. Wet.

Snow. Blood. On her face. In her mouth. The taste of her own blood on her swollen tongue.

Things were coming back, jagged flares of images. A black darting shadow. A white flash of muzzle fire. A collapsing brown body. And sounds. Water. A scream. *Shick-shuck. BOOM!*

And . . .

Oh, God. She could remember the rest. The cold of the barrel on her skin. The knife. His face above her.

Tears. She couldn't stop them. Falling, falling. Hot tears streaming over her forehead.

Wait . . . wait.

Her eyes were open, but she could see nothing. The swirl in her head, the sickening feel. She was hanging. She tried to move her legs. She was tied by her feet, hanging upside down.

Her arms were dangling over her head. Her hands were tied with something. God, the pain in her stomach and ribs. And the cold . . . she was so cold, and the air was so piercing it was like her insides were turning to ice. And then it came to her. She was naked.

But she was alive.

How long had she been out? She strained her ears, but it was so quiet. Just the soft sound of rushing water. Her head was pounding, but it was coming back now, what had happened, the ambush and . . .

"Rafsky."

Her mouth hurt. She tried again.

"Rafsky!"

Her voice echoed back to her, small and weak. "Rafsky! Sheriff?"

Nothing but the awful silence.

She began to shiver. How long had she been hanging like this? It was night, no moon, no stars. Just the suffocating blackness. She had to do something. Had to get down somehow before she froze to death here.

Move! Move! Do something!

She tried to move her hands again and then remembered he had used a belt to bind them. Twisting against the wet leather, she was able to slip one hand free. Her trembling fingers touched cold metal. The buckle. Slowly, she worked the end of the belt free and uncinched it. The belt fell away with a soft thud.

She clasped her icy hands together for a moment. Her struggle had left her swinging gently. She closed her eyes against the rising nausea of the motion and tried to take a deep breath.

A sharp pain tore across her abdomen. Slowly, she brought up one hand to its source. There was a gash just below her ribs. She was bleeding.

Red dots swam against her closed eyes. She couldn't feel her legs anymore. But she could remember how he had tied her. If she could somehow pull herself up using the hoist . . .

But every move brought another wave of nausea. And she knew instinctively that the cut on her stomach had rendered her muscles too weak.

The sickening swaying went on. The rope creaked against the tree limb in the blackness above.

Tears again. Hot tears running up into her wet hair.

No! No! I am not going to die! Not like they did!

The swaying . . . maybe . . .

Maybe if she could swing enough, she could grab something to pull herself up. She began to move her body, trying to get some momentum going. The motion made her sick, but she fought it back. After a while, she was swinging freely. She flailed her arms in the dark, but there was nothing to grab. She twisted, trying to change the direction of the swinging.

The gash on her stomach was so painful she could barely pull in a breath. Then, suddenly, her arm hit something hard. Then again on the downside of the motion. She tried frantically to catch it.

She twisted again, moving her arms. Her

palm hit, and she grabbed. The tree. She bounced against the rough bark but finally managed to wrap her arms around the trunk.

Her cold hands clawed at the bark, finding a knob. She pulled herself up, wincing, her other hand desperate for something to grab onto. Then a branch, wet with snow.

Gritting her teeth against the pain, she slowly pulled herself up another foot.

Another knob, another larger branch. Up to a limb. She had to stop, exhausted, but she knew she couldn't last much longer. With trembling arms, she climbed higher and could feel the pressure loosening on her legs as the rope holding the hoist grew slacker.

One last effort, one last wave of pain.

She was on the limb now. She rested her forehead against the rough bark, her arms wrapped tightly around the trunk. When she could pull in a breath, she slowly reached down to her right ankle. Rope . . . wet, tight.

She was shivering so hard. And her fingers were burning with cold. And she couldn't see anything. But she picked away at the rope until finally it began to loosen.

One leg swung free, the weight of the hoist almost pulling her off the limb. She steadied herself and worked on the other ankle.

Then, finally, the thing fell away with a thud. She clung to the limb, gulping in icy air.

How far up was she? The hoist hadn't fallen very far from the sound it made. He had hung the others up at least thirty feet, and she didn't know how she would take a fall of that distance, but she had no choice. She had to jump.

She took a breath and pushed off the limb into the black.

The snow and leaves broke her short fall, but still, she lay there for a long time, unable to pull in one full breath. The cold was numbing. She had to move, had to get help.

She began to crawl.

Her hands, her knees, everything beyond numb now. She felt herself drifting, her mind becoming fogged, and she had a fleeting memory, something she'd read in a book a long time ago, that a death by freezing was a gentle thing.

Her hand hit something soft in the darkness.

Cloth. A brush of fur. A solid form beneath. She drew back.

A body. But whose?

Don't think. Move . . .

She reached out, patting the form, searching. Flashlight . . . they all wore them on their utility belts. She reached under the parka.

Her fingers found first the cold metal of a revolver, then the flashlight. She jerked back from the body and clicked it on.

The beam caught the shimmer of snowflakes and the black trunks of the far trees. Then, about fifteen feet away near the water, a dark mound half covered in white. The face was turned toward her. Eyes open.

Mack.

She swung the light to the mound closest to her. Another brown parka. A stain of red in the snow. Cold blue hands outstretched. She couldn't see the face, but she knew it was Leach.

Rafsky . . .

She raked the darkness with the beam. But there was nothing but the snow. Tears burned her eyes.

No time now. She had to live.

Still on her knees, she slowly ran the beam over the ground looking for her clothes. If they were still here, they were long ago buried by the snow. She brought the beam back to Leach.

Setting the flashlight in the snow, she gripped his parka and rolled him over. A sob caught in her throat, but she forced herself to keep her hands moving. It took

her a while to get his parka off. It was shredded with buckshot and heavy with blood,
but she pulled it onto her arms. Once she
had it zipped, she moved on to take his
pants, his boots, and his gloves.

She was dizzy with exhaustion and pain
by the time she staggered to her feet. It was
only then that she saw the form lying over
by the stream, half hidden behind a rock.

She stumbled to it.

Rafsky lay on his side, a red stain spread
beneath his body. She knelt down beside
him, dropping the flashlight to the ground
and turning him gently to his back. He was
lifeless, the brown deputy's jacket ripped
apart with buckshot.

Hot, quick tears filled her eyes. A sob
escaped her, and she clasped a trembling
glove over her mouth, the pain inside her
drawing her forward over his body. She
clutched the sleeve of his jacket in her hand.

She heard a small, raspy breath.

It took a second to understand it, and she
grabbed the flashlight and pointed it at his
face. Blue and still, and she wasn't sure now
that she had really heard anything.

She ripped off a glove and worked her
hand inside the collar of his jacket and felt
for a pulse. It was there, a faint, dying flut-
ter under her fingertips.

She grabbed the radio from his belt and keyed it. Her voice was iced over. Hoarse.

"Help," she said. "I need help."

Static.

She pulled Rafsky onto her knees, cradling his head and brushing the snow from his face. She keyed the radio again.

"Help us, please."

A voice broke through the darkness. "Radio caller, this is state dispatch. Please identity yourself."

She choked back a sob and keyed the mike again. "Frye. Deputy Frye. Leelanau Sheriff . . . I need help now. Officers down."

She still couldn't get warm. That was the first thing that came to her as she struggled up from the blackness. Then . . . sounds.

A siren cried from somewhere very close. Ambulance, she was in an ambulance, and the siren was right outside, on the roof. And lights . . . she tried to open her eyes, and soft white lights bounced in her vision, making her dizzier.

When had she blacked out? The last thing she could remember was calling in on the radio. There was nothing after that.

She became aware of someone close. A man hunched over, his hands working furiously on opening a small white package. The ripping of the paper sounded like gunfire. Then she felt something pressing on her abdomen and a jab of pain.

"I'm cold," she whispered.

"Sorry," the man said. "I put a heated blanket under you."

She reached up to grab something, unsure of what she was looking for. A second hand covered hers. She tried to draw away, but he didn't let her.

"Deputy Frye." A voice somewhere behind her. Warm voice.

She tried to move her head to see it but couldn't.

"Deputy Frye, I'm Trooper Washburn. Can you talk to me?"

"What?"

"I need a statement."

She tried to concentrate and bring his face into focus, but he was somewhere above her head, and she couldn't see him. She wanted to see him.

"Who did this?" he asked.

"Roland Trader," she whispered. "Shotgun. Four shots. He was . . . he was behind the waterfall. I was looking at . . ."

Her arm suddenly lit up with a fluid fire, and she groaned, feeling whatever the EMT had given her surge through her veins.

"Did anyone return fire?" the trooper asked.

"No."

"He shot Ken Snider, too?"

She was still feeling the shot, and she gritted her teeth, managing a nod.

"Why?"

"He . . . he tried to help me . . ."

She heard his voice but didn't understand the question, a thick fog settling behind her eyes. The next thing she knew, the ambulance had stopped bumping and was moving more smoothly. The same voice drifted back, calm and gentle but still coming from somewhere she could not see. "Deputy Frye."

"Yes . . ."

"Why were you wearing Sheriff Leach's clothes?"

"He . . . he took mine. Roland . . . Roland Trader . . ."

Even in her pain, she didn't want to finish the sentence. She didn't want to say it out loud, and she shut her eyes against the lights, wishing he would just ask her so she could nod. But she heard nothing but the painful cry of the siren.

"He raped me," she said.

The siren seemed to grow louder, and somewhere in her head, she recognized the change in its tone. No longer pouring into the hollow black night and disappearing but ricocheting off buildings and concrete.

A crackle of static close by, coming from the trooper's radio. "Three dead on the scene. Two on their way to the hospital."

"Deputy Frye?"

She shut her eyes.

"Did you see a vehicle, Deputy Frye? Did he say anything to you to tell us where he might be going? Deputy Frye —"

She slipped into an icy darkness, and the warm voice was gone.

40

She had been drifting in and out of sleep all morning, her mind a fog of images and sensations. She knew some of it was the result of the sedatives. But she was awake and aware enough to realize what was real.

The hot tingle of her frostbitten fingers. The ache of the stitches in her belly. The pull of the IV in her vein. The bleach yellow of the November sunlight coming through the window that matched the bleach smell of her hospital room.

Some things didn't feel real. She was try-ing not to remember those things, at least for the moment. But she was hearing the radio voices that came after. *Three dead on the scene. Two on their way to the hospital.*

"You're awake."

She slowly turned her head on the pillow. Brad. She tried to smile but couldn't. Her lip was too swollen.

He came over to the bed. "I was out talking to the doctor," he said, as if apologizing for his absence.

She nodded. Much of last night, when they had brought her in, was fuzzy. But she could remember Brad being there. Or, rather, the bright red of his sweater, because the sedative was taking effect by the time he got there. He was still wearing the red sweater. He looked tired and worried.

She raised her right hand and made a circling motion, then pointed upward.

"The bed? You want it raised?" Brad asked.

She nodded and closed her eyes, listening to the whirring sound. Her head was pounding. When she opened her eyes, Brad was staring at her.

"I look that bad?" she whispered.

When he didn't even try to smile, she closed her eyes again. The dizziness took a long time to stop. When she opened her eyes, Brad was at the window, staring out.

"Do you know if Rafsky made it?" she asked.

He turned and gave her a strange glance that melted quickly to another silent apology. "I don't know," he said.

The wan sunlight from the window highlighted the lines around his eyes and sharpened the quivering at the corner of his lips.

Joe closed her eyes. A moment from last night drifted back. A hard exam table. The feel of the doctor's gloves on her skin. The touch of the cold steel instrument.

She opened her eyes to see Brad still staring at her. "They told you what happened to me?" she asked.

He nodded, his eyes closing for a second, then snapping open, as if he realized it was the wrong thing to do. He came back to the bed and took her hand. She thought he might lift her fingers to his lips and kiss them, but he didn't. Just held her hand in his, his eyes searching for somewhere to settle besides her face.

There was a tap on the door, and a man came in. It took her a second to recognize him. Kellerman, Rafsky's boss.

He came a few steps into the room and stopped. "The doctor said you could talk." He looked at Brad. "Would you excuse us?"

Brad started to protest, but Joe raised a

hand. "It's okay, Brad. Why don't you get a coffee for a few minutes."

"Joe, I —"

"I'm okay," she whispered.

Brad moved away from her, his eyes focused on Kellerman before he slipped from the room. Kellerman waited until the door eased shut before he came closer to the bed. Joe tried to sit a little higher, but it was hard with the IV. Kellerman waited until she was comfortable.

"How are you feeling?" he asked.

There was some compassion in his voice, but his eyes betrayed his other feelings — blame and anger.

"I'm okay," she said. "Can you tell me about Detective Rafsky?"

"He's out of surgery," Kellerman said. "But he lost a lot of blood. The doctors say it's fifty-fifty for him. If he does make it, he'll have little use of his right arm."

Joe's eyes brimmed with tears, and she turned her head toward the window. "Have you caught Roland Trader?" she asked.

"No," Kellerman said.

She looked back to him, hearing something in that word that told her there was more. And she realized it had been almost eighteen hours since the ambush. "Tell me what happened," she said.

Kellerman pursed his lips. "After you told us he was the shooter, we put out an APB on him," he said in a flat voice. "We didn't know until forty minutes later, when we finally got in touch with your department, that his sedan was still sitting outside his motel. Evidently, your deputies didn't see him leave."

"So what did he drive to the woods?" Joe asked.

"It took us another hour to find out he rented a second vehicle, a green Jeep," Kellerman said. "We got a second APB out on that, and around eleven-thirty, one of your deputies located the Jeep over by Bass Lake hidden in some brush."

"The Collier cabin," Joe said.

Kellerman gave her a moment, then went on. "We immediately checked out the cabin. The Colliers' vehicle was gone, and we got no answer at the door, so we went in."

"Oh, no," Joe whispered.

"All three Colliers were dead."

Joe closed her eyes, letting the tears come. Kellerman handed her the box of Kleenex off the table and kept talking, his voice a soft drone in her ears.

"He slashed their throats. Didn't look like he raped the girl, though. It appeared he was in too big a hurry. He took canned

441

food, blankets, things like that. By the time we got a third APB out on the Collier vehicle, he was probably already in Canada."

Joe was quiet for a moment, then looked at him. "Were Annabelle Chapel's bones in the cave?"

Kellerman shook his head, drawing a small notebook from his pocket. "I'm sorry to do this to you now," he said. "But I have to ask you some questions."

"I talked to a trooper last night," she said, "in the ambulance."

"I know. But your information was rather disjointed."

She pulled the sheet a little higher and crushed the edge in her hand. The numbness in her fingers was wearing off. She could feel the threads of the sheet.

"We have the tape of your interview with Ken Snider before you left the station," Kellerman said. "But we need to know if he said anything else in the cruiser."

"I don't know. I rode with Rafsky."

"Did Snider say anything after the officers were shot?"

"He tried to help me," Joe said. "That's why Roland shot him. I don't think Ken Snider killed any of the girls. I think everything he told us in the interview room was the truth except the part about the Indian friend. I think Roland Trader killed those girls."

Kellerman just shook his head. "All right," he said. "Let's go over this one more time. Tell me exactly what happened during the ambush."

Joe closed her eyes to gather her thoughts. It was important that she make things as clear as her memory would allow. Any one detail could help them find Roland Trader. She began to speak, slowly and clearly, faltering only a few times.

When she was finished, Kellerman set his pen down. He poured a cup of water from a plastic pitcher. He held the cup out to her, and she shook her head. He drank it himself.

"I know you were asked this last night, but now think hard. Did Roland Trader say anything to you that might help us know if he went anywhere but Canada?" Kellerman asked.

She thought for a moment. "No," she said.

"Did he say anything about the other victims?"

Again, she had to think. "No."

Kellerman's next question didn't come immediately, and she glanced at him, seeing in his face that same discomfort she had seen in Brad's.

"I need to know step by step what he did

to you."

She stared at the white blur of the sheet. But she was seeing the falling snow and feeling the cold across her back. When she opened her mouth, nothing came out.

"Deputy," Kellerman said, "stand away from it. Tell it as if you were writing a report."

She nodded absently, lowering her eyes. The words were in her head, but she couldn't say them. Ropes. Hoist. Knife. The cutting away of her uniform. The burn of the cold on her skin. The silent and cold way he raped her. The grind of the pulleys. The suspension of time as she drifted in and out of consciousness.

"He tied my hands with a belt," she said. "He tied my feet to the hoist and cut off my uniform. He raped me. He dragged me across the snow, cut me, and pulled me up into the air. Then he left."

She looked up slowly. Kellerman was staring at her, his eyes dark with something she couldn't immediately decipher. Disbelief? Or was it pity?

"Thank you," he said. "One last question. Whose decision was it to take Snider out of the sheriff's office into the woods?"

She looked at him, hearing again that edge of blame in his voice. *Whose decision?*

The chain of command left unquestioned responsibility with Sheriff Leach, but she knew it was more than that. It was Mack, trying to be the city cop he needed to be. And Leach, despite twenty-five years behind the badge, blinded to the thought that the pristine wilderness he loved could possibly hold any danger. And Rafsky, putting aside every cop instinct he had in order to protect her and her department.

And her? What was her part of the blame?

"Deputy Frye?" Kellerman said again. "Who made this decision?"

"We all did," she said.

Sleep would not come, chased away by the images flickering on the screen of her eyelids. She was aware of Brad always there, slumped in the chair, but it was too hard to talk or even keep her eyes open. She tried concentrating on the sounds outside her head. The squeak of the nurse's soles as she came in to check the IV. The rattle of a cart in the hall. The plaintive ring of a telephone.

Finally, she felt herself drifting off. But a touch on her arm brought her back.

"Brad?"

"No, baby, it's me."

Joe opened her eyes.

"Ma. Oh, God, Ma . . ."

Her mother's soft cheek was close, her cigarette-and-Shalimar smell everywhere. Arms enfolding her, fingers stroking her hair. For the moment, all the ghostly images were gone, chased away by the realness of her mother's touch. Joe clung to her.

When Florence finally pulled back, every feeling and every thought were there in her face for Joe to see. The green eyes behind the big pink-framed glasses welled.

"Ma, don't cry. Come on . . ."

"Don't tell me not to cry." Florence wiped a hand roughly across her cheek. She sat down on the edge of the bed, her purse sliding off her arm.

"Brad called me. I got the first flight to Detroit I could," she said.

"How'd . . ."

"Had to rent a car and drive from there."

"You hate to drive in the snow."

Florence shrugged. Her eyes hadn't left Joe's face. She reached out and gently touched her cheek, tears welling again.

"My poor baby."

"I'm okay, Ma."

Joe started to reach for the Kleenex box on the nightstand. Florence held it out.

"Blow your nose," Joe said, nodding.

Florence jerked two tissues out and blew her nose. Then she lifted her glasses and wiped her eyes, letting out a deep breath.

"Did you talk to anyone yet?" Joe asked softly.

Florence nodded. "Your doctor, that young fellow . . ."

"Did he tell you what happened to me?"

Florence nodded again, closing her eyes.

Joe could see her struggling to hold it together. She reached across the sheet and took her mother's hand. When her mother's tears came this time, Joe didn't say anything. She let her cry.

The nurse came in, stopping when she saw Florence. "I'm sorry, but I have to take her vitals."

Florence wiped her face as she rose from the bed. "I'll go wash up." She went into the bathroom, taking her purse.

When the nurse left, Florence emerged from the bathroom. For the first time, Joe got a good look at her mother. She had put on some weight, and it looked good on her, but nothing else had changed. Her hair was still its improbable brassy blond, Aqua Net–frozen in its Alice Faye style. Her pink lipstick, the same color she had been wearing for decades, matched her big tinted glasses. Gold hoops hung from her ears, but her blue pantsuit was wrinkled from the long trip.

A tiny smile came to Joe's lips.

"What?" Florence asked.

"You look great," Joe whispered.

Florence smiled and set her purse on the chair. She noticed a man's coat lying there.

"Is Brad here?" she asked.

Joe nodded. "Somewhere."

Florence came over to the bed. "Joe, is there anything I can do?"

Joe hesitated.

"Baby, please, let me help."

Joe struggled to sit up. Florence was there immediately to help her. Joe started to swing her legs over the side of the bed where the IV stand was.

"I need to go somewhere, Ma, and I need you to help me."

Florence's eyes swung to the door, looking for a nurse, but then back to Joe, who was trying to get out of bed. Florence put a hand on her arm.

"Joe, you can't —"

"I can, Ma. If you'll help me. Please."

Florence sighed and looked around. She spotted a robe and slippers that Brad had brought and gave them to Joe. Joe grimaced as her mother gently helped her to her feet and slipped the robe over her shoulders. Florence put an arm around Joe's waist and, wheeling the IV pole ahead of them, led her daughter out of the room.

The lone nurse, busy on the phone, didn't see them as they headed down the hall to the elevator.

"Where we going?" Florence asked.

"Intensive care," Joe said.

The hospital was small, the ICU easy to find on the second floor. Joe was stopped by a nurse, who said she couldn't enter unless she was family.

"I'm a police officer," Joe said. "I was with him last night."

The nurse hesitated, then nodded, telling Florence that she would have to wait outside. The nurse led Joe farther down the hall, helping her with her IV. She paused outside a small glass-enclosed room.

"He's in there," she said. "But you can't go in, okay?"

Joe shuffled to the small window. The small, dimly lit room was crowded with machines. Rafsky lay in a narrow bed, covered to the waist by a pale yellow blanket. His right shoulder, arm, and part of his chest were wrapped in heavy packing and gauze. His face was ashen and hollow, and he looked thin and weak under the tangle of tubes.

Joe wiped her eyes.

It was only then that she saw the woman

in the room. She had her back to the window, and all Joe could see was a blue sweater and a bouffant of dark hair. Then the woman turned, as if sensing Joe was outside the window. Lovely brown eyes, despite the shadows of exhaustion under them. Gina Rafsky.

The woman rose quickly and came out of the room, closing the door gently behind her. She clutched a handkerchief in her fist, and her eyes were swollen and red. They were tearing up again now.

"Deputy Frye," Gina said softly.

"I'm so sorry to intrude," Joe started. "I just wanted . . ."

Gina gave her a shaky smile. "Please don't apologize," she said. "I'm glad you came down here. I was going to come up and see you later. I wanted to talk to you."

Joe looked down, hoping Gina Rafsky did not want to ask any more questions about what happened at the waterfall or why they were out there.

"I wanted to thank you," Gina said.

"Thank me?"

"If you had not found the strength to survive," Gina said, "my husband would not have survived, either. I owe you for his life."

Joe felt more tears, and she shut her eyes. She felt Gina Rafsky give her an awkward hug, heard her whisper something about telling her husband that Joe had come by, and then she was gone, back inside the small room.

Joe turned and walked slowly away, wiping her face with her forearm. She saw her mother standing in the doorway ahead and quickened her pace.

When her mother put her arm around her waist, Joe felt herself go limp against her. She didn't fight it, letting her mother's hands keep her steady as they walked back down the corridor.

41

The cottage felt too full. Too full of smells — pumpkin pie, roasting turkey, cigarette smoke, and wet dog. Too full of sounds — the murmur of the Lions-Rams game on TV, the whir of the electric beater, the hush of carefully chosen words.

From her place lying on the sofa, Joe could see Brad and her mother in the kitchen. Brad was whipping up the mashed potatoes. Florence had the oven door open, peering at the turkey. They were speaking low, thinking Joe was napping, but their voices carried out to her.

"I think you should have put it in earlier,"

Florence said.

"It's fine," Brad said.

"It won't be done in time, Brad. Maybe I should turn it up a little."

"If you'd stop opening the door every five minutes, it would cook faster, Florence."

Joe shut her eyes. The tension had been steadily building since her arrival home from the hospital yesterday. That night, when Joe and Brad went to bed, Brad gently helped Joe get undressed. But in bed, they lay there in the dark not talking, listening to Florence, snoring in the small bedroom next door. Finally, Joe moved toward Brad, and he pulled her to his chest. His arms encircled her, but with a strange carefulness, as if he were afraid she would break in two if he held her too hard — or fall into a thousand pieces if he didn't hold her hard enough.

This morning, she had been awakened by the clatter of pans in the kitchen. Brad told her he wanted to make Thanksgiving dinner. She tried to talk him out of it, but he insisted. He said it would help them get things back to normal. She didn't ask him what that meant.

From the kitchen now, more hushed voices. Brad telling Florence not to give Chips any scraps. Joe closed her eyes.

She heard footsteps and opened them to see Florence standing over her holding a beer.

"You're awake," Florence said. "You want anything?"

Joe shook her head slowly. She started to ease herself up into a sitting position, and Florence was there to rearrange the pillows behind her.

"Ma, let Brad take care of dinner," Joe said softly.

"I'm just trying to help."

"I know. But he likes to cook. And I think this makes him feel like he's . . ."

"He's what?" Florence asked when Joe didn't finish.

"I don't know, helping," Joe said.

Florence started to speak, then just sat down in a chair and looked vacantly at the television. She took a sip of beer. "What's the score?" she asked.

"I'm not sure. The Lions are losing. Reed just threw another interception."

"Get the pillow ready," Florence muttered.

Joe smiled slightly, a memory skimming her mind. Nine years old, snuggled in an overstuffed chair with her dad, watching the Browns play the Redskins. Her dad tossing a throw pillow at the TV, missing and knocking over the parakeet's cage. The Browns won and went to the playoffs. After that, whenever the Browns were losing, her father would heave a pillow at the cage. Both the bird and the Browns made it to two more postseasons. Gerard Frye died a year later.

"Dennis called this morning," Florence said. "I didn't want to wake you. He said he'd call back tonight."

"You told him?" Joe asked, looking at Florence.

Her mother nodded, her eyes locked on the TV. "He was really upset. Then he got really angry," she said softly. "Said he felt like he wanted to come down here and kill someone."

Joe shut her eyes. Her brother was just like their father, a man whose big bear appearance hid a tender heart. Joe had a sudden memory of Dennis skidding his bike to a stop to scoop a caterpillar off the pavement and deposit it gently in the grass.

She looked over at Florence, who had a small smile on her face as she watched the game. "What's so funny, Ma?" she asked.

"I was thinking how much your brother hated football. Your father never got over that." She shook her head, still smiling. "Thank God you would watch it with him."

They fell into silence, the shared memory diverging into private ones. The phone rang. Joe heard Brad answer and say something about Joe not being able to come to the phone.

Then he came into the living room, holding a dish towel. "There's a Captain Kellerman on the phone. He says —"

Joe threw off the blanket and was on her feet before Brad could stop her. She went to the kitchen, holding her side, Brad following.

Brad said, "I told him you needed —"

Joe ignored him, grabbing the receiver. "Yes, Captain?"

She listened, nodding a few times, then hung up. Brad stood there, waiting.

"I have to go to Traverse City tomorrow," she said.

"What for?"

"I have to give a statement."

"A statement? I thought you already did that."

She met Brad's eyes, not wanting to see what she saw there. "This is different. This is to the shoot team investigator. They need me to give an official statement, tell them exactly what happened."

Brad just stared at her.

"Will you drive me?"

"I don't think you should do this," he said.

"I have to, Brad," she said. "It's my job, and I have to go do this. I need to do this. Will you drive me or not?"

Brad wiped a hand over his sweating brow, his eyes going past Joe to Florence. "I'm going to go walk the dog," he said quietly.

He left the kitchen, grabbing his coat and Chips's leash off the hook. Chips saw the leash and trotted after him. The door closed with a dull thud behind them.

Joe felt the burn of tears in her eyes and blinked them back as she hurried to the door and thrust her bare feet into a pair of Brad's boots. She grabbed a parka from the hook.

"Joe?"

"I'll be back in a minute, Ma. Watch the turkey."

She went outside, holding the parka over her nightgown. Brad was sitting in a chair on the far end of the porch. She went over to him. "Brad, we have to talk about this," she said.

He shut his eyes for a moment, then opened them. But he wouldn't look up at her.

"Why do you have to go back and relive it all over again?" he asked. "Why do they keep putting you through this? Why can't they let you put it behind you and let us get back to . . ."

"Normal?" she asked.

He sighed, shaking his head. She pulled up a chair and sat down directly in front of him, taking his hands in hers. "I can't put it behind me when he's still out there," she said. "And it's my job to help others catch him. I can't get by any of this without talking about it. Without you talking about it."

When he looked at her she was shocked to see tears in his eyes. "You're the one who won't talk, Joe," he said.

"Me? I've tried to tell you —"

"No," he interrupted. "You haven't told me, Joe. You haven't really told me anything. Yeah, you told me what happened out there, you told me what he did to you. You told me the same things I could hear on TV or read in the paper."

She was too stunned to speak.

He pulled his hands away, shaking his head. "But it's not like you really talking," he said. "It's like . . . I don't know, like you're telling it in some damn police report or something, Joe." He wiped a hand at his eyes. "It's like you . . . you can't . . . you don't . . ."

She sat back slightly. "Don't what?"

He shook his head.

"Don't what, Brad? Don't break down, don't cry? Is that what you want?"

"No, it's like I can't help you. I can't protect you. It's like you don't need me anymore."

The words had been said softly enough, but the sting was there. Brad held her eyes for a moment, then looked away. Joe heard Chips barking somewhere nearby.

"I need you, Brad," she said softly. "Just like I always have. This thing hasn't changed me, Brad. I am still me."

When he finally looked back at her, his eyes were dry, but there was sadness there, and Joe felt something break inside her, as if a bone that had been bruised long ago had finally given way. And she suddenly heard the hollowness in her own words. *I am still me.*

"Brad," she said softly, "maybe you should go home for a few days."

"You're pushing me away, Joe."

"I'm not," she said. "I just . . . maybe we just need a little break, a little air."

"I can't leave you alone right now."

"I won't be alone."

Chips started to bark again, and they both looked toward the trees. She was suddenly aware of the cold wind swirling around the hem of her nightgown. She started to shiver.

"You'd better go inside," Brad said. He rose slowly and stepped off the porch. He walked toward the trees, whistling for Chips.

Joe watched him for a moment, then went back into the cottage. Her mother came out from the kitchen, wiping her hands on a dish towel.

"Baby, you okay?"

Joe eased out of the parka and hung it back on its hook on the door.

"Joe, where's Brad?"

"He's . . ." She looked at her mother. "I have to go give that statement tomorrow."

"I'll drive you," Florence said.

42

She gave her statement in a small room with dirt-veiled windows. The shadows were soft, the faces of the officers expressionless. She spoke first into a tape recorder, then answered questions from the investigators, who, no matter how many times she gave her story, seemed to feel the need to make her tell it again.

Then they played Ken Snider's interview for her, asking her again what logic was behind the decision to take Snider to the waterfall. They took another photo of her abdominal laceration, slipping it into a folder she knew held all of the photos taken at the hospital.

They showed her a photo of Roland Trader. Asked her to make an official positive ID. Then, while someone typed her statement, she waited in another room she suspected was used to interrogate suspects. An hour later, a woman wearing a state police uniform and a look of pity brought her the typed pages to sign. It occurred to Joe, as she scribbled her name on each page, how bizarre it was that such a horrible event could be reduced to twenty-three simple pages.

When Joe set the pen down, the woman asked her to follow her down a hall filled with blue uniforms and radio noise. At the end of it, she opened a door and ushered her into a small office.

A man sat behind a desk. Slender, thinning, strawlike hair and small, round glasses that bugged his eyes. He rose slowly.

"Please come in, Deputy Frye," he said.

Joe glanced behind her, but the female officer was gone, the door closed. Her eyes went back to the man. He was smiling, a bland kind of smile that was meant to put her at ease.

"My name is Dr. Littleton," he said, motioning to the chair in front of his desk.

"Please sit down."

"I didn't ask to see a doctor," she said.

"I know," he said. "But Captain Kellerman has requested that you speak with me. I'm a psychologist."

Joe didn't move.

"Please," he said.

Joe walked slowly to the chair and sat down. The blinds on the window behind the desk were closed, giving the room a beige hue and putting Littleton in subtle shadows.

"Would you like to talk about what happened?" he asked.

"Do I have to?"

"I'm not sure I understand," Littleton said.

"Is this something I have to do to keep my job?"

"No," he said. "But Captain Kellerman feels you're not coping well with your trauma. He asked me if I would speak with you. That's why you're here."

Joe shifted in the chair, bristling at the thought that Kellerman hadn't even asked her if she wanted to speak with someone. He had just gone ahead and arranged it.

"I'll be okay," she said. "And if I'm not, I'll get some help in the future. But thank you for your time." She reached down to get her purse.

"Deputy," Littleman said.

The calm authority of his voice made her stop and sit back in the chair.

"It's important you talk to someone now," he said. "I've spoken with many police officers who have experienced trauma similar to yours, and I can help."

Joe tuned him out, first focusing on the blinds behind him, then dropping her eyes to her lap. A small shiver rippled across her shoulders.

"I'm really doing okay," she said. "I'm in mourning for my fellow officers, but I'm a police officer, and I understood the risk before I ever took the job."

"What risk?"

"Of being killed on the job," she said.

Littleton was quiet, the kind of pause she knew was intended to make her look up, and she did. "I'm okay with what happened to me, too," she added. "Or I will be. I just need some time."

He studied her for a moment and leaned back in his chair. "Can you be more specific about what you mean by 'what happened to me'?" he asked.

She stared, not understanding the question. Then she realized he wanted her to say it out loud, as if hearing her own voice was a way of facing it head-on. She could do that. She'd said it and written it a dozen times since it happened.

"I was raped," she said.

Littleton held her eyes for a moment, then glanced down at a folder on his desk. "You have a fiancé . . . Brad Schaffer?"

She wondered how he had gotten that information. She nodded slowly, thinking about how quiet Brad had been that morning before he left for work.

"How is he taking this?"

"Taking this?"

Littleton held up a hand. "Let me rephrase that. Have you been able to talk to him about this?"

It took Joe a moment to meet Littleton's eyes. Then she shook her head slowly. "He says I'm pushing him away," she said.

"Are you?"

"I don't know," she said quickly. "Maybe I am. It's just —"

Littleton was waiting for her to finish. Joe blew out a long breath. "He doesn't understand," she said finally.

"Understand what, exactly?"

Joe stared at the man, a slow simmer of anger building, but she couldn't figure out where it was coming from. She sat forward in her chair. "He doesn't understand that I am not —"

She stopped, shaking her head. There was a pressing feeling deep in her chest, as if something were trying to push its way out. Littleton was watching her from behind his steepled hands.

"This job," she said, "what I do, it was okay before, because I don't think Brad thought it was real." She looked up at him. "I don't think he ever thought I was real in it."

She looked away.

"Go on, please," Littleton said softly.

"But this thing," she said, "this ugly, horrible thing that happened, this made it very real, and Brad can't deal with that. He wants to protect me, just like he always has." She shook her head slowly. "But he can't protect me, because it's not his job. If I let him protect me the way he needs to, I can't do my job. I will be just . . . just a . . ."

She shook her head.

"Just what?"

She looked up, directly at Littleton. "A victim. And if I let myself be nothing but a victim, I won't survive this."

Littleton was saying something, but she didn't really hear it. The pressure in her chest was still there, and she pulled in a hard breath to ease it. When she looked back at Littleton, he seemed to be disappearing into the shadows. The room felt suddenly hot and cramped, and she needed to get out.

She stood up, interrupting the doctor in mid-sentence. "I have to go," she said.

"Deputy Frye, please —" He picked up a business card. "Take my card, at least."

She hesitated, then took the card. "Thank you for your time, Doctor," she said.

Joe walked back into the cold air, stopping outside the door of the state police headquarters to look for her mother. The smell of cigarette smoke drew her attention to the left. Florence was sitting on a concrete railing, a Salem in her hand, a white shopping bag next to her hip.

Florence slipped to her feet, tossing down the cigarette and grabbing the bag. "You all right? You look —"

"I'm fine," Joe said quickly.

"How'd it go in there?"

"Routine stuff." Joe was looking out at the street, and finally she came back to her mother's face and let out a long sigh. "They made me talk to a shrink."

Florence's eyes got bigger behind the pink glasses. "What'd you talk about?"

"Nothing. Come on, let's go home."

Florence fell into step with Joe, and they headed back to the car. They walked for several blocks until Joe finally broke the silence.

"Ma, did Dad understand your job? I mean, why you wanted to do it?"

Florence took a moment to answer. "He knew I wanted to do something to help people, and he understood it because it was the same thing for him being a fireman."

Joe nodded slowly. "When I was in with that shrink, I was thinking about Brad and how he always wants me to come to bed when he does. When I stay up, I get the feeling he's a little upset at me for it, like if we don't go to sleep at the same time, something is wrong."

She stopped and turned to look at Florence. "I never figured out why that always bothered me. But when that shrink was asking me about my job, it hit me. Some of us are meant to stay awake so everyone else can sleep."

Florence was staring at her.

"Does that make any sense to you?" Joe asked her.

Florence nodded. Then she held up the white bag she had been carrying.

"What's that?" Joe asked.

"I got you some medicine," Florence said.

"I have my antibiotics," Joe said.

Florence reached into the bag and pulled out a small box. "Remember these?"

"Chocolate cherries?"

"Just like you used to get."

Joe opened the box and took out one of the chocolate-covered cherries. When she bit into it, the memories flooded back. Every Christmas, a box of the drugstore candies under the tree for her mother, the only thing Joe could afford on her dollar allowance.

They finished the cherries on the drive home to Echo Bay. Joe felt drugged from the sugar, but maybe that was okay. She was exhausted, and she thought maybe tonight, for the first time, she might sleep through the night.

In town, Joe saw two vans from Detroit TV stations, and she suspected the reporters were hanging around to film the police funeral. The parking lots of the motels seemed emptier, and Joe wondered if the mothers had gone home.

As they pulled up to the cottage, Joe noticed Brad's truck wasn't there. She went into the cottage first, stopping near the door. Something felt different, and she took a long look around, trying to see what it was, but she saw nothing.

"Honey, what is it?" Florence asked, coming in behind her.

Joe walked away from her, drawn to the bedroom and to the closet. Brad's duffle wasn't in its usual place on the top shelf. She spotted a single piece of cream-colored paper on the bed and read the note he had left.

Dear Joe,

I have gone home to stay with my parents for a few days. I think you are right that we need a little time away from each other right now and I know you will be okay with your mother there. Call me if you want to talk. Don't worry about anything. I paid the utilities and the rent.

I love you, Brad.

Joe folded the paper and walked to the living room, toward the fireplace. She folded the note a second time and set it gently on the logs.

"Joe? What it is?"

She ignored her mother, lighting the fire. The paper caught and blazed, the pieces floating up the flue like black feathers.

43

The morning broke crisp and clear, the sky cloudless and the colors — cobalt-blue sky, ice-white sun, barren brown trees — vivid and solid.

The funeral procession began at the small Methodist church in town and made its way toward Beechwood Cemetery on the edge of Lake Leelanau. It was led by two cocoa-colored horses drawing a caisson with two white flag-draped caskets. The horses were reined by a trooper dressed in his ceremonial blues. The five remaining Leelanau County deputies walked behind the caisson.

Behind them came two riderless horses, symbolizing the missing officers. Finishing the cortege was a six-man state honor guard that would fire the graveside salute. And beyond them, stretching for the next half-mile, ribbons of blue and brown uniforms. Hundreds of officers, the swing of their white-gloved hands and the snap of their steps synchronized, their faces a shared mask of solemnity.

For a long time, Joe kept her eyes on the shoulder of the trooper atop the caisson, watching the play of the sun off his gold braids, trying not to think about anything but thinking about everything. The note

Brad left on the bed. The look on the investigators' faces in Traverse City. Rafsky lying in the hospital bed. The stiff feel of her uniform shirt this morning when she pulled it up her arms. The look on Holt's face when he stood at her front door yesterday, a small bag in his hand.

Your collar pins, name tag, and badge, Joe. They found them in the woods. Kellerman says you can have them back now.

She lowered her gaze to the ground and listened to the steady *clop* of the horses' hooves behind her.

As they made a turn, a church bell tolled. It was soft and respectful, and it moved through her, bringing an unexpected memory.

Mama, why are they ringing bells?

It's a fireman's bell, Joe. They're ringing it for Daddy.

Joe lifted her head, her eyes tearing from the wind and the thickening emptiness inside her. The procession made its way slowly past brown lawns pillowed with snow. Past porches huddled with people offering bowed heads. Past the school and its half-mast flag snapping in the wind.

They made another turn onto North Manitou Trail. Up ahead at an intersection, Joe could see where the troopers had blocked traffic. A few people had gotten out of their cars and were watching. One man in a flannel shirt offered a two-finger salute up to his John Deere cap.

She glanced at Holt, walking at her left. His face was streaked with tears he was not wiping away. She looked to her right, at Mike. Everything about him seemed crystallized. The stiff draw of his lips, the razor crease of his uniform, and the steeled set of shoulders. By default, he was now Acting Sheriff, forced into the role of a different man, a different cop.

The procession left the concrete of Manitou Trail and moved onto the soft grass of the cemetery. They passed under two sentry pines and into the swaying shadows of the graveyard. She saw a white canopy ahead, the riotous colors of the funeral bouquets, a lectern on a raised platform.

They broke ranks as they neared the gravesite, the officers from other agencies spreading out in a wide half-circle. The horses stopped, and someone barked a command.

Joe joined Mike and Holt at the rear of the caisson, and together, with three other officers, they slid Leach's casket off the platform, hefted it to their shoulders, and waited while six other officers did the same for Mack.

The casket was heavy, the ground uneven, her view blurred by tears she had no will to stop. She stumbled and felt the others raise the casket slightly, taking the weight off her shoulder. When they set it down, they stepped away and paused for a second before making the turn on their heels to assume their positions in the front row.

The Leelanau sheriff's office deputies lined up shoulder to shoulder. Joe stood in the center, between Mike and Holt. The mayor stepped up to make a short speech. He was followed by a minister from the Lutheran church.

Joe let her eyes drift, taking in the endless rows of uniforms, the colors more vivid now. The blues deeper. The browns more solemn. The hundreds of motionless white gloves.

When the minister finished his speech, Mike broke from the line of deputies and walked to the lectern, holding a sheet of paper. He flattened the paper with his white-gloved palm and started to speak, but his gaze was drawn to the cemetery entrance.

Joe followed it. A state cruiser moved silently toward them and came to a stop on the edge of the grass. A trooper emerged from the driver's side and opened the back door, sticking his hand into the rear seat to help someone out.

It was Rafsky.

He wore a state uniform. Blue campaign hat, dark blue trousers with a stripe, navy parade dress coat, with state patches and gold and black braids. The coat was draped over his shoulders to accommodate his heavily bandaged right arm and chest. He started across the grass, and when his step faltered, the trooper put a hand on Rafsky's elbow to steady him.

Mike stood poised and silent, waiting.

As Rafsky made his way to the front row, he stopped as if unsure where he should stand. Joe moved sideways, making room. He stepped in next to her.

Mike cleared his throat and smoothed his paper, holding his palm against it to keep it from blowing away. The crowd of family members, friends, townspeople, and law enforcement officers fell into silence, waiting.

"A week ago," Mike said, "we were a small department of seven. Today, we number only five. Our loss is great, and our sorrow is deep, but it comforts us to know that we are not alone in our grief. We are comforted to know that the pain we thought we were to shoulder as only five is eased by the sharing of it by so many others. And because of that, we will endure.

"We are angry, we are broken. We are leaderless, and we are lost. But because of the strength and the goodness and the gentle wisdom of the men we lay to rest today, we will endure."

Mike paused, his eyes down, his hands still spread across the paper in front of him.

"Our home, the home Cliff Leach and Julian Mack loved so much and protected with their hearts and their lives, has been invaded. Our beauty has been violated. Our serenity shattered. Our crystal streams bloodied. But in that same beauty we find our vision. And in the echo of gunshots we find our direction. And in the bloodiness of our waters we find clarity. And because of that, we will endure."

Joe closed her eyes against the sting of the wind.

"We say goodbye today to two family members. Two men who made law enforcement their life," Mike went on. "Julian Mack wore a badge for twenty-one years. He was stubborn, sometimes funny, sometimes harsh, often difficult. But he was a man with the purest of motives. He sought only to mend the hearts of other families by bringing home to them a loved one who had been lost.

"Clifford Leach . . ."

Mike paused and tried to clear his throat. The moment lengthened before he finally went on. "Clifford Leach. Our leader, our teacher, our friend. The hole he leaves in our department and in our hearts will never be filled.

"These men died in the cold, and today we bury them in the same cold. But I believe both these men would ask that you not stand angry at the cold images of how they died but wrap yourself in the warmth and kindness of how they lived."

Mike did not raise his eyes. He slowly gathered up the paper and walked away from the lectern.

They folded the flags into triangles. Since neither Leach nor Mack were married, both were presented to Mike. Then came the gun salute. The first one jarred Joe's bones, and she shut her eyes against the image that exploded in her head. She kept her eyes closed through the next two, not opening them until the echo faded.

It was over.

She grabbed a hard breath and wiped her eyes with the Kleenex she had been holding since Mike started his speech. She turned to Rafsky. He was fighting to stay on his feet, face drawn in pain and sadness, eyes gentle and dry. She wiped her face and stuffed the wadded Kleenex into her jacket pocket.

"How are you feeling?" he asked.

She looked away from him, at the caskets, the ribbons of brown and blue, the white mums, and finally back at him. "I don't know yet," she said. "I need some time. But I'll be okay. My mother is here with me now."

Rafsky took a quick scan of the crowd. "Where is Brad?" he asked softly.

"He's gone home."

A pause, then, "I'm sorry."

She shrugged and sighed, again meeting his eyes. There was nothing in them but exhaustion and a tightening grimace of pain.

"How are you doing?" she asked.

He gave her an awkward nod and a shake of his head, as if he had no true answer. "I'm going to Detroit for more surgery," he said. "Then home to Gaylord for a while."

He shifted his weight, letting out a small cough that seemed to trigger another spasm of pain through his body. He shut his eyes for a moment, letting it pass.

"I'm so sorry," she said. "If I hadn't called you —"

"Don't do that to yourself," he said quickly. "You were doing your job. I was doing mine."

She fell quiet, feeling more tears, wishing she still had the Kleenex in her hand. He dug in his pocket for a handkerchief and handed it to her. Behind him, the trooper stepped forward and spoke softly.

"Sir, we should get you back now."

Rafsky gave him a nod and turned back to Joe. "I guess this is goodbye."

She hesitated, then held out a gloved hand. "Goodbye, Rafsky."

"Goodbye, Frye," he said.

He squeezed her hand and then let it go. He turned, reaching for the trooper's arm. She watched him walk away, past the caskets and the mums. When he reached the car, the trooper took the coat off his shoulders and opened the door. Rafsky slipped inside. A few minutes later, he was gone.

III
HUNGER MOON

44

He had never seen a place so empty. Not a thing to see but the endless sea of ice and the tall pines, their branches bowed with snow. Not a thing to hear but the harsh breath of the north wind as the storm drifted in.

And not a thing to do but think. And remember.

Roland sat down on the floor in front of the fireplace, legs crossed, shotgun across his knees. His eyes drifted to the newspapers scattered on the floor. He had tried to collect all of them over the last few weeks, and it had been easy at first, because even the Canadian papers carried the story. But after a week or so, there was less and less mention of him, and he had finally resorted to writing to the Echo Bay newspaper and sending money for a subscription so he could find out what was happening down there.

The *Echo Bay Banners* came every few days, when the postman could get through. And Roland would snatch them from the mailbox and read each page two or three times. He read about the grieving mothers and how they had all gone home now. Read about the two dead cops and about the investigator with the ice-blue eyes and how he survived a blast that almost ripped his body apart. Read, too, about the woman cop he had left hanging in the woods. Read about her bravery and saw her picture so many times he thought he'd be sick.

And he read about Kenny and how he had been buried without a ceremony in the Leelanau County cemetery. The same place Dad was buried.

What do you boys want to do with your father's body?

We don't have any money to pay for taking him home, sir. Can he be buried up here in Leelanau?

Roland knew almost every article by heart. The newspapers didn't speculate about where he was, and he knew the cops would assume he had come to Canada. But they would never find him here, in this remote cabin at the end of this empty road. He'd been lucky finding this place himself. And finding that man living here alone, a man no one seemed to care about. He had let Roland in, thinking Roland was stranded in the snow. Two minutes later, the man was dead. Roland settled into the cabin, eating the man's food, using his firewood, and sleeping in his bed.

He had even used his name — Otis Deppert — when he called to get the *Echo Bay Banner* subscription.

Roland held his hands to the fire, hearing a soft rumble move his stomach.

There had been enough food and firewood so that he had not had to leave the cabin for two weeks. But when he opened the last can of stew, he realized he would have to go hunt his own food. It was then he started missing Kenny, because Kenny had always been good at things like that.

You're a fucking animal, Roland!

But Kenny was gone.

Finally, there had been no choice but to go into the woods. He had set out, shotgun in hand, desperate to hear the skitter of an animal. Any animal. But even they were silent and hidden, sleeping maybe in an attempt to stave off their hunger until spring.

Will you read the book to me, Mommie?

No, you are too young to know the legend. It will scare you.

Then, one night, sitting by the fire as he

was doing now, he watched the dance of the flames and listened to the howl of the wolves and the fierce rush of wind. And he suddenly knew what he needed to do.

He would use the weakened state of his body and his gnawing hunger. He would use it in a vision quest for salvation. Outside, he built his bed of pine branches, and for five days, he sat there looking to the sky, tired and hungry and hoping.

The spirit did not come.

I'm not scared, Mommie. Please read it to me.

It is a large creature, as tall as the trees, with big jagged teeth and fearsome breath. Its footprints leave a trail of blood. And when the hunger comes, it hunts, and it eats any man, woman, or child it finds. And those, my son, are the lucky ones.

Roland shivered and moved closer to the fire, bringing his hands up to his face. He felt the unfamiliar prickle of a ragged beard, and he could smell the stink of his unwashed body. There was no mirror in this cabin, and he wondered if he looked different, wondered what he would see in his own eyes, wondered if they now reflected what was inside him. He wondered, would he even recognize himself anymore?

He looked down at the shotgun in his lap.

Kenny's old gun. The one Kenny had shot his first deer with. The one he had killed Dad with.

Dad! Please don't tie me up. Don't tie me to the hoist!

I'm going to teach your whiny little ass that there's nothing out here in these goddamn woods to be afraid of.

Kenny! Help me.

Dad! What are you doing to him? What the hell are you doing? You know he's afraid. Why do you treat him this way? Stop it!

Mind your mouth, Ken. Go back inside the cabin.

No!

Get back inside.

Shick-shuck. BOOM!

Roland ran a finger down the shotgun and tipped it upright and stared into the barrel. The odor of gunpowder filled his nose.

Tell me more about the legend, Mommie.

Sometimes, my son, the Windigo will choose to possess a person instead. But then the person becomes a Windigo, hunting down those in his tribe and feasting upon their flesh.

He set the butt of the gun on the floor and rested his head against the barrel. No spirit would come here. He knew that now. It was too late.

He set the gun down and stood up suddenly. He walked to the back door of the cabin and threw it open. The man's body lay in the backyard, covered by a blanket of snow. He went to it and knelt down, brushing the snow from the man's face and neck.

The blood from his slashed throat looked like black mud on his face and collar. Roland drew his knife from his belt and pressed the blade against the man's face. He dug out a piece of frozen flesh, holding it in his palm.

Kenny?

Oh, God, Kenny!

Stop screaming, Ro.

You shot Dad! You shot him in the face. I got his blood on me. Get it off! Get it off!

Hold still, Ro. Hold still!

Oh, God. I have something in my mouth . . . oh, God!

Roland shut his eyes as he placed the flesh in his mouth. It was hard, tough, and almost tasteless, like pork cooked too long and left in the air. Not what he expected. He swallowed it, waiting for something to happen in his body. A feeling of power, or satisfaction, but there was nothing but the lingering dryness on his tongue.

He knew what was wrong. The man was dead. They weren't supposed to be dead when eaten. He went quickly back inside

the cabin and rummaged through the cupboards for the last few crackers. There were
three, and he took one out and nibbled on
it, to get the taste of the man's flesh out of
his mouth.

How do you kill a Windigo, Mommie?

*It takes a very worthy warrior, Roland. The
warrior must kill the Windigo and then burn
its body to ashes. Only then will it remain
dead.*

As Roland ate the last cracker, he turned
slowly, scanning the cabin. The fire was dying, and he knew there was no more wood.
The lamp was flickering and he knew there
was no more kerosene. Soon, he would be
left alone in the cold darkness, and he knew
he would die here.

The woman, the one he had left hanging
in the woods . . .

He went back to the living room and
spread the newspapers out on the floor. His
eyes locked on a photograph.

She stared back at him, daring him to
come back for her. Was she the warrior? Is
that what gave her the strength to get out of
the tree? Did she have powers the others
didn't have? And if she did, and he were to
consume her, what kind of power would he
then have?

He picked up the paper and folded it. He

thrust it into the dying fire and watched it burn.

45

Joe stood on the backyard deck, robe clutched tightly around her, watching the snow fall. The hours were drifting like the snow. The days were melting together. When she thought about it, she knew it had been twenty-one days. But most of the time, she didn't think about it. The strength she had found in the first few days after the ambush had waned quickly, and she wondered now how long it would be before she didn't wake up in sweat-soaked sheets or feel the need to escape into long afternoon naps.

"You're going to catch cold out there," Florence called.

Joe didn't move, her eyes drawn up to a small plane puttering across the gray sky. She watched it until it vanished over the tips of the pines, then she turned and went back inside the cottage.

The living room was strewn with Christmas decorations. A rainbow of flashing lights snaked across the floor. Chips ambled into the room, strips of silver hanging from his snout.

"Ma," she said, "Chips chewed open a box

of tinsel."

"At least someone around here wants to celebrate the holidays."

Joe picked the tinsel off Chips and wandered to the kitchen for her fourth cup of coffee. Florence gave her a look as she passed, then went back to her astrology chart. Her books were spread on the table in front of her.

"When are you going back to work?" Florence asked.

"I told you, Ma, I'm not sure," she said, pouring her coffee. The doctor had released her to go back this coming Monday, but Joe had not yet called Mike to let him know. Maybe it was because she knew there was nothing she could do to find Roland Trader. Or maybe it was the idea of having to put her hands on a suspect and not being able to physically deal with him. Or maybe it was the thought of facing the male deputies and seeing the pity in their faces.

Or maybe it was just the nagging question that still kept her awake night after night: Why had Roland Trader left her alive?

Her eyes wandered to the newspapers lying on the countertop. Three weeks' worth. Joe wasn't sure why she kept them. Maybe for the same reason Leach had kept all those articles on John Norman Collins.

She pulled the top one to her. Theo had given daily coverage to the case and the ambush. Yesterday, he had run a feature on local Indian lore and had printed all twelve moon symbols. She wondered what kind of chaos that was causing Kellerman. It was an open invitation for copycats to mark up trees all over the state.

"Do you know the birth date of this Trader guy?" Florence asked.

"Ma, come on," Joe said.

"What can it hurt?"

Joe took a sip of coffee, the idea of her mother doing an astrology chart on Roland Trader knotting her stomach. She didn't want Roland Trader anywhere inside her home in any form. But even as she thought that, a date popped into her head. She must have read it somewhere in the paperwork.

"October 17, 1948," Joe murmured.

"Do you know where?" Florence asked.

Joe shrugged. "Try Inkster or the Detroit area."

"I wish I had a time of birth," Florence murmured.

Joe moved to the string of lights on the floor and gathered them up. She would go ahead and finish stringing them. Keep her mind busy. While she worked, she could hear her mother flipping pages in her ephemeris.

"Good Lord," Florence said. "His sun and his Mercury are squared to each other and both retrograde."

Joe was quiet, remembering slivers of this stuff from her childhood, when Florence used to do charts for the neighbor women.

"And his moon and his Venus are in opposition," Florence said.

"What's that mean?"

"The moon — his moods and the women in his life — is at opposite purposes with Venus, his planet of love and relationships."

Joe glanced over her shoulder. "I already know he's a sicko, Ma. Now, if you could tell me where the hell he disappeared to, that might be helpful."

Florence ignored the sarcasm. "His chart is lopsided. I'd be willing to bet he's a Pisces rising. That would put . . ."

Florence was scribbling with her pencil. Joe opened a box of ornaments. She wished she had some of the ornaments her mother had stored in Cleveland. There was a toy fire truck in that box somewhere, given to them the first Christmas they were without Joe's father.

"Was this guy an orphan?" Florence asked.

Joe shrugged. "His father was killed when he was sixteen. I don't know about his mother."

"If I'm right at where I'm putting things, then I'd say he didn't get along with his father," Florence said. "There was violence in the home. Lots of failures. Isolation."

Joe suppressed a sigh. "I don't care how badly he was mistreated."

"I know you don't. But just like the victims, you need to understand him if you're going to find him."

"I'm not in charge of finding him, Ma."

Joe was glad when Florence didn't answer. She knew she sounded depressed and miserable, and she thought again about what that doctor in Traverse City had said. *It's important you talk to someone now. I've spoken with many police officers who have experienced trauma similar to yours, and I can help.*

Littleton . . . that was his name. She still had his card somewhere, probably in her jewelry box.

The crunch of tires on the snow made Joe look to the window. She went to it, pulling back the curtain to see a sheriff's cruiser in the drive. Mike got out with an armload of folders. By the time he got to the porch, she had the door open.

"Hey," she said.

"Hi," he said. "Can I come in?"

She nodded, and Mike slipped past her. He looked around and set the files on the kitchen table, catching the ones on top so they didn't slide off. He unzipped his jacket and took off his cap, setting it on the files. His black hair was recently trimmed. His tie was so starched it looked like cardboard, and his collar chevrons and star were polished to a high sheen. There was a piece of black tape over the badge.

Mike saw Florence. "You must be Joe's mom," he said, giving her a smile. "Nice to meet you."

Florence lowered her glasses, giving him a long look. "Michael Villella. I've heard a lot about you."

"Not all bad, I hope," Mike said.

Florence smiled. "Not all."

Mike flushed and turned to Joe. "I hope you don't mind me just stopping over. How are you feeling?"

"I'm okay," she said. "How are things in the department?"

"Well, you know the board made me acting sheriff, until they can arrange an election."

"I heard."

"And I don't have an undersheriff," he said. "So mostly it's just me and the other guys, doing regular patrols and things.

There's some state troopers in town, just keeping an eye out."

"No sign of Trader?" she asked.

He shook his head.

"Any news on the case?"

He sighed. "Kellerman's guys found two bones in the dunes this morning," he said. "They think it's a couple of hand bones."

Joe shook her head slowly. So that erratic-looking carving hadn't been a copycat after all. "Is Kellerman keeping you in the loop?" she asked.

"Not really," Mike said. "He says we just need to heal and return to our regular routine."

"So," she said, motioning to the folders, "if everything is routine, what's all this?"

Mike looked suddenly uncomfortable. "Well, a few days after the . . . ambush, Kellerman called and said he wanted everything we had on the case. I went into the sheriff's office to gather it up, and I found myself standing there at his desk and looking down at his stuff." He blew out a long breath. "Well, I realized I was about to give up any chance we had as a department to help bring his killer in."

Mike glanced at Florence, then down at the floor as he tried to find the words to finish. His head came up slowly. "I didn't want to do that."

Joe opened the top folder and gave it a quick glance. There were about fifteen pages, neatly typed and labeled, BACK-GROUND — ROLAND J. SNIDER/TRADER.

"This is new," she said. "Did you compile all this background information?"

"Holt and I did," he said. "I sent him to Inkster to dig stuff up. He talked to neighbors and even found a distant aunt in Detroit. We found out a lot about these two guys."

Joe closed the folder. "Why did you bring the files here?"

Mike sighed. "Because Holt and me don't know what to do with this information. You're the best investigator we got. We need you to look at it."

Joe said nothing.

"If you're ready," Mike added.

She opened the folder again and walked away from him as she read it. Roland had graduated from Cherry Hill High School, and despite scoring a 1460 on his SATs, he ended up at Henry Ford Community College. More colleges, six or seven different majors, but no diploma and twenty-some jobs in his twenty-seven years. His last known address had been an apartment on a street Joe remembered being near Ronnie

Langford's house.

She heard her mother asking Mike if he wanted some coffee, but their voices faded as she read on. Holt had interviewed a neighbor who described the Snider boys as rambunctious and bratty. Described the father as a yeller and a drinker who taught his sons to shoot blue jays in the backyard with BB guns.

She turned. "Mike, did you find anything more on how his father died?"

Mike set his coffee down and came forward, pulling off his jacket and hanging it on a chair. "I couldn't find the responding Deputy Miller," he said, pulling out a file. "But this is the original report you already saw, and I made some notes on it."

Joe took it from him. Mike had scribbled in the margin: "4:30 p.m. — almost dark. No one starts hunting at 4:30. Plus — why only 2 guns for three hunters?"

"Good points," she said.

Mike shrugged. "I don't think they were setting off to hunt. I think something else was going on. And I'm not even sure the shooting was accidental. Did you know they didn't even take their father's body home? They buried him up here in the county cemetery, same place Ken Snider is now."

"Were there any photos taken of the scene

where the father was killed?"

He nodded, slipping them from his folder and holding them out to her. "I finally found these last week. Kellerman didn't ask for them, so I didn't send them."

She sifted through them, stopping at one that showed the backyard of the cabin. The body was a dark form on the leafy ground. The father's shotgun lay near his right hand.

"Two guns for three people," she said softly. "What if Roland was the one who didn't have a gun, and maybe he didn't have one because he didn't like to hunt?"

"Then why would the dad bring him up to the cabin?" Mike asked.

"To force him," Joe said. "To teach him . . ."

"To be a man," Mike finished for her.

Joe nodded, moving on to other pictures. She stopped at another photo of the backyard. In the background, she could see a shed, an old covered well, more trees than were now there. And hanging not far from the father's body, on a low branch, a deer hoist. Roland Trader's voice was in her head.

Go get the hoist, Kenny.

How can you do that to her after what he did to you?

"You okay, Joe?" Mike asked.

It took her a second to bring herself back

from the woods. She held the photo out to Mike. "Look at the hoist in the tree," she said.

Mike glanced at it. "You think the father used the hoist on the kid?"

Joe shut her eyes, hit again with the memory of her feet being tied to the cold metal.

"Oh, God," Mike said softly. "I'm sorry, Joe."

"No, it's okay," she said quickly. Her throat felt dry, and she licked her lips. "Roland used the hoist for a reason when he killed. He learned it from somewhere."

"His dad would have been a real bastard to do that."

"Maybe that's why they killed him," Joe said.

"Good theory," Mike said. "But I don't know what it gets us."

"It gets us understanding," Joe said.

Mike said nothing, and Joe went back to reading the background gathered from the aunt and the neighbors. The neighbors didn't remember the mother at all. The only mention of her in the interview was her name — Mary Trader — and the fact that she had died when the boys were young.

"Mike," Florence said from her perch on the sofa. "You got Roland Trader's birth certificate in there somewhere?"

"Ma," Joe said quietly.

But Mike dug through another file, pulled out a piece of paper, and took it to Florence. "You do astrology charts?" he asked.

Florence eyed him. "Let me guess. You're an Aries."

"Scorpio," Mike said.

"Born late afternoon, though, right?" Florence asked.

Mike grinned. "Four a.m."

"I'm losing my knack," she mumbled, going back to her scribbling.

Joe looked up. "Mike," she said, "you didn't happen to get a copy of Mary Trader's death certificate, did you?"

He went back to her and pulled it out. Joe read it.

Name: Mary May Trader.
Born: Leelanau County, Michigan.
Died: Leelanau County, Michigan.
Manner of death: Car accident.
Cause of death: Multiple internal injuries.
Date of death: January 1954.
Home address: Inkster.
Age at time of death: 28.
Race: Indian.

"Good Lord," Joe whispered.

"What?" Mike asked.

"His mother was Indian," she said, facing Mike. "That's why those children's Indian books were in the basement. Roland was only five when she died."

Mike was quiet, and he was staring at her, his face crossed with bewilderment.

"What's the matter?" she asked.

"You sound like you feel sorry for him."

Joe started to snap at him, then stopped herself. "I hate this man with every ounce of my being," she said. "Don't ever mistake anything I say or do in this investigation for sympathy. I have none."

Mike was quiet for a moment, then his radio crackled, and Augie called to him. Mike answered and stuck the radio back in his belt.

"I need to run," he said. "Do you want me to leave all this with you?"

"Yes, please," Joe said.

"Maybe you and Holt and me could meet later and talk about what else we can do?"

"Sure. Come on, I'll walk you out."

Mike looked at Florence as he pulled on his jacket on. "Nice meeting you, Mrs. Frye."

"Flo," she said. "Call me Flo."

"Yes, ma'am."

Joe walked Mike out to the cruiser, arms

folded against the cold. He stopped to face her. "Joe, I didn't get a chance to say this before. I'm really sorry about what happened to you," he said.

"I know, Mike."

"I should've been there."

"If you had been, you'd be dead. Don't do that to yourself."

She knew there was something else on his mind, and she stayed quiet, letting him work out how to say it.

"I was going through your desk the other day looking for something," he said. "I found this."

He pulled a photograph from his pants pocket. It was the one of the pretty teenage girl posed on the hood of his cruiser.

"Thanks for not showing it to anyone. It was . . ." He shook his head.

"You don't need to explain anything to me."

"Yes, I do," he said. "I want you to know nothing happened. I was bored, and she was up here on vacation, and she said she'd never been in a patrol car, and I . . ." He blew out a long breath. "I guess I just wanted to steal a few minutes with a pretty girl. It was childish and stupid."

He kicked at the snow with the toe of his boot. "When I was your partner," he said,

"I know I was an embarrassment to you. I'm sorry."

"The sheriff would be proud of you now."

He looked away, over her shoulder, blinking away tears. He had to clear his throat to speak. "I miss him," he said.

"Me, too," she said.

"Shit, I even miss Mack."

Joe gave him a small smile.

They stood for a moment longer, listening to the chatter on Mike's radio. Augie's familiar voice. Holt's cheerful response. The faint wail of a siren as Holt kicked his cruiser into gear.

Mike turned and reached for his door, then looked back at her. "When you coming back to work?"

She hesitated. "Monday," she said.

"Good. We need you."

Mike got into his car and backed out of the drive. She stayed at the end of the walk, slippers growing wet, arms crossed, watching the cruiser. The lettering on the trunk still read, "Leelenau County SO, Sheriff Cliff Leach."

When she went back inside, her mother was penciling in planets on Roland Trader's chart. Chips was snoozing on a bed of tinsel.

Joe went to finish stringing the lights on the tree. She thought about dinner and made plans to go down to the market and splurge on a couple of steaks. And a bottle of wine. After dinner, she and her mother would watch *M*A*S*H* and maybe talk some about her father. She had a feeling that maybe tonight she would fall asleep early.

And tomorrow, she would go in search of Mary May Trader.

46

The dirt road came to an abrupt end. Joe shoved the Jeep into park and surveyed the barren landscape in front of her. She was high on a bluff above Lake Michigan, about five miles north of Echo Bay.

She got out, tugged the baseball cap down on her head, and set off toward the setting sun, knowing by the smell that she was close to the lake. But there was no path, and the brush and grass were so high she couldn't be sure of her footing.

The wind was pushing in hard and cold, the western sky a welling bruise of pale yellow and angry purple. She made her way another twenty feet, stopped, and looked down. Far below was the gray swirl of Lake Michigan, the waters choppy and white-capped. Through the spray, she could barely make out the dark sand of a beach. In summer, it was a favorite place for swimmers and sunbathers, but today it lay as cold and empty as some primordial shore.

Joe turned and looked at the bare aspen trees that formed the edge of the clearing. There was a giant dead oak tree standing alone in the weeds. It was cleaved in two, its insides blackened by the lightning bolt that had killed it countless years ago. This had to be the place. But there was nothing here. No houses, no fences, nothing to mark the fact that any human had ever touched this place.

She saw him coming through the tall brown weeds. In the whistle of the wind, she hadn't heard a car. He had seemed to materialize out of the gray sky and now was moving toward her, his dark hair whipping around his face. She didn't move. There was no place to go. There was nothing but the sky and the lake at her back.

"I didn't think you would come," she said.

Thomas Ahanu's eyes were slitted against the wind. He was bundled in a plaid wool jacket, old chinos, and heavy workboots. Strands of his hair flew like a torn curtain around his face.

"I am here," he said.

The same vague sense of unease she had felt around Ahanu on their first meeting came back to Joe. When she had called him yesterday to ask for his help with Mary Trader, she had expected him to refuse. But he had agreed and then surprised her by asking her to meet him here.

"You had no trouble finding your way?" Ahanu asked.

"Your directions were good," Joe said. "But why here?"

"You said you wanted to know about Mary Trader," Ahanu said. "She is here."

Joe was trying to figure out what to say without sounding disrespectful, when she realized Ahanu was smiling. Barely. But it was definitely a smile.

"Look, Mr. Ahanu, I didn't come all this way —"

"I know." Ahanu turned and gestured toward the clearing. "This is a cemetery," he said. When he looked back at Joe, the half-smile was still there, but there was a sadness in it she hadn't seen the first time.

"I told you I would tell you about Mary. Come, let's go," he said.

Joe followed Ahanu through the heavy brush, past the dead oak, and toward the aspens. She spotted something gray in the thigh-high weeds and stopped. It was an old headstone, the name and years erased by the wind and time. Ahanu hadn't stopped, and she drove through the brush after him. She spotted one more ravaged headstone and a toppled stone cross before she caught up to him.

She watched as he crouched down and pulled away at the brush with his rough hands. There was a stone marker lodged in the hard brown earth. The name MARY TRADER was visible and the years 1925–1954.

Joe surveyed the weed-choked meadow. A cemetery? But why here, in what seemed such a forsaken place?

"I expected —" Joe said, but then stopped. She shook her head slowly.

"Expected what?" Ahanu asked.

Joe looked around at the windswept dead grass moving like the waves down on the lake. "I don't know. I didn't expect the loneliness of it, I guess."

Ahanu got to his feet, brushing the dirt off his hands. "There are more than two hundred of our people buried here. Men who fought in the Civil War, the World Wars. Other men, women, and children who never fought in any wars at all. Unmarked, forgotten, but not lonely."

Joe looked down at the stone marker. "Did you know her?"

"Not well. We were of different clans, but

I heard about her life. Her father was a white man, her mother Ojibwa. On this place where we are now there was once a village called Onominee. This is where her mother's people came from long ago."

"She was half white?" Joe asked.

Ahanu nodded. "Mary Trader walked in two worlds, and when she married a white man, she chose that world."

"Then why is she buried here?" Joe asked.

"I don't know everything," Ahanu said. "I heard her husband was not good to her. I remember that she suddenly came back here one winter to see her mother and her brother. She brought two sons with her."

"She died here," Joe said.

Ahanu nodded. "An accident. The roads were icy. Their car went off the road near Omena. Mary and her brother were killed. There was a lot of talk at the time, because Mary's husband did not come here to take her back downstate."

"What happened to the boys?" Joe asked.

"Annie Redbird, Mary's mother, took them in. I remember seeing the boys at Mary's funeral. They looked very lost."

Joe was staring at the stone marker, trying to imagine Ken and Roland at their mother's funeral. They had been just little boys.

Why the hell didn't their father take them home?

"During the funeral, the older one walked away," Ahanu said. "But the little one, he stayed and watched everything. I remember watching his face when they put Mary in the tree."

Joe's eyes shot up. "The tree?"

Ahanu pointed toward the aspens. "In winter, if the ground was too hard, the body was wrapped and hung in the fork of a tree until it could be buried later."

Joe turned away. She had no sympathy. But a part of her could now understand. She could understand that somewhere in the sick, black swirl of Roland's mind, flashes of memory and madness ignited and exploded, propelling him on his murderous path. Or maybe — and this was something that she didn't want to think about — maybe it wasn't something that could be understood. Maybe there was just something that could only be called pure evil. She didn't want to think about it, because everything she had been taught, in school and at the academy, had made her believe that murderers were created. But that night in the woods, everything changed. She wasn't so sure what she believed anymore.

"I know what happened to you."

She looked back at Ahanu.

"I read the newspapers. I know what he did to you," Ahanu said. "And I know you are trying to understand why. That is why you are here. That is why I came here, to help you."

It took every bit of her will not to look away from Ahanu's steady eyes. "I don't think you can help me with that, Mr. Ahanu," she said quietly.

"I am of the bear clan," he said. "We are the healers of our people. I took some classes at the community college. In another place or life, maybe I would be a shrink with a nice office above a café on Front Street in Traverse City."

She stared at him. He gave her that odd half-smile again. She laughed softly.

A chilling gust blew in, sending Ahanu's trousers flapping. In the distance, the bare branches of the aspens clicked like old bones.

"Do you believe in good and evil, Mr. Ahanu?" she asked.

"My people believe everything is occupied by a spirit, every tree, every rock, every lake," he said. "There are many spirits, from the great Manitou to the simple spirits that inhabit every animal. But good? That, like survival, is up to each man or woman."

She nodded. "And evil?"

"The same. It is up to the individual."

She came closer. "Tell me about the Windigo."

Ahanu's eyes were steady on hers. "Let's walk," he said.

They went back through the clearing and toward the lake. When they drew close to the edge, Ahanu stopped and turned to her. "I believe evil is up to the individual."

"You already said that."

"It is the same with the Windigo."

"I don't understand," Joe said.

Ahanu looked out at the lake. "Some believe the Windigo was put on earth by the creator. Some believe the Windigo is dreamed into being. But most of my people believe the Windigo is one of us who has lost his way."

Joe waited, impatient for information she could use.

"Life has always been hard for my people," Ahanu said. "Through the centuries, we have needed great physical and mental discipline to survive in this land. When the lakes froze and food was scarce, we went hungry. The Windigo is a symbol of death stalking us during the long winters, a giant monster of cold and hunger. He represents our greatest fear, that any one of us may be forced by starvation to eat human flesh to survive. That any one of us, forced to live in the harshest winter without anything to sustain us, can turn into the monster."

Joe let out a long breath.

"I don't know if there is pure evil in this world," Ahanu said. "But to me, the Windigo is very real, because he is the embodiment of everything we most hate and fear, those things that are made all the more ominous by their reality. Real or not, you ignore such things at your own peril."

Joe turned away, looking out at the lake. The clouds had piled high, heavy with snow, iron-gray weights over the more fragile dove gray of the water.

"This man who killed, this man who hurt you. You think this man is a Windigo?" Ahanu asked, his words torn away in the wind.

"I think he thinks he is," Joe said.

"Then that is how you fight him."

Joe looked at Ahanu. "How?"

"If he is a Windigo, he hates what he is, and a part of him wants to die. If he is a Windigo, he won't die by his own hand."

Joe took a step closer. "Then how?" she asked.

"He can be killed only by a worthy opponent, a warrior brave. Only a warrior can put his evil spirit to rest. And he will seek out that warrior brave to do this for him, seek out the warrior who will kill him and burn his ashes so he can never come back. That is what he wants. That is the peace he craves."

Joe shook her head. "This man killed two cops and ran. That is not a man who wants to die."

"I read in the newspaper that he killed his own brother," Ahanu said. "Is that true?"

"Yes."

"I can only guess what is in his mind now. Maybe when he killed his brother, he crossed a line he did not want to cross."

Joe considered this. "Just like the Windigos cross a line that must not be crossed when they cannibalize."

Ahanu nodded. "He is alone now. Winter is coming."

Joe fell quiet.

"He must confront the worthy warrior," Ahanu said. "And that is you."

Joe's eyes shot up. "Me? Why me?"

"You survived."

Joe took a few steps away, turned, and looked down at the lake far below. "What do I do?" she said.

"Nothing," Ahanu said. "He will find you."

47

His feet were numb, but he didn't move. If he did, he might disturb the branches, and if she was watching from the cottage window, she might see it and sense he was out here.

She might be able to do that now. Feel his presence. As the others could when they were hanging there in the darkness, calling out to him. As his mother could that day when he had stood under the big tree and stared up at her.

Don't be sad, my son. I will always be with you.

Roland cupped his hands and blew into them. His eyes moved to the back door with its empty deck and the snowcapped evergreens that surrounded the cottage. Nothing was moving, and he looked back at the door, trying to will it open.

If she didn't go to bed soon, he would have to come back tomorrow. He needed her in bed, relaxed and unarmed, because he knew he couldn't let her get to her weapon. If she did, he might have to shoot her, and that wasn't the way this was supposed to happen. He needed her alive for a while.

Roland glanced down the road, worried

someone would see the truck parked in the trees. It was the dead man's truck. He had driven it down from Canada, amazed that the men at the border didn't see much difference between Roland's face and the blurry bearded man pictured on the driver's license. More amazed that he had made it all the way across the Mackinac Bridge from the Upper Peninsula without so much as a look from the state trooper who passed him, chasing someone else.

Finally, he had snuck a look at himself in the rearview mirror. He was shocked at the gray in his beard and hair and how sunken his face looked. He was different. He must be different for them not to see. Maybe he was even invisible now.

He concentrated on the drawn curtain of the bedroom window.

Turn off the lights and go to bed, bitch.

A silhouette paused behind the curtain. He knew it was her. Recognized the thin, long body and the ponytail. Then a second silhouette moved across the window. Roland jerked to attention, his head clicking with possibilities about who the other person could be. But then he realized it was another woman. Shorter. Fatter. And no threat.

He settled back against the tree, his mind

starting to wander again, strange images drifting through his head. The woman and how she had looked hanging in the tree. Kenny lying in the snow, staring up at him with dead, accusing eyes. The way his father had looked that day at the cabin. Hating him, even in death.

His mother . . .

He didn't have much of her in his memory anymore.

Roland dug down into his pants pocket, his stiff fingers coming out with a small wad of old tattered cloth. He set it in his palm and unfolded it carefully. It was too dark to see clearly, so he touched the strands of black hair with the tip of his finger, stroking them tenderly. He had taken the little bundle that morning so many years ago, stolen it from her body before they put her in the tree. He had kept it with him for his whole life, bringing it out to stroke the hair whenever he needed to feel her presence.

The lock of hair seemed thinner now, and he wondered how the hairs disappeared when he kept them wrapped so carefully in the cloth for so long. But maybe the lock of hair grew thinner with each life he took. Maybe that was how his mother stayed with him, giving a part of herself to those who hung in the trees as she did.

The bark of a dog drew his head back to the cottage. He quickly refolded the cloth and stuck it back in his pocket. The back door opened, washing the snowy yard with a long slant of yellow light.

A big dog bounded onto the deck, first barking and jumping, then running off into the yard. The woman closed the door, killing the light. The dog stopped halfway to the trees, nose tipped to the icy air.

No. No!

The dog came toward him, a suspicious tilt to its head, a small baring of its teeth. Then a low growl rolled through the darkness.

No, goddamn it. No!

Roland slipped behind the tree, but the dog followed, lunging at him, then jumping back, every bark growing more fierce.

God . . . God . . .

He didn't know what to do. He couldn't shoot the damn thing — the woman would hear. But he had a knife, and he started to reach for it when the dog jumped at him again, its teeth ripping into his sleeve.

He worked the knife free, pressing himself back against the tree, throwing his arm up in front of his face, because he knew wolves always went first for the face.

It came at him again, snarling, growling,

its teeth sinking into his hand, tearing at the flesh.

Roland choked back a cry of pain. He thrust the knife into the hard muscle of the dog's shoulder.

It yelped and jerked away crazily, crying as it jumped and twisted through the snow, spraying blood. Then the dog was gone, staggering into the black trees, its whimpers hanging in the air behind it.

Roland looked down at his shredded hand, then pushed off the tree and started to run.

"How long has Chips been out?" Florence asked.

Joe looked up from her book, then to the clock. It had been twenty minutes. Usually in this weather, he was back in seconds, scratching at the door to get back in.

"Want me to see if he's by the door?" Florence asked.

Joe pushed up off the sofa. "I'll get him."

She turned on the deck light and opened the door. The cold air rushed in around her, and she gathered her robe tighter as she stared out. The backyard was silent and empty, Chips's paw prints visible in the snow.

"Chips!" she called.

Nothing.

"Chips!"

Joe took a step onto the deck, scanning the yard, trying to see into the deep shadows of the trees, trying to hear something besides the wind moving in them.

"Chips!"

Still nothing.

She needed to go look for him. He could be caught somewhere, or, God forbid, some animal could have gotten him. She went back to the living room and picked up her revolver off the counter, flipping open the cylinder to make sure it was loaded.

"Joe? What is it?"

She slipped on her boots and grabbed a parka and a flashlight.

"Wait," Florence said. "Let me come with you."

"No, stay here. Lock the door."

Joe moved quickly to the deck, pulling the door shut and waiting until she heard it lock behind her before she clicked on the flashlight and shined it into the woods. The dark trees shifted with the wind, and she couldn't tell if the movement she was seeing was real or her imagination.

She lowered the flashlight beam and followed the paw prints. They trailed deeper toward the trees, and she paused again, alert for any sound, her eyes scanning the darkness.

"Chips!"

She followed the paw prints across the yard, her pace slowing as she neared the trunk of a large pine.

Dark droplets.

She took two more steps, then stopped, trying to hold the flashlight steady as the bright white circle moved over the trampled snow.

Blood.

Paw prints.

Footprints. Large. A man.

She lifted her gun and spun, unsure where to point the flashlight or aim the gun, seeing nothing but the moving darkness.

She had to find Chips. She leveled her gun, moving it in a wide arc as she edged away from the blood and followed the smeared paw prints deeper into the trees. Every nerve in her body was drawn tight, her eyes flicking from Chips's prints to the blackness of the forest and then, oddly, up into the branches, part of her expecting to see a body.

Then she heard something. First a whisper that grew to a soft whimpering that moved through the trees like the wind.

Chips.

Shivering, wet, and bloody, he lay sprawled in a puddle of pink snow. He looked at her, eyes liquid, belly heaving.

She knelt down next to him, then looked back to the yellow lights of the cottage. She started to scream for her mother, but she couldn't risk bringing her out here.

She took one last look around the trees, then worked her arms under Chips, keeping her gun in her hand. He was heavy and wet, but she managed to get him up against her. As she staggered back to the cottage, his breathing grew labored and shallow. She kicked at the back door.

"Ma!" she screamed. "Ma, help me!"

Florence threw open the door. "What's the matter? Oh, Jesus . . . what?"

Joe pushed inside, almost stumbling as she set Chips down on the kitchen table. "Get me a blanket. We're taking him to the hospital."

"Did an animal get him?" Florence asked.

Joe grabbed a towel and pressed it to the bloody hole in the fur. "No, there was someone out there."

Florence handed her a blanket, and Joe moved Chips so she could wrap him. He was looking up at her, his eyes dark with fear.

Florence pulled on her jacket and turned,

looking at Joe. "Are we safe leaving?"

Joe held out her revolver to her mother. "Can you shoot this?"

Florence took the gun. "Damn right."

"I'll carry Chips," she said. "You go first, and take the flashlight. Check the yard, then the Jeep before you get in."

Florence opened the front door and went outside, Joe close behind her. There were no footprints in the snow in the front yard and none around the Jeep.

But as Florence drove down the narrow country road, Joe noticed tire tracks about a half-mile from her cottage. It looked as if someone had driven off the road and parked in the trees. But there was no car there now. He was gone.

Mike stared at the bloody ground, then ran the flashlight beam back to the far trees. Joe's phone call had gotten him out of bed, and he wore jeans and his sheriff's parka thrown over an old flannel shirt. His face was slashed with shadows, his eyes jerky as they scanned the trees.

"He's gone, Mike," she said.

Mike glanced back at the ground and nodded slowly, as if he knew that but still couldn't shake the idea of a man in the darkness aiming a shotgun at them.

They heard a door close, and they both looked to the cottage. Holt was walking toward them, his own flashlight beam jumping across the ground ahead of him. He stopped and blew out a cloudy breath. "Your mom says to tell you the vet just called," he said. "Chips is going to be okay. And he said you were right. It was a knife wound."

Joe looked away, running a hand over her face.

Holt broke the silence. "The tire tracks up the road are from a truck. I'm no expert, but I'd say a big pickup. Pretty worn tread, though, so it might be an old vehicle."

"Nothing else there?" Mike asked. "Cigarette butts tossed out the window? Oil leak? Wrappers?"

Holt shook his head. "I don't think he stayed in the truck. Looks to me like he sat right here."

Joe stepped closer to the tree, shining her light directly onto the footprints. They were from a boot, size ten or eleven. Nothing special about them. But then she saw something else.

"Look," she said.

Mike knelt next to her.

Lying in the snow behind the tree was a shred of fabric, dark green. Chips had torn a piece of clothing from him. Mike picked it up and put it in an envelope he drew from his jacket pocket, then pulled himself to his feet.

"I'll get a team out here tonight to look around," he said. "See if we find anything else."

Joe nodded. They stood in silence for a moment longer, hands stuffed in pockets, gazes nervous and unsteady.

"What do you think this is, Joe?" Mike asked.

"I think it's Trader. He's back."

Mike glanced at Holt, and Joe thought she saw a glimmer of fear in his eyes — for her.

"He'd be crazy to come back here," Mike said. "Every cop in the state is looking for him."

"But not here. No one believes he'd come back here."

"But why?" Mike asked. "What does he want?"

"He wants to die," she said.

Mike looked at Holt again, and this time she was sure she saw doubt. "Come on inside," she said. "I'll explain it to you."

48

The uniform was laid out on the bed waiting for her. Joe's eyes traveled over the dark brown pants with their razor-sharp crease, the tan shirt with its starched collar, the brown tie, the thick leather utility belt.

The room was cold, but she didn't make a move toward getting dressed. She just stood there, staring at the clothes, lined up like some weird headless, deflated corpse.

She heard the floor creak and turned. Her mother was standing at the door, bundled in a pink robe, coffee in hand.

"You didn't have to iron my uniform, Ma," Joe said.

"It's your first day back. You should look good."

Joe smiled, went to the bed, and picked up the pants. She put them on, sliding on a belt and pulling it tight. It went in an extra notch.

She went to her dresser and opened her jewelry box, taking out the gold bar that read J. FRYE, the two SO collar pins, and her deputy star. She slipped the collar pins into the small preset holes in the shirt.

She turned to her mother. "You find the tape?" she asked.

Florence nodded and pulled out a roll of

black electrical tape from her robe pocket. Joe tore off a small piece, and placed it over the star. She inserted the star in its hole in the shirt. When she put the shirt on, it was tighter than normal. She turned, frowning, to the mirror.

"I sewed some darts in it," Florence said.

Joe looked at her.

Florence shrugged. "Why the hell not? Just because it's a man's shirt doesn't mean you have to look like one."

Joe smiled. "Thanks, Ma."

She clipped on the tie. There was just the utility belt left. She slipped on the attachments, the leather loop for the nightstick, a second one for the flashlight, the cuffs pouch, the pepper spray holder, the radio pouch, and last, the holster with the .38 revolver snapped inside.

She cinched on the belt. It was only ten pounds, but it felt heavier than she remembered. She turned to face her mother.

Florence had been sipping her coffee, and her hand holding the mug came down from her face slowly. Her mouth fell open slightly. Her eyes, behind the huge pink frames of her glasses, blinked and misted over.

"What's the matter?" Joe asked.

Florence shook her head slowly.

Joe's right hand touched the butt of her

gun and then came up to the star and the tie. "Do I look okay?"

Florence nodded quickly. "I never realized before how much you look like your father." She took off her glasses and wiped at her eyes. Then she turned suddenly and headed toward the kitchen. "I'm gonna make some fresh coffee. You want some?"

"Ma —"

"You should have some breakfast, you know."

Joe followed her mother into the kitchen. "Ma, I'm all right. It's time for me to go back."

Florence was standing at the sink, her back to Joe. When she finally turned, she was wiping at her eyes. "I know, I know," she said.

Joe came forward and hugged her mother. "I gotta go. I'm late," she said softly.

Florence held up a hand. "Wait a minute." She reached into her bathrobe pocket and pulled out a small holstered .22 revolver. "I want you to take this."

Joe's eyes went from the gun up to her mother's face. "Where'd you get that?"

Florence thrust the gun forward. "It's mine, and it's legal. And I don't want my daughter going out there without a backup weapon."

"Ma . . ."

"Take it!"

Joe took the gun and gave her mother a kiss on the cheek. She went to the door, reaching for her parka hanging on the back.

"Keep the doors locked, okay?" Joe said, slipping the .22 into her parka. "And if you want to go out, call me first."

"Joe, Mike has a cruiser parked at the end of the driveway."

"I know. But I can still worry about you for a change, you know," she said.

Outside, Joe squinted in the bright sun and pulled the cold air into her lungs before getting into her Jeep. She waved to the deputy in the cruiser as she pulled out and headed toward town. The only driver she saw was the woodcutter, Jack Jenkins, hauling cords of firewood in his old red pickup. She made a mental note to call him. It was something Brad had always taken care of in the past.

As she drove slowly down Main, she realized a sense of normalcy had returned. Emptied of the state police cars, the TV vans, and the morbidly curious, the streets were quiet again. Dirty snow was piled against the curbs, and people came and went from the grocery to the post office, heads shrouded in wool hats and hoods, pausing to chat in the cold sunlight. The somnambulant pace of Echo Bay in winter had returned, even if it was fragile, as if the smallest jostle could awaken everything again.

Joe had a sudden idea and parked in front of the Early Bird. She would take fresh doughnuts to the station. She was paying for her order when she spotted a woman in the corner booth by the window.

Dorothy Newton.

Joe went over to the booth. Dorothy Newton was gazing out at the street, chin in hand, and didn't look up. A copy of that morning's *Banner* and a plate of half-eaten scrambled eggs and toast sat at her elbow.

"Mrs. Newton?"

The brown eyes came up, blank for a moment, then clearing with recognition. "Deputy," she said softly.

"How are you?" Joe asked.

A faint smile. "I'm okay. Thank you." The smile faded. "I heard what happened to you. I'm so sorry. I don't even know . . ."

Joe gave a curt nod. "It's all right, Mrs. Newton."

Dorothy Newton's eyes drifted back to the window. "Everyone's gone," she said softly.

Joe hesitated. "May I sit down, Mrs. Newton?"

She didn't look up but nodded. Joe slid into the booth.

"I don't understand it," Dorothy Newton said.

"Understand what, ma'am?"

"I read they found more bones, somewhere up in the sand dunes."

"Yes."

"I don't understand why there are so few bones. I don't understand why the rest . . ."

"Mrs. Newton —"

"I know now Natalie's dead. But I know she's still out there somewhere."

"Mrs. Newton," Joe said, "you should go home."

Dorothy Newton shut her eyes briefly.

"There's no reason for you to stay here now. If there is anything . . ." Joe's voice trailed off. "You really should go home."

"Have you given up, Deputy Frye?"

Joe was silent, riveted by the strength in those brown eyes.

Dorothy Newton gave a half-smile. "I didn't think so. Neither have I."

She was surprised to see Brad waiting for her outside the sheriff's office. Hands thrust into the pockets of his jacket, his face red from the cold, his eyes tearing from the sun as they drifted to the sound of her tires crunching on the frozen snow.

They had talked on the phone two nights ago. He had gently told her he had accepted a position at a clinic in Marquette, saying without really saying it that he was not coming back. She had told him she was happy for him and she understood. He told her he would come back to get his things and hung up.

She didn't think it would be so soon.

She gathered the bag of doughnuts off the seat and got out slowly, not at all sure what she was feeling.

"Hi," he said as she stopped in front of him.

"You could've waited inside," she said.

He glanced at the sheriff's office door and tried a smile. "I was never comfortable in there."

She nodded, looking around for his truck. She saw it, parked in front of the drugstore. A canvas was draped over some boxes in back.

"Your mom helped me pack up," he said. "She was very kind. Tell her thank you for me."

Joe nodded, and they both fell quiet while a salt truck rumbled past. When it was gone, he stepped closer.

"I need to make sure you know that I'm not doing this because you were . . . because of what happened to you," he said.

"I know that, Brad," she said softly.

"It's just" — he shook his head and let out a long breath — "I don't know, Joe, it's just you wanting to stay in a world that hurt you so much. That's what I don't understand. I don't think I can ever understand that."

Joe forced herself to look at him. The stiff wind was fingering his hair, watering his eyes. It reminded her of how he looked the day they had foolishly ventured out onto a frozen Lake Superior. Scared to death but trying to be brave.

"This is where I belong," she said.

They both fell quiet. He reached out and pulled her to him for a hug. She closed her eyes, wanting to hold on to this one moment for just a few seconds longer. When he let her go, the space between them filled with cold air.

She realized suddenly that he was waiting, waiting for her to tell him it was all right to go, to leave her alone.

"It's okay, Brad," she whispered. "I'm okay."

His eyes teared. "If you need anything,

you call me, okay?" he said quickly. "You have my mom's number in Marquette."

She nodded. Again, the quiet. He looked down the street, sighed, and finally forced his eyes back to her.

"Take care of yourself, Joe."

"I will. I promise."

He walked away, and she stayed for a moment on the sidewalk, watching the truck until it turned a corner at the traffic light.

There was an ache in her chest, as though if she tried to take too deep a breath, something would break. And already she missed the feel of his arms around her, missed his voice, missed knowing he would be there when she came home at night. But she knew it had to end. Knew that as much as they had loved each other, he couldn't give her whatever it was she needed to heal.

She turned to the door of the sheriff's office. In the sun-glazed glass, she could see herself. She didn't know what she needed to heal. But whatever it was, she had to find it herself.

She pulled open the station door. The smell of burned coffee, leather, and pine air freshener greeted her, and she closed her eyes briefly at the familiarity of it.

"Joette!"

Augie sprang from his console and came

rushing forward, throwing his arms around her, crushing the bag of doughnuts. "Oh, my dear! I'm so happy to see you!"

Joe pulled back and handed off the doughnuts. "It's good to be back."

"Are you okay, Joette? You look a little —"

"I'm fine, Augie."

"Mike told me to tell you he needed to see you as soon as you got here."

Joe was still thinking about Brad, and it took her a moment to pick up on Augie's agitated tone. "Why? What's going on?"

"I don't know, but Theo just got here, and he's all excited about something, and no one will tell me —"

Joe was already on her way down the hall, throwing off her parka. The office door was ajar, and she pushed it open. The sight of Mike sitting in Leach's beat-up leather chair was like a punch to the heart. Mike and Theo looked up.

"Joe," Mike said, rising. "Boy, am I glad you're here. Theo, tell her what you found."

Theo had a paper in his hand. "I was going over some records, and I found this."

Joe tossed her parka onto a chair and took the paper. It was a form, filled in for a six-month subscription to the *Echo Bay Banner.* The name on it was Otis Deppert.

"So?" Joe asked.

"Look at the town," Theo said.

"Peterbell, Canada," Joe read.

"It's up in Ontario," Mike said, gesturing to the map spread on the desk. "It's about five hundred miles from here."

She looked at Theo. "When did this order come in?"

"I don't know. Carrie didn't record it. I only noticed it because the bank called me since it's a Canadian money order. The subscription started December 1."

"About a week after the ambush," Joe said. "Better call Kellerman."

As Mike made the call, Joe looked at the map of Ontario. Peterbell was nothing but a pinpoint in what looked like a forest or game preserve. The nearest town of any size was at least twenty miles away. If Roland Trader had been hiding out in Canada, an outpost like Peterbell would be the perfect place. She had a fleeting thought of some faceless man named Otis Deppert. As much as she wanted Roland Trader caught, she prayed Deppert was still alive.

Mike finally reached Kellerman, and she listened as he relayed the information. She was thinking about how Mike had reacted when he came over the night Chips had been stabbed. She had told him everything she knew — about the moon symbols, the

Windigo psychosis, what Ahanu had told her about the worthy warrior. She told him her theory that Roland Trader had targeted her as his mythic opponent in some twisted final confrontation. When she finished, Mike's face was etched with skepticism. But that same night, he had posted the deputy in their driveway.

Yesterday, Mike called her to say he had spoken with Kellerman and filled him in, not just on the stabbing of Chips but also on Joe's theories, including that Roland might be back in Echo Bay. Kellerman had told Mike just to send him a report.

"Joe?"

She turned to Mike. He was holding out the receiver. "Kellerman wants to talk to you."

She took the phone. "Deputy Frye."

"I want you to listen to me very carefully," Kellerman said. "First off, I don't think you should be back at work yet."

"Captain, the doctor —"

"I don't care what the doctor says. I have a lot of experience with this sort of thing, and I've seen officers — strong men — crack after being involved in a traumatic situation, and what happened to you goes beyond even that. I'm not sure putting on a uniform, let alone still working this case, is the best move for you or your department."

Joe felt a tightness in her chest, felt eyes on her, but didn't look at either Mike or Theo.

Kellerman coughed. "I've got someone on the phone now with RCMP, and we're going to catch this bastard. You leave it to us. I don't want you people doing anything stupid again."

"Sir, we aren't —"

"I mean it, Deputy. Don't go setting yourself up as some bait. Don't put yourself in any position where —"

He coughed again. When he spoke this time, the edge was gone. "Look, I'll send a man over. We'll do what we can, but we can't completely protect you."

Joe almost cringed at the paternal tone of Kellerman's voice. "Sir, if I may, I don't think sending your men here will help," she said. "If Roland Trader has come back here, any extra police presence will scare him off."

Kellerman was quiet again, considering this. "I still don't think he's stupid enough to show up there. But on the small chance he is, I want you with other deputies at all times. I want you to be careful."

Now Joe was quiet.

"Do you understand me, Deputy?"

"Yes, sir."

Joe hung up and turned to Mike. Holt had appeared. Augie was standing just outside the open door next to Theo. They were all staring at her. Kellerman's voice had a way of carrying, even from the telephone, and she wondered how much they had heard. From the look on Mike's face, they had heard every word.

"Okay, look," Joe said. "You heard Kellerman. You heard him say he can't protect me. And neither can you."

They were all just staring at her. She was looking at them, but she was seeing Brad.

"I don't *want* to be protected. I want to work. I *have* to work," she said. "I know you want to make things right for me, make things go back to the way they were. But that can't happen."

Holt looked at the floor. Mike shifted uneasily from one foot to the other. Theo glanced at Augie.

"If things are ever going to be okay again around here, you guys can't be walking on eggshells afraid something you say or do is going to upset me," she went on. "We will never be able to function as a department again that way."

She looked at them, at each of them. "I am all right," she said, carefully enunciating every word.

Mike hesitated, then nodded. "Okay, then we'll see this through together." He looked at the other men. They nodded awkwardly, and then, almost as one, they looked back at Joe.

She felt a small tightening in her chest. "Doughnuts," she said. "I brought you doughnuts. I'll go get them."

She pushed past Augie and went out into the hall. She paused to take a deep breath and continued out into the main office. She started for the doughnut bag on Augie's desk, but the sound of the door opening made her look up.

The cold air swirled in, sending the hem of the man's coat flapping. He let the door close softly behind him and turned.

"Hey, Frye," he said.

Her eyes focused on the bandaged right arm beneath the overcoat. She felt something hard knotting in her stomach, felt the memories of the night in the woods coming back. She fought them, pushing them down in the lockbox of her mind, slamming down the lid.

When she looked up to meet his eyes, she managed a smile.

"Hey, Rafsky," she said.

49

They sat in the cruiser, neither saying anything. Joe had suggested they take a ride, anything to get out of the station and away from the eyes of the others. The heater was on, the windows clouded, and in the cocoon of the car, she was suddenly too conscious of him, of the wet-wool smell of his coat, of the even rhythm of his breathing.

"What are you doing here, Rafsky?" she asked.

He shifted in the passenger seat to face her. "Mike called me."

Joe kept her eyes trained out the windshield. "Mike called you," she repeated softly.

"He's worried about you."

She didn't look at him. She didn't want to, afraid he would see something, a vulnerability or hurt that she wasn't willing to let anyone see. It had been okay so far; she had been able to hold things together. Even after saying goodbye to Brad, even after telling Mike and the others that she didn't need their protection, even then she had been all right. She had been able to convince herself that if she had other things to think about like the job, if she didn't think too long or too hard about what had happened, it wouldn't be *there* in the front of her memory.

But now *he* was here. Rafsky was here. And it was all there again, in the furrows of his cheeks, the set of his mouth, the broken-wing way he held himself in his sling, and the blue flame of his eyes. He was here — the other survivor — and every memory about the ambush was suddenly back, banging in her head to get out.

"Did Mike tell you what happened to my dog?" she asked finally.

"Yeah. How is Chips doing?"

It touched her that he remembered her dog's name, and for a moment she couldn't trust herself to answer. "He's going to be okay," she said.

"So you think Trader did it?"

"Yes, but I have no proof. Just a feeling."

Through the windshield, she saw Mike emerge from the station. He paused on the sidewalk, looking their way.

"I can't take this," she said softly. "Let's get out of here for a while."

She steered the cruiser out onto Main Street, and soon they were heading south on M-22. Rafsky didn't ask where they were going. She didn't know, really, but the driving gave her something to concentrate on instead of him.

They were entering the village of Lake Leelanau, and Joe eased off the gas as they cruised through.

"So you think Trader has come back to force you into some sort of final ritualistic confrontation?" Rafsky asked.

She glanced at him. "Mike told you that, too?"

Rafsky nodded. "He told me everything, about your talk with Ahanu, about Mary Trader. He told me that as much as he wants you back, he thinks it's too soon."

"Damn it," Joe said softly. Mike hadn't mentioned that.

"Mike's worried about you," Rafsky said. "I'm worried about you."

"Look, you didn't need to come all the way up here just to check on me," she said. "I'm okay, all right?"

"Joe —"

"I'm okay, damn it," she whispered. "I'm okay."

Rafsky was silent, but she could feel his eyes on her.

They didn't say anything for the next fifteen minutes. When Joe pulled the cruiser to a slow stop on the snowy road, Rafsky looked out the window at the tall pines and turned to Joe.

"What are we doing here?"

"I don't know," she said quietly. Her hands gripped the wheel. Her eyes stayed on the distant trees.

"Sometimes they come back to the place where they murdered," Rafsky said.

"I don't think he's here," she said.

"Then why are we?" he asked.

There was a murmur from the radio, one of the deputies reporting in from a late lunch break. Joe realized she was clutching the steering wheel so tightly her fingers hurt. She let go, closing her eyes.

"Do you want to see it?" Rafsky asked gently.

Joe hesitated, then nodded.

They got out of the cruiser. The doors closed with dull thuds in the snow-muted woods. Without a word, they started up the hill through the trees, Joe slowing her step in deference to Rafsky's pace.

"Do you have a gun?" she asked as they walked.

"No."

She stopped and pulled out her mother's holstered .22 from her parka pocket. She handed it to Rafsky. He slipped it into his coat pocket, and they walked on.

The sound of trickling water told them they were near. They slowed as they approached the waterfall. Joe drew to a stop.

The trees stood tall and unmoving, laden with capes of snow. The cold had frozen most of the waterfall's flow, but a stream still fell, making its slow way through the snowcapped rocks. The air was still and cold. It was hard to breathe.

She stared straight ahead, unable to look up at the tree she knew was only a few yards away. She kept her eyes on the water, trying not to see anything but instead seeing in her imagination the stream running red. She closed her eyes.

A sob burst from her chest. She fell to her knees.

He was there, quickly, pulling her close with his good arm, pressing her head to his chest, letting her cry.

Back in the cruiser, she sat spent and numb, eyes closed. Rafsky's handkerchief was wadded in her hands. She was thankful he didn't say anything, because she knew one word from him, one more kindness, would cut her in two. She was too fragile right now, and the realization of that was hard to accept. With one violent act, Roland Trader had stripped something away from her — her belief in her own strength. And she had to find a way to get it back.

"Joe?"

She didn't open her eyes.

"Are you okay?"

She felt his hand, rough and cold, cover hers.

"Are you okay?" he asked again.

She nodded, her eyes still closed.

"What do you want to do?"

The softness of his voice was piercing. It struck her in that moment, like a small but sharp stab to her heart. She wanted him, still. And in his question, she felt the same want from him. But she knew the intimacy they felt wasn't love. It was a bond born the night of the ambush and now living as two survivors' need to forget.

She slowly opened her eyes, drew in a deep breath, and faced Rafsky. "I want to find him," she said.

Rafsky pulled in a deep breath. "All right," he said. "Then I want to help you. If he has come back, I want to help you. I don't want you facing him alone."

She felt a small catch in her throat and kept her eyes trained out the windshield.

"If you want me to go home, just say so," Rafsky said quietly.

She shut her eyes.

"Joe?"

"No, stay," she whispered. "I want you to stay."

■ ■ ■ ■

For the next hour, they sat in the cruiser and talked. About Leach, about the ambush, about how her memories of it were so fragmented she sometimes wondered if she were going crazy. They talked about his boss's loss of confidence in him. They talked about his wife, Gina, and about how his son, Ryan, couldn't bear to be away from him anymore. They talked about Brad, and when she told him she and Brad had decided to stay apart, he just nodded. By the time Rafsky gently steered her back to Roland Trader, she felt spent but oddly calm.

She put the cruiser in gear, and they drove out of the forest, away from the waterfall.

"Where are we going?" Rafsky asked when they were back on the highway.

"If he's really come back, there aren't many places he can hide," she said.

"But if he's trying to provoke a confrontation, maybe he doesn't want to hide," Rafsky said. "At least, not from you."

She nodded, thinking.

"So where would he go?" Rafsky asked.

"Maybe to visit the grave," Joe said.

"His brother's?"

Joe nodded. "And his mother's."

Rafsky hesitated. "You're sure you're up for this?"

"I told you. I want to catch the bastard," she said.

The county cemetery was just south of Echo Bay. Joe pulled the cruiser into the gates and eased along the narrow, snowy road that wound between the headstones. She remembered reading in one of Theo's stories that Ken Snider had been buried in a part of the cemetery for indigents. They found the section in a far corner devoid of trees and headstones.

They trudged through the snow, brushing off the plain metal markers, looking for anything that resembled a recent burial. Finally, they spotted a snowy mound near a backhoe. The grave didn't even have a metal marker yet, just a paper sign on a post, hand-printed: K. SNIDER.

The snow looked undisturbed. Joe looked around at the other plots. No footprints around any other graves, nothing to indicate the grave had been visited by anyone. But still she felt a tightening in her gut, and her hand went automatically to her holster as her eyes traveled over the far trees.

Rafsky was also looking at the trees. "He hasn't been here, Joe. So where do we go from here?"

"His mother," Joe said.

A half-hour later, Joe pulled the cruiser to a stop on the road leading to the bluff where she had met Thomas Ahanu. Dressed in a full coat of snow, the place looked even lonelier than it had the first time she saw it. She led Rafsky up the hill and toward the huge dead oak. The old headstones were almost covered in the snow, but she was able to find Mary Trader's.

The only prints visible were the ones she and Ahanu had left several days ago, partially filled now with a dusting of fresh snow. She stared at the ground, her mind starting to itch with doubt about her theory. Maybe Roland Trader wasn't back at all. Maybe Chips had just been the victim of a panicked prowler.

She turned in a circle, scanning the trees, her ears pricked for any sounds.

"I don't think he's here," Rafsky said softly. "Or anywhere near here."

She nodded. "Maybe we should get back to the station."

They walked to the cruiser in silence. She headed the car back to the main road, slowing as they came up behind a salt truck. When she saw a sign, she hit the left blinker.

"Where we going now?" Rafsky asked.

"We're near the Collier cabin," she said.

"I don't think he'd be that stupid, but let's check it out."

Rafsky was quiet for a moment, then he looked at her. His face was drawn with uncertainty. Maybe a flicker of fear, too. "I don't think it's a matter of stupidity," he said. "It's need. It may be exactly where he'd go."

Joe thought about that for a moment, then hailed Mike on the radio. He and Holt were checking out a fender-bender south of town. She asked them to meet her at the Collier cabin. Mike said he was ten or so minutes behind her and clicked off.

They headed into the thick trees.

50

The cabin was waiting for him, empty and dark, as it always was in the winter time. Pillows of snow on the roof and icicles on the eaves, shimmering in the sun like thousands of tiny knives.

He stepped from behind the tree and looked down the long, unplowed road. There were fresh tire tracks, and his gaze followed them up into the driveway. He knew they must be from a four-wheel drive. Nothing else could make it through the snow.

The cops had been here, probably after the woman reported her dog dead. He wondered if anyone was inside now. He hadn't been in there yet. Instinct had told him to wait, and that was what he had been doing since returning to Echo Bay — waiting, spending the last few nights in empty hunting shanties.

This morning, he had dumped the truck, worried that the Canadian plates would attract attention. He had pushed it into a ravine and covered it with branches. Then he had hiked back here, because this was where he needed to be.

He looked down at his hand. The dog bite was swollen, pus oozing from the puncture wounds. He wondered what would happen if the pus got into his veins. Would it kill him or make him stronger?

When he looked back at the cabin, the glare of the sun off the snow made his eyes water. The hot tears felt good on his cold face. Felt human. Unlike the rest of him. The rest of him felt numb and sore, his bones so hard and cold he was sure they would crack if he moved too quickly.

Why couldn't he think? Why couldn't he just *sense* if there was someone inside?

Talk to me, Mommie. Help me. Be with me now, and tell me what to do.

He shut his eyes, the voice a whisper in his head.

Just go inside, son.

He moved forward, carrying his shotgun and the small bundle of newspapers. His heart kicked into a furious beat as he neared the front door. The snow was trampled with footprints.

Cops. Lots of them had been here.

The door was locked, and he followed the prints around the cabin to a back window, to the bedroom that had been his. The window was locked, and he started to pick up a log from the wood pile to break it, then remembered the kitchen. He had broken that window the night he had come here and killed the people.

He went back. The glass in the window pane was still missing. They hadn't even bothered to cover it up. He peered inside.

Snow had drifted into the kitchen, covering the floor and dusting the counters and the dinette set. It looked like one of those places in a movie where someone had gone away and draped white sheets over the furniture to keep things clean.

He carefully reached in through the pane, unlocked the door, and went in. Footprints on the snowy floor. He would step in those and stay invisible.

No one had bothered to clean anything up. Plates of half-eaten food still sat on the table. He needed to stop the gnawing hunger in his belly. He leaned the shotgun against the counter and searched the cupboards. He found a package of oatmeal cookies and ripped it apart, scattering them across the counter.

He shoved the dry cookies into his mouth. He found a Faygo cream soda in the fridge and was guzzling it down when his eyes caught movement outside the kitchen window.

A deer.

Standing by a white birch. Tawny fur shimmering in the sunlight. Its eyes round, black, and guileless.

Shoot it!

The animal seemed to hold Roland's stare.

Shoot it! What's the matter with you? Shoot it, you little pansy!

Roland set the can down, eyes still fixed on the deer but his mind shifting with different images.

Girls. All of the faces coming at once.

The first one. Ronnie, that bitch Kenny fucked in their dad's bedroom. That hadn't been his fault, and it hadn't happened the way he told Kenny. Ronnie had never come on to him. He had sat there on the basement steps, watching her fingers as they plucked panties off the line. Then she had looked at him over the clothesline, her eyes wide and dark as that deer's.

She didn't see him pick up the hammer. She didn't fight after he hit her. She didn't move when he took her.

He brought her body up here only because he needed somewhere safe to hide it. He dumped her in the woods and ran back to the cabin. And then he saw the carving under his bedroom window, the one he did the day Kenny shot Dad. He saw it, and all the memories came back.

The explosion of buckshot as his father's face was blown away. The sticky, warm feel of brains and skin on his face. The taste of those few small shreds of bloody skin that ended up in his mouth as he screamed.

And he knew then what was happening to him. And he knew what he needed to do to satisfy it.

He got his father's hoist out of the basement and hid it in his car. And then he found other girls. He tied their feet to the hoist and took their bodies the way Kenny used to do to Ronnie. He sliced them and pulled them up into the trees, because that's how women died, up in trees. Then he hid and waited, watching the blood trickle down their naked bodies onto the white snow below.

It was with the third girl that he discovered that if he waited long enough, if he was patient — if he was invisible — sometimes the animals would come. Bears, wolves, once even a cougar. And if he was careful, he could work the pulley from his hiding place and lower the body without frightening the animal away. And he would watch the animal eat.

Then, after a day or two, he cut them down, always leaving a piece of them for the animals but taking away the rest.

The girl with the red hair . . .

The one he had done last February. She had been the only one he tasted. He had waited a long time for the animals to come for her, listening to the wind from the lake crying like wolves. And when the real wolves finally came, he watched as they ripped her apart, their chewing and growling giving him an erection so hard and a climax so explosive, he screamed out like one of them.

The deer suddenly bolted away, vanishing into the trees.

Roland turned away from the kitchen window. He picked up the newspapers and the shotgun and went to the living room. No snow here, just smears of dried blood on the wood floor, the walls, and the sofa from where he had killed that couple and their daughter. The cops had left fingerprint powder, a plastic glove, and little yellow evidence markers.

He stared at the bloodstains. This is where Annabelle Chapel had died, too. Right here in this room. The story he had told Kenny about her had been true, about how he took her from the ski lodge and brought her here. How he cut off her head and threw it in the woods. It was all true, except the part Kenny had told the cops about helping him get rid of the body. Kenny had never done anything.

I'm sorry, Kenny.

Roland knelt and ran a finger along the wood planks of the floor. His fingertip came away with a pink-brown smudge. He stared at his fingertip, then stuck it in his mouth. It tasted only of dust and wood.

The ache was coming again, starting low in his body and moving through him like a rush of hot water. A face came to him, not one of the girls this time but the chiseled face of the woman cop he had left at the waterfall.

There had been no time to wait for the animals that night. He had time now.

But he didn't know where she was or what

she was doing.

The newspapers.

He spread them out on the floor. They were from the last three days, stolen from mailboxes, and he looked for her picture or any mention of her, but there was nothing.

It didn't matter. There were cop tracks outside, and she would be back. It was just a matter of time.

He had to be patient.

He had to be invisible.

He gathered up the papers and the shotgun. He remembered the cookies and the pop can. He couldn't leave any sign of himself. Back in the kitchen, he snatched up the can and the cookie wrapper. Dropping to his knees, he picked the crumbs off the floor, licking them off his cold fingers.

Confident that there was no evidence left, he stood, clutching the newspapers, looking around the kitchen. The trash can was dusted with snow. They'd know if he touched it.

He peered out the kitchen window, out at the white shed. Maybe he could hide them out there. He grabbed the shotgun and went out the back door. He was careful to walk in the prints that were already there, because he knew she had powers the others did not and would see.

He froze.

A noise.

The hum of a car engine riding on the thin, cold air. He turned, staring down the side of the cabin into a glare of sun and snow.

The engine grew louder.

Someone was coming.

There was a trash can out by the corner of the cabin. He went to it quickly, grabbed the lid, and stuffed the newspapers inside.

The engine was close now.

He dropped the lid back on the trash can, his eyes swinging out to the shed and back to the cabin door. He needed to become invisible.

And there was only one place he could go to do that.

51

"It looks deserted," Joe said.

Rafsky stood on the other side, squinting at the cabin, then taking a slow look around the yard. "Lots of prints here," he said. "They from you guys?"

Joe came around the front of the cruiser. "Yeah, Mike and Holt were out yesterday looking around."

Rafsky stared at the ground, maybe trying

to see a print that didn't belong. Joe looked, too, but saw nothing she could pinpoint as different. After a moment, Rafsky's gaze moved to the cabin.

"We can wait for Mike if you want," Joe said.

Rafsky shook his head and walked slowly to the front door, his hand dipping into his coat pocket for the .22 as he stepped to the porch. Joe followed, her hand poised over the unsnapped holster of her gun.

"You got keys?" Rafksy asked, taking the gun from its holster.

She dug into her jacket and came out with the keys no one from the Collier family had ever claimed. While Rafksy unlocked the door, she turned and watched their backs.

"Stand aside," he said.

He shoved open the door, then flattened himself against the outside wall. She was on the other side of the door, and they waited, breath held, for any sound from inside. Nothing.

They swung inside. Joe held her gun level, gripped in both hands. Rafsky held the .22 in his left hand, unsteady.

The living room was empty, the air cold but stale with the lingering smells of death. Joe was surprised no one had been here to start cleaning things up. But she knew the

Colliers' only relatives lived down in Detroit and after the funeral had left everything in the hands of the police and a Realtor.

Rafsky checked out the bedrooms, and Joe moved slowly to the kitchen, pausing at the door.

Snow. But then she saw the broken pane on the back door. Three plates of food sat untouched on the small Formica table. She pulled her gaze from the table to the floor. The prints in the snow looked fresh, but she couldn't be sure. She drew her radio from her belt and called to Mike. He answered quickly.

"Mike," she said, "did you and Holt come inside the cabin yesterday?"

"Yeah," he said.

"How did you enter?"

"I forgot the key, so I sent Holt through the kitchen. The window is busted back there."

She saw nothing to indicate anyone else had been here.

"Everything good there?" Mike asked.

"Yes, we're good."

She had just started to put the radio back into her belt when she caught a glimpse of something through the window. The Ski-Doo, still under its tarp. It looked secure, covered with untouched snow. Beyond it, about fifteen feet away, she saw the shed. The door was wide open, but the angle didn't allow her a full view of the inside.

"Rafsky."

He came up behind her, and she pointed to the window. "The shed door," she said.

He stepped closer to the window. Joe keyed her radio again. "Mike, did you guys go in the shed?"

"That's affirmative."

"Did you lock it back up?"

"That's a negative, Joe," he said. "Padlock was broke, and the door's off-kilter. Doesn't shut right, so we left it open."

She stared at it, feeling her heart shift into a higher gear. "How far away are you?" she asked Mike.

"Seven, eight minutes."

She stepped closer to Rafksy, and they stood at the window, cold air in their faces.

"What do you want to do?" she asked.

"Let's take a quick look at it from the backyard," he said. "Keep your eye on the snow in front of the door. Watch for shadows moving."

They moved to the rear door. Rafksy pushed it open with one hand, and they waited, guns ready. Again, they heard nothing, and he motioned for her to go first.

She slipped outside, her eyes sweeping

down the back wall of the cabin, then out to the endless rolls of snow that stretched into the trees. Nothing.

Rafsky edged out behind her, staying against the cabin as he took a quick look around. "No prints going out to the trees," he said. "Nothing unusual here."

"I think I can get a look inside the shed from over there," she said, nodding toward the corner of the cabin.

"Stay against the house," Rafsky said.

She moved carefully, stepping over a snow shovel and passing the high stack of firewood. When she got to the corner of the cabin, she was only about ten feet from the shed's open door. She had a good angle to see inside. It was empty.

She heard a sigh of relief and looked back at Rafsky. He was watching the trees that formed the far perimeter of the yard, the .22 at his side. He reached for the back door of the cabin to go inside.

Joe was about to follow him when she noticed a trash can sitting just beyond the firewood pile. The lid was tilted, something sticking out from under it. She holstered her gun and went to it.

Crumpled newspapers. *Echo Bay Banners.* She pulled at one of the corners to check the date. Yesterday.

"Raf—"

Something heavy and hard came down from above her, knocking her forward. But she didn't fall. A hand came around her neck, and something jabbed into her back.

"Don't you move," he whispered. "There's a shotgun in your back."

Rafsky's face was drawn tight with fear. He took two steps away from the door, struggling to keep the .22 level.

Roland pulled her farther out into the yard, the barrel of the shotgun digging into the nylon of her jacket. Right at her spine.

Her mind spun. Where had he come from?

Her eyes shot to the roof of the cabin over the back door. The snow was disturbed, icicles on the eaves broken. Oh, God, why hadn't she looked up?

"Drop the shotgun, Trader," Rafsky said.

"Fuck you," Roland said. "You drop that little piss-ass thing, and I'll let you walk out of here. All I want is her."

Rafsky started sidestepping slowly, but Roland turned Joe with him, using her body as a shield.

"Drop it!" Rafsky said.

Roland suddenly let go of her collar, his hand groping under her jacket. He grabbed her radio first and stuffed it into his pocket. He yanked her revolver from the holster and threw his shotgun to the ground. His arm slipped quickly around Joe's neck in a choke hold. The barrel of her .38 jammed hard into her face, just under her eye.

Rafsky edged closer. "No way you're walking out of here," he said. "Let her go. Now."

"You're hurt, old man!" Roland shouted. "You should've died at the waterfall. You want to live now, you walk away. No one will ever know."

"Drop your weapon, or you're a dead man," Rafsky said.

Joe stared at Rafsky's .22, at the tiny dark hole of the barrel. It was moving, from her face to behind her and then back again. Panic filled her chest, her head washed with cold images. The waterfall. The rope. Small bones in a red glove. She forced it all away, trying to think, and suddenly something came. She turned her head slightly to Roland, into the press of the steel barrel.

"You're not supposed to do it this way," she said.

"What?" Roland said.

"You're not supposed to kill me this way," she said.

Rafsky yelled something else.

Roland's head shot back toward him. "Shut up!" he screamed.

Then Roland's face was close to her again.

"What are you talking about?"

"I'm the warrior," she said. "You're supposed to fight me."

Roland leaned closer. She could feel the prick of his wiry beard, smell his sour breath.

"I know what you are," she said.

The cold gun barrel shifted against her cheek, and for a second she thought he might go for the idea of fighting her. But then he laughed softly, and the gun dug deeper into her cheek.

"You've wasted your time, bitch," he said. "There is no warrior, and there is no spirit. There is just me and you, and you will make me eternal."

Roland's hand tightened around her neck. "You got three seconds, old man!" he yelled to Rafsky.

Joe tried to grab deeper breaths, forcing herself to stay calm and think. Rafsky was edging closer. She knew every step he took lent more accuracy to the small gun, but still his left arm wasn't steady.

She knew he would never take the shot. It was up to her. She could drop to the ground. Roland would not be able to hold her dead weight, and he would be pulled down with her. Then he would either shoot her or let go and take aim at Rafsky. And in that one second before he could find his target, Rafsky could get a shot off.

Her eyes went to the shotgun near her feet. She would have to go for it when she dropped, roll back and fire it. She thought about the waterfall and how long it had taken her to draw her gun then. Three full blasts of Roland's shotgun, and she still hadn't been able to get her weapon out of the holster.

She shut her eyes, straining to hear anything above Rafsky's voice, praying for the sound of Mike's cruiser.

Nothing.

She looked back at Rafsky, at the .22 shaking in his left hand.

One shot. That was all they had.

She tried to draw Rafsky's eyes to her, hoping he would understand what she was going to do. But he wasn't looking at her. He was talking to Roland, repeating the commands to drop his weapon, his eyes fixed with fear.

"I'll shoot her right there!" Roland screamed. She flinched in pain as he jammed the gun into her cheek.

She steadied herself with another deep breath and looked back at Rafsky one last time. This time, their eyes met.

She glanced to the ground.

He gave her a tiny, almost indiscernible nod.

She dropped.

Roland's arm tightened like a vise, and the gun flew away from her head as he struggled to catch his balance in the snow. And suddenly, he let go of her.

She fell to her hands and knees.

A shot popped, splitting the air above her head.

Then a second bang. Louder. From her .38.

She rolled in the snow. A third shot splintered the wood of the cabin.

A fourth zipped over her head.

She groped for the shotgun. She snatched it up, trying to twist onto her back so she could fire it. But she saw nothing but blinding sun-glazed snow and a splatter of blood.

She scrambled to her knees, looking first to make sure Rafsky was not hit, then to the snow that stretched out in front of her. Roland was running away, stumbling through the drifts toward the trees.

Rafsky was at her side, extending his arm and taking aim for another shot. He fired.

The shot zinged into the trees. Roland kept running.

Joe struggled to her feet and lifted the shotgun to her shoulder, her heart pounding so hard she could barely focus on the sights. She pulled the trigger.

The explosion was deafening, the recoil jarring every bone in her body. She saw Roland dip forward and stumble, but he didn't fall.

She started after him, but the single yelp of a siren stopped her. She spun toward the cabin. Doors slammed. Anxious male voices.

"Joe!" Mike called. "Joe! Where are you?"

"In the backyard!" she screamed. "Hurry!"

She turned back to the trees. Roland slipped into the shadows. Gone.

She took a step.

"Frye, wait!" Rafsky said. "Call for backup. I can have fifty officers here in fifteen minutes."

"He'll be gone in fifteen minutes!" she yelled. "I won't let that happen again. No one else dies. You hear me, no one!"

She broke into a run.

52

His footprints were easy to follow. Deep punctures in the snow, speckled with blood. They hadn't even reached the trees when Joe stopped, looking down.

This was where Roland had been when

she had fired the shotgun. The prints here were sloppy, the snow splashed with a bright smear of blood. But there was a clear red path that would make it easy for them to follow safely.

The four of them advanced, quickly but cautiously slipping in and out of the trees, guns level and moving, their eyes never leaving the red trail that was leading them deeper into the woods.

Joe carried the shotgun, feeling naked without her own weapon but glad she had something in her hand that could blow Roland Trader in half if he stepped out in front of her.

She glanced to her left at Mike. His step was steady, his arms steeled out in front of him, fear, adrenaline, and anger etched on his face.

Holt was to her right. His movements were jerky, the raw panic on his face obvious with every flick of his eyes up into the trees. She had the thought that she should send him back to the cabin, but she knew he wouldn't go.

Rafsky was behind them, slowed by his wounds and something else she suspected was anger at her for not calling backup. She knew that was as wrong as allowing Holt to continue this hunt, but it didn't seem to matter right now. Nothing mattered but catching him.

The trees thickened, the bare branches casting long, thin shadows across the pillowed white ground. Roland's footprints had grown sluggish, the blood widening into pink slush. She could see where he had dropped to his hands and knees and crawled before finding his footing again and stumbling on.

A sound.

She stopped, holding up a hand to signal the others. A stream. She felt a spike of panic. If he managed to get in the water, they would lose the trail.

"Hurry," she said.

They drew closer together, quickening their steps, following the red trail until it came to an end at the bank of a half-frozen stream. From the cover of the trees, she could see that the snow on the other side was smooth and undisturbed. There was no sign of Roland's prints anywhere.

"Damn it," she said.

Mike eased away from her, staying in the trees as cover as he made his way downstream. Joe strained to see anything on the other bank. But her head was tripping with the sounds of the water and Roland's face over her as he tied the hoist to her feet.

"Joe?"

It was Holt, his voice directionless in the trees and muffled by the sound of the water. She had lost track of him and she couldn't tell where he was.

"Joe?" he said again. "I think I see his tracks."

Mike rushed past her toward the sound of Holt's voice, and she followed him. The ground was rocky and slippery, and she had to go slowly, using the tree trunks to keep her balance. Mike stopped. As she pulled up next to him behind a tree, she spotted Holt. He was upstream, standing under some low branches, pointing across the water with his gun. Her eyes shot beyond Holt to a patch of bloody snow that disappeared behind a large rock on a low bluff. She realized suddenly Holt couldn't see the bloody snow from where he was, and he was too exposed.

"Holt!" she screamed. "Take —"

A gunshot severed her warning. Holt dropped to his knees.

"No!" she screamed.

Another shot ripped into the tree she was behind, splintering bark and zinging up into the branches. Her chest was so tight she couldn't breathe.

Holt. God, no. Not Holt.

She had to get to him. But she knew she couldn't. No one could get to him without being a target.

Oh, God, why had she let this happen?

"Joe," Mike hissed. "Take a breath. Concentrate."

She nodded and pulled in some air, taking a quick look at the rock. When she turned back, Rafsky was next to her, face wet and pale, his breathing labored.

"He's fired four shots," Rafsky said. "That leaves him two."

"Any chance he has another weapon besides Joe's revolver?" Mike asked.

"I don't think so," Joe said.

Mike's eyes came back to her. "I'll draw his fire to use up those last two shots," he said.

Joe grabbed his sleeve. "No."

Mike pulled away. "I'm going. You get ready to take a shot at him when he sticks his head up from behind that rock. Make sure you hit him."

She stared at him.

"That's an order, Joe," he said.

She nodded.

Mike gave her a moment to level the shotgun and set her feet, then he took off, zigzagging between the trees. She fought the urge to look at Holt, keeping her eyes trained down the long barrel and on the top of the rock. But there was no movement.

And Mike was drawing no fire. Finally, he stopped behind a tree about twenty feet away from her and they waited. Ten seconds. Then twenty.

She felt Rafsky's labored breath behind her. But she kept her eyes on Mike. He was out in the open, walking toward Holt, gun held straight out in front of him.

What was he doing?

She tightened her grip on the shotgun, squinting at the rock, watching for the slightest movement. Then suddenly, there he was.

A blur of a green jacket. Wet, pale skin. Dark eyes.

She fired.

The buckshot shattered the top of the rock, sounding like cannon fire and sending a cloud of gray dust into the air.

A single shot rang back. From her .38.

She racked the shotgun, her eyes lasering to Mike. He was kneeling next to Holt, his gun pointed at the rock, his other hand pressed to Holt's body. Holt's arms were moving, grasping for Mike's sleeve. She could hear Mike telling him to stay down.

Mike rose slowly, and she pulled her attention back to her sights, seeing Mike move into her view as he stepped into the stream.

He was too close to Roland now, too easy a target for even a wounded man to miss, and she knew if she let Roland get his last shot off with any accuracy at all, Mike was dead.

"I'm coming to get you, you son of a bitch!" Mike yelled.

Something moved in the corner of her eye. Not at the top of the rock but on the side — a tiny flash of a shadow that skipped across the shimmering white ground and disappeared. Roland had moved. He was going to take his shot from down low, near the bottom of the rock.

Or was he? Had she seen anything at all? Or was it just the bowing of a branch? What if she was wrong?

Instinct. Trust your instincts.

"Rafsky," she whispered, "watch the top. I'm sighting low."

She centered her sights on the edge where the gray stone and blood-smeared snow merged. She drew in her breath and held it.

"You're finished, you bastard!" Mike shouted.

From behind the edge of the rock, a glint of blue steel.

She fired, sending an explosion of rock, snow, and blood into the air. Somewhere in the concussion, she heard another gunshot, then a third, and suddenly a man was screaming. She looked first to Rafsky, then to Mike, before she realized that the screams were coming from behind the rock.

"That's six. He's empty," Rafsky said.

Joe racked another shell and stepped out from behind the tree, keeping the shotgun level as she moved toward the stream. Mike was nearing the rock on the other side, gun pointed. She hurried after him, catching him at the top of the slope, pressed against the rock. He glanced at her.

"You go around the other side," he whispered. "And watch for cross fire."

She slipped around the rock, and when she was in place, she looked back at Mike.

"On three," he said.

He counted down, and they spun around the rock in unison, guns drawn.

Roland was slumped on the ground between them. Thigh shredded, jacket soaked a dark red. Ragged flesh dripping from his buckshot-peppered cheek. Joe's revolver lay at the tip of his bloody fingers.

Mike kicked the .38 away and dropped to his knees, grabbing a fistful of Roland's collar. He slammed Roland's head back against the rock, then shoved his gun into Roland's mouth.

"You're gone," he hissed.

"No! No!" Roland screamed.

"Mike! Stop!" Joe said, pulling at Mike's sleeve.

Mike shoved her off and Joe came back with the flat of her hand, pushing Mike so hard he tumbled back off his heels to the snow. His eyes swung up to her with angry questions.

"He's mine," Joe said, stepping closer and pointing the shotgun at his face.

Roland's eyes drifted up to her, filmed with pink, as if he were bleeding everywhere on the inside. She shoved the barrel into his cheek, hard enough to pin his head against the rock. Behind her, she heard the shuffle of snowy footsteps. Rafsky and Holt.

"Frye," Rafsky said calmly. "Back away."

She shook her head, using the weight of her body to force the barrel deeper into Roland's face, drawing the skin so tight it pulled back over his teeth.

His eyes were locked on hers. Then, to her amazement, he smiled.

"Do it," he whispered.

"Shut up!" she said.

Roland lifted a limp hand to wipe his mouth, coughing on his blood. His eyes never left hers. "Do it," he said. "Shoot me."

"Shut up!" She slammed the barrel into

his face, cracking bone.

"Shoot me!"

"Shut the fuck up!"

"Do it!" he screamed.

She pulled the trigger.

But she heard nothing but a hollow snap of the firing pin. The shotgun was empty.

She froze, her body stiff, still braced for the shot that didn't come.

"Use mine," Mike said.

She forced her head up. Mike was holding his revolver out to her.

"Use it."

She blinked, and pulled in a deep, ragged breath. "No," she said.

"Then what do you want to do with him?" Mike asked.

"We take him in," Rafsky said.

"I'm not dragging his ass back a mile just so he can rot in some prison for the rest of his life," Mike said. "I say we kill him now."

"You're cops," Rafsky said. "You can't commit murder."

"Watch us," Mike said, taking aim at Roland.

"Mike! Stop!" Joe said. "Just stop."

For a moment, it was quiet. Just the hiss of the stream and their own labored breathing.

"Then what do you want to do, Joe?"

Mike asked. "Your call."

What did she want to do? She stared at Mike, seeing only shifting images of him. His hand smeared with Roland's blood, pain and hatred carved deep in his face. Holt. The brown deputy's jacket ripped with a bullet hole, face ashen and suddenly so much older. Rafsky. Overcoat soaked with Holt's blood, his long body shivering and broken.

"We leave him," she said.

"Frye, that's the same as murder."

Joe turned toward the soft sound of Rafsky's voice. She looked back at Roland. He was conscious, his breathing watery and shallow. But he was watching her, his eyes filled with something she didn't immediately understand. Then she knew what it was. Fear — fear of being left out here. That was why he wanted her to shoot him, so he could die his twisted mythical death by her hand.

She took a step back. "We leave him," she said. "We leave him here for the animals and his fucking hunger moon."

"No!" Roland cried. "No! Don't leave me here! Shoot me!"

She took a slow look around her at the three men. "Are we in agreement?" she asked.

Mike holstered his revolver. "Yes."

"Holt?" she asked.

Holt gave Roland a long look, then managed a weak nod.

Her eyes settled on Rafsky.

Disbelief shadowed his eyes as he looked to them one by one. When his gaze finally came back to her, she met it, sure and silent, giving him time to understand — hoping he could understand — that this was what needed to be done.

"You'll be murderers," he said softly. "All of you."

No one said anything.

Rafsky set her .22 pistol on the rock, and without another word, he turned away, making his way down the slope and across the stream. Joe watched him until the dark overcoat disappeared into the trees.

"You can't do this!" Roland rasped, trying to crawl to her. He fell forward, his cries smothered in the bloody snow.

Joe stared at him. He couldn't move his arm, and blood was still dripping from the ragged wound in his thigh, melting the snow under him into a muddy, red mush.

"Tie him to a tree," Joe said.

Mike handed her his revolver, and she held it on Roland as Mike dragged him to a tree. Mike tore a strip from Roland's shredded jacket. Roland screamed as Mike tied his hands to the tree.

Mike turned to Joe. "We good?" he asked.

"We're good."

Mike walked to Holt, steadying him with an arm around the waist as he led him across the stream.

"Don't leave me here!"

Joe picked up her .38 from the ground, brushing off the snow before she put it in her holster.

"You bitch!" Roland screamed. "Don't you leave me! Don't let me die this way! This is wrong! You know it's wrong!"

She snapped her holster and picked up the .22 off the rock, slipping it into her pocket.

"Please . . . please . . . don't leave me out here! Don't leave me! You fucking bitch! You goddamn fucking bitch!"

Mike and Holt were waiting for her on the other side of the stream. When she reached them, Holt held out a hand, and she slipped her arm around him, just under Mike's. They held on to each other all the way back.

53

In the first hours afterward, they didn't talk about how to keep their secret. It wasn't necessary.

Mike drove them to a two-story blue clapboard house on Trout River Road, about ten miles from the Collier cabin. A bearded man with wine-scented breath opened the door and, without a single question, showed Mike and Joe the way upstairs. They laid Holt down on a bed with a yellow chenille spread.

An hour later, Mike's uncle Ernesto, a retired doctor from Detroit, had removed the bullet from Holt's shoulder and told them Holt was resting comfortably. He said Holt could stay in the upstairs bedroom as long as they needed him to.

Around three a.m., Joe and Mike sat down at Augie's radio console and copied the day's activity log onto the next empty page in the book. Leaving out, of course, the line that showed the three of them in service at the Collier cabin.

Then they ripped out the original page, poured two glasses of brandy from Leach's cabinet, and drank as they watched the paper burn in the station fireplace.

It was then that Mike remembered the

audio tapes of the radio traffic. They burned only one, the four-hour period from two p.m. to six p.m. Afterward, they shared a second brandy while Mike filled out leave-of-absence paperwork for Holt, giving him permission to attend a funeral downstate for a relative who didn't exist.

If Augie ever noticed the strange handwriting in his logbook or the missing reel of tape, or wondered about Holt's absence, he never asked.

The next morning, Kellerman called to say they had a credible sighting of Roland over near Alpena on the Lake Huron shore. Mike offered the assistance of the Leelanau County sheriff's office, but Kellerman turned him down.

Dorothy Newton called Joe that morning, too, asking if they had any news. Joe told her no, there was nothing new. No more bones had been found, but some carvings, suspected to be done by copycats, were still turning up all over the state. Dorothy told her she'd be at the Riverside if there was any news. Joe told her she knew the number.

Brad called her at around four. He said he wanted to know how she was doing. She told him she was fine and asked about his mother. He didn't ask about hers, but he did tell her to call him if she ever wanted to talk. She told him she knew the number.

Rafsky did not call.

She had told him to take her cruiser from the Collier cabin, wanting to go with Mike and Holt to the uncle's house. Rafsky had left the cruiser parked in front of the station, keys in the ignition. He had not left anything inside. And his was the one phone number she didn't know. Nor could she call it, even if she did.

On the third day, they went back.

The three of them — Joe and Mike helping Holt along — made the same walk through the woods, guns resting in their holsters, their hearts thumping with the memory of three sudden shotgun blasts fired seven weeks ago in a place very much like where they were now. They trudged up the slope to the rock and looked down.

Part of him was still there.

His head was gone, chewed off at the neck. His insides had been eaten out, leaving only a partial rib cage and frosted tatters of red flesh hanging on the bones. Another piece of him lay nearby, but it no longer bore any resemblance to the human leg it was.

There was nothing else, except for animal tracks.

54

She stopped just inside the front door of the station, stomping the snow off her boots. Augie was standing at his radio console, taking down a silver banner that read HAPPY NEW YEAR 1976. The small Christmas tree that had spent most of December on the front counter was partially dismantled, ornaments lying on the console. Leach had purchased both items with his own money a few days before he died, and for weeks they had lain untouched on a shelf. Finally, Augie had put them up a few days before Christmas.

She noticed something else new. The print of Mackinac Island that normally hung over the coffee station was gone. In its place were two new framed photographs of Clifford Leach and Julian Mack. Both bore plates that read, "Killed in the Line of Duty, November 1975." They were the first memorial pictures ever to be put on the Leelanau sheriff department's wall.

"Are they all right?" Augie asked.

"Yes," she said.

He smiled sadly, and she knew he had chosen the pictures and had them enlarged and framed himself, with Theo's help.

"Did you do anything special last night?"

he asked.

"I was here until eleven," she said. "Then I went home, my mother and I shared a bottle of Maker's Mark, and I was asleep before the ball hit the bottom."

Augie started to say something, but the phone rang, and he turned away. She heard the name of Mrs. Elsinore and smiled as she walked toward the back offices. She realized that the smile was possibly the first one she had allowed herself in more than two weeks. It felt good. It felt normal.

She paused at the conference room door.

The desk was stacked with files and envelopes. She knew what it was — all the reports, evidence, and photographs from Ken and Roland's case. She gathered a breath as she moved to the desk. Paper-clipped to the top folder was a note.

Joe: Can you please do the evidence log, case summary, and prepare this file for permanent storage? Thanks — Mike.

She looked down at the folders. She hadn't realized the case file had gotten this large. There had to be a thousand pages in almost twenty folders. And three or four fat envelopes of photographs.

She took off her jacket and sat down in

the chair, picking up one of the envelopes. It held more than a dozen eight-by-ten color photographs. Crime-scene photos of the woods where they had found Annabelle's jawbone. The ground was leafy, the trees scarlet and orange with autumn. Suddenly, it seemed like a very long time ago.

She opened a second envelope, her stomach tightening when she saw the top picture. It was the Collier cabin murder scene. She put those away and picked up a third envelope that had writing on the outside: "Joette Frye/November 26, 1975/Body shots/Rape/Traverse City Hospital."

She set it down and sat back in the chair. Once she filed all this away, the case would be officially over, at least for the Leelanau County sheriff's office. Kellerman was still actively seeking Roland Trader, but the leads were growing cold, and his calls reporting in to Mike had tapered off. It was just as well.

She often thought about what would have happened if someone had found Roland Trader alive and they had been exposed for what they had done. But finally, in the quiet last days of the year, his face had begun to fade from her dreams. Instead, there seemed to be a slow settling of something else, a fragile kind of peace that she had welcomed.

She had no regrets. Except one.

She wished they had found more of the girls' bones. Enough to give Dorothy Newton, Arthur Chapel, and the others something to take home and bury. It would have brought them comfort to be able to stand over a grave and speak to their daughters, in the way it brought her comfort to be able to stand over Leach's grave and speak to him.

Grabbing an empty accordion folder, she started sorting the reports and statements, deliberately working fast so she needed only to scan the first few lines.

Then she moved on to the photographs, making sure each envelope was properly sealed, initialed, and labeled. She picked up the final envelope — this one from the Rexall in town. It was dated November 1964. She frowned, trying to figure out what they were. Finally, she dumped them onto the desk.

They were the photos the Leelanau sheriff's department had taken eleven years ago, on the day Ken Snider, Sr., had been shot. They showed the backyard of the cabin as it had appeared when the Sniders — not the Colliers — owned it. Joe had first seen the photos the day Mike came to her cottage asking for her help with all the background on the brothers. Then, Joe had focused only on the photograph of the deer hoist in the tree.

She stared at the hoist photograph for a moment and then set it aside. She slowly sifted through the other photos, stopping at a wide-angle shot of the backyard. There was a corner of the shed in the picture — a drab gray before the Colliers had repainted it white. The picture also showed thicker trees before Don Collier had cut them down. And in the center of the photo was what looked to be an old wooden well.

She frowned. She couldn't remember seeing a well on the Collier property in any of the times she was there.

So you changed the place a lot after you bought it, Mr. Collier?

Had to . . . no plumbing to speak of, just a well out back.

Joe pushed up from the chair and took the picture out into the main office.

"Augie," she said, standing over his console, "do you know what people do when they shut down old wells?"

"Wells?" he asked.

"Yeah, wells like you'd use to get water. What happens to them when they're not used anymore?"

"They're supposed to be filled in with

dirt," Augie said, "but most folks here just put something over the top and cover it with a layer of sod."

She hurried to Mike's office. He looked up, startled.

"Look at this," she said, thrusting the photo at him.

"What am I looking at?" he asked.

"The Collier backyard and the well," she said.

"What?"

"The well," she said. "It's not there anymore."

He studied the picture. Then his eyes came up again. He still didn't see it.

"What if that's where Roland put the rest of the bones?" she asked.

"Joe, we searched that yard," he said.

"We did a surface search," she said. "And most of the search was concentrated in the trees, away from the shed and the well."

He rose slowly. "You think he put them all in one place?"

"Why else didn't we find more than one or two bones from each girl?"

Mike reached for his jacket. She hurried back to her desk to get hers. She was halfway out the door when she spun back to Augie. "Augie," she said, "radio Holt, and have him meet us at the Collier cabin."

They took shovels from the shed and used the photograph as a guide to determine where to start digging in the two-foot drifts of snow. It was slow going, moving the snow and then chopping at the frozen ground for evidence of something underneath.

About thirty minutes in, Holt radioed another officer to bring them a thermos of coffee. Finally, after two hours, Holt hit metal. Mike's and Joe's heads snapped up when they heard the dull clang. Holt dropped to his knees, clawing at the hard dirt with his gloved hands. Mike stepped in and started chopping with his shovel.

Twenty minutes later, they stood looking down at a square of wet, rusted metal. Mike wiped his brow and looked at Joe.

"You ready?" he asked.

She nodded. Mike and Holt worked their fingers under the edge of the metal, and in sync, heaved it up and over.

The well was a small dark hole, finished around the upper rim with crumbling concrete. The concrete sides of the well were visible for eight or nine inches before everything turned to black. The three of them stepped to the edge and trained their flashlights down into the hole.

From the stark beams of the three white lights came the ivory glint of bones.

Despite Kellerman's objections, the Leelanau County sheriff's office retained possession of the bones. Kellerman had insisted they didn't have the capabilities, but the county put out a call for help and got it.

The experts came from all over the state, some paid, some volunteers, everyone from retired doctors to gravediggers. They brought their equipment, microscopes, and chemicals, and the day after the well was discovered, boxes of bones began arriving at the high school gymnasium to be sorted out. The students were still out on vacation, and it was the only place big enough.

The process began with the laying of eleven black tarps out across the polished parquet of the basketball court. With nowhere else to start, they began with what they knew.

The jawbone was placed on tarp number five in the same position a head would have been. A paper was placed nearby that said, ANNABELLE CHAPEL, FEB. 2, 1969.

Of the ten skulls found in the well, only one showed any sign of trauma — a deep, jagged gash that punctured the bone. It was assumed that belonged to Ronnie Langford, killed with a drywall hammer in the Inkster basement. Her skull rested now on tarp number one: VERONICA LANGFORD, FEB. 1965.

The other skulls had been placed on tarps according to the expert's estimated date of death, which was vague at best. Papers rested at the foot of each, a different year written on each one, from 1965 to 1975.

Stainless steel tables were set along the recessed bleachers to hold the bones for examination after they came out of the locker room, where they had been carefully cleaned. Other tests were being performed on the opposite side of the gym, three medical examiners from the state trying to find the slightest variation in size, gender, or race and looking for any scars, breaks, or diseases that might indicate a possible link to another bone.

But except for an occasional exact match in height, there was little to help them link any one bone to another. The only conclusion was that all the victims were girls, all Caucasian, and all between the ages of seventeen and twenty-four. It appeared all had been relatively healthy.

By the end of the second day, Joe stood

near the double doors to the gym, her eyes locked on the small, incomplete skeletons, so stark against the black tarps.

She leaned back against the wall and closed her eyes.

They had found no clothing in the well. But they did find other things. One pair of hoop earrings and one pair of silver studs. A class ring from a high school in Battle Creek, no initials. One shriveled contact lens. A gold barrette with the name ROBIN. Ten fake nails, all painted red, all broken. But it was the hair that still gave a churn to Joe's stomach.

Clumps of it. Blond. Brown. Curly. Straight. A few strands dyed bright pink. One intact braid, tied with a moldy white ribbon. All of it was being meticulously separated, strand by strand, on a third set of tables.

"You okay?"

Joe looked up. Mike was standing next to her. His uniform was starched and neat, but his face held the ragged look of a man fighting both sleep and demons.

"I will never forget what I am looking at right now," Joe said softly.

Mike nodded but said nothing.

They stayed near the gym doors, watching. A man in a white coat was kneeling by tarp number three, comparing the bone in his hand to one lying on the tarp. He measured it in every direction, and finally, with a subtle shrug of his shoulders, he set it down next to the other.

"The mothers are coming back," Mike said. "And Mrs. Newton is outside now."

"Oh, God," Joe sighed. "How can we show her this?"

"We can show her the jewelry and . . . the hair."

Joe shut her eyes again.

"I'll do it if you like," Mike offered.

"No," Joe said. "I will."

Joe turned and walked to the small lobby outside the gym, past the trophy cases. She saw Dorothy Newton standing on the icy sidewalk, her blue coat pulled around, her head wrapped in a flowered scarf. Joe pushed open the door and waved her past the officers.

Dorothy Newton pulled off her scarf when she got inside. "Is Natalie in there?" she asked, pointing to the gym.

"We don't know," Joe said. "I'm sorry, but there's so little to go on. We only have a few pieces of jewelry, and even if you could identify that, we don't know which bones are hers."

"The newspaper said you think you have

eleven girls."

"Yes."

Dorothy Newton's face suddenly softened with a strange kind of peace, as if she already knew her daughter was in the next room, warm and cared for now, already on her way to coming home.

"I want to see my daughter," she said.

Joe couldn't find her voice even to say no.

"Please, Deputy Frye."

"I have to prepare you," Joe said.

"There's no need. I know I will only see bones."

Joe took her arm and led her back to the gym. Dorothy Newton stopped a few feet inside the door, and Joe stayed behind her, prepared to react if she darted from the room. But she didn't. She put her scarf in her coat pocket and started toward the long row of black tarps.

But then Joe saw her stop, her gaze going to the table with the clumps of hair, and she went to it.

"Oh, heavens," Dorothy Newton whispered.

Joe came up behind her. "I'm sorry, Mrs. Newton," Joe said. "Please —"

Dorothy Newton held up a hand to silence her and bent to look at the piles of hair. The technician looked at Joe but then stepped back.

Dorothy Newton picked up some long strands of brown hair, laying them across her palm and smoothing them with her fingers. Her eyes came up to Joe. "These are hers."

Joe had no idea what to say.

Dorothy Newton turned and, taking the hair with her, moved to the tarps. All of them held bones now. Most just a few, one with nearly half a skeleton. She saw the signs with the years on them and walked slowly down to the tarp labeled 1968. She looked down at the bones for a long time, then she knelt, reaching out to touch one.

Joe started to tell her not to, but she couldn't get the words out, afraid she'd sound harsh. But before she could say anything at all, Dorothy Newton turned to her.

"This is Natalie," she said.

"How do you know?"

"These bones are slightly bowed," she said. "So were Natalie's legs. She inherited it from her father. She had to wear leg braces for a year when she was ten."

Joe didn't see any bend to the legs, but she drew a marker from her pocket and knelt down and picked up the sign. Under the 1968 date, she wrote Natalie Newton's name. She laid the sign down by the leg bones.

Dorothy Newton leaned forward and set the long strands of brown hair near the skull. Then she placed a soft kiss on her fingers and gently touched them to the skull.

"I've missed you," she whispered. "And I'll see you soon."

She rose slowly and turned to Joe. She was a blur, and Joe had to blink her into focus.

"I'm so sorry we don't have more of her," Joe said.

Dorothy Newton's fingers touched Joe's.

"There are two hundred and six bones in the human body," she said. "Natalie was born with only two hundred and five. Missing that one bone did not make her any less my daughter than missing a hundred now."

Joe blinked against tears.

"This is enough, Deputy Frye. So thank you for what I do have."

Joe wiped her face, her gaze drifting again to the black tarps and steel tables. Dorothy Newton's voice brought her back.

"I'm going home now," she said. "I have arrangements to make. Will you let me know when I can come back and get her?"

Joe cleared her throat. "Would it be okay if I brought her down myself?" she asked.

"You would do that?"

"I'd be honored."

"I'd like that," she said. "You have my number in Indianapolis?"

"Yes."

Dorothy Newton gave her a small hug and walked away. Joe stayed where she was for a moment, then went back to Mike. He held out a handkerchief. She pressed it to her face and dropped back against the wall.

She felt a nudge. "Joe," Mike said softly.

Joe looked in the direction Mike was pointing.

Rafsky.

He was standing just inside the far door, hands in the pockets of his overcoat, scanning the room. When his eyes found hers, he started over to them.

Mike pushed off the wall and stood almost at attention. Joe stuck the handkerchief into her pants pocket. Rafsky's walk was stronger, and there was no bandage on his shoulder. But his right arm seemed to hang a little limply.

He stopped in front of them. "Hello, Sheriff," he said. "Deputy Frye."

"Detective," Mike said.

Rafsky glanced at the bones. "Congratulations," he said. "Case solved, right?"

"Yes, sir," Mike said, ignoring Rafsky's

sarcasm.

Rafsky's eyes moved to Joe. They were filmed with lingering disapproval. And it made her wonder, if he still felt so strongly about what they had done, why had he stayed silent? She was about to ask him, but he spoke first.

"If you're about to thank me for not saying anything, please don't," he said.

She was quiet.

"I made a choice about what I could more easily live with," he said. "Letting you get away with what you did or sending three young . . . decent cops to jail."

"He was going to die anyway," Mike said.

Rafsky started to say something but just gave a small shake of his head. "And you had an obligation to try and prevent that, not bring it on sooner," he said. "And not make it any more horrible than it would have naturally been."

Mike's eyes were steady on Rafsky. "I can live with what I did," he said.

Rafsky turned to Joe. "What about you?"

The ice-blue eyes were steady but with an odd sadness that told her he somehow knew the answer and she did not.

"I wanted —" she began.

Rafsky waited.

"I needed . . ."

He was quiet, giving her time to finish her thought, and when she didn't, he looked to the tarps. She could tell from his expression that he didn't want to be here anymore.

She slowly stuck out her hand. "Goodbye, Rafsky," she said.

He took her hand, his fingers closing around hers. "Goodbye, Frye."

She watched until he disappeared through the gym doors, then turned to Mike. He was talking to a technician, a small piece of paper in his hand. When the technician left, Mike turned to her.

"They're done," he said. "The well is empty. There were nine hundred and sixty-seven."

She leaned against the wall, staring at the tarps. Nine hundred and sixty-seven. Fewer than half of what they should have for eleven victims. And they knew they had eleven victims with the ten skulls and Annabelle's jawbone.

"Why do you think we have so few?" she asked.

Mike shrugged. "We have one victim from the dunes," he said. "That means at some point, he changed his territory, and we have no idea where else he might have gone. The rest of the bones could be scattered all across the north."

Joe shook her head, and they fell quiet for a long time. Then Joe sighed, still staring at the tarps. "Nine hundred and sixty-seven," she said softly.

"No," Mike said. "Counting the twenty-seven little bones in the red glove, the two we found in the dunes, and those four we found last fall, we have an even thousand."

Joe looked at the tarp labeled NATALIE NEWTON, 1968.

"It's enough," she said.

55

Natalie Newton and Annabelle Chapel were the first girls to go home. Less than two weeks after the discovery of the bones in the well, Arthur Chapel took possession of his daughter's remains and left Echo Bay. A few days later, Joe made the drive to Indianapolis and stood by Dorothy Newton's side in a cemetery much like Beechwood as Natalie was put to rest.

Over the next few weeks, three more girls made their own journeys.

Susie-Q, whose hand bones were discovered in the red glove near the Collier cabin. Robin, who had left a personalized barrette in the well as the one link that would eventually bring her parents to Echo Bay, her dental records in hand. And a young girl named Mariah, pictured in her family portrait with long, thick braids tied with white ribbons.

By the end of March, four more were identified and sent home. But as the winter began to wane, so did the trickle of relatives searching for their daughters. Eventually, only two sets of bones remained unidentified, and as the final snow of the season fell, the two skeletons were moved from the county morgue storage vault and turned over to Witherspoon's Funeral Home for burial. The sheriff's office made the decision to bury both girls together.

A pearl-colored casket was donated by the mayor's family. The plot was paid for by the citizens of Echo Bay who had begun contributing to Theo's burial fund back in the autumn when the first bone had been discovered. The headstone was purchased by the deputies of the Leelanau County sheriff's office. The inscription read, "Somebody's Daughter."

In the spring, just after a warm April shower, two hikers happened upon some bones in the woods west of Bass Lake.

They were white, cleaned by crystals of ice and sanded smooth by the Michigan winds. There weren't many. A few finger bones. An arm and three small knobs from the toes.

The sheriff's office went out to investigate. In their search, they picked up other pieces of evidence. Shreds of a green parka. A boot. A few tufts of brown hair, hundreds of pellets of buckshot, and a single .22-caliber bullet.

The bones were determined to be those of a Caucasian male, age twenty-five to thirty-five.

They sent all the appropriate flyers to neighboring agencies, asking for help in identifying the victim. They did not send one to the state.

The buckshot was stored and logged as unrelated to any possible homicide, more likely from hunters.

The .22 bullet was never matched to any weapon.

No one came forward to identify the victim.

His cause of death remains unknown.

EPILOGUE

Captiva Island, Florida
December 1988

The sun was starting its descent into the gulf as Joe finished. She had talked, told her story, the entire time she and Louis had walked. They had walked all the way down to Bowman's Beach, where the inlet narrowed to separate Sanibel Island from Captiva. They had walked back, bare feet in the surf's foam, weaving between the shell seekers and the sandpipers.

Louis had not said much during her recital. Just asked a few questions when she faltered. When the *words* faltered, not her memory. Thirteen years, and the memories were still clear. But finding the words was hard, because she had never talked about the whole thing before. Bits, pieces, police statements, shards of nightmares. That was all it had been before now.

But now. Now she had given it a shape

it never had before, given her experience and pain a context that had come only through the distance of years. And through the love of the man who was looking at her now.

She could trust him.

She knew that now.

She could trust him to understand her job. She could trust him with everything bad and wrong and defective about her soul, and he would still love her.

"You never talked to anyone about this?" Louis asked finally. "I mean the rape, not even a doctor?"

She shook her head but didn't look at him, because she heard something in his voice that told her he meant a psychiatrist.

"Just that one doctor in Traverse City," she said. "After the bones were buried . . ." She shook her head slowly. "I don't know, it was like I just buried everything."

"How long did you stay there after?" Louis asked.

"About a year. I wanted to make sure Mike was going to be all right, that everyone was going to be okay." She paused. "But after a while, I couldn't stay there anymore. I loved that town, but I couldn't look at anything without seeing the scars."

"So you quit?" Louis said.

She nodded. "I packed up my stuff and left. I stayed with my mother in Cleveland over Christmas and then just started driving south. I didn't stop until I felt warm. I put in some apps in Tallahassee, Tampa, and Lauderdale. Everyone was looking for women, so I had my pick. I took Miami-Dade because when I got down there and saw the place, I knew it was as far away from Echo Bay as I could get. Miami's not the kind of town where you get attached to things easily."

They started walking again. They were almost back to the cottage. An elderly couple sat in lawn chairs facing the setting sun. They nodded and lifted their wineglasses in greeting as Joe and Louis passed.

"Why did you tell me all this, Joe?" Louis asked.

She stopped and faced him. "Because I knew you wouldn't think . . ." She shook her head, her eyes falling to the sand.

"What, that you murdered him?" Louis asked.

She couldn't look at him.

"I can't judge you on that, Joe," he said. "I'm the last person to judge anyone on something like that."

He took her hand, and they walked on, not saying anything else until they were back at the low dune in front of Louis's cottage.

"Sit down," Louis said gently.

Joe dropped down to the sand. Louis sat down beside her. They looked out at the sun, now bleeding onto the shimmering horizon.

"What happened to the others?" Louis asked.

"Holt stayed for two more years and then took a job with the Grand Rapids PD. I think he got married," she said. "Mike is still Leelanau County sheriff."

"You're still in touch with him?"

Joe hesitated. "I wasn't until this week. He called me the other day." She closed her eyes and pulled in a deep breath. "He wants me to come back and work for him as undersheriff, Louis. He's taking an early retirement next year and wants me to run for sheriff."

She had expected an outburst of surprise, but when Louis said nothing, she opened her eyes and turned to him.

"I was waiting for you to say you turned him down," he said.

"I didn't," she said softly.

The incredulous look on his face tore at her heart. "Louis, listen to me," she said. "I told him I had to think about it. And I needed to talk to you first."

She could see a veil descending over his gray eyes, and she knew it was because it had been so very hard for him to open himself enough to love her.

"You're free to make your own decisions, Joe," he said finally. "We haven't promised each other anything here."

"I know," she whispered.

The hiss of the waves filled the silence.

"Why did you tell me this whole story?" he asked finally.

She sighed. "I don't know. Maybe I expected you to . . ." She shook her head slowly, looking out at the water.

"Expected me to what?" Louis said. "Tell you what you did was okay? Make you feel okay so you can go back and make things right? What, Joe, what did you expect from me? Some sort of absolution?"

She closed her eyes against the sting of tears. Rafsky was there in her mind now, the way he had looked when they said goodbye. He had not contacted her in thirteen years. But he knew where she was. The cards had started coming the first Christmas she joined the Miami-Dade police department. From Gina, not Rafsky. Five cards, and then they stopped. She understood why Rafsky had to keep his distance. He had been her mentor, her priest, and when she had sinned, she burdened him with her secret. He had no choice in turning his back on her. That was the kind of man he was, the kind of cop he was.

If it was absolution she was seeking now, she knew neither Rafsky nor Louis could give it. She had lost something out there in the cold. Roland Trader had taken away her belief in her own strength. But she had lost something even more important the day they left him to die. Once the heat of vengeance had faded, she had felt a coldness in its place. It had served her well for thirteen years, made her the kind of cop she needed to be to survive in Miami, brought her a detective's gold badge. But the coldness had cost her too much.

"Joe," Louis said softly.

She didn't move.

"Joe, look at me."

She opened her eyes. He was turned toward her, his face dark in the slanting red light of the setting sun.

"What do you want to do?" he asked.

"I want . . ." She faltered.

"What do you *need?*"

"I need to go back," she said. "Just for a while, maybe a year or two."

He shook his head. "It's an elected position, Joe, a four-year commitment," he said gently. "You don't walk away from people who put their trust in you."

Now he looked out over the water. "Besides, I heard something in your voice when you talk about that place," he said. "Despite what happened there, you love it and you want to go home."

"And you won't leave here, will you?" she said.

He shook his head slowly. "I have a commitment here, people who've put their trust in me, and I can't walk away from that."

She knew he was talking about Ben Outlaw, the boy whose kidnapping had brought them together. Ben was twelve now, a fragile age for any boy, especially one without a father.

Joe was watching Louis's profile, thinking now about how hard it had been for him to find a place where he felt at peace. And that place was right here.

She looked out at the water. The sun was just above the horizon now, melting into the purple water of the gulf. There was a soft breeze blowing, redolent of salt. And coconut oil lotion, she realized, although there were no other people on the beach except them.

"Ever heard of something called the green

flash?" Louis said.

She could barely hear his voice above the whisper of the surf. She shook her head. "No."

"It's an atmospheric phenomenon where if conditions are just right, the top edge of the sun will turn green just as it disappears," Louis said.

She was quiet, watching him.

"The Celts believed that anyone who saw it could never be hurt in love," he went on. "Jules Verne wrote a story about it. 'He who has been fortunate enough once to behold it is enabled to see closely into his own heart and to read the thoughts of others.' That's what he wrote about it."

A small smile tipped his lips as he watched the sun. "I've been watching for it for years now, but I've never seen it."

He turned suddenly to her, took her face in his hands, and kissed her. She closed her eyes, memorizing the feel of his lips on hers for when she would need it.

She pulled back slowly. "Can we make this work, Louis?" she asked.

He smiled and pointed to the horizon. "Watch," he said.

ACKNOWLEDGMENTS

Echo Bay, Michigan, is not a real town. It is a creation of our imaginations, a compilation of many places in northern Michigan. It stands as our homage to the towns, forests, and lakes of our childhood. If we took some license with our use of the Leelanau Peninsula's geography, we hope our Michigan readers will forgive us and understand that we were trying only to capture the spirit and beauty of this special place.

We have some friends we need to acknowledge who have kindly lent their expertise to our books: legal eagles Bradley R. Weiss and Mark J. Loterstein; our good buddy Dr. Doug Lyle, who keeps us on track for all things forensic and medical; and our favorite weapons wizard, Fred Rea.

And last, we need to thank three people who make our books possible. To our talented and patient editor, Mitchell Ivers:

Your vision helped give this book its shape. To our agent extraordinaire, Maria Carvainis: Thank you for being at our side through the marathon ("It's not a sprint!"). And most of all, to my husband, Daniel: You believed in us before anyone did, including ourselves.

ABOUT THE AUTHORS

P. J. Parrish is actually two sisters — Kristy Montee and Kelly Nichols — who pooled their talents and their lifelong love of writing to create the character of Louis Kincaid. Their *New York Times* and *USA Today* bestselling novels include *An Unquiet Grave, A Killing Rain, Island of Bones, Thicker Than Water, Paint It Black, Dead of Winter,* and *Dark of the Moon.*

Their collaboration is unique in that the sisters live in separate states (Kelly in Mississippi, Kristy in Florida). The sisters were born and raised in Detroit, Michigan. Kristy graduated from Eastern Michigan University with a teaching degree but went on to journalism, working as a police reporter and a features editor; she also served as the Fort Lauderdale *Sun-Sentinel*'s dance critic for eighteen years. She now lives in Fort Lauderdale with her husband.

Kelly attended college at Northern Michigan University in the state's remote upper peninsula. Kelly has lived in Arizona and Nevada, and currently lives in northern Mississippi. She worked in the gaming industry for the last twenty years, and was a senior specialist in the human resources department of a Native-American casino in Mississippi. She has two daughters, a son, and three grandchildren.

For more information, visit www.pj parrish.com.

The employees of Thorndike Press hope you have enjoyed this Large Print book. All our Thorndike and Wheeler Large Print titles are designed for easy reading, and all our books are made to last. Other Thorndike Press Large Print books are available at your library, through selected bookstores, or directly from us.

For information about titles, please call:
    (800) 223-1244

or visit our Web site at:
    www.gale.com/thorndike
    www.gale.com/wheeler

To share your comments, please write:
    Publisher
    Thorndike Press
    295 Kennedy Memorial Drive
    Waterville, ME 04901